AUTO

Books by Alexander Plansky

Safari
Arcadia
Auto

AUTO

A **CRAY & FRASER** NOVEL

ALEXANDER PLANSKY

A MEQ MEDIA BOOK

First edition August 2021

Jacket artwork by Lauren Budney © 2021 by Meq Media, Inc.

Author photo by Samii Stoloff Photography

Published by Meq Media, Inc.
4409 Hoffner Ave #254
Orlando, FL 32812
www.meqmedia.com

ISBN: 978-0-9992399-2-6 (paperback), 978-0-9992399-5-7 (ebook)
LCCN: 2021912196

BISAC: Fiction/Thrillers/Technological | Fiction/Thrillers/Suspense

Subjects: LCSH: Automated vehices--Fiction | Hacking--Fiction

Hell is full of good meanings, but heaven is full of good works.

PROVERB

The only thing more dangerous than ignorance is arrogance.

ALBERT EINSTEIN

MONDAY

9:18 PM

"**Y**our wife doesn't need to find out about this."

Graham sounded tired, weary. Spencer wasn't surprised. The past several months had taken a toll on all of them. He stared out the rain-streaked window beside him, watching headlights speed through the dark.

The voice on the car's speakers continued. "It was bound to happen given how hard you've been working. Long nights up late at the office, you and her close together..."

Spencer nodded, even though the other man couldn't see him. "My wife and I have been growing apart for a while, but I've...I've never done anything like this."

He didn't have many close confidants anymore, and never expected to be talking to Graham about these things. Probably wouldn't have if, earlier tonight, Graham hadn't come into his office while she and Spencer were still half undressed.

But Graham was discreet. He'd always defended Spencer to the board. He'd keep quiet about this. He had too much at stake and there was no need to stir the pot, anyway. What happened was between two consenting adults. Sure, Niall Spencer was her superior, but these things occurred all the time. It would cause a scandal—and Asimov Automotive certainly didn't need another one of those—but it would stir embarrassment more than anything if it got out.

"To be honest, I think we've all got bigger things to focus on. You were both stressed and needed a release. That's all that happened. It was a one-off. It won't affect your ability to work together, right?"

It wasn't a one off, but no, it hadn't affected their jobs. If anything, it had enhanced them. It was so good to *feel* something for someone again. He'd taken refuge in his work before, but she'd reminded him life was more than that. From the way they looked at each other when no one else was around, he wondered if she felt the same way too.

Maybe they'd make it official, once his current marriage was over. That seemed inevitable, certainly now. Kayla had never really seemed to bond with her stepmother, so at least she shouldn't be too upset. Maybe she'd like his next wife better.

"Niall...?"

Spencer shook his head, snapping out of it. "No, it'll be fine." He looked toward the front of the car. Aside from the dim white glow of the dashboard instruments, the brightness of the center panel touchscreen was the only light inside the vehicle. On the display were the words *Edward Graham* and, below them, the current duration of the call—just over ten minutes. "She and I are both adults. We'll handle this maturely."

"Good. Because all three of us know that Friday is much more important."

"Yes," Spencer said, smiling with the thought of it. Friday *was* much more important.

Friday was everything.

She and his wife would both be there, he realized. That could get awkward, but in the face of what was coming, it wasn't a real concern. The focus would be on the keynote. The big reveal Silicon Valley had whispered about for months was almost here, and in just a few days he would pull back the curtain on the company's most ambitious move yet. His technological magnum opus.

Waymo, Uber, Tesla, Detroit—they wouldn't know what hit them.

"It's been a long road, but I'm glad it's led us here. You deserve a fair share of the credit. Your help has been invaluable."

Graham chuckled. "A lot of them said I was crazy to back you, said Asimov was just another Tesla wannabe. After this, Tesla will want to be *us*."

Spencer was already certain of that, but he liked to put on a show of modesty. "We'll see," he said. "Disruption is what Silicon Valley does best. We're about to become the new leaders of the pack, that's all."

He could hear Graham yawning. "Alright, I've got to get some rest. I'm glad we had this talk, though. I trust both of you. Just remember that no matter how advanced a world we create, at the end of the day, we're all still human."

Spencer paused. "Of course... Goodnight, Ted. I'll see you tomorrow, but I won't be in until closer to ten. I'm going to spend breakfast with Kayla and take her to school. Then it'll take me a while to get back up the coast, especially with morning traffic."

"Hey, you've earned it. And remember, we're almost at the finish line."

He rubbed his forehead, laughed. "That's true. Goodnight, Ted."

"Same to you." Graham hung up.

A synthetic female voice replaced him on the speakers: "Call ended."

The same words popped up on the touchscreen, then the display went black. It would only activate again if Spencer addressed SALLY or tapped on the panel. Now the interior of the car was dark. The only sounds were the patter of rain on the windows, the gentle *swish* of the windshield wipers, the *whooshing* of cars in the left lane. Spencer allowed himself a sigh of relief as he relaxed back into the chair, taking in his surroundings.

All four seats currently faced each other, as was the default setting when the SUV was on AutoDrive, but Spencer liked to sit in the back. It made him feel like he had his own virtual chauffeur, which in effect, he did—as did everyone else who owned an Asimov Automotive vehicle. It was to be a brief transitionary age before a new day, when no one owned a car and ridesharing fleets stretched as far as the eye could see. A more efficient world, devoid of advanced vehicles sitting idly in garages. Steering wheels and combustion engines would vanish, taking gridlock and city smog along with them.

The Asimov Automotive T-Series sped through the pouring night. Spencer glanced outside again. Traffic was thinner here, as usual. Highway 1 dwindled to a two-lane road in the Monterey Peninsula and now wound its way through the darkened California countryside. He was getting close to home.

Home. Not the quiet, lonely apartment in Palo Alto he had been spending so many nights in lately to get to the office before sunrise. His real home. Spencer closed his eyes and pictured it, the ultramodern house with a sweeping view of the shore, his wife and daughter waiting for him.

His wife, to whom he had been unfaithful.

Spencer thought of what Graham said: *At the end of the day, we're all still human.*

It was a human error he'd made, the kind reason warned against. Yet he'd been unable to resist the impulse. She had been, too.

We're all still human.

That's the problem, Spencer thought. A world run by imperfect beings could never become a perfect world. He sometimes envied those who were less ruled by their emotions, for whom detached, cold calculus was the logic of their lives.

He sighed. If only years of childhood torment had washed away his emotions instead of solidifying them.

There was one thing, he thought, that made it bearable. He wouldn't trade all the progress in the world to give up how he felt for his daughter. It was rough on Kayla with her stepmother gone almost every week and her father spending most nights up in the Valley. Even rougher given that her real mother died of a rare heart condition when Kayla was only four.

Now that this unveiling was almost upon them, Spencer knew she must become his primary focus. He couldn't leave his own flesh and blood on the backburner any longer. There were less than two years until she was off to university, and even if she went to school close by things would be different.

He'd start making amends tonight, he decided, as soon as he got home.

Spencer opened his eyes, then frowned. The SUV was still traveling south on CA-1. He was certain it should have turned onto Ribera Rd by now. Peering out into the rain, he saw waves crashing against the seashore to the right. Spencer blinked, unbelieving.

The car had missed its turn.

"SALLY," he said. "State destination." The center dashboard screen remained black. "SALLY!" he barked.

Nothing.

Spencer froze, his mind searching for an explanation. It found none. No production-model Asimov vehicle had ever taken a wrong route to a destination. And he'd never had an issue with SALLY's voice activation, either.

"SALLY!" he repeated, only to get the same response.

Suddenly, Spencer realized the headlights on his left were whipping by more rapidly. Raindrops smacked the windshield with an increased frenzy.

He disengaged his seatbelt and tore it off, the metal latch slapping against the window as it retracted. Spencer launched himself into the seat across from him and reached around behind it under the steering wheel, where the AutoDrive lever was located. He pulled down on it twice.

Nothing happened.

The driver's seat should've turned back around and manual driving—a dirty phrase—should've activated.

He tried it again. And again.

And again.

Finally, he resorted to frantically jerking the lever up and down. Still, the SUV remained in AutoDrive.

And it wasn't slowing down.

Jesus Christ, Spencer thought.

There was only one logical explanation, but his mind struggled to see how it could even be possible. He shook his head. *Solve the breach later. Get the fuck out of here.*

The vehicle was speeding up a hill now, away from Monastery Beach. Trees flanked the road on either side. The speedometer had him going more than 90 now.

The T-Series was an electric car. It could accelerate *much* faster than this. Whoever was in control didn't want him dead. At least, not just yet.

They were taking him somewhere.

Maybe this was a kidnapping. There had been threats against him, but anyone with a social media account got death threats from somebody these days. Had one of those anti-automation loons somehow gotten into the system? The car was protected against spoofed 5G towers. Or at least, it was supposed to be.

Focus.

The human problem again, emotions getting the better of him. He needed to stay calm.

Breathe in, breathe out…

As he exhaled, his eyes swept the car's interior. The doors would be locked. Windows were all around, a moon roof above.

Break the glass and escape.

No, at this speed that was far too dangerous. But, he realized, it was the only option. Maybe the car would decelerate at the next turn.

Spencer stood up and pounded against a window with his fist. He'd never thought to keep sharp objects in the car in case it ended up in a body of water because, he'd figured, it never would. AutOS was the best Level 4 autonomous driving system on the market. It didn't make those kinds of mistakes, not even in the rain.

And it wasn't making one now. This car was no longer self-driving.

Spencer smashed his fist against the glass over and over, making his knuckles bleed. He didn't care. He gnashed his teeth through the pain, waiting to spot a crack in the window. But, of course, one wouldn't appear, not without a severe blow. Safety was one of the selling features.

Asimov Automotive. Driving your future.

Cars streaked by in the other lane, metallic blurs led by light. The SUV was going well over a hundred by now, but he didn't dare look at the speedometer. He kept smashing his fist into the rear-left window. *Break, goddamnit, break.*

Suddenly the car lurched left, into the other lane. Spencer flew back and felt weightless, just for a moment, but the vehicle swerved right again—*hard*—and he flew face-first into the glass.

Spencer fell to the floor, clutching his head. His skull throbbed and his nose was broken. Blood gushed all over his face and hands and he struggled to gather his bearings. The car kept swerving in and out of the lane. Honks erupted and tires squealed.

But none of that bothered Spencer anymore. He was staring up past the darkened touchscreen panel to the spot where the webcam resided. It was too dark to make it out in this light, but he knew it was there. It hadn't been on for his call with Graham, but whoever gained control of the car's systems would have access to it. The bastard had watched him trying to break the window, as futile as that was, and nearly killed him.

Maybe this wasn't a kidnapping. Maybe they were just toying with him before…

It suddenly occurred to Spencer that this might be it. Actually it.

No, no, no…

He hadn't gotten to say goodbye to Kayla. That's all that mattered now. The project, the keynote, the affair—all were suddenly irrelevant.

No, it couldn't be over. Not yet.

Despite his definite concussion, Spencer hauled himself up to the touch panel and stared into the webcam.

"Fuck you," he spat.

There was no response.

Blearily, Spencer looked out the windshield and saw he was zipping past the Point Lobos Reserve. The trees were higher here, woods all around. You wouldn't guess this was a coastal road, not from this section.

He knew what was coming. It was inevitable.

Tears sprouted from his eyes, and he buried his face against the screen, smearing it with blood.

"Who the hell are you? And *why*?" He said the words quietly, and part of him wasn't expecting a response.

Then came the voice.

It was electronically distorted and emanated through every speaker, as if the car itself was alive and speaking to him.

"You already know."

The sound chilled him to the bone. It didn't sound human at all, but as Spencer racked his brain for an answer, it suddenly hit him.

Gripping the sides of the panel, he raised his head and stared into the webcam. He knew whose face watched him on the other end.

He swallowed. "Killing me solves nothing."

"On the contrary, it solves several problems at once."

"Please...we can work this out." He forced a smile, but inside he was shaken with despair. How had it come to this? None of it seemed real, save for the physical pain racking his nose and skull.

Outside, the car cleared the Point Lobos forest, following the curve of asphalt left toward Carmel Highlands.

"You brought this on yourself, Niall." A pause. "Enjoy the ride."

The car accelerated again, flying around the next curve, arcing back toward the ocean. The speedometer returned to the triple digits and kept climbing, climbing. Now the SUV sped past coastal villas hidden in the trees, fences on both sides of the road. Spencer watched in horror as the vehicle veered right, up a driveway incline into a private estate—

And kept going, barreling over muddy ground, slaloming past trees, the lights of a house off to his right. Where the trees ended up ahead was a low fence. Beyond that was only blackness and rain.

He gripped the reverse-facing seats beside him tightly, as if they would do him any good. Then the SUV smashed through the barrier, and as it plunged down, down, toward the foaming sea and sharp rocks reaching up to meet the headlights, Niall Spencer opened his mouth to scream.

TUESDAY

8:32 AM

Cray awoke slowly, sore and aching all over, and realized her left wrist was still handcuffed to the bedpost. She groaned, watching a ray of sun glint off the metal as she moved her hand this way and that, then glanced beside her.

A raven-haired woman lay facing the other direction, her bare back toward Cray. Last night she'd been wild and vicious, but asleep she was suddenly boring. That was the problem with hookups. If she got to like a longer-term partner enough, just having them around could make things interesting. Sometimes, she could even pretend she was normal. Not that she wanted to be, having seen what normal people were really like.

Turning to the nightstand beside her, she pulled open the top drawer and rummaged around, not caring if the other woman stirred. *Shit, what's her name again? Mary? Marcy?*

Right, Marcy, that's it.

Finally, Cray grasped the tiny metal key and slid it into the lock. Moments later, she was free and rubbing her wrist, aches stitching across her body. Groggily, she got up. At nearly twenty-seven years old and just shy of six feet tall, Cray was both younger and taller than the woman lying in her bed. She rubbed her face and brushed golden blonde hair out of her eyes, heading to a full-length mirror to inspect the damage.

The date, time, and weather forecast were displayed in the upper right corner.

Marcy had done a real number on her, and a smile came to Cray's face. High pain tolerance was one of the few benefits of her brain's wiring. Her neck was covered in hickeys. Rope marks crisscrossed her chest. Purple welts stretched from her rear down much of her legs.

Well, someone's dressing conservatively this week.

As bad as it was, she'd done worse to her usual toy, a studio executive, last week. She liked him because he let her go completely animalistic, biting him all over, pinning him to the bed, going at his neck. She wondered what it would be like to tear out his jugular, just to see what would happen. Cray knew she'd never go that far, but it was still fun to think about.

Wouldn't be the first time she'd tasted someone else's blood.

Said toy was the longest relationship she'd had since Simone, and it had only been a casual thing going for a few months. They were free to see other people. He was in his early thirties and between marriages. Unfortunately, he was also away for the rest of the month in Australia, overseeing a film shoot.

Bored by his absence, she'd turned to one of the dating apps on her phone and matched with Marcy, a graphic designer, last evening. Marcy wanted to meet at a bar in West Hollywood, not far from Cray's apartment. Then one thing led to another.

It had been a while since anyone dommed her. On one hand, she could have a person begging her to do as she pleased. On the other, handing the reins to someone else was relieving from time to time. And the uncertainty it sparked always kept boredom at bay.

Even Dr. Perkins thought it was a good idea. "A lot of people like you turn to drugs and sex for stimulation. I think it's obvious which one is healthier. If it's safe, sane, and consensual, I'd say go for it."

The first and third, she always followed. The sane part was often a little ambiguous.

Standing in her bedroom, morning sunlight glowing beyond the blinds, Cray looked at the mirror's time display and was struck by a thought.

He might've logged on by now. He might've clicked the email already...

Her excitement surged. Sex wasn't the only thing that staved off monotony.

Throwing on some underwear, a T-shirt, and a pair of pajama shorts, Cray left the bedroom and entered the main open area of her apartment. The dining table stood to her left by the window, the kitchen at the back, and a sofa in front of a TV to her right.

Her laptop was on the kitchen counter. She snatched it and brought it to the table, logging on with a password she changed every few days. The welts made her wince as she sat down, but Cray quickly settled in.

Opening her favorite application, she saw a new IP address listed among the others she had access to. She couldn't help but smile. All it had taken was an email pretending to be the legal firm the property and casualty insurance company had on retainer. The senior vice president she sent it to had clicked the PDF link without question. It *was* a legitimate document from a real law firm elsewhere, though she'd doctored the heading. Whether the SVP realized the legalese had nothing to do with his company was irrelevant.

What was relevant was the remote access Trojan virus she'd attached to the file, which had installed itself on his computer the second he downloaded the PDF.

Cray clicked his IP address and a terminal window popped up, displaying his logs in command prompt, green text on black background. She could remotely view his screen too, but that would require more bandwidth and might get her detected on the insurance company's network. She'd only resort to that if it became necessary, but this shouldn't be too hard. For her, it rarely was.

She pawed her way through directories. It only took her a few minutes to find the one she was looking for. Since this SVP was the head of cybersecurity, he had access to the active directory containing every password for every user in the corporate network—as well as previously used passwords for each account.

Which now meant Cray had that access.

Of course, the passwords were masked by hash functions. No big deal. She pulled up fgdump, a long-reliable hacking tool, and began extracting them.

Cray sat back in her chair, watching the progress bar begin its slow crawl. This would take a while. Then she'd need to run the hashes through a rainbow table, which should be able to decipher most of them. After that, she'd be able to get to the billing department, where her ultimate goal lay: the database of credit cards for every single one of the company's clients.

Once in, a hacker would be able to use them at will, charging payments here and there to the thousands of different policyholders. Or they could sell the numbers and scatter them to the winds of the darknet.

The insurance company didn't want that to happen, which was why they'd hired Cray to breach their network and see where the weakest points lay. Penetration testing, a core tenet of whitehat hacking.

A few years ago, the breaches she performed weren't always so ethical. Now they were safe, sane, and consensual. Dr. Perkins would approve.

By now, Cray's stomach had finally woken up and started rumbling. She sighed. It was always at least one thing or the other, hunger or boredom. Her worst impulses came out to play whenever they crossed paths.

Groaning from her bruises as she stood up again, Cray made her way to the kitchen, retrieved an egg carton from the fridge and a small bowl, and began cracking the eggs in. One, two, three, four...five? She thought for a moment. *Yes, definitely five. And toast, yogurt, and cantaloupe. Fuck it, maybe some waffles too. With maple syrup. And whipped cream.*

Doctors had diagnosed her with, among other things, a well-above average metabolism. No one on either side of her family ate as much as she did, but then again, there were a lot of things different about her. She and her younger sister and brother had been conceived through in vitro fertilization, and yet Benita and Iain somehow turned out completely normal. Isabella Cray was the tallest in her household, born to a five-ten Scottish father and a five-three Cuban mother. Thanks to a pituitary issue, Cray had grown to five-eleven and three-quarters. She was also born with complete heterochromia, her right eye blue and her left amber.

But the most crucial difference was her mind. MRI scans taken when she was in college showed parts of her brain had formed a little differently than other people's. Her ventromedial prefrontal cortex was slightly smaller, and it had *communication issues*, they said, with her amygdala. Both were instrumental in regulating social interactions and feelings.

Genetic mutation, everyone told her. Luck of the draw.

All things considered, Cray didn't feel she turned out too badly. She had a higher IQ than anyone in her family. After her parents' harping on her for years, she finally pushed herself to do better and graduated near the top of her high school class. Up until tenth grade she'd been lanky and slightly awkward looking, especially with braces, but by graduation she'd certainly glowed up. It made the boys and girls she liked considerably easier to manipulate.

By the time Cray finished making her enormous breakfast, the hunger pangs actually hurt. She glanced back toward the bedroom. Marcy wasn't visible from here but didn't appear to be up. Cray put the cut-up omelet onto several slices of sourdough and began devouring them as fast as she could.

Back when she was still mastering the art of social interaction, circa ninth grade, a group of girls had decided to pick on her for eating ravenously at lunchtime.

"You alright there, Izzy?" one had sneered. "Do you have a tapeworm or does your family just never feed you?"

"I thought your mom runs a restaurant," another said.

"Don't you at least get the scraps?"

"Of course she doesn't," said a third. "Look how fucking thin she is. I've seen anorexics with a better ass."

Cray sat there, frozen and glaring, not saying a word, not even swallowing the bite of overcooked cafeteria food. The girls had finally given up and walked away, laughing.

A few days later, they opened their lunchboxes to find pieces of a dismembered squirrel scattered evenly among them. The third girl had gotten all the entrails. Her scream was heard across campus.

Soon the omelet sandwiches were gone, along with two waffles doused in maple syrup and a container of pre-sliced melon from Safeway. She was downing a glass of orange juice when Marcy walked out of the bedroom wearing an over-sized T-shirt. Cray had gotten it from the studio executive, and it displayed his company's logo.

Marcy yawned and rubbed her eyes, looking around. "Morning. How are you feeling?"

Cray detected none of the ice cold domme from last night. Now here was the caregiver, checking in. Cray herself had only started doing that a few years ago. Either she was gone by the time they woke up or went on like normal. Whenever *she* subbed, she felt fine afterward. Why would anyone else be different? The thought never used to cross her mind. But once she realized the things she did to people might leave them a little shaken, she'd started putting more effort into the morning after. After all, she didn't *want* to be careless.

Instantly, the mask from their date was back on. "Hey," she said softly, lowering her gaze. "Feeling alright. Just...a little sore." She laughed, made it awkward on purpose.

Marcy tilted her head, smiled warmly. She came around the kitchen counter and got up on her toes to give Cray a kiss. She was about half a foot shorter, in her early thirties, and had freckles.

"You were great," Marcy said, looking up at her eyes. Did she notice, Cray wondered, how her smiles never quite reached them? "Really, really great. How's the bruising?"

She forced a blush and shrugged. "I've had worse." *I've given worse.*

Marcy gave her a warm look and gently began lifting Cray's shirt. She let her. Marcy traced the marks across her chest, worry flashing across her face. "This is actually worse than I thought. You sure you're alright?"

Said the woman who, less than eight hours before, had trussed her up and beat her with a riding crop, calling her a filthy fucking slut.

"I'm fine," Cray said, secretly annoyed. Marcy probably wasn't doing this because she cared. Deep down, she probably just felt bad and wanted to make sure Cray was alright so it didn't horrify her later. Cray had never been disturbed by the things she'd done, even if she tried. Her brain just didn't work that way.

And yet neurotypicals liked to pretend they were so much better. So what if they felt guilt? If it didn't change the things they'd done, did it really matter if the NTs felt sorry or not?

Marcy ran her fingers across the red fox tattoo on Cray's left side, right below her bra. "When'd you get this?"

"A while ago," Cray said, keeping her voice soft, leaning closer.

Briefly, she wondered what actual intimacy was like. Did anyone ever achieve it or was it just people deluding each other? Did mutual delusions cancel each other out? She thought she'd achieved it once before. Losing that was one of the few times she'd ever felt sad.

Cray couldn't decide if she wanted to fool around more or get back to hacking. Marcy worked freelance from home, just as Cray did. She didn't have to leave yet. And fgdump was still working. It would be a while before she needed to run data through the rainbow table.

Why not? You'll be bored until then.

Marcy looked past her at the empty plates and let go of Cray's shirt. "You ate breakfast and didn't make any for me?"

Cray smiled and looked away. "Maybe."

Marcy poked her full stomach. "You're a terrible servant."

"What are you going to do about it?" Her smile morphed into a playful grin.

Marcy returned it. "I've got some ideas."

Cray's phone rang, buzzing on the kitchen counter where she'd left it last night.

She stared at the device, wondering who was calling. Marcy suddenly grabbed her chin and pulled her head toward her.

"You'll only answer that if I say so, got it?"

Cray smiled again. "Yes."

"Yes, who?"

"Yes, *Mistress*." A clichéd title. Cray wondered how new Marcy was to the scene. She preferred different titles herself, depending on the kind of roleplay.

The phone kept ringing as Marcy guided her back to the bedroom. It rang again immediately after. And again immediately after that.

By the fifth consecutive call, Cray's curiosity piqued. She wanted to see if she recognized the number but was already out of her clothes again and bound to a wooden chair, the ropes so tight it was almost uncomfortable. Almost.

Marcy sat astride her, their lips locked. She pulled back and smirked. "Somebody *really* likes you."

Cray laughed. "Clearly."

Marcy tilted her head. "Want me to bring it over?"

"I don't think they're gonna stop until you do."

She sighed, stood up, and disappeared to the other room, leaving Cray to stare at herself in the mirror again.

With Marcy gone, she let her mask down and examined herself, the *real* Isabella Cray.

Simone told her that her eyes looked soulless like this. Said it was unnerving, even though she'd been the one who wanted to see Cray's natural state. *That was my fault, letting her get too close in the first place.*

A moment later, Marcy came back in, and Cray readopted a friendly, submissive demeanor. The phone was buzzing again. "Sixth straight ring." She sat astride Cray once more, swiping her thumb across the Answer icon before Cray could read the caller ID. Marcy held the device against her captive's ear.

Cray cleared her throat. "Hello?"

"Izzy?" A sigh. "Thank God you're there. I've been calling like crazy…"

It was Ted Graham. She hadn't heard from him in over half a year. Last time, he'd gotten her to pen test a Valley startup he'd invested in.

"Ted, hey, sorry. I've been a little tied up this morning."

Marcy rolled her eyes.

Sorry, Cray mouthed, smirking.

But Graham sounded desperate. "It's been crazy here— Hold on Casey, I'll be with you in a minute… Have you heard? Never mind, of course you have. Everyone has. It's all over the news. Jesus, what a *mess.* Wait." Quieter now. "What about the feds?"

Cray's mask slipped, and concern washed over Marcy's face. "Ted, what's going on?"

"Oh wonderful, just fucking wonderful. Exactly what we needed before Friday." It sounded like he was speaking to someone else, off the phone.

"Ted?"

"Sorry, Izzy." His voice was clearer now. "It's chaos here. There's going to be an investigation and I need someone I can trust. They've made me Interim CEO until this gets cleared up. We're not confirming it in the news, but some of the speculation *is* correct. It had to be a breach through the OTA system. We don't know how far it goes, but I need you on the team. I don't want the FBI poking around in things they don't need to poke around in. You're well respected. You'll make a great addition to the task force. I'll bring you on as a consultant. How busy is your schedule this week?"

"I…um…"

"Because I'll double your usual pay."

"It's…pretty tight right now." It really wasn't. The insurance company pen test was the only thing she had locked in for the next little while. She'd been corresponding with some other potential clients, but nothing was official yet. However, by the tone in Graham's voice, she knew she could get more out of him. Right now, money wasn't his priority.

Which meant that whatever happened was very fucking bad. "I'll triple it."

Cray paused, just long enough. "Well… Okay, Ted… I'll make it happen. Just for you."

"Thank you, Izzy. I've already sent the corporate jet. It'll pick you up at LAX in a couple hours. Pack for at least the week. After Friday, there won't be much point in you staying, whether it's been solved by then or not. I'll send you an email with the details."

"I'm getting my suitcase as we speak."

"See you soon." His voice was bone tired. The line clicked off.

Marcy lowered the phone, looking apprehensive. "What's wrong?"

"Untie me," Cray commanded.

Marcy glowered. "Is that how you talk to—?"

"Un. Tie. Me." Their eyes met and Cray let the mask stay down. It was enough to chill her partner, who began undoing the ropes. When she was done, they fell around her ankles and Cray shot up, storming out of the room.

She made straight for the open area and snatched the remote off the coffee table, turning on the TV and switching to a news network.

She saw a helicopter view of the California coast. It looked like the Monterey area. The footage was labeled *Earlier this morning*. A boat with a mounted crane pulled a partially submerged SUV out of a rocky cove, an Asimov Automotive model. The back end was still recognizable, but the entire front half of the vehicle was a mess of twisted metal and shattered windows.

"…really is unbelievable," some off-camera expert was saying. "It's horrible, but I'm not surprised something like this has happened, if there *was* foul play. I've been saying for years that computerized vehicles, autonomous or not, are susceptible to hacking. This is definitely a worst-case scenario, though. It's just shocking that it was done to such a visible figure."

Cray stared at the *Breaking News* headline in disbelief. It read *ASIMOV AUTO CEO DEAD IN ACCIDENT,* and below it, *Vehicle may have been hacked.*

"Izzy?"

She turned. Marcy was staring at her from the bedroom doorway, confused and worried. "What's going on?"

Cray brought the mask back up, relaxing her shoulders, offering the woman a weak smile.

"I'm really sorry," she said. "But I need you to leave now."

10:07 AM

Sova pressed his gun to the man's head and gazed out the window, toward the lake.

"Beautiful, isn't it?" he said, leaning closer.

Outside, it was a cold day in Tahoe. Snow dusted the ground and trees. Ice lined the shore but didn't extend too far into the water. Not yet anyway. This was just a little taste of winter, whetting the skiers' appetites.

But Markus Sova hadn't come here to ski. Neither had the man whom he'd come to kill. The man who now sat bound to a chair and gagged with duct tape in the expansive family room, a fireplace sitting empty not far behind them, an elk's head stuffed above it. Sova kept the oblong silencer against the side of the skull, just above the left ear.

He looked at the man now, cowering and simpering, tears spewing from his eyes. Sova sighed. It wasn't supposed to be like this. None of it ever was.

He crouched beside his target. "Listen," he said. The man kept staring forward. "Personally, I don't have anything against you. You've never wronged me, never hurt anyone I know. But your Vegas friends *really* didn't like you skipping town with their money. And they *really* don't want that to happen ever again. They need to make an example. So if they *don't* kill you, they're fucked. You left them with no other choice."

He stood up again, repositioning the 9mm. "Luckily for you, they sent me. They could've sent someone else, someone real fucked in the head. The kind that'd dismember you before they'd even killed you. The kind that'd do other things I don't even wanna think about. But I'm not like that." He looked back out at the frigid November day. "I don't know why you took their money. Maybe you had good reason to. But you still fucked up. They found you, and from that point you were always gonna have to die."

Sova looked back to the man again, who still wasn't making eye contact with him. "So here's my philosophy: You didn't ask to die, but you made some bad choices and now you're going to get killed whether I'm the one who pulls the trigger or not. So what I do is try to make it as painless as possible. The best out of a horrible situation. You don't want to die, and I don't want to kill you. But I'm going to. I have to. That's how this works."

With his free hand, he gestured out the window. "Your safehouse has a pretty nice view, you know? There are worse ways you could shuffle off this mortal coil. So take it in. Take your time. And when you're ready…I'll make it quick."

The man's nostrils flared with each sharp breath, beads of sweat rolling down his forehead. His eyes focused on the scenery and Sova stepped back, keeping the gun aimed at his head. He watched him like that for a while, saw him take it all in. Gradually, the breaths came slower and deeper, his shoulders seeming to relax. It was quiet in the house save for inhalations and exhalations. After what seemed like a long time, he was completely lost in it all. The trees, the snow, the distant mountains—

Sova squeezed the trigger.

The bullet punched through the back left of the man's head, escaping his cranium through the right temple. Blood and bits of brain sprayed across the plastic tarp covering the floor. Some splattered the sliding door and part of the wall beside it.

The man tipped sideways, dragging the whole chair to the ground with him.

Then there was total silence.

Sova lowered the gun and sighed, his arm tired from holding it out for so long. He walked to the sofa behind him, where a briefcase lay open with his usual set of tools. He drew out a washcloth and some soap, then stepped over the corpse and knelt by the window. If he hadn't shot him so close, the bullet might not have gone all the way through, or at least as far as it did. Now there was more mess, all for the convenience of a point-blank kill.

You deserve to be on your hands and knees, he thought. *Imagine if Tereza could see you now.*

His sister never learned what he did to pay for her treatments. As a veteran, finding a job in this country was one thing. Finding one after you were dishonorably discharged was another. The United States Army maintained a strict code of conduct to instill discipline and duty in its members. They hadn't seen Sova's tendency for bar fights and insubordination as a benefit to their cause.

These days, he was a good soldier. He followed rules, but they were loose rules, set by people who paid far more than the military ever did. They gave him parameters and he operated within them. Mission success, every time. All parties satisfied. Except for the target, who usually would've preferred to still be alive.

Toward the end, however, he'd realized that no amount of money in the world would've been able to save Tereza. He'd kept her on the machines, kept her alive as long as possible no matter what the doctors said. Eventually, the truth had stared him in the face, looking up from the hospital bed.

It was too deep in her system by the time they'd first found it. He'd killed for nothing.

And yet, years after her death, he kept on killing. For a while, he didn't know why. Still didn't, not really. He supposed it was a part of him. He'd always been good at violence, even though he never liked it. It came easily, but guilt always crept in afterward like a thrown stick washing back ashore with the tide.

It was an awful way to make a living. Then again, he'd lived an awful life.

Sova finished scrubbing the blood off the window and wall and tossed the rags onto the plastic tarp. He didn't worry about leaving fingerprints. He'd had his surgically removed years ago.

He began picking up the plastic and wrapping the tarp over the body, still tied to the chair. As he did so, his phone buzzed. He immediately ceased what he was doing and drew it out.

At any given time, Sova had a few contacts from whom he received urgent notifications. Everyone else was left on silent, something he could read at his convenience and respond to when he was free.

Vibrations were saved for ongoing contracts, and right now he only had one aside from this job.

Sure enough, it was Racer, messaging him through an encrypted darknet channel.

Sova's heart beat faster as he opened the text. He'd been waiting to hear back from them. Their last job together had been a couple months ago, but Racer told him to be on standby for later this week. Now, the plan seemed to have changed.

How soon can you be in SV?

He thought for a moment. It wouldn't take too long to stash the body up the chimney. Securing it would be the most difficult part. Nobody would be visiting this place for some time and above the hearth probably wasn't the first place they'd look. Even if they did find the man's body, it didn't matter. Sova would never be tied to this, and his employers had taken steps to ensure that they wouldn't be either.

Late afternoon, if I hurry. Just finishing up another errand, he texted.

Racer responded a minute later.

New complications have arisen. Your assistance is requested. I have a new person of interest for you.

Next came a file with info on the new hit. He studied her picture, something taken from her website for freelance cybersecurity consulting. Racer had added other information too: height, weight, date of birth. It evidently hadn't taken long to find. So much was publicly available these days. Internet privacy had always been an oxymoron.

Sova examined the photo. She was a tall blonde with different colored irises wearing a suit jacket over an open-collared shirt. He would've said she looked cute, friendly—if not for her eyes.

There was something about them he couldn't place, but he'd seen it before in the gazes of men and women who killed without remorse, a feeling which they simply could not grasp. In all his thirty-seven years, he found it was their one consistent tell-tale sign.

Such people terrified him. He felt his conscience was the only thing still tethering him to humanity, even after all he'd done. People detached from that... Well, were they even human at all?

A surge of emotion swelled through him. He couldn't be certain, but if he was right about this target, then Racer hadn't simply given him another job. They'd given him an opportunity, a rare one in his line of work. A chance to remove a dangerous individual from society.

Yes, he was going to enjoy ridding the world of Isabella Cray.

12:16 PM

It was raining in Silicon Valley.

The attendant handed Cray an umbrella as she stepped onto the jet's stairs, trailing a carry-on behind. She descended to the tarmac, downpour pelting her personal canopy. When she reached the bottom, she looked up to see a sedan waiting for her beneath the dark gray sky. Small traces of light pock-marked the clouds, but the sun did little to pierce the overcast. Downtown San Jose and the Santa Cruz Mountains rose in the distance beyond.

The vehicle displayed the Asimov Automotive logo on its grille, a sideways A reflected horizontally to form a diamond shape. With the As' internal lines, Cray had always thought it looked like a polygonal eye. The silver car resembled an elongated hatchback, with large LED lights wrapping around the front and back in place of standard head and taillights. The saloon-style doors opened automatically as she drew nearer, revealing four facing seats and a white woman in a cashmere sweater awaiting her.

"Hello, Ms. Cray," she shouted over the rain. She looked about thirty-five. "How was your flight?"

"It was great! Been a while since I rode in a corporate jet, but I could get used to it." She laughed.

Cray wore a different mask than she had this morning.

Now she was Corporate Izzy—cool, confident, with just enough levity to seem relatable. She drew this personality out whenever she was on business and found it incredibly ironic. If someone had told her three years ago that she'd one day work to protect the very entities she used to hack, she'd have burst out laughing.

Cray had never breached any of the self-driving or electric car companies though, so this wasn't a homecoming. It also meant she had no clue what Asimov's internal network looked like. Still, it would probably be easy for her to find her way around it.

Clearly, it had been easy for someone.

She stepped into the car and the woman gestured across from her to what would otherwise be the front passenger seat, when it wasn't turned around. Cray sat down, managing not to visibly wince from her bruises, and placed the suitcase on the chair beside her. She shook out her umbrella before pulling it in.

"I'll take that," the woman said, placing it at her feet. She raised her head to the ceiling. "SALLY, close doors and take us to HQ."

"Closing," said a synthetic female voice, and the saloon doors sealed them inside. "Confirm destination: HQ?"

"Confirmed."

The car began moving and Cray settled into the plush black leather, glancing around the cabin.

It was more spacious in here than the exterior suggested, but that was the marvel of electric cars. With batteries replacing engines and no need for exhaust, the interior cabin finally exerted its grand expansion over the chassis. Only took it a hundred and thirty years.

The interior was mostly black, but glowing red lights ran along the doors and dashboard. Cray allowed herself to relax in her chair, which was as large and comfortable as the one she'd sat in on the jet.

Thanks to Marcy, she wore a black turtleneck, completing her outfit with a gray skirt, dark tights, and Oxford shoes.

Black and gray always went together and meant she didn't
have to waste as much time picking good outfits. It was also
a holdover from her goth phase, which, according to her
mother, had never completely ended.

"I'm Cheryl Acheson," the woman said, extending her
hand. "I was Mr. Spencer's personal assistant. I'm now filling
the same role for Mr. Graham."

"Nice to meet you," Cray said, shaking her hand. "I wish it
was under better circumstances."

Cheryl was a short, mousy brunette, and Cray discretely
took her in while she glanced out the window, the car passing
through a gate and departing the airport grounds.

"We're all in shock." Cheryl looked very pale, accentuated by
the vehicle's dimly lit interior. "Everything's been happening
very quickly today. I'm still processing it." She forced a laugh.

I could take your mind off of it, Cray thought, still staring at
her. It would probably be half an hour before they got there.
They had time. Acheson turned back and Cray averted her
eyes at the last second, watching rain hammer the windows
on the other side. *Get a grip on yourself. You have no right to be
bored. Not today.*

That much was true. Today had been the most exhilarating
she'd had in years. Cray still had no clue what the fuck was
going on, but she was grateful for every second of it. If she
could feel giddy, she probably would be.

"You must be wondering how much the press is saying
is true." Acheson either hadn't caught her looking or didn't
show it.

"Have you confirmed it's a breach on your end?"

She sighed. "We've ruled out any other possibility, but we
have no clue how they got into our system, whoever they are.
The police aren't equipped for this kind of thing, so the FBI's
coming in with a digital forensics team."

Cray tensed a bit. She'd never worked *with* the feds before.
"Makes sense. But they've got the best tools for this in the coun-
try. I'm still not really sure what you need *me* for." She laughed.
"I simulate break-ins on computer systems, not figure out

how they got breached. I've got more experience with *inductive* reasoning than *deductive*."

"But that's exactly why Mr. Graham wants you on the task force. We need someone who thinks like a hacker. We're pulling out all the stops on this thing. If there's any way we can solve it quickly, we'll do it. The whole situation is...well, honestly, it couldn't have come at a worse time."

"How so?"

Acheson looked at her as if it should be obvious. "The keynote. It's this Friday, opening night of the Auto Show."

It all hit Cray at once. "Ah," she said slowly. "Right."

Anyone with even a remote interest in tech had heard about the keynote. Asimov had been hyping it up for months and rumors were flying across the Internet.

"You're still going forward with it?" she asked.

Acheson scoffed. "Of course we are. It's what Mr. Spencer would've wanted. And if his killer was trying to stop us, that would just give them what *they* want."

Cray paused for a moment. "So...what is it?"

Acheson sat up straighter, clamming up. "I'm not at liberty to discuss, but you'll find out Friday with everyone else." The way she said it reeked of practice.

Awkward silence hung for a moment, then Cray gave a little laugh. "Well, I'm pretty sure the FBI is gonna wanna know before then."

Acheson glowered. "Well, they won't need to. It's not relevant to the investigation."

Cray did her best not to show surprise. "Doesn't sound like the timing is coincidental."

"I mean the *digital forensic* investigation. The project was worked on over air-gapped systems. There's no way they could've been breached. This intrusion was something separate."

Cray remained silent and looked out the window. They were turning onto Interstate 280, heading down the on-ramp. She was reminded again how impeccably smooth autonomous driving was, every turn a precisely calculated arc, every acceleration a graceful motion.

Except when they had to break suddenly. Though that wasn't necessarily a bad thing, even on vehicles you still had to mostly drive yourself.

She remembered that night well. Her friend's car, which she'd borrowed, coming to an abrupt halt, the other vehicle just a few feet away. The driver screaming at her out the window to watch where she was going. He'd sped off with a squeal of tires. Cray didn't get scared—couldn't, not with her wiring. But she did get tense, anxious even. She'd been shaken that night, not just by the near miss but by the relief that a cop hadn't witnessed it. Hadn't pulled her over and smelled the alcohol on her breath. Without automatic breaking, she'd probably have a DUI.

Consequences, Izzy, Dr. Perkins had said. *Never forget them, because they'll never forget you.*

She turned back to Acheson, allowing her to see confusion on her face. "The FBI will find it highly suspicious if you don't turn it over to them. They can always get a warrant or a subpoena."

"I doubt they'd be able to convince a judge it's relevant. No one gets to see the project until Friday. Mr. Spencer was crystal clear about that."

Cray paused again, considering what to say next. "What was it like working with him?" she finally asked.

Acheson stared straight at her. "He was a visionary, a genius. Unparalleled."

Cray nodded slowly. *I'm definitely back in the Valley.* "So you'll want me to assist with the digital forensics?"

"I think I've told you too much already, actually." She managed a laugh. "Mr. Graham wants to go over everything with you at the board meeting."

"Board meeting?"

"Yes, they're waiting on us to arrive. He's going to give them a rundown before the FBI shows up."

Cray nodded along again, concealing her bafflement. Everything about this was so strange. And yet before it, life had been a monotonous sprawl, peppered with flings and soured by boredom. For the first time in years, she had no idea what she was heading into, a situation where she had no control.

The car continued along I-280, remaining perfectly in the center of its lane. Acheson stared out the window beside her and Cray could tell she was thinking of something to say. The only sound was rain lashing against the exterior. The electric motor was virtually silent.

Finally, Acheson turned to her. "So...where are you from?"

"Miami," she said, trying not to sound bored. Cray realized there probably wasn't much more to be gleaned from her, not until they got to Graham.

"Ah, nice," Acheson said, smiling. "Did you learn any Spanish?"

Cray laughed, a genuine one this time. "Not as much as my mother would've liked. She's a first-gen Cuban-American."

"Oh." The other woman tilted her head, as if examining her from a new angle. "You don't look Latinx."

Cray did her best not to roll her eyes. Acheson seemed like the type to call herself cosmopolitan for vacationing in Cancún. All that was missing was a latte in her hand. Not to mention Cray's entire family hated the term *Latinx*.

But Valley dime was worth putting up with Valley talk, so she forced a smile. "Yeah, I get that a lot," Cray said without bitterness. "My father is from Scotland. He came to Miami to study marine biology, met my mom while she was working at her parents' restaurant. Now she runs it. He's still a scientist."

Her skin tone and blonde hair weren't the things that stood out most on her mother's side of the family. It wasn't even the color of her eyes. It was how *tall* she was. Isabella stuck out like a sore thumb at reunions and get-togethers.

"*Dios mío,*" her grandmother had said, staring up at her at the beginning of high school. She'd turned to Isabella's mother. "What the hell are you *feeding* her, Angela?"

"Pretty much everything," she'd laughed. Then, a little more tiredly, "Izzy's eating us out of house and home."

Though Cray never felt embarrassed, the specter of

awkwardness had crept up on her then. It was strange, thinking she should be feeling something that she couldn't actually process.

Back then she'd thought most people were like her, that empathy was a polite fiction employed to maintain society. In retrospect, Cray was surprised how long it took her to see how fucked up she was.

"That's really neat," Acheson said. "What brought you to California?"

"Did coding in Miami after college—lots of tech there after the pandemic—but I found some even better opportunities out here." Not quite accurate, but then Cray added, "I settled on L.A. because the palm trees reminded me of home." She laughed, but it was true.

Acheson smiled. "The weather is really something out here." She looked out the window and sighed. "Usually, anyway."

The highway wound its way through the Valley, tree-covered hills and suburban sprawl passing by. Cray found herself growing bored. She kept on a pleasant face, an attentive gaze, but her mind was preoccupied with her growing hunger. They'd given her a sandwich and a bag of chips on the plane, as if that would be enough. If they didn't have at least a granola bar for her by the time she arrived, it could become a problem. Masks tended to slip when there was a gnawing in her belly.

Finally, the car began following the curve of an off-ramp. Cray had to hand it to Asimov's AutoDrive system. So slick was its chauffeuring that she hadn't even realized they'd entered the turn lane.

The sedan merged onto Page Mill Road and continued north through some more hills. She recognized the area now. A few miles to the west was the Stanford Dish, though it wasn't visible from here.

Soon they arrived at Deer Creek Road. The hills gave way to open space with lower slopes stretching off, heading down toward the distant bay. Cray turned around to see it through the front windshield. It didn't look like one of the most technologically advanced places in the world. It looked like the frontier days, when it had been known as the Valley of Heart's Delight instead of Silicon. A land where crops grew, a remnant of the Old West.

Then, as the car turned onto Deer Creek, a sign of unmistakable modernity loomed ahead in the rain. The yellow glow in its windows struck Cray as ominous.

Behind her, Acheson sighed with relief. "And here we are."

12:45 PM

Asimov's Palo Alto headquarters was wedged into the hillside, a two-story structure of glass panes and right angles. From above it looked like an L. Chain-link fencing enclosed the other sides of the property to form a large rectangle.

The sedan hung a right and entered the parking lot, passing rows and rows of various Asimov models sitting idle in the monsoon. They swung left and approached a curve at the structure's vertex, where a large set of automatic doors waited.

"There were some tech reporters here earlier," Acheson said as the vehicle slowed. "But really, I'm surprised there's not more news coverage, given who died. The media seem to be focusing on the hacking angle."

Cray nodded, but internally scoffed. Spencer was a known entity in the tech world, but he wasn't a Musk or a Zuckerberg. Certainly not a Jobs. The average person was more concerned with whether the metal death machine in their garage could be hacked. The press would happily sell them that fear in exchange for ratings.

The car came to a stop. Acheson reached for the umbrellas on the floor. "Mr. Graham will meet us in the lobby."

"You let him know we've arrived?"

"No, he'll be notified by the system that my car arrived. GPS tracking."

Cray paused. "Do you track every car you sell?"

"It's part of the agreement everyone signs when they purchase our vehicles." She held up her hands, offered a weak smile. "Don't worry, it's just for analytics. We don't make profiles of drivers so we can sell them new cars. We're not like the *social media companies*." She said it like a dirty phrase. "We sell *real* products that help the world."

"Of course," Cray said, nodding.

Acheson handed over her umbrella. "Let's head inside. SALLY, open passenger side doors."

"Opening."

They folded out into the rain.

Cray grabbed her suitcase and followed Acheson to the sidewalk, opening the umbrella as she stepped onto the curb. She looked back and saw the car doors closing automatically. The sedan rolled off to find a parking space.

They went through the entrance and entered the lobby. The walls were charcoal gray. Cylindrical lamps were mounted along them, spewing gold light toward the ceiling. Potted plants added greenery by the windows. Directly ahead of them stood a reception desk. A woman sat behind it, wearing a mixed-reality headset and scrolling through something mid-air. The wall behind her was emblazoned with the corporate logo, and beneath it the words *ASIMOV AUTOMOTIVE*, then beneath that, *Driving your future.*

Whether you like it or not. Cray rolled her eyes.

To the right was a display of three different Asimov models, labeled on the ground—the F-Series sedan, the T-Series SUV, the K-Series hatchback. On the wall behind them was a screen where Niall Spencer stood, a sly smile on his face. Beside him was the word *DISRUPT.*

She looked at the dead man's image for a moment. With short, dark hair, brilliant blue eyes, and a strong jawline, he'd been rated one year as the Sexiest Tech CEO by some magazine Cray forgot the name of. That had been as close to celebrity as Niall Spencer had gotten. Outside the Valley, anyway.

"Ah, there you are!"

Corridors flanked the reception desk, heading off deeper into the building. From the one on the right, someone emerged, wearing a button-down shirt and chinos. He was a handsome white man with graying hair and a salt-and-pepper beard, mid-fifties.

Cray smiled. "Good to see you, Ted."

Edward Graham walked up and shook her hand. He was a bit shorter than her. "The flight was good?"

She nodded.

"Excellent." He turned to Acheson. "Thanks for picking her up, Cheryl."

She beamed. "My pleasure, Mr. Graham." She took Cray's suitcase. "I'll put this at the reception desk for you. Your suite at the Sheraton downtown won't be ready until later."

"Thank you," Cray said, turning to Graham. But he was already heading back toward the corridor he came from.

"Sorry," he said, calling over his shoulder. "But we need to hurry. The board is waiting."

The conference room sat at the end of the building's western wing, on the second floor. It had a sweeping view north, rolling hills beyond the parking lot descending toward suburbia and the water. It must've been quite something on a sunny day, but the November sky was somber. Rain drizzled down the glass.

Modernist paintings adorned the walls. The table was a long, thin rectangle of zebrawood. Leather rolling chairs sat around it, all occupied save for two at the left end.

Graham took the head of the table and gestured Cray to the other free space. She lowered herself down carefully but still winced. This chair wasn't as plush as the one in the car. Had she known she'd be in the Valley today, she wouldn't have been so carefree last night. She'd expected to be home and bored for the whole week.

The bruises were worth it, though, for both last night and

this. Cray hadn't been this elated in ages, but she maintained a calm face. Corporate Izzy was not impulsive. Corporate Izzy was dependable, reliable, and always got the job done.

This time though, she still wasn't exactly sure what the job entailed. Did they want her to solve a murder? Jesus Christ, she wasn't a detective. She liked crime shows, but that was as close to police work as she'd gotten.

Well, assisting it anyway.

"Ladies and gentlemen," Graham sighed. "Within the next half hour, the FBI will arrive with an Evidence Response Team to collect Niall's personal belongings, and computer forensics technicians will comb through our network and databases. They don't have a warrant for any of this. We've invited them and are cooperating fully to help them solve this as quickly as possible."

A slim woman with jet black hair and circular glasses stared at Graham. She looked to be in her late thirties. "Except for everything on Catalyst." It seemed like she was clarifying it for the rest of the board more so than for herself.

Graham leaned over to Cray and whispered, "That's Mallory Ritter, CTO." Then he turned back to the others. "Yes, that's correct. If they want to muck around in Catalyst, they're going to need a court order. But by the time they get one, the keynote will have happened. We'll gladly turn everything over to them on Saturday if they need it. But the systems are air-gapped, so there's no reason why the forensics team should need access to them."

Cray glanced around the room at the other faces, trying to peg who else was in the C-Suite and who was just an investor. Some of the figures farther down the table flickered occasionally, and Cray realized they were holographic images. Several projectors were stationed across the ceiling.

Graham's button-down shirt looked formal compared to everyone else, save for a heavyset South Asian man in similar attire. He was probably legal counsel. The others wore polo shirts, sweaters, or blouses. The Chief Technology Officer, Ritter, wore a black top under a suit jacket.

The woman across from Cray caught her attention, a red-head with green eyes. She was incredibly pretty. Cray found herself sitting up straighter as Graham continued.

"I've brought a cybersecurity consultant, Isabella Cray" — he gestured to her — "up from L.A. to be our eyes and ears on the investigation. I've worked with Izzy before and I assure you she's top notch. She'll provide a hacker's perspective and will help the authorities find this bastard as soon as possible."

Thanks, Ted. No pressure.

"Do we know the extent of the breach?" An old white-haired guy at the back leaned forward intently, his hologram lagging for a brief instant.

The redhead looked down the line of chairs toward him. "Not yet, but Security Division's been on that all day running our diagnostic software. We haven't found anything so far, but —"

Ritter gave a dismissive wave. "The FBI will have better forensics. And anyway, they'll have to go through the whole system all over again. None of our evidence would be court admissible." She turned to the heavy-set South Asian man. "Right, Adi?"

He nodded. "The FBI will have to establish chain-of-custody of any forensic images it takes of our servers. That's the only way digital evidence is accepted in a trial."

Graham whispered, "Aditya Pawar, CLO."

Cray nodded, glad she'd guessed right. "What about…?" she muttered, gesturing to the redhead.

"Casey Kaplan, COO."

She nodded again, leaning back in her seat.

"So," the white-haired man continued, "there's still no indication whether or not the global fleet is compromised?"

Cray's stomach clenched. She looked around the table and saw several other board members having similar reactions. The only people with measured responses were in the C-Suite.

"No," Kaplan confirmed, looking down. "We're not sure yet if they have access to the global fleet, but if the hacker breached Niall's car through a virus sent via over-the-air update—which is the most likely explanation—then theoretically they would have access to any car which also downloaded the same patch."

Tension rose in Cray's shoulders. "When was the last patch?"

"We sent one out last Wednesday. But two weeks ago, there was a major update: AutOS 6.5."

"And how many cars downloaded those patches?"

Kaplan looked up at her. Fatigue flickered in those gorgeous eyes.

"Over 300,000 worldwide."

12:58 PM

The boardroom went quiet. Cray figured they knew the number already, but having it tied to this really put things in perspective.

She was in disbelief.

Holy fuck are you in over your head, Izzy. She almost laughed. Four and a half hours ago, she was still in bed. Now she was hundreds of miles from her apartment learning that some maniac had the ability to kill any of 300,000 people world-wide at the push of a button, any moment they felt like it. More if there were other passengers in the car. More if the vehicle rammed into pedestrians or fellow drivers.

"Have we rolled back those updates?" a fortysomething woman said, sitting down at the other end of the table.

"Yes, we put out a new patch this morning," Kaplan said. Cray noticed the fingers of the COO's left hand were clutching the table edge, her knuckles white. "We rolled back the updates for the past three months, just to be sure, but there's no telling when the breach happened. And no telling how deep the virus buried itself in the cars' systems."

"Didn't the incidents start happening in July?" White Hair said.

A bald white guy wearing a green sweater leaned forward, a finger raised. He was late twenties, early thirties at most, and had a goatee. "There's no indication our security was breached in those incidents. We've reviewed the logs. The glitches are still unexplained, but there was no evidence of intrusion."

"Who are you again?" the fortysomething woman asked.

"I'm Adrian Johnson, Chief Security Officer."

"Oh," White Hair said. "Nice of you to finally speak up."

"What incidents?" Cray asked, looking between the two of them.

Johnson sighed. "They were software issues. Not my department."

"What incidents?" she repeated. Now that she thought of it, Asimov Auto had been in the news a fair bit this summer. She'd been thinking too much about what happened to Niall Spencer. And about last night. *Come on Izzy, wake the fuck up.*

"They were on the news. First, an F-Series in Florida braked too soon and caused a pile-up. Five were injured. Then one of the A-Series big rigs we sold to Sunbelt Trucking wrecked another in its convoy, but mercifully no one was hurt. Then there was that ridesharing startup A-2-B that hit a pedestrian in Vegas—minor injury, but it happened in broad daylight in front of a bunch of people."

Cray nodded. Right, she had heard about those. But none of them had stayed in the news very long. They'd been quickly dwarfed by a political scandal, followed by some Hollywood actor's divorce.

"The people injured all made full recoveries and we paid settlements, made sure they didn't talk to the press," Pawar said. "There wasn't much for the media to discuss after that. Also, autonomous accidents have been happening since the mid-2010s. The industry's pushed on each time."

"Yeah, but we thought we'd have full autonomy by now," the fortysomething woman said. "It's nearly the end of the decade. We thought we'd have Level 5 years ago and that we'd be witnessing mass adoption these days. The industry has moved the goal posts several times."

"Yes, but that's usually what happens in tech," Graham said. "Look at how long it took VR to get a foothold in gaming. They've been hyping it since before the first dotcom boom."

"How do you know there was no breach, back in the summer?" Cray said quickly, wanting to get back on track. This was bothering her. Something felt very wrong here. A number of things, really. She hadn't been this anxious in a long time. Almost forgot what it felt like.

"Well, with Niall it couldn't be anything *but* a breach," Johnson said. "His car was driving home along the highway and ended up several miles south, with eyewitnesses saying it was speeding and swerving like a madman was in control. Then it drove onto private property and off a cliff. A glitch doesn't do that. Code doesn't do that. But with the incidents this summer—they began in mid-July and went to early August—it was different. Part of the system had just failed. We still don't know why, but glitches just happen sometimes."

"Jesus fucking Christ," White Hair said. "What if a glitch killed somebody? You wanna go on record telling a family their loved one died because 'glitches just happen sometimes'?"

"No, no," Johnson said, getting defensive. "Obviously not. But we put out patches after each of those incidents and there haven't been any more since. Like I said, we know Niall's death wasn't an accident. So that doesn't count."

"But glitches *don't* 'just happen,' " Cray said, trying to hide her exasperation. "It's always because of some bug in the code, and bugs can be fixed. A code without bugs works exactly as programmed. And Asimov cars are known for being the safest on the market. So how can you be sure those weren't intrusions?"

"*I* thought they were." Ritter, the CTO, took a big breath, looking flustered. "But nobody wanted to believe me." She shot a look at Johnson.

He sat up straighter. "*Calm down,* Mallory. You're always getting hysterical over security. This is our first major cyber-incident."

"Yeah," she said, glaring at him. "And our CEO is *dead* because of it."

All eyes were on Johnson. He gave an awkward laugh, held up his hands again. "Look, I've been over the corporate fire-walls at least a hundred times since then and we've found no holes. We've run virus scans, combed through databases for infected files, all of it. Every time, we found nothing. Okay? So the fuck up wasn't on our end."

"This time it was," Ritter said, glowering.

"And I have no clue how that could've happened. Our systems were as secure as they could be."

"They're never as secure as you think." Everyone looked to Cray. "Trust me. You can have the best firewalls money can buy. You can have layers and layers of security, encryption, you name it. But at the end of the day, the human link is always the weakest in the chain. All it takes is one employee clicking on an email URL that looks legit, and *boom*." She snapped her fingers. "You've just let a hacker into your system. And once they're in, they can use that compromised account to send emails to other accounts, and get viruses downloaded there too. Before you know it, they've gotten what they want—credit card numbers, R&D files, anything. And it all starts with human error. It's called social engineering and it's always been the most important part of hacking. It's all about manipulation."

Her stomach growled but she didn't shift in her seat or glance around to see if anyone heard it. She didn't care.

"I know what social engineering is," Johnson said, looking her up and down with distaste. "Obviously. But since you're such an expert on what happens on my computer systems, why don't *you* tell us what you think happened."

Cray put her palms on the table and leaned forward. "I'll tell you what I would've done. If I was some anti-autonomous cars nut and I wanted to kill Niall Spencer or sabotage your new product launch or whatever, I wouldn't do it all at once.

"I'd breach your system with a phishing email. I'd do my research and make it look really good. Then, once I was in

your system, I would phish my way to your software department and embed some Trojans in the software update."

Johnson shook his head. "Nothing goes *into* Software
Update. Data only flows out. Everything we put in that subnet
is from manually transported hard drives and flashdrives."

"And there are still ways of infecting those. I'm sure it's not
as hard as you think. And once I was in there, I would start
testing things, maybe a little accident here, a truck fuck-up
there. And once I was sure I could do it and get away with it,
then I'd plan for the big score, the head honcho. I'd figure out
which car was his, and when opportunity presented itself—
say, driving along a coastal road, I'd make my move."

Everyone had gone pale, staring off into space. Ritter took
off her glasses and rubbed her eyes. Kaplan looked sick, covering half her face with a palm. Down at the other end of the
table, White Hair shook his head slowly. "Jesus Christ."

Pawar turned to her. "But the last of those accidents was in
August. Why wait until mid-November to kill Niall?"

Cray shrugged. "Maybe they wanted to sabotage the
unveiling this week, so they timed the murder to over-
shadow it."

"Well," Kaplan said, sitting up straighter. "Good fucking
luck to them. They haven't stopped anything. The Catalyst
presentation is ready and the—" Her eyes flicked to Graham,
who brought a finger to his lips. "Right." She turned to Cray.
"I'm sorry, but we can't talk about that even with the NDA
you're going to sign."

Cray turned to the Interim CEO. "Ted, come on. If I'm
signing a—?"

Graham shook his head. "I'm sorry, Izzy. Niall was ada-
mant about keeping it secret. He had a zero-tolerance leak
policy. Not even everyone in this room knows what Catalyst is."

White Hair sighed. "I trusted Niall. I'm sure I won't be
disappointed Friday, and neither will the shareholders. But
this…" He shook his head and looked down. "This is just…
crazy. I still can't believe it."

Graham cleared his throat. "We don't have much time before the FBI arrives. We'll keep you updated throughout the investigation."

The board members nodded. The holograms abruptly disappeared while those with physical presence started getting up. Cray stood too, putting a hand to her empty stomach. Right now, it shouldn't have been her main concern, but it was starting to bug her.

Playing High Functioning is more fun when there's a challenge, Izzy.

She sighed and walked over to Graham, who was whispering something to Kaplan. He turned around as she approached. "Let's go to my office. I need to talk to you."

1:15 PM

The CEO Suite was at the other end of HQ, at the tip of the northern wing. It was a spacious corner office on the second floor.

Graham sat down behind the desk and gestured to the chair across from him. "Here, take a seat."

It had a rectangular bottom and backrest, both fashioned from black leather. The legs were chrome steel. She sat down a little too quickly, winced.

"You alright?"

"Yeah," she said, regaining composure. "Just hungry, that's all."

"Right. Forgot about that appetite of yours. Should've sent the jet with an extra sandwich." He laughed, buzzed the intercom. "Cheryl?"

"Yes, Mr. Graham?"

"Can you have someone get Izzy a snack?"

"I could grab something for her from the breakroom."

"That would be wonderful. Thank you so much, Cheryl."

"My pleasure." She clicked off.

Graham sighed and put his face in his hands. Suddenly, he stopped and looked up at Cray. "This must all be quite concerning. The murder, the number of people at risk..." He managed a laugh. "I know it freaks me out."

Cray nodded slowly and said, "It's just shocking, that's all." Which was true.

He put a hand on his forehead and rested his elbow on the desk, staring off at the rain. "It's been a rough year for the company. I've been in and out periodically to check up on Catalyst—that's what we codenamed the project. But Niall's not the only person we've lost. A couple months ago there was Greg, Greg Furman. Engineer. Good guy, only met him a few times, but he took his own life."

Cray looked down. She felt nothing from him telling her this but knew, cognitively, that it was sad. She could tell how much it troubled Graham by the look on his face. She could never sense a mood in a room, but if she studied the individual people in it closely, she could infer what they were feeling. It was surprising how much people gave away unintentionally.

"I'm sorry," she said. Part of her wished she were. She knew the 300,000 vehicles at risk was an awful situation, but knowing that felt like a detached observation rather than something she could intrinsically feel. *Think of the families who could be killed. Think of the innocent people.*

Holding those images in her mind, she could logic through it. Whoever was behind this needed to be stopped—and deserved to be. But personally, she couldn't help but notice how it didn't directly affect her.

I don't own an Asimov car. As long as I stay away from them until this gets sorted out, I should be fine. No one is trying to kill me. *I'm safe here.* And that was good. That meant her fight-or-flight response wouldn't get in the way of solving this problem.

And she *was* going to solve this problem. Not just because it would cure her boredom, but because it was the right thing to do. *High Functioning is a game that doesn't play itself, Izzy.*

"It was carbon monoxide poisoning," Graham said, still looking out the window. "All employees get a discount on Asimov models, and he'd bought one. But his wife didn't. Her car had an exhaust pipe. One weekend she took the kids to Disneyland and—" He breathed in and out. The only other sound was rain on glass. "They found him when they came back that Sunday night. I guess the stress just got to him. It's been awful for everyone working on Catalyst, these last months especially. And now, in the eleventh hour, in the final *minutes*—this happens. I just can't believe it. Just can't…"

He looked lost in a trance. Cray wanted to say something but wasn't sure what. She decided to keep quiet, which was the safest option. Usually.

"Why are you so quiet?" one girl had sneered at her in high school, junior year.

"She's just weird," another said. "I mean look at her. Can't even do goth right. Like, where are your fucking piercings?"

"I don't like them," Izzy said calmly, paying the girls little attention as she pulled something from her locker. She'd never even gotten her ears pierced. It was just never her thing.

The fox tattoo had been something different. And it came later, anyway.

"That's another good thing about electric cars," Graham said, turning back to her. "No exhaust pipe. Can't kill yourself with them, not like that. And with automatic breaking you can't drive yourself off a cliff." He stopped, paled. "Unless… someone else does it for you."

"I know what you mean," she said, trying to sound sympathetic. And she wanted to be, but it was as if everything she wanted to do had to be run through a filter of deliberate logic first. *I'm going to be kind now. I'm going to be considerate now.* Only indifference came naturally.

Graham looked at the desk as if he expected to find something there. "You know, I think that's why autonomous cars are taking off faster than electric cars did. You sell electric cars to people on how much it'll benefit the environment, how it'll save the world for future generations. But people don't care what happens decades from now. They want short-term gratification. 'What does this do for me in this moment?' But a self-driving car can help you *today*. It can make your commute effortless *today*. It can save your life and the lives of others around you *today*. So the more that people get over their fear, the more they'll see what these things can do for them. Because at the end of the day, that's all people really fucking care about." He looked back out the window.

Cray sighed. It was conversations like these that had built their friendship. Three years ago, when she'd begun making the switch to whitehat work, she wanted to build her rapport quickly. So she hacked a growing Valley company. Not Big Tech, not yet, but some at the time said it could get there. She'd breached their network all the way to the top and sent out an internal memo notifying them that they'd been hacked. Fortunately for them, it was a whitehat. But maybe if they wanted to prevent someone more malicious from getting in, they should contact her to safeguard their systems.

They'd hired her less than twenty minutes later.

One of the board members was venture capitalist Ted Graham, and he was impressed with her work. She became his go-to pen tester over the years.

There was a knock on the door. "Come in," Graham said. Acheson entered with several bags of vegetable crisps and an organic cola. "Ah, thank you, Cheryl."

"Any time." Acheson put the food down in front of Cray.

"Thanks," she said, tearing one of the bags open. Acheson walked out of the office and closed the door behind her. Cray took a handful of chips and shoved them into her mouth, but Graham didn't seem to mind. He looked dejected.

"I'm worried," he said, "that this is going to set us back years. People were just starting to accept autonomous cars, to see the benefits. Now even if they trust the technology, they won't trust that it can't be breached. The entire driverless car industry will take a hit."

He looked at her. "*That's* why we can't delay the keynote. If we don't keep pushing on, Niall will have died for nothing." Then, quieter, looking down, "Laura will have died for nothing."

Now Cray wanted to feel sad. At least Graham could properly care about those close to him. She would never even enjoy that kind of misery.

Graham's wife Laura had been killed by a drunk driver during the pandemic. He'd risked catching coronavirus to stay by her side in the ICU, but nothing the doctors could do would save her. Making roads safer got personal after that. He'd bought a sizable stake in Asimov and joined the board, the second largest shareholder after only Niall Spencer himself. Graham had always talked about autonomous cars as the thing he was proudest to work on.

She put down the bag of chips and sat up straighter. "They didn't die for nothing, because we're going to catch who did this."

Graham nodded slowly.

"Do you have any idea who it could be? Anyone who would've wanted to destroy Spencer or the company?"

He looked up at her. "Actually...yes, I do. I've been thinking about it since I first found out he was murdered. If there's one person who would've—"

A knock came at the door.

Graham sighed. "Yes?" he said, annoyed.

Acheson poked her head in.

"Hi, Cheryl. What is it?"

She looked anxious. "Sorry to interrupt, Mr. Graham, but the FBI is here."

1:23 PM

When the door opened again, a stocky black man entered the room. Everything about him screamed fed—the crisp suit, the closely cropped hair, the military posture.

When Cray saw him, she swiftly turned around and ducked her head, even though she realized that would be pointless. Her pulse soared and color flushed through her face. Butterflies in her stomach fluttered so high she felt hiccupping might set one free.

How? she thought. *No, not how.* Why? *Why did it have to be* him?

She heard him reach into his suit jacket and draw out the badge. But she knew his name even before he announced it with his deep, booming voice. "Special Agent Luke Reed, San Francisco Field Office, Cyber Squad. I'll be serving as the lead case agent on this investigation. And this is my junior partner, Special Agent William Fraser."

Now Cray turned around and did her best not to look startled. A second, younger man had entered the room. He was dashingly attractive with Asian-Caucasian features and shock blond hair, clearly a dye job. She'd never seen an FBI agent so young. He had to be mid-twenties at most. His suit appeared vintage and a bit broad-shouldered on his tall, fit frame, yet somehow it worked. The man looked as if he'd stepped straight out of 1986.

Fuck it. She sat up straighter, throwing both of them a warm smile. *This day,* she thought, *just keeps getting better and fucking better…*

Reed recognized her and froze but didn't say anything. His gaze returned to Graham, who said, "Right. We spoke on the phone earlier. This is Isabella Cray. She's a whitehat we've hired to assist with the investigation."

Reed seemed to suppress a laugh at the term *whitehat* but said nothing of it. "That's fine, Mr. Graham." His eyes flicked to hers, then back to the Interim CEO. "I've got a team from the SVRCFL in the lobby ready to get started, but there's a few more things I need to ask you first."

Graham looked confused at the term. Cray already knew what it stood for.

"Silicon Valley Regional Computer Forensics Laboratory," the other one—Fraser—said. He was standing up just as straight as his senior partner. "They assist us and local law enforcement with the digital side of investigations."

Graham nodded. "What questions can I answer for you?"

Reed exhaled. "Since a Trojan in an over-the-air update is the most likely vector of intrusion, the hacker may have access to other vehicles in your global fleet, right? Potentially…all of them?"

"Yes, we've put out a patch rolling back the software to several versions ago, earlier in the year. The intrusion most likely happened after then."

"Sadly, that's irrelevant. If the hacker breached your company and gained access to the OTA department, wouldn't they be able to plant a new Trojan in whatever software update you sent out this morning?"

He grimaced. "We've considered that, and we've sent out a warning to Asimov owners to be careful and that their safety is our top priority."

"I don't think that's enough," Reed said. "I think until we can identify the hole and patch it definitively, you need to treat any and every Asimov Automotive vehicle on the road as infected."

"That's—that's patently ridiculous."

"I'm sorry, sir," Fraser said, "but these cars have become a national security risk. International, really. We need you to release a statement advising owners to keep their cars powered down for the foreseeable future."

"We don't know for certain that's how the breach happened. We don't know how many people are actually at risk."

"Doesn't matter," Fraser continued. "We can't wait until this person uses a swarm of hacked cars to kill hundreds in a city center, here or abroad. If this was politically motivated cyberterrorism, then Spencer's murder could be just the beginning."

Graham shook his head. "I don't think this was cyberterrorism. Or for money. There have been no threats or any groups claiming responsibility. We've detected no ransomware. We can't detect any sign of intrusion at all, actually. It's as if a ghost possessed Niall's car and drove it off the road."

"We think sending it over a cliff was a deliberate move, not a convenience," Reed said. "At the speed witnesses said the car was going, simply ramming it into a tree would've killed Spencer whether he was wearing a seatbelt or not. But by crashing it into the ocean, we have no way of running forensics on the car's systems."

"Exactly," Graham said. "If this was a cyberterror incident, then I think somebody would've wanted to show how easily the cars can be hacked. I bet that cliff was chosen because it was the most accessible one closest to Spencer's house. I believe this was personally-motivated murder, pure and simple."

"By whom?" Fraser asked.

Graham composed himself. "Lucas Declan."

Fraser raised an eyebrow. "Wasn't he the original CEO?"

"And founder. Before Niall bought the company. Niall made money in crypto and AI, then wanted to get into autonomous vehicles. He and Lucas never really agreed about the direction of the company, and so Lucas...agreed to depart after a while."

"He was fired," Reed said bluntly.

Graham spread his hands. "You know how these things go."

"But that was ages ago," Fraser said, thinking back. "Near the end of the pandemic."

"I've seen Lucas at various events over the years. He's never looked well since then. I think he was jealous the company took off so much more after Niall became CEO, with a new headquarters and everything. He's at some lithium-ion battery company over in Cupertino now, but I think Declan still hates Niall. And he probably wouldn't mind sinking Asimov along with him. It's no longer his."

Fraser produced a notepad and pen and began jotting notes. "We'll add him to the interview list. The homicide detective from Monterey County should be here soon. It's officially his case, but because of the cyber angle the Sheriff called us in to form a task force. They don't have the resources to handle this themselves."

Cray felt lost sitting there, watching the conversation fire back and forth over her head. She was torn between thrill and self-preservation. *Don't be ridiculous. You're not a suspect this time. Reed is not going to arrest you. You're on the same side now.*

Which was something she wouldn't have believed three years ago.

"Even if this was meant to be an isolated incident," Reed said, "we can't risk it for public safety. We need the cars shut down."

"There's a small problem with that." Graham swallowed. "Even if I wanted to, there's no way of turning them completely off."

The FBI agents were gob smacked.

"What the hell do you mean?" Reed said.

"I mean they can be reactivated remotely even when powered down." Graham took a deep breath, not meeting their eyes. "It's how people summon the cars when they're parked, from their phone, watch, or smart glasses."

Fraser leaned against the wall, put a hand to his forehead. "Holy *shit*. And nobody ever thought that would be, you know, a *problem*?"

Graham stuttered. "I...Niall always assured me our cyber-security was top notch. I was just a board member and a project consultant before this. I wasn't informed of security updates, that was Adrian Johnson's purview. I had no reason to believe that it would ever become an issue."

Reed shook his head calmly. "Yeah, well it sure did, didn't it?"

Fraser was in disbelief. "How the hell did *no one in this company* ever question why that might be a bad idea?"

"They...they were busy creating *life-saving* technology." Perspiration appeared on Graham's forehead. "They were making sure the computer systems didn't glitch or fail."

"What? They thought the only threat was the limit of their own abilities? They never considered what would happen if this fell into the wrong hands?" Fraser looked at him with disgust.

"Of course they considered it. We've always recognized that vehicular cybersecurity is a major issue. Even non-self-driving cars with computer systems can be hacked. We've been aware of the issue for a while. In fact, we're considered an industry leader in countermeasures. The most common way of trying to hack a car is convincing it that it's connected to a cell tower instead of a hacker's antenna and using that to gain access. But Asimov cars have the most secure firewalls and threat-detection systems in the industry."

"Okay," Fraser said. "But what about general corporate cybersecurity? You must've realized what kind of risk you have here, if you have access to 300,000 vehicles worldwide whether they're powered on or off. All it takes is one phishing email to get into your network, even with a firewall. Have you made sure your people are trained to spot those kinds of dangers? Because those have always been the weakest links."

Graham massaged his temple. "They...they were sup-posed to." He put his face in his hands. "None of this was ever supposed to happen."

Cray exhaled sharply. "Look, there's no point bullying him for what's already happened. That's not gonna help us catch who did this."

Reed glared, but Fraser nodded.

"She's right." Graham pulled himself together. "All that matters now is solving this as quickly as possible. We can sort out blame later."

"Fair point." Reed sighed. "But I have one last question." He walked closer, stared down at Graham. "Have you considered the possibility of insider threat?"

There was silence in the room. Graham looked down. "I mean...it certainly warrants looking into...but..."

"Because," the senior FBI agent continued, "the greatest risk to any organization is an enemy within. A disgruntled employee, someone who didn't get a raise, someone who was passed over for promotion. Someone whose debts got the better of them. Or someone just doing it for kicks. Whatever the cause, it doesn't matter. They already know your networks. They already know where sensitive materials are located. They know when over-the-air updates will be sent out and how to access the computers that send them."

Graham stared off into space, turning over a pen in his hand, thinking.

"There's something else." Everyone turned to Fraser, still leaning against the wall. "Statistically, most homicide victims are killed by people they knew."

"Like I said, Niall knew Lucas Declan. They weren't exactly friends."

"True, but you said their falling out was years ago."

"I think—if it *was* Declan—that he wanted to sabotage the keynote this Friday."

Fraser nodded. "Maybe. But most likely Spencer was murdered by someone who he interacted with on a fairly regular basis. Possibly someone at this company or on the board." Both he and Reed stared at the man behind the desk.

Graham froze, swallowed again, knowing what they were implying.

"No one is above suspicion here," Fraser said, suddenly cold even with his relaxed position against the wall. "No one."

He didn't look at her, but Reed did, his stare piercing deep. Cray's stomach tightened as she got to her feet.

"If we can't shut the cars down, then every minute we're not spending solving this thing is a minute lives are at risk."

Fraser turned to her, pushing away from the wall. He nodded. "Then we better get started."

1:39 PM

"**A**lright everyone, we don't have much time, so I'm going to go over this very quickly—just to make sure we're all on the same page."

Fraser strode toward the smartboard covering the entire back wall and picked up an electronic marker. He scrawled *DIGITAL FORENSICS* on the screen.

"A lot of people get this term confused with cybersecurity, but it is not. Cybersecurity is about preventing a breach. Digital forensics—cyber-forensics, computer forensics, whatever you want to call it—is what we turn to when prevention fails."

He spun around. "Cybercrime is never the crime itself. It is merely the means of the crime. The crime, in this case, is murder. Outside of military or intelligence operations, homicide committed remotely via computer is virtually unheard of. So brace yourselves, everyone. We're in uncharted waters."

Asimov had set aside a conference space on the lower level as a war room and they were all gathered here now—the high-level execs, several engineers from the Security Division, and two digital forensics specialists from the SVRCFL. The FBI's Evidence Response Team was currently upstairs going through Spencer's office, trying to find anything among the dead man's items that might point to who killed him.

The detective from Monterey had arrived too, a man named Connor Quinn. He sat farther down the table at the other end from Fraser—a paunchy guy in his late fifties with brown hair, wearing a trench coat. He looked like he'd either been a smoker or still was.

Up near the head of the table, Reed watched his partner with measured admiration. The room was dimly lit, and the only windows were up high, against the hillside, a rainy day gloom leaking in.

"Usually, digital forensics is used to pull evidence off an arrested suspect's computer. In cybercrime, we use it to detect evidence of intrusion and see what the hacker or hackers got up to inside the system. Once we find the point of entry, we can trace the chain of IP addresses back to the hacker's own computer. Today, we're going to start combing through the Software Update Department's databases and see if we can find any signs of the virus that allowed a hacker to kill Niall Spencer. However, it's been over half a day since the crime, so the murderer may have cleared their breadcrumbs already. If advanced enough, certain computer viruses can delete traces of their existence as they move through databases, like living organisms covering their tracks."

"Jesus." Pawar, the Chief Legal Officer, rubbed his eyes.

"Fortunately, even these covered tracks can be detected with forensic software. Some is government-developed, but a lot of times we resort to commercially available products. Today we're using PrivateEye, which came out only three years ago but is already an industry standard. It works just as well as FTK and EnCase, but it's even more intuitive and is easily customizable. The FBI modified its version to process large amounts of data faster than the standard edition."

Cray glanced back at the Monterey cop, Quinn, and realized he was staring at her chest, one side of his lips curled higher.

Really, pal? They're not even that great. Still, she shot him a look.

Startled, he snapped out of it and resumed focus on Fraser.

Cray sighed. It was going to be a long day.

"We're going to take bit-for-bit images of individual servers and networks. These images will be protected with hash functions to ensure that they haven't been tampered with and are court-admissible…"

Cray started zoning out. She reached for the last bag of vegetable crisps but discovered, to her dismay, that she'd already eaten everything inside it. There was still a bit left in the soda can, which she downed in a single gulp.

Fraser was still going on about digital forensics as if anyone here actually gave a shit. All they really wanted was to catch the person who did this. Cray liked watching him though, specifically when he was turned facing the board. Those suit pants fit him well. Unlike Quinn, she knew the trick to staring at someone was to not get caught.

Really though, her mind was more preoccupied with Reed. Surely, he wouldn't tell Graham she'd been a suspect in a federal investigation, right?

What would that serve at this point?

A vendetta, maybe. He'd never had shit on her, though he knew she was part of the group that pulled it off. He must be the only other person in this room who found her becoming a whitehat ironic. Granted, the crime he'd nearly busted her for was more gray than black.

And Graham probably wouldn't care even if Reed told him, not at this point. Not with everything at stake. She wasn't going to get fired from this.

And certainly, Reed wouldn't consider her a suspect this time. *No way. You have no connection to the victim whatsoever.*

She hoped he was good enough at his job to recognize that.

He hadn't been good enough to catch her, but then again, no one had.

Not yet anyway.

1:51 PM

"**S**o what's the deal?"

Holding an umbrella with his other hand, Quinn inhaled deeply from a cigarette and exhaled smoke. They were standing just outside the HQ lobby doors, by the drop-off curve in the corner of the parking lot.

Quinn said, "Monterey County Sheriff's Department went through Spencer's house, got as much as they could for evidence—his computer, some physical notebooks in his desk, all that kind of stuff—but so far they've turned up nada. I told 'em to leave his computer to you guys. They'll be shipping everything up to the Palo Alto...uh, what's it called again?"

"Residence Agency," Fraser said. It was cold out here in the rain, even with his own umbrella. Reed stood beside him under a third, reading the expression of the man across from them. Quinn had insisted they stand outside. Only place to smoke.

"Right, right. So yeah, everything Monterey's got is getting sent to you guys. Should be there in a day or two, but I think you've got enough to go on for now. The ERT leave yet?"

"Not yet," Reed said. "They've picked apart Spencer's office, but that's all we've been cleared for by Asimov. Anything else we'd need a warrant."

"Wonderful." Quinn took another drag. "Gotta love these Valley assholes. You think they're hiding something?"

"The company itself? No, not really. I used to work in tech. The Valley is skeptical of anyone interfering with how they do things. Anyone that might fuck up the glorious utopia they're building for the rest of us. But an individual *within* the company hiding something? Now that's more likely."

"Of course, of course." Quinn laughed, gazed out at the parking lot. "So...I finished all the road witnesses this morning. There weren't too many. Other people just saw a blur speeding by, so that's not worth much to us. But the thing I didn't get to do was interview the wife. I figured she'd be too distraught last night. But I was planning on interviewing her when I head back down there this afternoon."

Fraser and Reed exchanged looks. "If you don't mind," Fraser said, looking back at him, "I'd like to accompany you, mainly for the wife interview and to look over some of the evidence. Maybe even drive by the crime scene. I'll stay at a hotel down there for the night."

Quinn considered for a moment, nodded. "It's a long drive."

Fraser smiled. "I've been needing an excuse to get out of the Valley for a while."

"Alright," Quinn said. "We should leave in the next twenty minutes or so if we wanna make it there by four o'clock."

"Works for me." Fraser turned to Reed. "I'd like to see the forensics get set up before I go, though."

Reed nodded. "Bailey and Levine are in the Software Update Department right now."

"Excellent." Fraser gestured back toward the lobby. "Let's go pay them a visit."

1:55 PM

Kaplan tapped her badge against the reader and led the group into a substantial, dimly lit computer lab where technicians sat before terminals with oversize monitors. Along the back wall, a series of enormous panels displayed dots across the globe along with real-time analytics. In the bottom right corner was a screen playing CNN. Dozens of staff were at work around the room, hunched over their keyboards, faces lit by the glow of their screens.

The COO sighed and turned around. "This is the main Network Operations Center. The separate NOC for the Software Update Department is over here."

"What are all those dots?" Cray asked, though she had a pretty good idea.

"Those are all the Asimov vehicles worldwide. We track everything from passenger cars to ridesharing services to cargo trucks in real time."

"Even when they're turned off?"

"They're rarely ever completely turned off. If one is plugged in charging, we can access it here as long as it has juice in its battery. If one went offline, we'd see for how long and where and when it appears again." She turned and walked down a row behind seated technicians and engineers. The group continued along.

Jesus, Cray thought, looking at the wall of screens. It was like something she expected the NSA to have. Or a really big sports bar.

"Wait," she said, catching up with Kaplan. "If you're constantly monitoring every Asimov vehicle worldwide, what are you doing with the data?"

"It's just for analytics. To improve safety." She'd said it quickly. Just a little too quickly for Cray's liking.

They arrived at a windowed door, itself located next to a large pane of glass. The smaller NOC was visible through both inside.

"Come on," Kaplan said, tapping her lanyard badge against an RFID panel on the wall. The door clicked open. "Every second counts now."

They entered the room.

It was essentially a smaller copy of the area they'd just entered, though there were only six technicians. Each of their workstations was spaced out to accommodate four monitors per terminal, but it reminded Cray of years ago, when standing or sitting far apart had become the pandemic norm. *Fucking Rona,* as she'd called it back then. She rolled her eyes at the memory.

"This," Kaplan said, "is the Software Update Department Network Operations Center. Whether the breach started in this subnet or not, it had to at least end up here."

A scrawny guy approached them, wearing an old graphic tee for the video game *Cyberpunk 2077* and some acid washed jeans. He extended his hand. "I'm the sysadmin for Software Update."

She shook it. "Isabella Cray. I'm the whitehat Graham brought in."

"Ah, great." He looked past her. "Where are the FBI guys?"

The only other people in their group were the two forensics technicians from the SVRCFL. One of the techs was a boyish-looking guy in his mid-twenties with red hair, name of Bailey. The other was a black woman in her early thirties called Levine. Bailey dragged a carrel behind him with a computer the size of a large suitcase, a small screen on its front.

"They'll be here in a moment." Cray turned to the forensics techs. "You two are the experts," she said, smiling. "Where should we start?" She'd taken the opportunity to act nice to these two while the FBI agents were still out of sight.

Bailey blushed, avoiding eye contact with her. "Well, I heard Asimov's already run some diagnostics of their own. I'd like to know what's already been looked for before we get started ourselves."

The sysadmin scratched the back of his neck. "So here's the thing. We've already accessed our SIEM terminal and there was nothing suspicious in the firewalls for the past month, nothing showing in the IDS, nothing anywhere."

"In English, please?"

Cray glanced behind her and almost groaned. It was Quinn. He walked right up behind her, looking over her shoulder. Evidently, he had his own definition of personal space. She shuffled a little to the right as the sysadmin replied to him.

"SIEM stands for security incident event manager. It's a program we run that basically centralizes all our cybersecurity stuff in one place. The IDS is the intrusion detection system noting any anomalies."

"Right." Quinn nodded blankly.

Cray saw Fraser and Reed through the window, arguing with Graham about something, the three of them standing out in the main NOC.

"How far back did you guys look?" Levine, the other technician, asked.

"Past thirty days," the sysadmin said. "We were thorough."

"But there were vehicle malfunctions in the summer," Cray pointed out. "Why not run tests back further than mid-October?"

The sysadmin folded his arms. "There was no evidence those were the result of an intrusion."

"No evidence *yet*," Quinn said. "I'll leave it to the Geek Squad here to be the judge of that."

"Look." The sysadmin sighed. "We upload our VM archives to cold storage in the cloud. We can access it, but it'll take you guys forever to go through it all."

Levine smirked. "Welcome to digital forensics."

"That's what this is for." Bailey reached down and patted the large computer in the carrel. "It's a Snowball edge machine."

The sysadmin paled. "Jesus, RCFLs are using Amazon products now?"

Bailey laughed. "No, no. 'Snowball' became the generic term for these things. Amazon just pioneered the first."

"What the hell are you talking about?" Quinn broke into a laugh. "Amazon's selling snowballs? 'Fuckin world do we live in?"

"It's a data transferring system," Cray explained. "You can store five hundred terabytes on that thing. They'll process the archive data on there and take digital images of it encrypted with hash functions back to the forensics lab for analysis. That way they'll have established a chain of custody so that they can prove the data wasn't tampered with."

Quinn didn't look like he was really listening to her, but he hadn't taken his eyes off of her either. "Right," he said, a wry smile forming on his face. His gaze traveled down to her shoes and back again, quick but not at all discrete.

"I don't know if Graham's cleared access to the archives for these guys." The sysadmin looked hesitant. "I should go ask him before we do anything—"

Cray spun around, looking him right in the eyes. "Graham put me in charge of overseeing the investigation on behalf of Asimov. I am the FBI and RCFL's corporate liaison, and *I* say we give them access. And right now." She didn't blink once, nor did she raise her voice.

He nodded, shrinking back a little. "Right. There's an open terminal back there by the wall that we can use to access the archives. How far back do you wanna go?"

Cray thought for a moment, turned to Levine. "Six months?"

The technician nodded. "Sounds like the best way to be sure."

Bailey wheeled the Snowball carrel over to the only empty terminal in the room, its four attached monitors all turned off. "Fortunately," he said, "this Snowball is an edge computer, which means it can start running our forensics software, PrivateEye, while it's still ingesting new data."

"Sounds like it'll still take a long time," Quinn said, looking not completely unimpressed.

"These types of investigations almost always do," Bailey said. "Digital forensics isn't sexy."

"Aww," Cray said, smiling. "Give yourself some credit."

Bailey's entire face flushed red. He laughed awkwardly and set about connecting the Snowball to the computer terminal with a cable. Levine moved to help him.

Cray glanced back at Quinn, who looked angry. She shot him a thin smile.

He glared back. "I've gotta deal with some shit in Monterey still today. I'll see you all tomorrow. Have fun with the nerd work." He strode out the door back into the main NOC, where the FBI agents were still talking with Graham.

Kaplan watched the technicians setting up the Snowball. She sighed and turned to Cray. "This looks like it's gonna take a while. Does anyone want me to grab some snacks for them, or something to drink?"

You are officially my favorite person now. "I'll take a snack," Cray beamed. "Come to think of it, I didn't really eat lunch." She laughed, placing a hand on her stomach.

Kaplan smiled at her. "I can get you something. Are you vegetarian or vegan?"

Motion in the corner of her eye caught Cray's attention. She glanced out into the main NOC, where Quinn and Fraser were parting with Reed. As Fraser moved to follow Quinn, he stopped and turned toward her, partly cast in shadow by the glow of the screens. Their gazes met. He averted his quickly, then spun on his heel. He hurried off, following the detective.

Cray turned back to Kaplan.

"No," she said, grinning. "Definitely not."

3:40 PM

Rain lashed against the windshield as Sova pulled into the parking lot. Even with the rapid-fire wipers and the deluge, he couldn't miss the red neon sign shining from the structure ahead.

El Camino Motel.

Two stories of cheap rooms—well, cheap by Silicon Valley standards—bordered the parking lot on three sides except the road. Sova drove into a spot before the lobby, straight ahead.

His sedan wasn't too old or too new, a 2024 model Toyota with a California license plate. An out of state one would've been a memorable detail. Normally, he would've disposed of it somewhere in the woods of Central California on the way back to his safehouse. But he'd snuck through the forest away from his last target's lake house and walked several miles in the cold to get to this car. He was confident no one would connect it to the Tahoe slaying—the discovery of which would probably be at least several weeks from now, anyway. By then, everything Racer wanted him to do this week would be a distant memory. And he'd be well compensated for it.

Sova opened the door and stepped out into the rain. He wore a cream sweater and jeans. With sunglasses and a baseball cap, he managed to look fairly nondescript. But nobody was wearing sunglasses in Silicon Valley, not today. Not all week by the look of the forecast. But his outfit wasn't bad. He easily passed as just another casually dressed techie.

He closed the door, locked it, and headed inside. The receptionist was a woman in her late forties with curly hair.

She looked up. "Can I help you?"

"Hi, checking in." You had to avoid memorable politeness and memorable rudeness. Memorable anything, really. To this lady, he would be just another customer. And that's the way he needed it.

"What's the name?" she said, looking at the computer in front of her. It was the most modern thing in the room.

Thirty years ago, East Palo Alto had been the kind of place where cars got shot at just for driving through. But as Silicon Valley became increasingly expensive, the people living in it turned to anywhere they could afford. Now East Palo Alto was just like anywhere else around here: a sprawl of corporate campuses intermingled with glorified, overpriced suburbia. Sure, rising prices had slowed a bit in the wake of COVID, after many software engineers and coders fled to places where small condos didn't cost a million dollars. Places where they could work remotely and better enjoy the fruits of their labor. But Silicon Valley was still Silicon Valley.

"Hutcherson," he lied, pretending to check his phone with disinterest. Racer had booked him into this motel under an assumed name in the morning.

"You're early," the woman said tiredly. "But it's ready, so here are the keys. It's on the second floor, west side."

She handed them to him. The physical metal seemed an anachronism in this place, given he was just two miles from Facebook's headquarters.

"Thanks," he said, taking them. Then he headed back outside into the downpour.

◄··►

The room was nicer than he expected.

Sova stood in the doorway with his briefcase and carry-on suitcase, impressed by the cozy furnishings and palm tree upholstery. NorCal wasn't SoCal, but it had similar postcard aspirations. Out the window he could see the sign of a chain restaurant glowing across the street. It was a bleak day, but the suite looked much warmer when he flicked on the overhead lights. He set his belongings down and shut the door, locking it tight.

Sova kept the suitcase in whatever car he was using at all times. He never knew where he'd be headed next and sometimes a job called when he was finishing up another one. Today wasn't the first time this had happened.

It's all just part of the routine, he told himself, breathing out. *In a way, it's normal. Or at least, to be expected.*

This was always the hardest part, he felt. The surveillance, the planning, the gearing up to the hit. The actual kill itself wasn't so bad. You just had to do it. Get it over with. There was a certain thrill to be enjoyed in covering your tracks, fleeing the scene. If you made it into a game, it didn't seem so barbaric.

Sova closed his eyes. *This girl needs to die. It's not her fault, but it has to happen. And maybe you're right about her eyes. Maybe she's done things before, bad things. Maybe she deserves this. Maybe, in some way, she brought this on herself, and you are the universe's agent of karma, coming to give her a comeuppance.*

He retrieved the briefcase, set it on the bed.

Opened it.

There they were—his tools. The guns, the silencers, the ammo, the knives.

He drew out a pistol and began attaching a suppressor.

Whether you deserve this or not, Isabella, you should be thankful Racer sent me.

I always make it quick.

3:44 PM

As the car continued south along the coastal road, the clouds finally broke to reveal a blue sky tinted orange by the waning sun.

Quinn never tired of Monterey County, even as he increasingly felt it tired of him. The views were impeccable, worth putting up with rich Californians, yappy dogs, and beach bums. And there was more crime than one might expect from such an affluent area, mainly in Monterey proper, so work stayed interesting. He'd served in the Sheriff's Department's Homicide & Robbery Unit for twenty years now.

But this was the strangest case he'd ever had.

What bothered him most wasn't the murder itself or the Valley ponce who'd gotten whacked returning to his mansion. It was that he shouldn't have been given this case at all.

Everyone in the department knew about his problems by now. Hell, the Sheriff even told him last week if he ever needed anyone to talk to, or wanted to come over for dinner some time, just let him know. He'd done good work for the department over the years, but since his divorce there'd been a decline in investigative quality. He made sure no one ever saw the bottles, but they had to have noticed the suspicious amount of mouthwash he used. And he couldn't do anything about the sweating. The damn smell came out of your pores after a night of drinking.

No, Connor Quinn was no longer the best homicide detective in Monterey County. That was now Richie Liu, but he was off sick this week. Quinn had known Richie for fifteen years. Richie didn't take sick days. The timing of this thing just seemed too coincidental, and Quinn had thought about it all the way up to Palo Alto today. He just couldn't shake the suspicion that someone wanted him on this case, but he had no clue why. If one thing was for sure, though, he was gonna find out.

The highway curved toward the peninsula and off to the right, Quinn could finally see the ocean. Turning to look at it meant glimpsing his passenger, Special Agent Fraser. Quinn didn't know what to make of him. He recognized the eighties style—hell, he'd lived it back in the day—but that was forty-odd years ago. This kid couldn't be more than twenty-five, twenty-six. How the hell was he an FBI agent, anyway? Were they making G-Men that young these days?

And he was quiet. He'd barely said anything the whole ride down, looking lost in thought. That was actually alright by Quinn. He used to dislike the silent types, thought them weird, but they were actually great listeners. They just sat there taking things in and you only realized later just how much they knew. Quinn had learned it was useful to befriend people like that. So no, it wasn't too bad that he was stuck with this weird eighties kid who wasn't from the eighties. Who was somehow a federal fucking agent.

Of course, he'd rather be aided by someone else from the investigation task force. A natural blonde, not whatever bleach Fraser had dumped on his scalp. Cray was just playing hard to get, he could tell. He liked that, in a way. You didn't want them to be too submissive up front. Where was the fun, the challenge? No, you wanted them to make you work for it, earn it.

He pictured the reward, maybe one late night working at the Asimov headquarters, in a darkened room when no one else was around. Her sitting on some Valley nerd's desk, stripping off that turtleneck, then her bra, running her hands across those small, perky—

"Quinn!"

He snapped back.

The car was veering off the road, speeding toward the guardrail—

He jerked the wheel at the last second, the car careening back into the lane. The Rivian truck in the next one over swerved, honked loudly. Quinn's heart hammered as he regained control, bringing the unmarked cruiser back into the center of its lane.

"Jesus Christ," Fraser said, one hand clutching a ceiling handle. "What the hell happened?"

"I…uh…" Quinn wiped sweat from his brow. "I spaced out there for a little bit." He laughed, turning to the FBI agent. "Maybe having one of those self-driving cars wouldn't be so bad."

Fraser didn't look impressed. "Or, you know, you could"— he laughed—"pay attention to the road."

"Ha-ha," Quinn said, his mood souring.

They drove on in silence, and he got thinking that maybe, just maybe, he didn't like this retro prick after all.

Just before four, they arrived.

The driveway off Ribera led down toward the sea, the property obscured by fence and foliage. Fraser watched Quinn roll down the window and press the intercom button at the gate, two giant rectangular slabs of polished wood.

"Hello?" came a woman's voice.

"Mrs. Spencer? I'm Detective Connor Quinn, Monterey County Sheriff's Department. We spoke on the phone earlier today. I'm here with Special Agent William Fraser, FBI. We won't take long."

"Yes, of course. Come right in."

There was a buzz, then the gates opened.

Quinn drove forward and around the bend, and the house revealed itself as they came out of the turn. It looked like a cross between a modernist mansion and a Mediterranean villa, painted white with large square windows on both stories. A three-car garage jutted off to the left and a firepit surrounded by wooden chairs stood to the right.

The car rolled to a stop and Fraser climbed out, looking beyond the firepit to the sea. Water stretched off to the golden horizon and seagulls circled above, cawing in the fading light. He could hear waves lapping against a rocky shore.

"Pretty sweet digs," Quinn said, glancing around. "For this price in the Valley, you'd get a walk-in closet."

He laughed and Fraser nodded, knowing it wasn't entirely untrue. The two investigators made their way to the front door, shoes crunching on gravel. Fraser rang the bell and a few moments later, it opened.

Before them stood a brunette of medium height in her early thirties. She wore a yellow sundress and held a vape designed to look like a cigarette. Fraser had seen Tatum Leigh Spencer on billboards before, advertising the TV series *San Diego Med*. He wasn't sure if she was still on the show.

"Come in," she said, looking exhausted. Fraser didn't blame her.

He and Quinn followed her inside and shut the door behind them. She led them through the house to the rear living room, with an expansive view of the ocean through floor-to-ceiling windows. The shore of Monastery Beach was visible with CA-1 continuing along the coast to the Point Lobos Reserve. The point itself stretched into the water, like a rocky hand reaching out into the sea.

Tatum sat on a sofa while Quinn and Fraser took armchairs. A glass table rested between them. Tatum took a puff on her e-cig, the tip glowing blue. In the kitchen behind her, a Samsung cleaning bot was quietly doing the dishes.

"Mind if I smoke?" Quinn asked, drawing a pack of Marlboros.

Tatum held him with a detached gaze. She exhaled vapor and said "Yes," her lips curling into a smile.

Quinn looked pissed but stowed the pack away. "Mrs.

Spencer, we'd just like to ask you some questions about what happened last night, and to see if you might know anything that could point us toward your husband's killer."

"Alright," she said, sighing. She looked bored. "Fire away." She took another pull on the vape.

Quinn pulled out a thin tablet from his jacket to type notes on, but Fraser already had his notepad and pen out.

"This is pretty far from the office. Did your husband usually come home on weeknights?"

"No, he usually spent most of the week up in Palo Alto and came back on weekends. But sometimes he made exceptions, like last night. Said he hadn't been spending enough time with Kayla and me, said he'd try to come home more this week."

"And what time was he supposed to arrive last night?" Fraser asked.

She scoffed, looked out the window, then back to them. The setting sun gave her an orange hue from behind and her face was shadowed—except for her amber eyes, which seemed vibrant against her silhouette.

"I always added two hours to whenever Niall said he was gonna be home. And sometimes even that wasn't generous enough."

"And was last night any different?" Quinn asked.

She paused. "Actually yes, but I didn't know it at the time. He said he'd be home by nine, and I guess he would've been home just before nine-thirty if he hadn't..." Her voice trailed off, her eyes starting to water. Tatum forced a laugh and sat up straighter. "At first I just thought he was late again." She took another drag of the vape. "He didn't arrive by eleven, so I thought he was just tardier than usual. I started getting ready for bed, but then the phone rang. I thought it was him at first, explaining why he was taking so long, but..."

Tatum swallowed. "It was the police. A diver had pulled Niall's body out of the car. They identified him by his driver's license. His face was too smashed up." She bit her lip, took another vaporous drag.

"Did—?" Quinn began.

"I'm sorry for your loss, Mrs. Spencer," Fraser said.

There were tears in her eyes now. "Thank you," she managed, wiping them away.

"I'm terribly sorry, Mrs. Spencer," Quinn said, though it sounded like an afterthought. "That's why we're here: to find out who did this."

Tatum nodded.

"Was Niall acting strangely in the weeks leading up to his death?" Fraser asked.

She hesitated. "Well, he was very stressed about his new project—Catalyst, he said it was called. It's been in the wings for years, but he wouldn't even tell Kayla or I about it, said he was keeping it a big surprise for us. The past few months had been really hard on him, trying to get everything ready in time for the unveiling, but..." She looked off toward the front of the house, laughed quietly. "It sounds stupid saying it out loud, but...it seemed like it was more than just the stress of the project. He acted...distant around me and, given how many nights he was spending away I...I..."

"Wondered if he was having an affair?" Quinn blurted.

She nodded, suddenly morose. "It might just have been paranoia on my part. But then again, I'm down in L.A. almost every week for filming. I figured he probably had the same worries about me. Maybe I just wasn't giving him enough credit, but..." She sighed, deflated. "I wasn't Niall's first wife, and he wasn't my first husband. We were both on our second marriages, and I really hoped with him that it would be, you know, *it*." She put a hand to her forehead. "No matter what, something always goes wrong."

Quinn looked ready to jump into the next question, but Fraser cut him off. "I'm sorry, Mrs. Spencer. Can I call you Tatum?"

She looked up. Smiled, nodded. "Yes."

"Do you have any idea who your husband might have been having an affair with?"

Tatum thought for a moment. "Well...he always spoke of

his assistant, Cheryl, very fondly. But I don't know." Tatum laughed. "She's older than me and not nearly as... I mean, surely he wouldn't..." A sadness had suddenly come across her and she looked very, very tired again.

"People never cheat for logical reasons," Fraser said, sympathy in his tone. He knew what it was like to face that kind of betrayal. "It could be with someone more or less attractive than their partner, wealthier or poorer, kinder or meaner. The main thing is that they do it without regard for who they're with."

She nodded slowly. "I never had any proof. It's awful of me to say something like that. I mean, he could've been perfectly faithful. I guess we'll never know now."

Quinn jumped in. "Did he ever tell you anything about his work? Anything bothering him? Anything he was worried about?"

"Just that he was stressed about Catalyst. Kept talking about how it was going to disrupt transportation as we know it, that kind of thing."

"You don't sound too impressed," Quinn said. He pulled out his pack of Marlboros. Realizing what he was doing, he put them back again.

Tatum sighed. "I loved Niall, but he drank deep from the Valley Kool-Aid. I suppose it worked for him." She gestured around. "But I've always found Silicon Valley a strange place. I grew up in L.A. and work in Hollywood, which definitely has its own supply of arrogance, but the Valley..." She paused, searching for the right words. "It's a special breed of self-superiority. It's tiring, honestly. And the whole place is so *boring* and overpriced. The Monterey area is lovely but it's far from anything. I've always found SoCal much more interesting."

"Well, there are a lot more pretty girls there, I'll give it that," Quinn laughed. "Bet you fit in better down south anyway."

Fraser shot him a look, but he didn't seem to catch it. He was too busy ogling the victim's wife, whom Fraser felt inclined to remind him was a *suspect*. Spouses always were.

Tatum gave a thin smile. "I get a lot of unwanted attention in my industry, Detective Quinn. I don't need it in the investigation into my husband's death."

He soured. "Of course. My apologies, ma'am."

"Did he discuss anything bothering him beyond Catalyst?" Fraser asked, wanting to get them back on track. He jotted down some notes.

"Not in the last little while... Well, during the summer he was concerned about all the AutoDrive accidents, said there was no way the system should be malfunctioning, but..."

"Did he think the vehicles had been hacked?" Fraser said, leaning closer.

"He..." Tatum took an exceptionally long drag of the e-cig. "Oh fuck, what's the point in hiding it? Yes, yes he did. He told me not to tell a soul, not even Kayla, but there's no use keeping it secret if he's dead now. Yes, he was worried they'd been breached, even though the CSO—Johnson's his name—kept insisting everything was secure. Said they couldn't find anything any time they looked and that there were no traces of any viruses in the cars. Niall stopped talking about it after that, but when the police told me his car went off the road, that's what I immediately thought. That he'd been hacked. And when they started saying it on the news this morning, it didn't surprise me at all. And then of course Detective Quinn called me earlier today to tell me that was the current theory."

"So you think the accidents several months ago are related to his murder?" Quinn said.

"I don't know," she spat. "Isn't that your job to figure out?"

"It is," he said. "Do you have any computer experience, Tatum?"

"I was born in 1997," she scoffed. "I practically grew up on the goddamn Internet."

"Any *hacking* experience?" Quinn asked.

Tatum laughed, bitterness in her voice. "I did not hack my husband's car and drive it off a cliff, if that's what you want to know."

"Maybe it is what I want to know."

"Then I gave you your answer."

"Maybe you did."

She looked to Fraser for support. He shrugged. "Tatum, it's routine to ask these types of questions to a victim's spouse. We're not saying you're a suspect"—he almost winced at the lie, hated not telling the truth—"but we just want to rule you out. Would you mind telling us what you did last night?"

"Well, I *already* told you. I was waiting for Niall to come back. I read a script my agent sent me in the bedroom."

"Is it sitting upstairs?" Quinn asked.

"It's on my iPad."

"And where did you read it?"

"In the master bedroom. On the bed."

"Any witnesses?"

"Kayla was off in her room, but she walked by once or twice to get water downstairs."

"Is she around?"

"I don't know. She comes and goes without telling me. Spends most weeks at her aunt's place in Monterey, then comes here on the weekend when Niall and I are back. I think she was here earlier."

Quinn scoffed. "Sounds like you really know how to keep an eye on your own daughter."

Tatum burst out laughing. "Please don't tell me I *look* old enough to be a high schooler's mother."

"No, just the trophy wife of some Valley dickhead billionaire who's going to inherit all his money now that he's dead."

Fraser shot him a look. "Cut it out, Quinn."

The detective fired one back at him.

Tatum restrained her rage, red flushing across her face. "Inherit *some* of it. Most will go to Kayla and various charity causes."

Quinn tapped his tablet. "I think I read somewhere once that Niall Spencer was worth $24.6 billion or something. Even a chunk of anything in the Three Comma Club's still gotta be pretty nice."

"That's enough," Fraser said, glaring. He turned back to

Tatum. "Do you mind if we take a look around his office?"

"Sure," she said, leaning back angrily. "The cops already took all of his computers from there earlier today. *With my permission*, might I add, so that they didn't need to get a warrant."

"That's fine," Fraser said. They weren't going to get anything else out of this conversation. Not after Quinn's outburst.

"It's on the next floor," she said. "Pretty much right above us. Stairs are back there." She nodded behind them.

"What the hell do you want to look around for?" Quinn said as they tramped down the upper hallway. He looked on edge, like he badly needed a smoke. "She's right. Sheriff's Department came through earlier today and got everything."

"I'd just like to get a sense of his workspace," Fraser said. "It'll help."

"Help? What, are you gonna sit down and meditate in the middle of the office? Play some Duran Duran on your phone?"

"I prefer listening to music on my Walkman, actually."

Quinn rolled his eyes, but Fraser ignored him. He opened the door at the end of the hall. Inside, the blinds were not entirely closed, and twilight bled into the room with horizontal shadows. Spencer's desk was occupied only by his monitor and a laser keyboard, but everything else was missing. The drawers of a filing cabinet off to the left were partially open and empty.

However, the posters on his walls had been untouched. Fraser walked to the center of the hardwood floor and slowly turned in a circle, taking in each image. An isolated tropical beach, reminding him of one he and his friends had stumbled upon in Oahu as kids. A map of constellations. A painting of a shining future metropolis. Some modernist art. A diploma from Caltech. A framed *Wired* interview with Spencer himself.

"Notice anything strange about these?" Fraser said. He walked to the window and gazed down at the shore.

"Not particularly." Though by the sound of his voice, Quinn was trying to figure it out.

"Strange maybe...for the CEO of an automobile manufacturer's office?"

The detective was silent for a moment. Then he said, "Huh. None of these show cars."

Fraser remained looking at the sea, thinking. Then a voice came from behind him, and it wasn't Quinn's or Tatum's.

"I don't think you're supposed to be in here."

4:03 PM

Cray turned away from the screen and yawned, leaning back in her seat. Before her lay several empty bowls, scattered across the workspace. Kaplan had brought micro-wavable ramen out for all of them, but nobody really seemed interested, so Cray ate three, the plastic fork still sitting in the bowl closest to her.

That had been nearly two hours ago. She'd spent the rest of the time overseeing the technicians' digital forensics work with the sysadmin and Reed. The FBI agent kept throwing her the occasional glance, suspicion in his eyes. He had yet to say anything to her, though, and she wondered how long he was going to keep playing it that way.

Only two other computer engineers for the Software Update NOC kept them company in the darkened room. Kaplan had come back with access badges and lanyards for her, Reed, and the technicians. Later, the CLO, Pawar, had brought an NDA for Cray to sign, but nobody else had stopped by since.

She got up and headed over to the two techs. They sat by the Snowball computer, plugged into one of the NOC ter-minals. The PrivateEye software was analyzing data as it came in. It displayed a progress bar as it scanned the virtual machine archives for inconsistencies, taking images of data-bases and logs at different times and cross-referencing them.

Bailey had connected a laptop to manage the software and Cray glimpsed the program's logo in the upper right corner, a silhouetted figure with a fedora.

"How's it coming?" she asked.

Bailey looked up at her and gave a tired smile. "No discrepancies yet, but there's still a *lot* of data to download."

Cray nodded, glancing around the lab. Reed had stepped out a little while ago to make a phone call. A man appeared at the door and entered, looking antsy. It was Johnson, the CSO.

"Find anything yet?"

Bailey shook his head.

Johnson sighed and walked over. "You know, I don't really think you're gonna discover much on there."

"Why not?" Cray said.

"Because our systems are air-tight." He looked at the laptop screen. "There has to be a way to check for an alternate source of the breach."

"Don't listen to him," came a voice. "He's just upset because this makes him look bad."

Cray turned to the door and saw the CTO, Ritter, leaning against the frame. She adjusted her circular glasses and something flickered across the lenses. Probably AR, though subtler than the lobby receptionist's headgear.

Johnson forced a laugh, turning back to them. "You see, Mallory's in charge of R&D. R&D was responsible for the hacking countermeasures we added to each vehicle, making sure they couldn't get breached by some asshole spoofing a cell tower. Mallory doesn't want to believe her system isn't perfect. She wants it to be *my* fault."

"Because it is," Ritter said, coming closer. Her eyes bored into Johnson with a stern gaze. "I've been telling you and Niall for the past several years that we need to increase internal cybersecurity, that we need to more thoroughly train staff of all departments against social engineering and phishing, that there are still zero-day exploits in our systems that need to be patched. And every single time, both of you dismissed me."

"We've patched close to a hundred zero-days in the past

year," Johnson said. "Everyone in my division is well-versed in the dangers of social engineering, okay? And reminders to watch for phishing emails and strange network activity go out all the time in internal emails."

"It's not enough to just spit those things out," Ritter hissed, anger burning in her eyes. "Nobody reads those emails. They skim them and nod along at most. You need to put up physical flyers, have regular company-wide meetings about this. Otherwise, it doesn't matter how secure we make a system if a stupid mistake on our end can bring it all down."

"I bet the forensics software hasn't found anything yet *because there's no virus* in our system. I'm willing to bet the car was breached through other means."

"Even if it was a zero-day, it was still your job to fix it, Adrian," she said. "Someone out there has access to 300,000 vehicles and—"

"Not if Niall's car was breached independently."

Ritter shook her head. "They would still have a technique that would allow them to crack other cars."

"Yeah, but not everywhere in the world at once. They'd have to do it one at a time."

Cray sighed, watching the shots volley back and forth. Boredom had found her again. She never got too far away before it caught up, but sometimes she could beat it back with the right tools. The past hour had been fucking tedious, though. She didn't know how these forensics technicians did their jobs without falling asleep at the keyboard. She greatly preferred intrusion to detection.

"I'll be right back," she said, leaving the two executives to continue bickering.

She headed out into the main NOC, past the attentive engineers glued to their machines, and finally made it back to the exterior corridor. The restrooms were right around the corner, and she made her way inside. A janitor bot roved around, looking for stalls to scrub. She picked one at the end and found it spotless.

A few minutes later, she finished up washing her hands

and headed back out into the hallway. Reed was headed toward the NOC entrance from the other direction. Cray almost doubled back into the washroom, but he spotted her, narrowing his eyes.

"Hello, Ms. Cray. What's it been, three years now?"

It was just the two of them here in the passageway. A slide-show of corporate images played silently on a large screen to the right. A smiling family, unloading surfboards from a T-Series at the beach. A suited woman climbing out of an F-Series downtown. A K-Series rounding a highway bend at night.

"Almost," Cray said. It had all happened before Christmas. Ruined her birthday that year.

He nodded, remembering. "How's Simone?"

Cray tensed. Fury began boiling deep within her. "I don't know. I haven't talked to her in ages."

"Aww. Bad break-up?"

It hadn't been a good one. "This doesn't have anything to do with who killed Niall Spencer."

He raised an eyebrow. "Does it? I wonder what Ted Graham might think if he found out his little whitehat pen-tester is really a known anarchist hacker suspected of—"

"Actually, I'm an anarcho-*capitalist*." She smirked. "Which you should know from your case files, if you ever bothered to review them."

Reed paused. He wasn't used to being talked to this way, not in his line of work. Maybe not ever.

But then he cracked a grin too. "I've always thought it was strange that there are so many different subsets of anarchism. Anarcho-communism, eco-anarchism, anarcho-syndicalism…"

She shrugged. "Disdain for society's a big tent."

Reed scoffed and stepped closer. "People who commit crimes come in all shapes and sizes, of all backgrounds, of all opinions. It doesn't make any difference to me *why* they do it. My job is to keep the public safe from them."

"Well, you're doing a bang-up job so far." She gave him a mock salute, eyes narrowing, mouth smirking. "I feel more secure already."

He shook his head in disbelief. "You've got some balls talking to a federal agent like this."

Cray laughed. One time a fling had called it off with her, citing her personality. Told her ego was "a man's game."

She'd shaken her head and said, *No honey, you're just jealous I'm better at it than you are.*

"When's your partner Fraser getting back?" One side of her smile curled higher than the other. "Or did he find his time machine back to the eighties?"

Reed glowered. "You stay away from him. And if you had anything to do with Spencer's death, you won't get away with it this time."

"I don't know what you're talking about," she said, smiling. "I've never committed a crime in my life."

He stepped even closer. "We both know that's not true." A pause, then, "I saw your records last time. That expunged misdemeanor doesn't surprise me, but your psychiatric evaluations... Well, I think anyone would find those concerning. Might even make your buddy Graham look at you differently."

She swallowed. "You're not supposed to be able to access that."

Now it was Reed's turn to smile. "We have access to everything, courtesy of the PATRIOT Act. And what we don't have, we can easily get. But your diagnosis would send chills down anyone's spine. And the fact that you turned up here right after the murder..." He shook his head. "Some would say that looks pretty suspicious."

Heat rushed to her face. "You know I didn't kill Spencer. I was *brought* here. I have no motive and, besides, I'm not a murderer."

"Maybe I do know that, or at least can figure it." His gaze turned toward the NOC entrance door. "But maybe *they* don't know that. Maybe you should avoid pulling any funny business with me and help me solve this case before anything really bad happens."

Now she was livid, doing her best to keep it inside. *High Functioning, Izzy.* High *Functioning...*

"That was my plan."

"Good. Don't deviate from it."

He tapped his lanyard badge against the reader and opened the door, gesturing Cray into the main Network Operations Center. She walked through without a word, keeping the Corporate Izzy mask on tight in case anyone looked. Smiling, relaxed, not bothered at all by the FBI agent close behind her.

When she badged back into the Software Update antechamber, she stopped cold. Everyone was standing around the Snowball, reading something off the laptop attached to it.

"What's going on?" she asked.

Beside her, Reed looked on edge too.

Bailey glanced up at both her and the fed. "We've found something."

"How bad?" Reed asked, moving closer.

Bailey looked pale. "Let's just say it's very concerning."

"You must be Kayla," Fraser said to the girl in the doorway.

She looked about sixteen or so. It occurred to him that she, him, and her stepmother were all born in the same generation, albeit at opposite ends. Fraser noted the resemblance to her father, particularly in the eyes. They were the same ones that stared at him from the screen in Asimov HQ's lobby. She was a bit above average height and wore a T-shirt and jeans, looking between him and Quinn as if they were intruders.

"I'm Special Agent Fraser, FBI." He smiled, trying to stay as polite as possible. He couldn't imagine what she was going through. Didn't even want to try. He'd worried about that as a kid frequently, whenever his father went off on business trips to Asia. Each time he feared he wouldn't come back. "And this is Detective Quinn, Monterey County Sheriff's Department."

Quinn nodded. He didn't look her up and down. *Thank God*, Fraser thought. *At least he has* some *decency.*

"What are you doing in here?" she said, appearing distant. Her eyes were red but there were no tears. "The police took all of his stuff this morning."

"We're just taking a look around, that's all," Fraser said. He paused. "Listen…Kayla, was there anything your father said to you that might help us with—?"

"No," she blurted. She looked much sadder now. "I wish he did... I wish I could help you, but I don't know why someone would kill him. All he cared about was the stupid project. All he..."

"I'm sorry for your loss," Quinn said, and it looked like he was.

Tears sprouted from her eyes, and she sniffed, trying to keep it together. "Thank you." Kayla swallowed and stared at something past them, narrowing her eyes. "It's strange, he..."

Fraser turned around. He couldn't tell what she was looking at. When he glanced back, she was shaking her head. "Is there any way I *can* help you? I'm good with computers. And I've read a lot of mystery books." She managed a laugh, a tear streaking down her face.

He smiled. "If there's anything you think of later, you can call us." He fished a business card with the FBI emblem out of his pocket as he walked closer, handing it to her.

She took it and nodded to herself.

Someone appeared behind her, and Fraser looked up to see Tatum, still holding her e-cig. "You two find what you needed?"

"I think so. We were just about to leave."

Tatum nodded, putting a hand on Kayla's shoulder. "Come on," she said, guiding her out of the way as the two investigators walked past.

Before they got to the stairs, Fraser looked back at the office, at the sundown streaming through the blinds. He pictured Niall Spencer sitting there at his computer, typing away. Then the mental image vanished, and there was nothing there but a chair basking in the early evening light.

<··>

When they got back to Quinn's car, Fraser found he had several missed calls from Reed. He swiped the contact to redial, climbing into the passenger seat.

Reed answered on the second ring. "Will, how'd the wife interview go?"

Fraser glanced at Quinn, who started the car. "Didn't glean too much, but she thought Spencer might've been having an affair."

"That definitely warrants looking into," Quinn said, shifting into reverse.

"Do you think the wife killed him?"

"Neither of us are sure. I thought her sadness seemed genuine, but then again, she is an actress. Here, I'll put you on speaker." He did so.

Quinn turned the car around on the gravel and headed back up the hill toward the gate. It opened automatically as they approached, and Quinn nosed the vehicle back up onto Ribera Rd.

"Acting is one thing," Reed said. "Coding a polymorphic virus is another."

Fraser was taken aback. "Jesus, did the techs find something already?"

"Only a few things, overwritten logs. But that indicates a breach in the Software Department, something capable of leaving very few breadcrumbs. It's been extremely hard to trace, but we've found a path leading from the big AutOS 6.5 update. That appears to be the one that was infected."

"By what?"

"That's the question. But whatever it is, it's very advanced."

"So we're not dealing with a script kiddie," Fraser noted.

Quinn slowed the car. He looked lost. "A *what*?"

"A low-level hacker who downloads viruses coded by other people and employs them for their own purposes."

"Instead of, like, designing a virus themselves?"

"Pretty much."

"Okay. And what on God's Earth is a polymorphic virus?"

Reed chimed in. "It's a self-mutating computer program that copies itself, re-encrypts itself, and deletes any trace of itself. Well, almost any trace. Advanced programs can pick up little breadcrumbs here and there."

"And that stuff you guys are using—the snowball machine or whatever—can do this?"

"Yes. It's detecting signatures of an advanced polymorphic virus, based on similar types of viruses that have been discovered in previous investigations. We haven't actually found the virus code for analysis yet, but…think of it this way: there's a monster in the woods. We haven't seen it yet, but we've found some strange footprints. We're sure something's out there. We just haven't gotten a picture yet."

"Alright," Quinn said, nodding.

"So that narrows our field of suspects considerably," Fraser said. "The unsub is a highly-skilled hacker with the coding expertise to make their own polymorphic virus, that is capable of breaching several layers of corporate network security in order to install a Trojan that gives the hacker root access to any Asimov vehicle."

Reed paused. "That's the current theory, yes."

"Have you located the source of intrusion yet? Any idea how it got into the Software Update Department?"

"Not yet. Snowball's still running. And there's a lot more data to get through. We're looking at every change made on the virtual machine systems for this subnet for the past six months, every log, every artifact moved—everything."

"Subnet?" Quinn asked, driving.

"Subnetwork," Fraser said. "A section of a larger computer network, in this case for Asimov Auto, but reserved for a specific group of servers."

"So this is the Software Update Department subnet they're pulling all the archives for?"

"Yes."

"Okay, got it." Quinn turned the wheel as Ribera Road curved back along another row of houses.

"This gives me a bad feeling, Will." Reed hesitated on the phone. "I want to see their stuff on Catalyst, but Graham and the others won't let me near it. Someone went to a lot of trouble to create a virus like this to kill Spencer and I've got a feeling it's over something more than an affair or a personal vendetta."

Quinn laughed, shook his head. "You'd be surprised. I've worked homicide for over twenty years. I've seen all kinds of motives and all kinds of effort. The one takeaway I can pull from it, the one thing that stays consistent..." He looked to Fraser, shook his head chuckling. "Is that people are fucking crazy."

9:54 PM

The rain had slowed to a drizzle, but Cray still put the hood of her sweatshirt up as she left the taco restaurant, heading northwest along Emerson. Finding a place to grab food at this hour had been a chore. Nearly everything in Palo Alto closed by 9pm, so discovering something that stayed open an hour later had seemed like a miracle. It was strange for a college town. Stranger for the municipality that vied against San Jose for Capital of the Valley.

Cray had bought enough tacos for two people. The cashier had asked if she was having a date night. Cray lied and said yes, that she and her girlfriend were spending a night in, watching a movie. Not that Cray would've cared if the lady knew the truth. She found it amusing when servers over the years raised eyebrows at everything she ordered, or the impressed look on their faces as they cleared away empty plates.

No, it was just fun concocting stories sometimes. She liked to go along with it herself occasionally, imagining a brunette waiting for her back at the hotel room or the apartment or wherever. Of course, even when there was someone, she still devoured most of the food. Simone had eaten like a bird, always letting Cray finish her entrees. She'd bring back leftovers just for her sometimes, when she went out with other friends.

Then, as Cray walked down the street in the rain, it sank in again that she lied to the cashier. Simone wasn't waiting for her back at the Sheraton. Neither was Marcy from this morning, who was far less interesting than Simone or even Tom had been.

A while back she realized that it wasn't so much her lovers she missed, but the feelings they gave her. The convenience of having a shoulder to lean on, to always have a toy around when you were bored. A toy that somehow felt like more than just a toy, in a way she couldn't quite place.

Dr. Perkins had explained to Cray that she would never be able to experience love like neurotypicals could. Her brain simply wasn't wired to process the chemicals that way.

But she could care about her partners, and only really two of them had brought her joy. It had been a long time since Simone though, and she found the ones actually worth caring about were harder to come by than she once thought. There seemed to be so many options whenever she opened a dating app, so many choices to swipe through. Yet nearly all of them turned out to be bullshit or boring.

Cray came to the intersection of Hampton and Emerson. The lights in the Palo Alto Creamery were still on, but it looked like the staff inside were cleaning up. She continued left onto Hampton, back toward the train tracks.

To her left was the eight-story Nobu Hotel, the tallest building around. She'd heard regulations now forbid anything over four stories in downtown Palo Alto. It was ridiculous that after decades of global prominence, the city still clung to its small-town America feel. Nobody wanted taller buildings around here, not in *their* backyard—or least visible from it. For a place constantly pushing disruption, the Valley itself seemed remarkably averse to change.

Continuing along the sidewalk, Cray wondered what the RCFL team would find when they finished parsing through the Software Update Department data. They hadn't found the polymorphic virus before they let her go for the day, but they'd uncovered more traces of it. Logs shifted here and there, files opened and closed at strange times by users who weren't at work. It was subtle, graceful, the kind of things most people would miss. But once a digital magnifying glass was put over them, they seemed obvious.

The other thing Cray couldn't stop thinking about was her conversation with Reed.

Your diagnosis would send chills down anyone's spine.

It pissed her off that he knew, but of course the feds would've been able to access that. Especially once she became a suspect in the Picturesque case.

She thought past three years ago, back to college. The summer after junior year when, after months of sessions, Dr. Perkins had finally diagnosed her.

That afternoon, Cray had come in and sat on the sofa as she always did. Upright, not lying down like in the movies. Dr. Perkins had sat across from her in an armchair, palm trees and sunlight out the window. Her office was in North Miami Beach.

"So Izzy, how are you today?"

Cray nodded, calm. Dr. Perkins had encouraged her to drop the masks around her, to express her true self. At first Cray had been wary, but over time she came to enjoy it. So much of her life was pretending to be someone who she wasn't, just because she came across as cold or unnerving. The masks were a burden NTs placed on her. Around Dr. Perkins she was free to say what she really thought, to act as she really was.

And she knew the psychiatrist wouldn't fuck her over. Dr. Perkins had gone to undergrad with her father at Florida International. He'd continued on into marine biology while she'd gone to med school at the University of Miami, where Cray was attending at the time on a merit-based scholarship.

"I'm doing well," she said, not bothering to smile. She didn't need to express happiness to feel fine.

"Any incidents…?"

Cray thought for a moment. This was a couple weeks before senior year began. The summer had been mostly uneventful.

She was working at her mother's family's restaurant again, as a waitress. She hated the customers, who were often unnecessarily rude, but it was good practice for fashioning masks. Pretending you cared got you more tips, which was a nice incentive.

"No," she said. "I only spat in one customer's food this time."

Dr. Perkins sighed. *"Izzy…"*

Now Cray smiled. "What? The way he was eyeing me, I think he wanted me to."

Dr. Perkins made some notes, no judgment visible on her face. That was why Cray appreciated Dr. Perkins. She wore masks too. Cray wondered what she was thinking then, probably questioning how her pal could've produced such a mentally disturbed offspring. She wondered if the two of them had fucked back in college. Cray had few people she could call friends over the years, but she'd slept with several of them, male and female.

"Still eating bugs for fun?"

Cray shrugged. "Only when I'm bored. And if I catch them alive."

More notes. "But no significant events?"

Cray sighed, scratched her stomach. "None really come to mind."

Dr. Perkins lowered her notepad. "Izzy, the main thing I wanted to talk to you about was the result of the test we took last time."

Cray nodded. Two weeks ago, Dr. Perkins had asked her a long set of questions that she had to respond either *yes*, *no*, or *somewhat* to.

"I have your records from the child psychologist you saw growing up. I saw she diagnosed you with both attention deficit disorder and oppositional defiant disorder at age ten."

Cray nodded again.

"This was on account of you getting in trouble with teachers, being aggressive with other kids, constant irritability, etc."

"I got better. I learned to control it by high school." She scoffed. "I wouldn't be going to college where I am now if I didn't."

Dr. Perkins smiled. "I know, Izzy. And you should be proud of yourself. You've come a long way on impulse control, and that's a lot better than most people can say for themselves."

"I wouldn't describe myself as impulsive," Cray said, annoyed. "Not anymore."

Dr. Perkins raised an eyebrow. "Then what do you call the cheating?"

"That was just—we've already *talked* about that, okay? I didn't *mean* to hurt anyone."

"You didn't *think* it would hurt anyone."

"I didn't. *Want.* To hurt him," Cray said, leaning forward, gripping the edge of the sofa. Her lips curled into a snarl.

She was taller than the woman across from her, and not for the first time fear flashed in Dr. Perkins's eyes. That made Cray smile, just a little. It was fun scaring people who thought they were above you. You had to remind them of the pecking order once in a while. Of course, this had been back in college. She'd gotten off on that sort of thing more back then.

"Izzy, there's no need to get angry." Firmness had entered the shrink's voice.

Cray relaxed and leaned back on the sofa, throwing one arm over the pillow beside her. She smirked. "You told me to tell you when I'm getting bored, Dr. Perkins."

"Alright, given everything we've talked about over the past several months—your arrest, the other criminal acts you were never charged with, and a troubling pattern of behavior dating back to childhood—I think you clearly meet the criteria for antisocial personality disorder."

Cray was quiet for a moment, looking down. She'd done a little poking around on the Internet these past few months and suspected as much.

"Alright."

"There's more," Dr. Perkins said. "You scored very highly on the test you took last week."

"I score highly on a lot of tests." She smiled.

"You got thirty out of forty, a 75%."

Cray frowned. "Ouch. That's actually pretty bad by my standards." She laughed.

Dr. Perkins had gone pale. "No, Izzy. Very few people score thirty or above on this test. It's estimated that only about one percent of the population meets the criteria."

Unease materialized in the pit of Cray's stomach. She sat up straighter. "What was the test?" she asked, her voice serious now.

Dr. Perkins met her gaze. "It's called the Psychopathy Checklist-Revised, or PCL-R for short. It was designed to be an objective assessment, usually administered to people in prison—but it can be used to assess noncriminal individuals, as well as those displaying similar traits. Those individuals are generally considered high functioning. Psychopaths are almost always diagnosed with antisocial personality disorder, but not everyone with ASPD is a psychopath. Some people just refer to them as sociopaths, but that's not an official medical term."

Cray nodded slowly. "So, am I...?"

"Yes, Izzy," Dr. Perkins said. "Thirty is the cutoff score, though some use twenty-five. By the PCL-R metric, as well as our talks these past several months, and the behaviors you've both exhibited and admitted to me, I am clinically diagnosing you as a psychopath."

Cray looked down at the floor, her arm still slung over the pillow beside her. Her brain was still processing the information. Even sitting here with the shrink she felt isolated, strange. She'd known for years that she was different than others, but there was a certain coldness that came with having a term for it. A term she'd always associated with serial killers and slasher movie villains.

"It's even rarer in women," Dr. Perkins continued. "Although some studies indicate that females with ASPD or psychopathy might be mistakenly diagnosed with borderline personality disorder. That could account for some of the discrepancy. Psychopathy manifests itself differently between the sexes."

Cray looked up. "Did you think I might have that?"

Dr. Perkins shook her head. "Not really. You've demonstrated anxiety problems and some obsessive behaviors, but I never actually thought you have BPD, Izzy. Though some people are diagnosed with both. They're Cluster B personality disorders, so they do have some overlapping traits, but people with borderline don't suffer from a lack of empathy. At least, not more than anyone else. I wondered if you might be comorbid with NPD—narcissistic personality disorder—which is also Cluster B, but most psychopaths have a high opinion of themselves. You don't seem to have a burning need to be the center of attention, though, which rules out NPD."

Cray scoffed. "I don't give a shit what other people think of me." She smiled. "Unless it gets in my way."

Dr. Perkins managed a thin smile. "Spoken like a true psychopath."

Cray paled, sat up straighter.

"It's unnerving to hear yourself called that, isn't it?"

She nodded, looking down at the floor again, at her sneakers. She swallowed. "Yeah."

"Most psychopaths aren't murderers, Izzy. A number of them are quite successful and live normal lives, have families even. This doesn't automatically make you a bad person, it's just a scientific explanation for some of your…behavior."

"What do you think caused it?"

"Nothing you've told me about your childhood seems particularly traumatic beside the burglary incident, but that would've triggered PTSD more than anything else, so I'd imagine it's genetic. If it doesn't run in the family, then it's probably a mutation, like your eyes, height, and metabolism. We can get MRI scans done to confirm this. Usually, psychopaths' brains form a little differently than normal."

"Is it considered a legitimate defense?" Cray asked, thinking. "In the court system?"

Dr. Perkins shook her head. "No. Neither psychopathy nor ASPD are considered valid legal defenses. You are responsible for your actions, Izzy, just like everyone else."

Rage seared through her. "So how the fuck does this help me?! If I tell anyone about it, they'll think I'm a monster! They won't care if I have a medical reason for why I do what I do. They'll hold me to a standard of decency they don't even hold themselves to."

"I'm sorry, Izzy. The older you get, the more you realize that life really isn't fair. And it's not like you've got nothing going for you. You're tall, good looking, and highly intelligent. A lot of people would kill to be like you."

"Minus the mental disorder part, I'm assuming." She folded her arms across her chest.

Dr. Perkins sighed. "You'd be surprised. Some people fantasize about not feeling guilt. They think those like you have it easier."

Cray burst out laughing. *"Easier?* What the fuck is wrong with people?"

The shrink smiled. "A lot of it stems from misinformation about psychopathy. You *can* feel emotions, just not as intensely as the average person—usually. You *can* be empathetic, just not by utilizing *affective* empathy."

"What do you mean?"

"You can still practice *cognitive* empathy. You can't intrinsically feel sorry for other people, but you can learn that something awful happened to a friend and logically recognize why they must be sad. And then, following this realization, you can go and make a conscious choice to comfort them. Not because it *feels* right, but because you know it is. You basically have to emulate kindness."

Now she was angry again. "Do you know how much fucking effort that is for someone like me? What, I have to work overtime to—"

"Make up for your shortcomings? Yes, you do, Izzy. I'm sorry. It's not fair, but society can't function without empathy."

She paused. "Is there any treatment? Any way to make it easier?"

Dr. Perkins sighed. "Psychopaths are notoriously hard to treat. Most therapists or psychiatrists won't even take them

on because they never feel motivated to improve. You yourself have to decide to act better."

The fury swirled within her, and she had trouble keeping
it in. "Everything's always *my* fucking fault and I'm not even
allowed to blame this...this...*thing*? Every day I see normal
people making excuses, blaming society for their problems,
blaming other people, acting entitled—but *I'm* not allowed to
make excuses?! Why the fuck, if I have a mental illness, am *I*
held to a higher standard than every other miserable shithead
on the planet?!"

There was genuine empathy in Dr. Perkins's eyes.
"Nobody is born a good person, Izzy. It's a choice people
make no matter how underprivileged or deserving they are.
I would describe you as fairly high functioning, but you can
do better. And I think I've found a way you can convince
yourself to do so."

Cray narrowed her eyes. "Alright. And what's that?"

"It'll appeal to your sense of pride. Every time you feel
yourself giving in to impulse, any time you're not sure if
you're considering other people's feelings, think to yourself
what a high-functioning person would do in those circumstances. It's not easy, and many psychopaths are far from
high functioning. They often go to prison early in life because
they don't think about *consequence*, not just for themselves,
but for others."

She leaned closer. "So every day, to keep yourself from
getting bored, to keep yourself from getting into trouble,
I want you to play a little game. Whenever you feel your
impulses flaring up, I want you to tell yourself: *Let's play
High Functioning.*"

Walking down the quiet Palo Alto street, the rain soaking
through her hoodie, Cray remembered those words well. The
only person she'd ever told them to was Simone, and that had
been the beginning of the end. Now she kept them locked
tight, close to her. Nobody needed to know that her interactions with them were all part of a game. She wasn't sure if it
was more for their protection or for hers.

She'd walked several blocks in her reverie and was now approaching Alma St, the tracks just beyond and the lights of the Sheraton past them. She hung a right, heading toward the tunnel that took University Ave under the Caltrain station so she could get to the hotel.

Alma was deserted at this hour, save for herself and some parked cars lit by streetlights. She continued along, keeping the top of the takeout bag twisted shut so the tacos wouldn't get wet.

It was about a block to the tunnel still and Cray suddenly felt a strange prickling sensation, like she was being watched.

She stopped and turned around, casually. She didn't mind walking along darkened streets by herself. She pitied those who did, NTs with their lives constantly ruled by fear. Online, she'd found other women with ASPD who had similar attitudes. Plus, Cray was tall and in good shape. She pitied the stupid fuck who tried to jump her, but no one ever had. It would be a good excuse to kill someone.

Not that she wanted to. It had just always been a curiosity of hers.

She glanced around. Nobody else walked the sidewalk behind her. On the other side of the street, the train station parking lot was dark and devoid of life. Only the silhouettes of parked cars were visible.

Cray turned around and continued on, boredom catching up with her again. At least some creep following her would've spiced things up. All she'd been working on this evening was continuing her pen test of that insurance company. The rainbow table had yielded a number of passwords and she had now obtained access to the billing department. Their security was surprisingly depressing. She looked forward to the fee she'd collect for fucking around with their systems.

There, again.

Behind her, left side of the street.

The sound of footsteps.

Cray stopped and turned around, peering into the darkness of the parking lot. It looked just as it had a moment ago.

This is ridiculous, she thought. *It isn't like you to jump at shadows. You're better than that.*

Maybe it was just the Spencer case getting to her. But there was no reason whoever killed him would want her dead. She didn't have any information any of the other investigators didn't.

Cray continued on toward University Ave, wanting to get back to her hotel room so she could eat the tacos. She couldn't be up too late if she wanted to get up early and work out before—

Now it was just the sense again, that feeling of unease, but she spun on her heels.

It happened so fast she questioned if her mind was playing tricks on her. But no, she was sure she saw it.

A shadow darting behind a car in the parking lot.

10:00 PM

You just had to ask for it, didn't you?

Her adrenaline spiked, but Cray remained calm, turning around slowly. *Make them think you haven't seen anything.*

She walked along at a steady clip, just slightly faster than she had been before. The closest traffic was a few cars heading up and down University, still half a block ahead. There was more light over there. It would be harder to nab her if she made it that far.

Cray's heart beat faster, heat flushing to her face. Her muscles tensed, her body ready to spring forward.

Fight-or-flight. The closest thing a psychopath had to fear.

Maybe she didn't have an advantage in this regard. Maybe an NT would've thought twice about walking down a darkened lane while working a murder investigation.

Where's the fun in a life without risk?

She focused her perception, training her ears for any noises behind her, anything at all.

So far, nothing. That was good. He was probably still over there.

Step. Step. One foot after the other.

Calm breaths. In, out. In, out.

Staying focused was key. She had the advantage in that whoever it was still thought they had the drop on her.

Cray was almost to the lights now. Almost there. *Just keep going.* She looked up, watched raindrops illuminated by a lamppost as they fell.

She hadn't felt so alive in a long time. Not even sex compared to this. There was no safe word out of this one. If she screwed up, it was game fucking over. *Terminada.* Done.

Concentrate, Izzy. Stop being reckless. You're playing High Functioning. This is just a new level.

Her ears picked it up. If she hadn't been paying attention, she might not have heard it at all.

Rapid, but stealthy footsteps, getting closer.

The hoodie had awful peripheral. She turned around, looking back at the road.

A shadow sprinted toward her across the asphalt, keeping low. A glint of silver flashed in his hand.

Cray didn't keep looking long enough to see if it was a knife. She turned and ran, sprinting as fast as she could, the takeout bag swinging from her hand.

Her pursuer wasn't trying to hide his footsteps anymore. They thudded loudly behind her on the sidewalk, growing closer and closer and closer.

Cray dashed past a parking garage, past the glass panes of an office building, and onto the circular road as it curved down toward University. She jumped up onto the curb just before a Tesla whipped by. Hurtled across the grass, down to the entrance of the tunnel.

She ground to a halt and looked back, ready to duck if he was still flying after her.

There was no one there.

A few cars passed by behind her, heading into downtown Palo Alto. She paid them no attention, scanning the way she had come for the assailant.

For a brief second, she glimpsed a shadow by the railing over the tunnel, disappearing toward the train station.

Shit.

Cray caught her breath, standing there in the rain. She had two choices now: She could head into Palo Alto and try to get help. Or she could head into the sidewalk tunnel adjacent to the one for the road.

It had a ramp leading up to the train station inside. He could be waiting for her there. Part of her wanted to turn the tables, to get the drop on him and slam him against a wall. If he had an unfamiliar face, she'd threaten to kill him if he didn't tell her who he worked for. Just like in the movies.

Not gonna happen. He probably ran away like the scared, little NT bitch he is.

Cray tore her hood off, letting rain spatter her hair. Curiosity willed her forward, closer, into the tunnel.

Soon the cement surrounded her on all sides. No one else was down here. Just the occasional car speeding by on University, visible through some gaps in the sidewalk tunnel with railings.

The ramp up to the station was near the other end. Cray walked forward, her entire body tense again, breathing slowly in and out.

Step after step, she drew closer to the branching ramp tunnel.

Closer, closer.

Before she knew it, she was about halfway there. An SUV sped past on her right, its beams shining through the gloom. The pavement was grody. A ceiling light flickered ahead. The air was damp and cold.

Her pulse quickened as she approached the ramp.

Cray flattened herself against the wall, inching closer. Then, carefully, she peered around the corner.

The sloping corridor was empty, leading up to the open air of the station. Precipitation pattered the pavement outside. There was a lamppost somewhere beyond, casting shadows along a wall.

Tension flowed out of her shoulders, breath releasing from her lungs.

Then footsteps came behind her, and Cray realized she hadn't looked back since entering the tunnel.

She spun on her heels, her heart accelerating again —

As a couple made their way toward her, chatting and smiling. They wore Stanford sweaters. Cray took out her phone and pretended to check something on it as they passed. Once they had continued back into the raining night and unfolded an umbrella, Cray peered back up the ramp to the station. Then back toward downtown Palo Alto again.

No sign of him.

She realized she was shaking. In the rush, she hadn't noticed how cold she was, a chill caught in the rain. Her teeth began chattering and her hand trembled, but she wasn't sure how much of it was just nerves.

Cray laughed out loud, standing in the tunnel by herself. She glanced at her watch and saw it had been just a few minutes, but time felt different when your life was on the line.

She headed out into the drizzle again, her senses on high alert, and continued along University Ave. It sloped upward and she kept looking over her shoulder as she walked, making sure he wasn't standing there up at the train station, ready to leap over the railing. It was still fairly dark in this area. She jogged along, trying to catch up with the Stanford students.

The street rose back to ground level and became Palm Dr ahead, leading off to the university on the other side of the overpass crossing El Camino Real.

Cray hurried after the couple, crossing the entrance to the train station bus loop. She reached the students waiting at the light for the El Camino off ramp, the Sheraton to her left. The hotel entrance was along the El Camino exit ramp, she knew, and El Camino was busy, even at this hour. If she stayed along here, he shouldn't have an opportunity to jump her.

The pedestrian signal blared a white walk logo and the students continued on, laughing at some joke beneath their umbrella. Cray looked around before moving on to the left. There was a dark patch at the corner of the Sheraton parking lot with a cluster of trees.

Easy for someone to hide in.

However, there were several cars on the off-ramp beside her. Even people on their phones with autonomous systems behind the wheel would hear a scream. All she had to do was shout. Hopefully, someone would see a darkly clad figure hauling her into the bushes.

Right?

Who the fuck are you kidding, Izzy? You're gonna leave your life in the hands of some absentminded NTs?

Fuck no.

She drew out her phone and turned on the flashlight, shining it forward into the dark as she walked closer to the dimly lit area.

No one was hiding in the bushes, or visible in the parking lot beyond. At least, not as far as her beam could pierce.

Cray hurried along, past the parking lot, along the side of the hotel, the windows obscured by more trees. Cars whisked by off of El Camino, coming up the off-ramp to head to Stanford or downtown Palo Alto.

The hotel entrance still seemed so far away. She spun around, shining her flashlight behind and around her, glimpsing nothing.

This continued as a pattern. A brisk stride forward, then a turn and sweep with the light, still walking. Cray did it another four times before she made it to the entrance. She didn't even bother to turn off the flashlight, sprinting for the circular drive around the porte-cochere.

She stumbled into the lobby through the automatic doors, dripping wet and half surprised she was still holding the takeout bag. She glanced back out the entrance, but saw no shadows lurking out there.

"Excuse me, miss," a male receptionist asked, standing behind a desk to her right. "Are you okay?"

Cray turned, put on a smile. "Yeah... Yeah, I'm good."

She was still processing it all, the rush having rattled her nerves. Tension abandoned her shoulders. She turned off the phone's flashlight and headed out to the central courtyard and the pool, trying to figure out what the fuck had just happened.

Markus Sova stood at the railing of the Caltrain station bus loop, looking down at cars passing by on University Ave. He'd watched Cray continue around the street corner to the hotel from a shadowed vantage point but hadn't gone anywhere near her.

She had looked thoroughly spooked, but in a way that reminded him of a defensive animal rather than a frightened human being. He didn't have proof of his theory yet, but he'd bet money that there was something off about her, something dangerous.

When he'd seen her alone on Alma St, he thought he'd had the perfect opportunity. Run up, grab the target, hold a knife to her throat or chest, convince her to do exactly what he said, lead her back to the darkened parking lot—looking just like someone helping a drunken friend.

Get her in the trunk lined with plastic tarp, do what he had to. Throat slashing was messy. Stabbing was too. At that point, a headshot from a silenced 9mm would've been the best bet. Clean, efficient, painless.

He'd done it that way several times before. Every single one had gone smoothly.

But not this time. No, this time the target had been more perceptive than he'd anticipated.

This changed things. She knew there was danger now. It would be harder next time.

He wasn't even sure he'd go in for the kill tonight. Surveillance was important. You had to gauge the target and their habits, how often they checked over their shoulder and so forth.

Instinct told him to seize the opportunity. He'd thought he had her. He was wrong, and now Racer would have to hear about it.

He didn't like the thought of that, but it needed to happen. You had to come clean with your employers, maintain that sense of trust. Racer saw how well he handled their last job.

This was a very salvageable situation. Cray hadn't gotten a good look at him, he was sure of that. To her, he would've been but a shadow, a blur in the night.

Sova turned away from the cement railing and the vines decorating it and walked back toward the station. His car was parked over in the lot on Alma. He would go back to the motel and re-strategize. Tomorrow there would be no fuck ups. Tomorrow he'd get his target.

Tomorrow was a new day.

WEDNESDAY

7:26 AM

"**A**nd you're absolutely sure it was a person?"

Cray sighed. "Yes Ted, I was not jumping at shadows. I saw the shape of a man. He looked pretty tall, was running down the street after me, and had a sharp object in his hand. When I got to University, I saw him sprinting away on Alma toward the train station, but I didn't see him again after that."

She sat in the backseat of a Cruise Origin autonomous taxi. Well, back was a relative term. The vehicle's front and rear were identical. It looked like a sleek rectangular prism with wheels and bus-like doors, four seats facing each other inside. A personal shuttle.

The rest of the cab was empty except for her satchel on the seat beside her. She'd ditched the turtleneck for today and concealed her hickeys with make-up, wearing a burgundy cardigan over a white blouse and black jeans. She'd opted for sneakers today too. Better to wear comfortable shoes in case she needed to run, something she never thought she'd tell herself in Silicon Valley. Her hair was done up in a messy bun, which was harder to grab than how she usually wore it, at shoulder length. It was less effort that way, but any advantage you could give yourself in a fight was worth it.

She'd gotten up before dawn and exercised in the Sheraton's gym, showered, and ate a hearty breakfast. Last night, Graham offered to send her home via an Asimov car, but she took an auto-taxi instead—which she was still expensing to the company, of course. After what happened by the train station, she was glad she opted for other transportation. If whoever killed Spencer wanted her dead too, they could've hacked her chauffeur and driven her off the road. Then again, if they truly had a backdoor into every Asimov vehicle, why not just hack one in the Caltrain parking lot or one tooling around Palo Alto and have it ram her on the sidewalk? Why have a physical human being try to take her out?

She hadn't really seen the assailant's face, but what she had glimpsed didn't ring any bells. That meant he was probably some kind of hitman. She knew there were murder-for-hire sites hidden on the dark web. It was known to be a large industry, had been for years. She'd never browsed those regions, but she had experience with the shadier side of the Internet and had heard stories. Most were scams or FBI agents trying to catfish people, but if you looked hard enough, there were underground networks where unsavory deals were forged. Even moderators who verified purchasers and sellers.

Which meant whoever was behind this wasn't fucking around. They'd coded a polymorphic virus to infiltrate a major corporate database to give themselves access to hundreds of thousands of vehicles globally. They'd taken the CEO's car for a remote joy ride with him inside, then sent it off a cliff. And now they had seemingly tracked down a darknet assassin to personally wipe her off the face of the Earth.

Cray was almost flattered.

"I think we should tell the FBI this," Graham's voice said in her wireless headphones. "Whether it was just a random mugger or something more, we should be cautious."

"A *mugger*? It was ten o'clock on a Tuesday in *Palo fucking Alto*, Ted."

"You'd be surprised. This is America, Izzy. Crime happens even in unsuspecting places."

"A mugger doesn't chase you down with a knife. This guy was trying to sneak up on me and kill me, Ted. It was a hit. Or at least, it was supposed to be."

Graham didn't know her experience with this side of the world. He did know she'd done some less than legal things as a hacker, but then again, who hadn't? She enjoyed their friendship, but he'd only seen the softer side of Corporate Izzy. He didn't know the real her and she was sure he wouldn't want to.

"I just don't know what killing you would achieve for this person."

"I have an idea. Think about it. Whoever murdered Spencer clearly put a lot of thought and effort into it. They made plans. They would've had to anticipate the FBI showing up with a digital forensics team. The local cops wouldn't have had the resources to solve this. So they could foresee that, but then you brought in *me*. I'm an unaccounted-for variable. They don't know how I might affect whatever they've got planned. So maybe they figured it would be better to take me out of the equation altogether."

"Then why not just hack a car to kill you?"

"I don't know. Maybe they wanted to make it look separate. I don't know."

"How did this person even find out you're part of the investigation?"

"There's a pretty easy answer to that question, Ted: Spencer's killer is someone within the company."

He was silent.

"Ted?"

"It's just...I've considered it, but I can't believe that anybody at Asimov would want to kill Niall. Everyone at the company wants Catalyst to succeed—hell, wants autonomous cars to succeed period, no matter who makes them. The way Niall was killed will be devastating for public trust in this technology. If Catalyst doesn't go off without a hitch, driverless cars will be set back for years. We all know the consequences of that here. More unnecessary road accident deaths, more traffic inefficiency, more—"

"Well Ted, maybe someone doesn't want you to succeed as much as you think they do."

Graham went quiet again. "There are ways it could be someone outside the company. If they've infiltrated our systems, maybe they've hacked listening devices, like phones. They'd have access to other emails potentially, and you were mentioned in a memo I sent to board members yesterday morning. Maybe that's how the killer got wind of you."

Cray thought about it. "Maybe."

Graham paused. "I'm sorry I got you into this, Izzy. I had no idea you might become a target. I'll prepare the corporate jet for you to leave this morning—"

She laughed. "Sorry Ted, there's no *way* I'm leaving now. I don't know why this asshole tried to have me killed, but they're gonna regret that they did. I am fucking *pissed*."

And, she admitted to herself, just a little bit enthralled. Spencer's murderer didn't realize it yet, but they'd fucked with the wrong psychopath. The FBI wasn't going to need court admissible evidence on this piece of shit. There wasn't going to be a trial. Hell, there might not even be enough of a body to bury.

Congratulations, motherfucker. You have my full, undivided attention. Thank you for curing my boredom. I will be sure to repay you with interest.

Graham gave a nervous laugh. "Okay, Izzy. But I want you out of Palo Alto tonight. I'll send someone to the hotel to collect your things. A friend of mine has a loft in San Jose, but he's out of town this week. He might lend it if I ask nicely."

"That sounds...great, actually."

Graham laughed again. "He owes me a few favors, so I should be able to snag that for you. And of course, we'll talk to the FBI too. I think anyone who's part of the investigation should have some protection."

"I doubt they'll do that for us. Reed will think I'm making shit up."

"Why would he think that?"

Cray hesitated. "I don't really get the sense that he likes me."

Graham chuckled. "I don't get the sense that he likes many people. But he's known you for less than twenty-four hours. I can't imagine he's formed an opinion of you either way."

"Yeah...I guess you're right." Graham was on a need-to-know basis. And he didn't need to know about Picturesque, though he certainly would've heard the news a few years ago.

"Anyway, the main thing is that you're safe, Izzy. I'll see you soon."

"See you," Cray said. She tapped the End Call icon on her phone and sighed, staring out the window. The vehicle smoothly turned left onto Deer Creek, her destination coming up on the right. She leaned back in her seat.

When the car rolled through the parking lot and up to the drop-off, Cray took several deep breaths. The vehicle stopped. The doors automatically opened and a sign on the screen opposite her thanked Cray for riding. Slinging her satchel over her shoulder, she got up and stepped out onto the curb. There was less rain than yesterday, but forecasts said downpour intensity would fluctuate throughout the week.

Cray headed for the front doors and soon was inside the gloom of the lobby. The receptionist wasn't currently at the desk. No one else was around. She drew her badge out of the satchel and continued toward the corridor on the left. Graham would know where the task force was. If they'd pulled the data they needed from the Software Update division, the forensics team probably wouldn't be in the same place again today.

Suddenly, there was a *thwack*, like something hitting wet pavement.

"*Fuck.*"

Cray looked back over her shoulder and saw a woman out at the drop-off curve, bending down to pick up her briefcase. It was Casey Kaplan, the redhead. The briefcase had opened on impact. A laptop and an assortment of paper were scattered across the cement. Kaplan got down on her knees, scrambling for the laptop. Her Asimov car behind her drove off to find a parking spot.

Cray supposed she should feel pity, or at least something, watching her grab her things in desperation. Instead, it was like staring at a picture in a gallery, one that sparked no meaning to the beholder.

She glanced around her. Still no one around. If she turned and walked away, not even Kaplan would know that she hadn't come to help.

That's not very High Functioning, Izzy. What would a good person do?

Was that a hypothetical?

Focus. Besides, she's cute. You don't know for sure if she's straight.

Cray sighed, looking back toward the corridor where she wanted to go, then again outside at the woman scrambling to reassemble her sopping wet belongings.

She made her decision.

7:35 AM

Kaplan glanced up as she heard footsteps approaching. If Cray had a heart, she supposed the pleading look in those eyes would've melted it. Instead, she felt a charge sending her mind to a place between the sheets.

Focus.

"Hey," Cray said, getting down and picking up a legal pad and some pens. "Rough start to the day, huh?"

Kaplan managed a laugh, hugging her laptop close to her, shielding it from the rain. "It's not been a good week."

"Really? Can't imagine why. Wonderful weather, too."

Kaplan laughed again, this time easier.

Together, they swiftly got everything back into the briefcase. Any sign of earlier organization was gone and the pages were soaked.

Both of them stood up and she noted Kaplan had to be about five-ten, just a couple inches shorter than she was.

"Thank you *so* much," the COO said, wiping damp hair out of her face.

Cray found herself staring at the soft green of her irises. "No worries, really," she said, mustering the most charming smile she could manage.

Kaplan glanced away, awkwardly laughing. Cray smiled, still staring. Dr. Perkins had told her it was a hallmark of the psychopath, sustained eye contact. People like her had the ability to make others feel like they were the only ones who mattered in the world, and all it took was bursts of undivided attention.

"We should probably head inside," Cray said when their eyes met again. "It's too dry out here."

Kaplan gave an endearing laugh, and together they made their way to the lobby doors.

Inside, Cray walked to the potted plant which she'd leaned her satchel against and picked it up.

"I think Ted was going to wait until the FBI agents and the forensics people got here before we have a meeting," Kaplan said.

"Did the technicians make any more progress last night back at the forensics lab?"

The COO shrugged. "I'm not sure. I think we'll just have to wait for them to get here."

Cray nodded calmly, concealing her impatience. "Are there coffee machines in any of the breakrooms?" She'd barely slept last night, staring at the hotel room door like a fox awaiting an intruder in its den.

"Yeah, in all of them. There's a breakroom on the way to Graham's office. I can show it to you, if you'd like."

"Sure."

They continued down the left corridor and badged in, then made their way up a multi-landing flight of plexiglass steps to reach the second floor. The CEO Suite was down at the end of one wing, but Kaplan pointed her through a door on the right to an open area. There were foosball tables, air hockey, and video game consoles set up in a corner with bean bag chairs. Along the back were several sleek vending machines and two coffee makers. The walls sported gray hexagon patterns with bright green edges.

"We have several spaces like this throughout HQ. Most of the high-level execs work in this wing, so you'll see the C-Suite and a number of SVPs frequenting this one. But employees can use any of the breakrooms," Kaplan said.

"Looks pretty sweet."

Cray moved to enter, but Kaplan said, "Wait." She turned around. The COO looked tired. "Thanks again for helping me back there. I really appreciate it."

"Hey, no worries." She mustered up that charming grin again.

Kaplan's eyes darted away. "You're...Izzy, right?"

She beamed. "That's what they call me."

Kaplan lent a warm smile. "I heard Graham calling you that. Figured it was a little more personable than 'Ms. Cray.' "

She laughed. "And you're...Casey, right?"

Kaplan nodded, still smiling. "That's what they call me. I'll see you around, Izzy." She continued on down the hall.

Cray headed into the breakroom, wondering how the same conversation would've felt without her disorder. Would she have come away glowing inside, relieved she hadn't messed up, excited by the possibilities?

Ulterior motivation was the only kind that led her to something good. Sometimes when she was nice to people she had just met, she acted that way solely to applaud herself for how well a mask fit her face.

It was exhausting to wear them. Exhausting to have to manually think through what came to most people so easily. But the reward was nice. *I'm a good person,* she could tell herself in the mirror, and it would fill her with pride. *I am High Functioning.* How many people like her could say that about themselves? Most were probably so self-absorbed they didn't care. But she did. That's what made her better.

"You can't be a good person, Izzy," Simone had told her, toward the end, "if you only ever do kind things for selfish reasons."

"Why not?" Cray had asked, frustrated. "Whether they admit it to themselves or not, doesn't everyone do good things just to convince themselves they're a good person?"

Simone paused, swept her bangs away. "No, some people do things because they are actually decent people."

"I don't believe that," Cray said, shaking her head. "I don't believe that for a *second.*"

"Of course you don't." Simone's voice grew bitter. "You can't grasp normal people because you're a fucking freak."

Cray reached one of the breakroom coffee machines and tapped the touchscreen, began filling up a cup. She heard someone approaching and turned to see Ritter, the CTO, walking toward her, looking frazzled.

"Ah," she said, adjusting her circular AR glasses. "I'm glad I'm not the only one who needs this shit to survive."

Cray laughed, smiled. "I think I'm an addict at this point." Psychopaths actually couldn't get addicted to substances, the way they were wired. But disclosing faux vulnerabilities got other people to let their guards down. And that was always useful.

"I think I have more coffee in my veins than blood at this point." Ritter filled a cup from the next machine over. "It's funny, I didn't use to need it. But these past few months, it's all that's been keeping me upright. And now *this* happens." She gave an exasperated sigh.

"I'm guessing Catalyst was pretty stressful to put together?"

Ritter put a lid on her coffee. "It wouldn't have been bad if Niall didn't ride us so hard to get it done by this month. I told him we should just wait for CES in January. But *no*, we gotta have it ready for the San Fran Auto Show. CES is a *tech* event, Niall said. The Auto Show is a *car* event. If we unveiled Catalyst at CES, it would be just another tech announcement. But if we unveiled it at a car show, especially the biggest one in Silicon Valley's backyard, then we would, wait for it…" She mimicked Spencer, staring off and dramatically sweeping her hand across the room. *"Disrupt* the automotive industry." She sighed and took a sip of coffee.

Cray raised an eyebrow. "I thought the whole Big Three vs. Silicon Valley thing ended like a decade ago."

"Oh, it pretty much did. But not for Niall. To him, Detroit just figured out the way the wind was blowing and didn't want to be left out. He never believed they were capable of innovation. He was a Valley supremacist. And in his mind the only way to get things done was to pretend we're still a startup and have everyone stay awake till four in the morning, working like our lives depend on it."

Ritter set the coffee down. "Of course, he was too busy screwing Casey Kaplan to appreciate what it did to the rest of us. It's sad. I was actually happy with how Catalyst's been shaping up, but now that all this has happened, it feels like it's for nothing. Niall could be a real prick, but for some reason I kept thinking that on Friday we'd all bask in success together, after the keynote. It just feels strange now that he's dead." She took another sip, slower this time, looking off deep in thought.

Cray was still processing what she'd just heard. "Wait, he was having an affair with Kaplan?"

Ritter turned to her. "Oh yeah, everybody knew about it. They'd be seen leaving together, showing up the next morning in the same car... You could feel it in the way they talked to each other, see it in their eyes. They were always more discreet whenever Graham came by to check on things. Some of us agreed not to tell him out of courtesy. I'm not sure if he ever put it together, though." She seemed very casual about this.

Cray recalled Kaplan's words outside just a few minutes ago: *It's not been a good week.*

No fucking shit.

"Do you think Spencer's wife found out?" she asked.

"What? And killed him?" Ritter laughed. "I doubt it. I've only met Tatum a few times and Spencer barely talked about her himself. I got the impression they were no longer that close. And she spends half her time in L.A. anyway, filming that doctor show or whatever. I don't think she has the technological prowess to hack our systems, but with a dipshit like Johnson running security, I wouldn't rule it out."

Cray thought for a moment. "Is Kaplan married? Her spouse could be a suspect."

"No, I think she divorced a few years ago." Ritter sighed. "I've been there myself. Not doing *that* again, no way."

Cray nodded, filing information away. "What was Spencer like?"

Putting herself into the headspace of another hacker was easy. But she'd never committed murder. If she was going to get to the bottom of this thing, she needed to understand why someone would kill the man. Though she already had a few ideas.

Ritter looked sadder as she sipped more coffee. "He was incredibly smart. And he had vision, I'll definitely give him that. But good luck to you if you questioned him. He would get this crazy, brilliant image of the future in his head and then decide that just because he thought of it that way, *that's how it would become.* As CTO, I run R&D. I kept telling him that just because he could think something and even make something didn't mean people would accept it, let alone *want* it. I mean, we all remember Google Glass. Nobody wanted to wear those headsets because it made them look like dorks. It wasn't until Apple came along and made AR cool that everybody else finally got their shit together.

"Niall told me the endgame was a world without steering wheels or people who owned cars. That's why he got rid of the Z-Series a few years ago. Said sportscars were for recreational driving, and that wasn't going to be around for much longer. Said one day it would be outlawed because it wouldn't be safe."

She rolled her eyes. "I told him nobody's going to accept that. Nobody's going to *trust* that. But Niall just looked right at me and said: 'People will accept anything with the right social conditioning.' Can you believe it?"

Cray nodded, wondering how the Valley Kool-Aid hadn't killed Spencer before someone else did.

"So is that what Catalyst is? A car without a steering wheel?"

Ritter paled, then laughed. "I've signed the world's most iron-clad NDA. Niall was completely paranoid that someone would spoil his big surprise. If I told you, his ghost would probably come through the wall and scream at me."

"Did he think anyone would actually care that much?" Cray paused, realizing that had been a little blunt.

Ritter looked slightly hurt. "Well, maybe I'm a bit biased because I've been overseeing it for three years from the pipe dream to running the—" She caught herself. "You'll see it Friday and you can judge for yourself." She glanced at her watch. "Graham's gonna start the meeting soon. We should probably get going."

"Right." Cray nodded and the CTO headed off, leaving her alone in the room.

She quickly emptied a pack of sugar into the coffee, poured some cream in, and slapped a lid on it. Best not to be late.

As she headed out of the breakroom and down the hall to Graham's office, she considered everything Ritter had told her, sorting info into different piles, re-organizing what she already had.

People will accept anything with the right social conditioning.

She could appreciate Spencer's logic, but he'd been too forceful. Cram something down someone's throat too fast and they choke. If you want them to swallow it, you need to spoon-feed it to them, sweet talk them into it. Make themselves feel *good* about taking it.

Now she wondered if Spencer's lack of tact could've gotten him killed. Ritter was the only executive who'd openly voiced discontent with the CEO so far. But that didn't mean there weren't others who had been displeased with him, people who were keeping their feelings closer to their chests.

Cray knew she wasn't the only one who wore masks.

8:05 AM

Sova sat in a spot far from any cameras that would catch his face—so long as he stayed in the car, anyway. Vehicles stood idle around him, caressed by the rain.

He'd parked near the end of a row of storage units. That's all there was in this part of town, warehouses and cargo trucks. He looked like just another civilian coming by to check on his locker. Maybe picking something up, maybe dropping something off. Nobody would glance at him long enough to care. He was only supposed to be here five minutes or so anyway, but his contact was running late.

That had him on edge. After he messaged Racer last night and alerted them to what went wrong, they had been understanding—or at least had tempered their disappointment and sent carefully worded messages back.

Racer was taking no risks with this target. Last night Cray had displayed aptitude, so now Sova's employer decided it was time for some assistance. Racer had another asset primed, which surprised Sova at first. Then the more he thought about it, the more it made sense. Racer didn't fuck around. He bet their contingencies had contingencies.

They had warned him, however, that this was last minute. Racer could not verify the asset's effectiveness, only that they would certainly be able to provide some support.

Sova hated working with others. They added too many complications, made errors he couldn't control. However, he'd had some successful hits working with people like him. Friendship hadn't emerged from those ops, but instead the closest thing approximating it in his line of work: mutual respect.

He had no clue how this one would go. Given that they were already five minutes behind, he didn't think well. Racer told him that if things went south, he had permission to terminate this man. He was probably going to have to when this was all done, anyway.

A sedan turned off Leghorn St and into the parking lot. It crept closer, pulling into a spot a couple spaces down from him.

Keeping his eye on the other vehicle, Sova reached for his silenced pistol, sitting on the passenger seat. Cocked it, held it low.

A man climbed out of the car and shut the door behind him. He strolled around the trunk and continued on straight, casually, like he was just heading to one of the storage units. Then, as he passed behind Sova's car, he hung a left.

Sova hid the gun down the side of his seat, keeping the grip within reach of his fingers. His trench coat would obscure the weapon.

The passenger door opened and a man leaned his head in, smiling. He held up a cigarette.

"Mind if I smoke?" asked Detective Connor Quinn.

"Actually, yeah. I kinda do," Sova said.

Quinn took a seat and closed the door, then drew out a lighter and lit the cig anyway. Sova thought about shooting him right then and there, but that would be too much mess to clean up. And what vehicle would he flee in? The other man's car might be unmarked, but it was still a police cruiser.

"You know, I couldn't believe it when I got that message last night. But then it all made sense." The detective took a deep drag. "It was strange that Richie Liu was out sick right when the biggest Monterey murder in ages hit. Then the case fell to me." He looked at Sova. "I'm guessing this...*Racer* had something to do with that?"

The hitman shrugged. "I've learned not to doubt their abilities."

Quinn laughed. "Fucker somehow knew about my gambling debts. Figured I wouldn't be above doing less than legal things to pay them."

Sova gave a thin smile. "Well, here you are."

The other man grew angry. "You kill people for a living, so don't fucking judge me."

"How do you know what I do for a living?"

"Put it together myself." He tapped his temple, flashed a grin. "I'm a detective, see."

"Well, you've just entered the same line of work as me, so let's not have the pot calling the kettle black."

Quinn held up his hands, nonchalant. "Hey, I've spent enough years solving murders to know that sometimes people just gotta die. They get in the way, they become a burden, they wrong you..." He looked out the windshield, raindrops drizzling across the glass. "But this girl... I'm all too happy to take her out. I see it in the way she walks, the way she talks, dresses—hell, the *nerve* of the things she says." He laughed. "She's asking for it, I'm telling you."

Sova shook his head. "Nobody asks to get murdered. Like you said, sometimes people just gotta die. It's sad, but it happens all the time. Our job is to get it done. Quick, professional, with as little pain as possible. It's the least we owe the victim, no matter who they are or what they've done."

Quinn took another long hit on the cigarette, blew smoke out into the car's cabin. "Yeah, but just so you know..." He looked at Sova. "This time, things might get a little...*un*professional."

A grin broke out across his face.

10:19 AM

Cray stared blankly at a computer screen in the Network Operations Center, thinking back to the time she got arrested.

Of all the things she'd done, she was still surprised it was the only one she'd gotten caught for. Fucking possession of marijuana, less than twenty grams. It wasn't even hers, and she was high on something else at the time, hanging out with some high school kids who she thought were like her. They preached the meaninglessness of life, the fakeness of love, and other revelations from the Gospel of Edge.

But Cray was wrong. They weren't like her because their bark was worse than their bite. Once she scratched the surface, got to know them better, she realized just how insecure they really were. She probably would've moved on from them sooner if the ringleader hadn't been a hottie. Cray got easy lays and free drugs and the best part was she kept it all from her parents. They thought the clothing was just a phase. But most goth kids didn't do the things she did or think the things she thought.

One Saturday afternoon in mid-April, near the end of junior year, the group was hanging out by the canal just off Miami Springs Dog Park. In retrospect, it had been brash to pick such an open spot to smoke. Pretty soon someone called the cops and a patrol car rolled up. They all bolted when the officers got out. Cray started running for the dog park but stopped as soon one of the cops shouted "Freeze!"

There was no point resisting arrest. She knew that would only make things worse. Also, she was starting to feel weird, worried she'd overamped on the coke the ringleader gave her. She decided playing innocent was the best route to go. She hadn't smoked weed with the others. She was just with some people who did.

Of course, there was an implicating brownie in her pocket. She'd been saving it for later, not wanting it to mess with the coke. Cray debated scarfing it down right there before they could stop her, but she didn't want to risk it given how strange she was feeling. Fidgety, anxious. She did her best to hold herself together, to avoid sniffing.

One of the cops was female and patted her down right there. She pulled the brownie out of Cray's pocket and raised an eyebrow.

"Let me guess: You're gonna say you got this at a bake sale?"

Cray mustered up an embarrassed smile, shrugging, tilting her head just so slightly. "I was holding it for a friend. They said it was a snack for later. They didn't say anything was in it."

"Right." The female cop didn't look impressed. She cuffed her right there, and Cray remembered thinking that part was kinda fun.

The boredom had been obliterated now. Her anxiety rose as they put her in the backseat of the car, her heart beating faster. She was getting shakes and hoped they would think it was just nerves, certainly not anything else.

When she got to the station and was permitted the infamous one phone call, her mother was confused by the strange number.

"Where are you, Izzy? What the hell's going on?"

"They took my phone. I could only call you this way."

"Who's *they*? Where are you?"

Cray sniffed, and not from tears. "I'm...um...I got arrested."

There was a pause, then her mother's voice roared back, so loud the officer watching her turned his head.

"ISABELLA ELSPETH FERNANDEZ CRAY, WHAT THE FUCK DID YOU DO NOW?!"

She winced, looked to the officer for sympathy. He grimaced and shrugged, offering a smile.

Her parents scrambled to get a lawyer, but Cray knew the drug test would seal the deal. Several kids from school had been caught with weed before, and they'd been given an option to go to something called Teen Court. In Miami-Dade County, this meant you admitted guilt in exchange for the crime never appearing on your record. However, you then went to a court overseen by an adult judge with student prosecutors, defense attorneys, and jury members to decide punishment. This included a minimum sentence of community service hours, Teen Court jury duties, jail tours, drug courses, and sometimes you even had to write an apology letter to your parents. Prosecution argued for harsher punishment, defense for less.

However, that was only for misdemeanors. With cocaine she'd be sent straight to juvie court. Cray hadn't had a stable social life through high school, but she had managed to do incredibly well in her classes. That hadn't been the case in middle school because she'd been so fucking bored, but her mother cracked down on her, saying she wasn't achieving her full potential. Cray preferred to focus on the present than the future, but she knew it would arrive eventually. She wanted to go to college and get a high-paying job, which was the exact same thought as everyone else in her generation. With a cocaine charge, she could kiss those prospects goodbye.

The cops were surprised when the drug test came back positive not for marijuana, but coke, and at that point Cray knew she was fucked. She did the only thing left she could.

Surprising even herself, she burst into tears and pleaded the cops to let her go to Teen Court. Admitted to the weed charge, said she didn't know where the cocaine came from.

Must be a false positive. But she knew the brownie had weed and she never ever should've taken it.

Please, Officers, please. It was a stupid, stupid mistake. I didn't know what I was doing. But you don't understand. This will destroy *me. My parents will* murder *me. I never wanted to hurt them like this. I just want to make this right. Please, I swear I will never ever touch drugs again in my life. I just—I just—Please, let me make this right.*

The cops left the room to discuss things after that. Sending people to real court was expensive and the whole point of the Teen Court program was to prevent youth from becoming more fucked up—read: liabilities—down the road. She didn't actually have any coke on her. There were just traces of it in her saliva. But she *did* have a weed brownie.

That's what Cray kept thinking, sitting there in the interrogation room and shaking. Her throat was sore and scratchy and she felt sick.

Eventually, the officers came back in.

"Where did you get the coke?"

"What coke?"

"Don't play dumb. You tell us who the distributor is, you can go to Teen Court."

"I don't know the distributor. I don't know where my friends got it."

"Then give us their names and we'll ask them."

She glared. "I'm not ratting them out."

"Doesn't look like you have much of a choice. *You* backed yourself into this corner, Isabella. We're giving you an out, which is pretty fucking generous considering the cocaine. I mean, you're only seventeen. What the hell are you doing with stuff like that anyway?"

I was bored, she almost said, softly. Cray was disappointed in herself. Not just for getting caught but for being so reckless in the first place. Now a whole skein of consequence was laid out before her that she hadn't even considered before. She never thought it would catch up with her.

"Come on," the female cop said. "I'm assuming your

friends aren't selling the shit. We can make deals with them too, as long as they testify against the dealer."

Cray thought about it. She didn't particularly like any of those people. The ringleader could be a bit aggressive with her and wasn't good enough in bed to make up for it. And now they'd all gotten away while her entire future was on the line.

"Okay," she said. And she told them.

Teen Court felt strange.

There she was up on the stand with the prosecutor grill-ing her, like something out of a movie. But he wasn't some charismatic scene-stealer played by a Hollywood A-lister. He was a high school senior with a cocky grin and the build of a football player. And her attorney wasn't exactly Perry Mason either, a gawky nerd from her school's debate team.

Her parents and siblings sat in the back row in suits, look-ing stern. The show she put on was as much for them as it was for the judge and jury.

"Were you aware that the brownie your friend handed you contained marijuana?"

"Yes," she said, sure to look as scared as possible.

"And what did you intend to do with that brownie?"

Cray looked down, as if ashamed. "I...I was going to eat it." The prosecutor opened his mouth to say something, but she launched in, "It wasn't the first time I'd done that. I've smoked it, eaten brownies with it, cookies, you name it. I did it because my friends all did it, but I know that's not an excuse." Anger flashed in her expression, still staring down. "I should've just said no." Her mother would love that. She was a big Nancy Reagan fan.

"I've done a lot of thinking since I got arrested. Not just about what would've happened if I hadn't gotten to come to Teen Court, but what it's done to my family. My sister and brother are so perfect compared to me. I've been an awful big sister to them." That she knew was true. "I've disappointed my parents and they've never done anything to me to deserve that."

She looked up, not at the wanna-be lawyer, not at the jury of her peers, but at her blood relations. "I'm really sorry." She said it softly, but still loud enough to hear. It wasn't a lie. Cognitively, she believed everything she was saying. She just didn't *feel* it.

Cray turned to the jury. "I deserve whatever sentence you give me."

The prosecutor opened his mouth to speak, then froze. She'd derailed his entire list of prepared inquiries.

"No further questions, Your Honor," he said, returning to his table.

When the jury came back, she was given the minimum community service, jury duties, and a jail tour. The clerk, another student from the debate team, read the sentence and the judge gave her a further admonishment.

"It seems the jury and I both agree, Ms. Cray," she said, adjusting her glasses. "I've looked over your report cards. You're a bright girl and you could have a very bright future ahead of you if you don't slide down the wrong path. It seems you understand the weight of your decisions. I'm glad you had this experience before your eighteenth birthday, at which point you would've been tried as an adult. And even if you get arrested again before that, you will not have the chance to return to Teen Court. You will be sent to juvenile court, and it will appear on your permanent record. I hope the severity of this forces you to carefully consider your life choices going forward."

Cray nodded, doing her best to look shy and timid. "I will, Your Honor. Thank you."

The severity did force her to consider things. The jail tour was a vivid image of consequence that resurfaced years later, when Luke Reed and the FBI nearly caught her and several others for the largest corporate data breach since the Sony Pictures hack of 2014.

She didn't want to come that close again.

It turned her from grayhat to whitehat and brought her to where she was now, leaping from defending companies against cyber threats to helping the same agent who nearly arrested her solve the murder of a Silicon Valley CEO.

10:24 AM

"How's it coming?"

Cray snapped out of her reverie, turning away from the computer screen.

Special Agent Fraser stood there. Despite the hard edge he'd shown yesterday, he seemed softer this morning. At least around her.

"It's coming," she said, smiling. His blond hair was combed back neatly and his suit this morning, less eighties than the one yesterday, looked good.

He'd spent the night in a Monterey hotel after looking through Spencer's computer and belongings. Quinn had driven back with him, then went to drop off the materials at the FBI Palo Alto Residence Agency.

Bailey and Levine had come in this morning saying they still hadn't found the virus code, but it appeared logs were deleted around the time of the summer accidents and on Monday evening when Spencer was killed. Based on their analysis, the virus was either installed manually by someone at the company via a flashdrive onto the Update Department subnet, or the hacker sent the virus into the Update Department through an Asimov car.

"That would be impossible," Johnson, the CSO, had told them. "The cars don't send software update confirmations—

or any data, actually—to the Update Department. Their data goes straight into the Telemetry servers in the general Network Operations subnet. Anything that was sent from a car to our servers would be logged in Telemetry."

And so now the forensics techs were combing through the Telemetry archive for the entire company's network operations. Everything Asimov monitored on its cars worldwide came through the Telemetry servers. Miles driven, battery charge level, hours used, time spent on and off, average speed—and what software version the cars were using, along with when they received their last update.

Bailey and Levine had a Snowball hooked up to one of the terminals in the main NOC and were harvesting data from the Telemetry systems to analyze.

Fraser sighed, looking around. The usual NOC staff were at work, keeping watch on Asimov vehicles around the globe. "I wonder what they do with all this data…"

Cray shrugged. "Spencer's assistant Cheryl told me it's for 'analytics.' Kaplan insisted the same thing."

"Gotta love vague answers," Fraser said, staring toward the giant monitors on the back wall. "They're always so helpful."

"Kaplan assured me it was to improve safety."

"Of course she did." He turned back to Cray. "People here think they're saving the world."

She smirked. "Doesn't everyone?"

"Do you?" The question seemed honest.

Cray laughed. "Not usually. But if over 300,000 lives are at risk, I'd like to stop someone from hurting them." She tilted her head. "How about you?" She still didn't know what to make of Fraser. He gave off a typical tough fed exterior, but there was a softness, a woundedness that flickered in his eyes from time to time.

"If I was younger, maybe I'd believe I was. I like to think that every little bit of order restored helps."

"Younger?" She laughed. "You've gotta be younger than *me*. How are you so jaded?"

He smiled. "Well, you don't *look* older than me. And I

wouldn't call myself jaded. I just know first-hand that tech-nology creates as many problems as it solves."

Cray leaned back in her chair, resting her arm against the desk. "It's rare to meet someone in my generation who's afraid of tech."

"Oh, I'm not afraid of tech, Ms. Cray. Just the people who think it's going to save us." He looked up past her and nodded.

She turned around and saw Reed and Quinn entering the NOC. The detective was beckoning to Fraser.

"I've gotta go, but Reed will supervise. Let me know as soon as you find anything. I've got a suspicion about the Telemetry database." He walked down the row of computers.

"Wait, where are you off to?"

He glanced back over his shoulder. "Cupertino, to inter-view Lucas Declan, founder of Asimov. Your pal Graham thinks he's our best suspect."

"And what do you think?"

"I guess I'll decide that after I talk to him. Take care, Ms. Cray."

Reed was heading toward her and the forensics techs, while Quinn stared at her by the door, a look of disdain etched across his face. He seemed to take getting brushed off really fucking personally. There was something about him that bugged Cray, but as long as he only kept pouting, there was no need to do anything.

The senior FBI agent stood over her, not impressed with her laid-back posture. He turned and addressed the forensics techs.

"Found anything yet?"

Bailey shook his head. "This is a *massive volume* of data. We're going through the backups of everything Asimov col-lected on its global fleet for the past half a year." He laughed. "We might need two Snowballs. And it's gonna take a while for PrivateEye to find any discrepancies between this and the current database. But if the virus got in here, we should see divergences."

Reed nodded, turned back to her. "Ms. Cray, since this is the most fun part of cyber investigations, I'll leave the supervision to you. Bailey and Levine know what they're doing, so all you really have to do is sit tight."

She glowered. "Don't you need me for anything more..." — she didn't want to piss off the techs — "I don't know...*involving*?"

Reed smirked. "This is very, very important, Ms. Cray. Putting you as supervisor while I work on a report is the highest trust I can bestow upon a civilian." He cocked an eyebrow. "What's wrong? Getting bored?"

Cray narrowed her eyes but smiled. "No, of course not. I rarely ever get bored."

"Wouldn't want you jumping at any more shadows tonight, would we?"

At that, she gritted her teeth. When Graham told Reed about what she saw last night, he'd said she might just be getting a little paranoid, that there was no logical reason why she'd be a target to Spencer's killer. Cray bet he thought she was making the whole thing up. Fraser had seemed more concerned, recommended she spend the night in a different area.

"No," she said. "You're right. The less jumpy I am the better."

Reed's smirk widened. "Good. Society really appreciates you doing this."

She almost clenched her teeth. "You know how much I love society."

Reed strode off toward the exit. Fraser and Quinn had already left.

Sighing, Cray got up and walked over to the Snowball machine. The technicians were monitoring the flow of data, searching through the Telemetry backups in cloud storage and selecting specific folders to download for analysis. They were mainly focusing on the software updates for each car. Every time a vehicle downloaded one, it sent an update receipt to the Telemetry system so that the company could know which version any given Asimov car was running at any time, as well as what versions it had run in the past and when.

So far, the file transfer was sitting at 28%.

Bailey and Levine were completely absorbed in their work, but boredom crushed down on her. Cray stared off toward the giant screens displaying active cars around the world, thinking back to after the Teen Court trial.

She'd thanked her defense attorney profusely, said she'd see him around at school. Then she went to the football-star prosecutor, who was fairly attractive.

"You did well back there." She slipped him a piece of paper with her number on it. "Good projection."

Before he could say anything, she'd gone back to her family, who looked relieved at the lighter sentence but disappointed and even embarrassed to be there in the first place.

"What were you doing, Izzy?" her mother asked, eyes flicking between her and the prosecutor.

"I was just congratulating him on a good job. It seemed the right thing to do."

Her father nodded, like he wanted to believe her. He still had a Scottish accent. "Given the things he said about you in his closing statement, that showed good sportsmanship, Izzy."

She'd given a shy, but proud smile in response.

That weekend she found herself in the backseat of the prosecutor's mom's SUV. They were on the top floor of a West Miami parking garage and the sun was setting out beyond the Everglades, bathing the inside of the car in an orange-yellow hue. The jock was going down on her, but Cray kept herself upright, gripping the driver's seat headrest. Teen Court and the arrest seemed far away.

After a while, he pulled back, gasping for breath and trembling.

Cray looked down at him with disappointment, tilting her head. "That it?"

He stuttered, "No, no, of course not."

She grabbed him by the hair and pulled him back down. He went at her with renewed vigor, her boredom finally starting to wane. She moaned louder to encourage him, to get him to get her there, and when he did, she was watching herself in the rear-view mirror. And it struck her even then, years before the diagnosis, how rarely smiles reached her eyes.

10:52 AM

The engine of Fraser's Crown Victoria rattled as the vehicle came to a halt. He put the gear shift in neutral and pulled up the parking brake.

"Jesus," Quinn laughed. "How old is this thing?"

"Nearly twenty years. They always give the junior agent on a case the most beat-up car they have. Reed got a late model Suburban."

"And they didn't have anything newer, or even an automatic?"

Fraser shrugged. "I requested it, actually. And I prefer manual."

Quinn stared at the gear shifter. "I've never seen a Crown Vic with one before."

"It was an aftermarket feature. This car got impounded during a bust back in the day and painted black."

"And you *requested* this?"

He shrugged again. "The fewer hackable parts, the better."

"But it's not self-driving. How could it be hacked?"

"Doesn't matter. If a car's computerized, it can be compromised. I don't trust any of them. Don't even really trust this one, but they wouldn't let me drive my own." He turned off the car and climbed out.

Quinn followed, shutting the passenger door behind him. "What do you drive off-duty?"

They walked across the parking lot toward the corporate headquarters before them.

"1983 DeLorean. Bought it a few years ago and restored it myself. Learned a lot about mechanics while doing it." He laughed.

"So you're a car guy?"

"You could say that, though I've been told I don't give off the vibe."

They arrived at the one-story structure, which was bordered by a cluster of palm trees at each corner. Above the front doors was the glowing logo of LIon, Inc.

The two investigators entered the building, which seemed the antithesis of the Asimov offices. Everything was brightly lit, and the walls were stark white. Out the giant window behind the reception desk, a rectangular courtyard was visible with a Japanese zen garden, complete with rocks, bonsai trees, and a koi pond with flowing water.

The receptionist stood up as soon as she saw them and smiled. "Mr. Declan is waiting. I'll take you right to him."

Fraser glanced at his watch. They were about seven minutes early.

The receptionist led them down a hall to the right all the way to the other side of the building, then to the left. She knocked, then opened the door and beckoned them inside.

The conference room was positioned at the other end of the courtyard from the reception desk. The entire back wall was a window looking out into the zen garden.

A man stood by the glass. He turned around as they entered, and Fraser examined him. He was in his early forties. Medium height. Reddish-brown hair. Goatee and a man-bun, a style Fraser had hoped would die with the 2010s.

"Hey, man. You must be Special Agent Fraser," Lucas Declan said, coming around the conference table. He extended his hand and smiled. "We spoke on the phone."

Fraser shook it, nodded out at the zen garden. "That's really wonderful. My parents have one at home in Hawaii."

"Oh yeah, I love it." He put a hand to his chest. "I really respect Asian culture." He paused. "I mean, I respect other cultures too. But, like, especially Asia. And especially Japan."

Fraser managed a smile, nodded. "I find it fascinating myself."

"Do you watch anime?"

"Not really."

"Oh." Declan managed something between a laugh and a wince.

Quinn sighed loudly. "Why don't you take a seat, Mr. Declan?" He patted the chair at the head of the table. "We wouldn't want to take up too much of your day."

"Of course, of course." Declan laughed nervously, sitting down.

Fraser took the chair by the window, Quinn on the other side. They both angled their seats to face the executive. Fraser drew his notepad and a pen. Quinn took out his tablet.

"Mr. Declan," Fraser said, "you are the CEO of LIon, Inc., correct?" He pronounced it like the animal.

The other man nodded. "We're in the business of making more efficient, recyclable lithium-ion batteries. We started out designing them for laptops, but we're branching into electric vehicles now."

"Getting back into the auto market?" Quinn asked, holding his pen like a cigarette. Evidently, he knew better than to ask if he could smoke in here.

"Well, that was always the goal, man." Declan leaned back into the seat, trying to relax himself, tenting his fingers. He watched rain fall into the garden and his expression grew darker. "I know you're here because of what happened to Niall Spencer and...you want to see if I had anything to do with it."

"Not necessarily," Fraser said. "You worked with Spencer for several years, him as Chairman and yourself as CEO. We know you disagreed with him and left the company. Maybe you can give us insight into why someone would've wanted him dead."

Declan sighed, still staring out the window. "Man, who *wouldn't* have wanted him dead? He always thought he was right and everyone—*everyone*—else was wrong. It was his way or the highway."

"What disagreement finally drove a wedge between you guys?" Quinn asked. He seemed more invigorated on this second day of the investigation, Fraser noted.

Declan rubbed his forehead. "We had a lot of disagreements, but the last one was turfing the Z-Series. The sportscar. I knew Tesla was coming out with a new Roadster and I wanted us to get ahead of them on that market. But Spencer kept saying, 'let them chase it, it won't matter one day.' And I looked at him and I said, 'Man, what the hell are you talking about?' And he was just like, 'Sportscars are gonna be a thing of the past ten years from now. Driving will be illegal by the end of the 2020s.' And he was dead serious, man, *dead serious* about it. I don't know how so many people in the Valley can say stuff like that with a straight face, but Niall was one of the worst offenders. The Z-Series was a Corvette competitor. Once the T-Series and F-Series started selling, I wanted us to upgrade the Z to being a supercar, like the Tesla Roadster. But Niall was so convinced that cars with steering wheels weren't gonna be around much longer, he felt we should turf the Z entirely. And that was pretty much the last straw for me.

"You gotta remember, this was just after the pandemic. It was only around then that the industry realized driverless cars would take a lot longer to go mainstream. I mean, look at today. Sure, we've got autonomous trucks, but highway driving is a lot easier to automate. There's way fewer variables to control for than in a city or a suburb. I read a little while ago that the A-Series, Asimov's big rig, is still its biggest seller globally. It was the easiest to implement worldwide. And yeah, we've got autonomous ridesharing apps, but they're not ubiquitous like everyone was saying they were going to be by now. Tech is crazy. Some changes happen faster than you expect and others take a lot longer. We've progressed a lot with driverless cars, but we still don't have true, honest-to-God Level 5 autonomy."

Quinn raised an eyebrow. "Everyone keeps talking about these levels of self-driving cars and whatnot. What the hell do they mean?"

Declan turned to him. "So basically Level 0 is a car with no automation. You do everything yourself. Level 1 is, like, cruise control. Barely automation, but it technically counts because the car is maintaining a speed you set for it. Level 2 only went commercial in the 2010s. It's basically automatic breaking and the car being able to drive itself on the highway for certain stretches. You know, like the old Tesla Autopilot, that was the one that got the most public attention, both for popularity and because of some accidents. Back then it didn't count as self-driving because humans still had to be behind the wheel to take control. The car didn't *start* or *end* driving itself, it was basically just really advanced cruise control.

"Level 3 is where things start to get interesting. Now the human-computer control balance shifts to the computer side. The car can start making decisions in how it drives, not just braking if something comes up ahead of it. It can read the *environment around it*. It can choose whether or not to change lanes and overtake a slower car. When I left Asimov, we were about to launch the next gen F-Series and T-Series with Level 3 capabilities, the first on the market. Audi and Mercedes almost beat us to the punch, but we got there. And even under Niall, Asimov started commercially offering Level 4 capable cars in 2025. Waymo was already testing ridesharing with Level 4 vehicles in the late 2010s, but they weren't selling the vehicles to consumers."

"How did you beat the other companies to Levels 3 and 4?" Fraser asked.

"LiDAR." Declan smiled, reminiscing. "That was our big entry in the market. Halfway around the 2010s, once everyone started pouring money into driverless cars, that was our major standout feature. We had the best LiDAR sensors. They could work even in difficult weather conditions like rain and snow. Our cars still used a combination of LiDAR, radar, and cameras to read the environment, but the LiDAR was definitely what allowed us to advance faster than anyone else."

"And what exactly does LiDAR do?" Quinn didn't look impressed.

"It uses laser light to scan an environment and create 3-D images. In Asimov cars, it works over 200 feet in each direction. It's so accurate it can even capture facial expressions. With our software, we figured out how to get the system to factor out precipitation. But it's not perfect. That's why even Asimov vehicles are still at Level 4. Even the trucks."

"You still haven't explained what Level 4 is," Quinn said, tapping his pen on the table.

Declan looked increasingly nervous with each of his interjections. "The best way to describe it…is that it's full autonomy, but not quite. The reason why cars have advanced to higher levels is that coders have observed what works and what doesn't. That's half of what we did at Asimov, collected data, ran analytics, and thought 'How can we make this safer?' Where did the car not respond well enough? Why did it have to alert a human driver to take over here? Usually it was weather, but I hear Asimov cars have more trouble with snow than rain nowadays. It's thicker and it piles up on the roads, it's much likelier to make things slippery, that kind of stuff.

"So Level 4 is very high-functioning autonomy, but it's not quite perfect. There are still certain instances where it needs human control. But for the majority of city and highway driving, you don't need anyone in the driver's seat. That's how Waymo, Uber, Cruise, and all of them do it with ridesharing. They're technically not Level 5, which would never need a human in any circumstance. At that point, you wouldn't even need a steering wheel installed in the car."

"And that's what Spencer wanted, right?" Fraser asked.

"Yeah. We got into a lot of disagreements over what that would mean for the auto industry, and for society. He was sold on this idea that driving should become illegal one day because self-driving cars would be just so much safer. And

I kept telling him that people weren't going to accept that. They're always going to want some control. They like driving.

"Niall said people liked horses and carriages and the traditional car replaced those, so therefore the autonomous car will replace the human-driven ones we have today. But that's a fallacy. The traditional car gave people *more* control over their transportation. With the autonomous car, they're relegating that control to a computer. And not everyone is cool with that."

"But if self-driving cars become safe and affordable, wouldn't people eventually just grow tired of driving?" Quinn asked. "After a while, they probably wouldn't mind a car with no steering wheel if they never use it."

"Maybe. And I do believe a lot of cars on the road one day will lack steering wheels. But Niall and I disagreed on something even bigger than having a manual option: ownership. Niall wanted a future where no one owned a car, where we all subscribed to ridesharing services and could order different sizes or styles of car based on what we were doing, like taking the kids to school or going out on the town. He thought that would significantly reduce the number of cars on the road.

"But the thing is, part of the economic appeal of electric and autonomous cars is that they're going to get cheaper in the long run. Electric cars have far fewer parts than combustion engine cars because there's just a battery. They don't even need air intake or an exhaust pipe. That's why you can have small electric cars with big cabins—less space is taken up by all the machinery. So cars are going to get cheaper and cheaper the more electric cars are mass-produced. But if electric, self-driving cars become cheaper, why wouldn't people just buy them for themselves? People like to personalize their cars. For many, it's an extension of their identity. Yeah, there are cities like New York where owning a car is a hassle, but look at L.A. That city thrives on the personal automobile. There's a certain kind of freedom to it.

"Not to mention families, who would have to install car seats every time they get into a new Uber, or bring a bag of toys with them in and out for their kids. Even adults leave things in their cars all the time. Glove boxes aren't just for manuals. If you can own a car, it's a convenience to have one. So what if it sits in your garage for most of the day? When you need one, you're thankful you have it. And if cars become cheaper, more people will be able to afford them. So I definitely think ridesharing services are a good idea—we all need to grab a taxi sometimes—but I don't think they're the only type of personal transportation people are going to have in the future. And when the next pandemic hits, you don't want to be stuck taking transportation that a sick person might've just been inside, whether it's a subway car or an autonomous taxi. Even after COVID, Niall still talked about things like a virus killing millions globally didn't make us wary of sharing vehicles with strangers."

Fraser nodded slowly, jotting some things down. Just abbreviations to trigger the memory of thoughts later. "So what do you think the keynote on Friday is all about?"

Declan sighed. "With the amount of hype Niall built up around it, it really better be Level 5 autonomy or everyone's going to be disappointed."

Quinn looked surprised. "How? You said the advancement to each new level was because coders programmed the cars to respond to everything they could think of. But how could they account for every possible event on the road?"

Declan sat up straighter. "That, I believe, is why Niall was so secretive about it. To figure it out, you don't really have to look that far. Niall was invested in several other companies besides Asimov, but the biggest one was a startup called Wintermute."

Fraser nodded, a piece of the puzzle falling into place. "Artificial intelligence."

Declan nodded. "Niall was big into that. Ted Graham is invested in it too. I always figured to reach Level 5, he'd have to cross-pollinate his companies eventually. In order to have a car that can respond to any and all road events, you'd need a car that can think for itself. Machine learning."

Quinn had paled. "What? Something like *Terminator* or *The Matrix*?"

Declan laughed. "Nah man, not like Skynet or any movie AI villains. Those always have self-awareness. They're artificial *general* intelligences, AGIs. An AI for a Level 5 car would be way simpler than anything like that."

The detective looked relieved. "Alright, so you think this big announcement is a car without a steering wheel or something?"

"I wouldn't put it past Niall. Nearly a decade and a half ago, Google unveiled the Firefly car without a wheel, but that was just a concept. If Niall actually developed a version of AutOS—that's the software running on Asimov vehicles—capable of Level 5, I can see him being brash enough to introduce it in a car with no steering wheel. And selling it to the public."

"Can't imagine investors would be thrilled," Fraser said. "Consumers might not even want a car like that yet."

"That's what I was thinking, but it's the Valley, man. They always put a spin on it. They say it's the future and that you'll be ahead of the curve, ahead of everyone else, if you buy it. Many get off on that, thinking they're more *advanced* than other people. It makes them feel special." He laughed. "Spencer wouldn't have made that kind of move without making sure the marketing department could work their magic with it, whatever it is."

"What else could it be, if not a Level 5 car?" Quinn asked.

"I don't know. Most of the speculation I've heard in the Valley is that it's just some software, and that's why nobody's seen any spy photos of Asimov testing a new car. You usually see upcoming models driving around with coverings to hide what they look like. But there haven't been any spy pics of new Asimov models. And tech journalists have *looked*. There's a lot of interest in what's going down Friday. But some have taken this as a sign that it isn't a new car.

"Really, I think they're just overlooking the obvious explanation. Niall was obsessed with secrecy. If he'd designed a new car—and it wouldn't just be an updated F- or T-Series with him, no he'd make it new and flashy—without a steering wheel, he'd probably test it at some incredibly remote site in the Nevada desert or somewhere. Anyone involved in the project would have NDAs up the wazoo."

"But how would they test the car on city streets?" Fraser asked. "Testing in the desert or on a closed track would only prove the hardware worked, not that the software could respond to anything in a civilian driving environment."

Declan sighed again. "There's still an explanation for that. And I wouldn't put this past Niall either, though I think it would be reckless if he did it…" He took a deep breath. "Asimov could test the car in a simulation. The more accurate the simulation, the more accurate the results."

"That wouldn't be street legal for regulators, though," Quinn said.

"Yes, but they would begin street testing *after* the keynote. It would still be a concept car when it's unveiled. But they couldn't claim it has Level 5 autonomy unless they've done *some* kind of testing to back it up. And I believe with all the data Asimov collects from its cars, they would be able to make an extremely detailed simulation."

"Wait," Fraser said, suddenly tense. "Do you mean that they would take data from the Telemetry servers and then run that in whatever databases they were using for the new project?"

Declan paused for a moment. "Well, I mean, I have no clue what they're doing there, man, but yeah, that's how I'd do it. Knowing Niall, he probably has his new stuff air gapped from everything else in the company, but yeah you could still transfer it using Snowballs or something like that."

"So if there was a virus that had breached the Telemetry servers, it would then be transferred into this new air gapped system, the one used to simulate the Level 5 car?"

Declan held up his hands. "Man, I don't even know if it *is* a Level 5 car. That just seems the best explanation to me. But yeah, if there was a virus hiding in the Telemetry data and that data was put into the Level 5 project servers, then yeah, it would be in there. Wouldn't do much good if it was a Trojan or something, since the hacker wouldn't be able to see into the air gapped systems. *But* if the virus was well designed enough, a polymorphic code, then yeah, it could maybe replicate itself and do some damage. I could see that."

Fraser's heart was racing. They needed to wrap this interview up, *fast*.

"Just one last question," Quinn said, tapping his stylus on the tablet. "How exactly did you leave Asimov? Was it abrupt or—?"

"After the Z-Series argument, he just looked at me and said, 'Maybe we don't see as eye to eye on this as we thought.'" Declan had grown angry. "Which was pretty damn obvious by that point. I knew what he was really saying. But then the next day, he came into my office, and talked about me leaving and when I wanted to go. He said it would be better that way, without having to force a board vote to oust me."

Quinn narrowed his eyes, studying Declan. "You still sound a bit bitter all these years later."

Declan scoffed. "Yeah, man. Asimov Automotive was my *child*. I named it after my favorite author—loved reading *Foundation* as a kid, but *Caves of Steel* was always my personal favorite. The voice assistant, SALLY, is named from his short story about a sentient car. I really believe autonomous and electric vehicles are the future. And when Niall Spencer became the majority shareholder, I thought it was the best thing to ever happen to the company. He'd already made his name in crypto. He was a Valley hotshot... Looking back on it, I was naïve. Yeah, real naïve. Even in the early stages, he was micromanaging me, but I kept thinking how his money would make the company better. And I guess it did. Its stock rebounded this morning because of all the anticipation for Friday. Not even his own death could derail the hype train. But he still took something from me that I cared about."

He gave a long exhale, deflating. "You're right, though, that was years ago. It was only when I heard he'd died that all these emotions started swirling back. Honestly, I'd thought I was over it. I was looking forward to Friday. Still am, I guess. But Asimov Automotive without either of us sounds like an alien place to me. I don't even own one of the cars anymore. I've got a Tesla and an i4 these days."

Fraser finished jotting some notes and stood up. "Thank you for your time, Mr. Declan. You've been of great assistance." He handed him a business card. "We may contact you again."

Declan nodded, still a little shaken. "Anything I can do to help, man."

Quinn stood up too and they left the room. When Fraser closed the door behind him, Declan looked lost in thought staring out at the garden.

<··>

They strode across the parking lot back to Fraser's black sedan. As they began climbing in, Fraser glanced behind him to the corporate offices.

"You know, it's funny he named *Caves of Steel* as his favorite Asimov novel."

Quinn stopped, halfway into the car. "And why's that?"

Fraser turned to him. "It's a murder mystery."

"You need to see this."

Cray came around behind Bailey, staring at the laptop screen over his shoulder. His computer was hooked up to the Snowball, and PrivateEye displayed a window with two separate columns of files. The details of most rows were highlighted green for both sides, one labeled *Telemetry* and the other *Backup*.

However, three rows were highlighted in red.

"What am I looking at?" she said.

"Okay, so Levine and I wanted to specifically cross-check all logs for the past week, as well as the logs from mid-July to early August, when those previous accidents occurred."

"I'm assuming the red ones are discrepancies?"

"Yeah, but here's the thing. There's only a few differences between what's currently in the Telemetry system and what was in the backups."

"And that is?"

He turned around and looked up at her. "Three vehicles in the summer were sent unscheduled over-the-air updates. One in Florida, one in Texas, and one in Nevada."

She nodded. "The ones that had the accidents."

"But get this." He turned around again. "The accidents occurred after each car reported an *Unknown Error* to the

Telemetry database. The Florida car's error occurred at 02:04:23pm UTC. Then an update, one we didn't see in the Software Update subnet logs, was sent to *that car only* at 02:04:45pm UTC, twenty-two seconds later. We see the same thing with the Texas truck and the Nevada car. *Unknown Error*, followed by a software update less than a minute later."

"What was the update?"

"The most recent patch the cars had downloaded."

"So the affected cars re-downloaded the same software version they already had when they crashed?"

"Looks that way."

Cray started pacing. "Nothing strange was found on those cars when Asimov ran diagnostics. So the virus must've wiped itself from each vehicle by downloading an uninfected version of the most recent software. That confirms there's a virus infecting the Update subnet. But if the Telemetry servers don't match their backups, then that means the virus copied itself, sent the copy out into the general Ops network, infected Telemetry, and is programmed to delete any confirmation of updates sent to cars."

She looked back at Bailey and Levine. "What about Spencer's car?"

"There was an Unknown Error logged a few minutes before the vehicle went off a cliff," Levine said. "But no update confirmation was sent."

"Hmm." Cray stared at the wall, thinking. "Each of the summer accidents was faster than what happened with Spencer. The hacker just drove them off the road or forced them to crash. But with Spencer, they drove him several miles before killing him. Probably they logged out after each of the summer crashes and the virus automatically sent an update once they stopped using the remote access Trojan. But there was no need to log out with Spencer. The impact and the salt water would've destroyed the electronics. Even if an update was sent, there wouldn't have been a receipt relayed back to Telemetry."

Bailey nodded. "Right. There was nothing for us to find in Spencer's wreckage, anyway. No need to cover up the virus at that point."

Levine rubbed her chin. "So the summer incidents tell us more. But since we didn't find any of their unauthorized update logs in the Update subnet archives, that means the virus must be embedded deeper in Update than it is in Telemetry. It either wasn't able to delete the backups showing the update confirmations, or whoever coded the virus didn't think we'd dig this deep into Telemetry."

"I doubt that last part," Cray said. "Sure, now we know Telemetry was breached, but we still don't have any virus code to analyze. And we don't know what else it's infected. We don't even know how it got into the system in the first place. The hacker is still several steps ahead of us."

Just then, the NOC entrance door swung open. A familiar blond FBI agent stormed in, Quinn on his heels.

Cray smiled as he came closer. "Ah, Fraser. Guess what we just found?"

"Is it good or bad?"

She gave him the rundown, pointing to the files as she did so.

Fraser put a hand to his head. "*Shit.* We need to find out if Telemetry data has been used in Catalyst. The virus might've gotten over the air gap if they're using it for a simulation."

Cray's brow furrowed. "A simulation of what?"

"That's the right question." He turned around and shouted to the room, "Where's Kaplan?"

A South Asian man with tousled hair stood up from a computer terminal behind them. "She's not here, but I'm the Ops sysadmin. What do you need?"

Fraser headed over to him. Cray followed.

"I need to speak to someone who worked on Catalyst or someone in the C-Suite."

The sysadmin laughed. "Nobody on Catalyst will tell you anything. We've all been asking them for months, trying to get any little nugget we can."

"I don't need to see the data, or whatever it is. But its servers may have already been compromised by the person who killed Niall Spencer."

Cray detected Quinn standing behind her and tried not to look. Carefully, she stepped around to the other side of Fraser.

The sysadmin ran a hand through his hair. "Jeez...I'd say talk to Ritter. She's probably your best bet."

The FBI agent nodded. "Where's her office?"

"It's in the C-Suite wing, right before you get to the COO and CEO offices." The man pulled out his phone. "Here, I'll call her."

"Just tell her I'm on my way." Fraser turned around and made for the exit. "I prefer speaking to people *in person.*"

Cray was left standing there with the detective and the sysadmin. Quinn leered at her with a self-satisfied grin, like he knew something she didn't.

She shot him a look of disgust, then hurried after the FBI agent.

11:40 AM

Fraser didn't even knock on his way into the CTO's office. Cray rushed in after him, just as Ritter looked up, startled. "Vijay said you'd be coming. What can I help you with?"

"Are you using Telemetry data for Catalyst?"

She froze, then forced a laugh. "I really can't say. Graham will kill me."

Fraser leveled his gaze with hers. "Telemetry was compromised months ago. We have evidence that the summer accidents were caused by the same hacker who killed Spencer."

Ritter paled. Her mouth opened and she looked like she really wanted to say something, a debate raging in her mind. She looked up at both of them.

"Yes, we were using it for simulation purposes." Her voice was quiet.

"What were you simulating?" Cray asked.

Ritter gave them a pained look. "I really can't tell you more. But yes, we've been using Telemetry data. *However*, the last time we transferred data to the Catalyst servers to feed into the simulation was just before last Christmas." She looked hopeful. "The breach doesn't go back that far, right?"

"We're not sure," Fraser said. "But it goes back at least four months."

Ritter slouched and put a hand to her head.

"What's going on?"

It was Graham's voice. They all turned to see him in the doorway, Reed beside him.

"Why are you harassing my executives about confidential material?"

Ritter sat up straighter behind them, shaking her head. "Ted, really, it's fine."

Reed turned to Graham. "Detective Quinn notified me that your Telemetry systems have been breached and there's a concern infected data may have been uploaded into Catalyst servers."

Graham shook his head angrily. "That's impossible. The last time we took Telemetry data was—"

"Christmas," Fraser said, growing impatient. "Last year. But we don't know how far the breach goes. It's been swimming around in your servers since at least July, probably before then."

"Yes, but even if the breach goes back half a year—"

"It could easily be longer," Fraser continued. "It seems to have started in the Update subnet, which implies insider threat. Someone at the company probably installed the virus with a flashdrive, and there's no telling when that could've happened. Sometimes the people coding systems leave backdoors just for their own amusement, or for corporate espionage if they leave the company. Corporations sometimes find viruses in their systems planted *years* earlier, just sitting there beaconing, waiting for their creators to send them updates to carry out some sinister purpose."

"We would've detected a virus beacon if it had been sitting there for that long," Graham scoffed.

"Only if the beacon sends out a signal on a regular interval," Cray pointed out. "Some viruses are coded to emit beacons using a random distribution. That way, irregularities aren't detected by cybersecurity measures."

Ritter massaged her temples, exhausted. "Fuck."

Graham held up a hand. "Now hold on. We don't have any *evidence* the virus has been there that long. But we'll run some additional checks on our Catalyst servers just to be sure there are no irregularities."

"I'd really prefer if we could run our forensics software on it as well," Fraser said. He looked to Reed for backup.

His superior nodded. "There's really no point in hiding Catalyst from us," Reed said to Graham, his tone calm, friendly even. "We're not going to leak it to the press. We just want to make sure a bad actor isn't going to make things worse for you on Friday."

Graham laughed. *"Worse?* How could they make it *worse*?! The CEO and chief architect of the project has been *murdered*. If not for the hype around Catalyst, the stock would be dead too. The company's future is barely hanging by a goddamn *thread*. Friday is our last chance to redeem not only ourselves, but the autonomous car industry as a whole. Catalyst will outshine Niall's passing, martyr him even."

"We want to help you," Fraser said. "Let us do our job so you can do yours."

"I know what Niall would've wanted, and under *no* circumstance would he have let you inside the Catalyst servers. Not even his own death."

Fraser stared at him in disbelief. "He was *that* fucking obstinate?"

Ritter burst out laughing behind them. Everyone turned to her. "Sorry," she said, looking embarrassed.

Graham shot her a look, then turned back to Fraser. "Niall always said the rest of the world didn't understand the way we do things here. Said people who don't comprehend the nuances of emerging, complex technologies would destroy better futures out of fear, whether they realized they were doing it or not."

"Alright, let me re-phrase." Fraser put a hand to his forehead, then looked up. "If you don't show me the Catalyst servers, I'm going to charge you with obstructing an investigation."

But Graham gave a thin smile. "I know you can't charge me with that, and if you try to, I'll have Pawar in here to represent me in a flash. As Interim CEO, I *granted* you access to all our data systems except Catalyst so that you wouldn't waste time getting a warrant. If you want to see Catalyst, you will need a court order, which I doubt you will be granted. I will happily let you poke around those servers come Saturday morning—or even Friday night if you're that set on it."

Fraser shook his head. "Do you *want* us to solve who did this?"

"Of course. That's why you've had our full cooperation."

"If this is full cooperation, I'd hate to see half."

"Sorry to interrupt, but we kind of have a problem."

Johnson poked his head up behind Graham and Reed. They turned around, letting him into the room. It was starting to get crowded. Cray found herself backed against a wall. At the sight of the CSO in her office, Ritter gave a look of annoyance.

Graham seemed aggravated too. "I can think of several problems, Adrian. What is it now?"

Johnson glanced between him and the two FBI agents and said, "We've detected activity on Niall Spencer's account. In our network. Someone using his credentials logged on remotely."

Cray pushed off the wall. "Can you trace them?"

"We did." He looked straight at her. "Someone is actively looking through his files *right now*, from a computer terminal at the Lathrop Library. On Stanford campus."

11:57 AM

Reed's Suburban tore down Palm Dr, rocketing toward the distant grounds as tropical trees whipped by.

Cray sat in the rear right seat, gripped by anxiousness and excitement. She glanced over at Kaplan beside her, who looked deathly pale clutching one of the roof handles.

Graham had insisted that Cray and at least one other Asimov representative tag along. Kaplan burst into the office and volunteered, though she now looked like she regretted it. Her terrified expression made Cray want to slide over to hold her hand and—

Focus, Izzy.

Reed was nodding, saying something on his phone. Then he threw the device down into a cupholder and turned to Fraser. "Stanford Department of Public Safety has been notified. They're ready to assist us in any way they can."

"Who?" Cray asked.

Kaplan turned to her. "They're the campus police." She gave a shy smile. "I went here."

Cray gave her a warm one back—

As the SUV abruptly lurched to the right. The seatbelt strained to keep Cray upright and her head jerked left, pulling a muscle in her neck.

"Jesus," Fraser said, grabbing one of the handles.

They had come out into the ring road around the Oval, a gigantic grass lawn. Sandstone buildings with archways and red roofs lay before them, Hoover Tower reaching up into a pale gray sky to the east.

Reed accelerated past parked cars toward the front of the campus. The engine roared, vehicles blurring by. Massaging her neck, Cray was struck by how enormous Stanford was. Palm Dr itself was a mile long. The University of Miami had been nowhere near this size.

Finally, they veered around the bend. Reed took the turn a little easier this time but slowed only as they rode up onto the curb, a sidewalk separating the ring road from Jane Stanford Way. The SUV lurched to a stop. Quinn's police cruiser came up right behind them and screeched on the brakes just in time.

Several students gathered near the entrance, some holding umbrellas, stepping closer to get a better look. Reed threw open the door, grabbed his phone, and climbed out.

Fraser did the same. "Real stealthy, Reed. Next time we should bring some helicopters. And a SWAT team." He closed the door behind him.

Cray got out and followed them, nudging the earpiece they had given her into a more comfortable position. She'd left her cardigan back at HQ. The wind had picked up, pelting her with raindrops, blowing her hair into a mess. She swiped strands out of her face, trying to keep up with the FBI agents and not wanting to see if Quinn was behind her.

She wondered where Reed had been after he left her with the forensics technicians. Had he really been sitting in some corner working on a report? Had he been interviewing software engineers and executives, trying to glean more details about the case?

Or something else?

As she watched, he stopped and answered his phone, speaking while looking around in the rain.

Bracing herself, Cray looked back. Quinn and Kaplan were walking toward her, the COO seeming anxious and upset.

Cray wondered about what she'd heard earlier, about Kaplan having an affair with Spencer. She hadn't gotten to probe deeper yet, but now was not the time to bring it up.

Reed hung up the phone and turned around, coming back toward them. He seemed oblivious to the ten or so students watching.

"The cops have got a perimeter around the library, but I told them not to lock it down just yet. We've informed them what terminal it is and they're sending a security guard to walk past casually, to see if anyone is there."

Fraser put a finger to his earpiece. "Johnson, are they still active?"

The CSO's voice spoke in Cray's ear. "Yeah, they're still in Spencer's account. They're looking at his R&D folders. Don't worry, nothing on Catalyst is there. The directory's still open, but they haven't opened anything new for the last three minutes."

"Alright." Fraser nodded. "Keep us posted."

Ritter's voice gave an exasperated sigh. "I swear to God, if this is all because some comp sci brat didn't get a fucking internship—"

"Cool it, Mallory. I'm trying to work."

"Easy, Adrian. We all just want to get through this." Graham's voice.

Reed led them along Jane Stanford Way at a brisk pace. The library was up ahead on the left, obscured by some trees. They came around the corner and headed up a path called Lasuen St to the entrance. Several men and women in bulletproof vests stood by an art installation, firearms holstered at their sides. The word *Sheriff* was emblazoned on each of their backs. They looked a lot more intense than the campus police at Miami.

One of them turned around as they approached and walked up to Reed, who introduced himself as the lead case agent. "What's the sitrep?"

"There's someone sitting at the terminal you specified wearing a white hoodie, but they're hunched over. We can't see their face."

Reed nodded. "Central Casting hacker attire. Sounds like we got a true original on our hands."

"There are several ways we could play this. But I wanna know what you're thinking," the Deputy Sheriff said.

"We play it calm," Reed said. "Let them think we're not onto them yet. Then, when they try to leave the building, we snag them."

Quinn laughed. "Case closed."

Fraser looked concerned. "Well, hold on a second. Something's not right here. I mean so far, this hacker's been ultra-careful. Why are they trying to access Spencer's account in a way that's so easy to track?"

"I don't know," Reed said. "Why don't we ask them ourselves?"

"But what if this is some kind of diversion, or a trap—?"

"Cool it." Reed turned back to the Deputy Sheriff. "What are they doing now?"

The officer took out his handheld transceiver. "Underwood, do you copy?"

A moment's silence. Then, "I'm making another pass right now. Hold tight."

Cray bit the inside of her lip. She felt anxious just waiting here in the rain for someone else to do something. What were they waiting for? Just grab the fucker and go.

But what Fraser said was right. This didn't make sense at all. Why would the killer put themselves in a situation where they could so easily get caught? Unless, of course, it wasn't the killer themselves.

Her mind flashed back to last night, the silhouette of a man running for her, knife out and ready to strike.

Don't be ridiculous. This is not a ploy to kill you.

But whoever was behind this seemed to want her out of the picture, if that really was a hitman who came after her yesterday.

Cray looked around her. She was surrounded by cops. Even Quinn, as much as she detested him, was on her side. Nobody was going to try to kill her here.

The transceiver crackled. "Allen, you there?"

"Copy," the Deputy said.

"They're gone. Vanished." The voice came quickly, anxiously.

Reed immediately turned and began striding toward the entrance doors. The Deputy changed the channel on his transceiver and spoke into it as he followed Reed.

"All units, lock down the building. No one gets in or out."

Quinn and Kaplan headed after the others, but Cray followed last. Unease gripped her and the anxiety surged. It was one of the few strong feelings she ever experienced.

She quickened her pace to keep up with them, but as they approached the doors, a voice came over the lead Deputy's radio. Even from here, she just made out the words, "...*open window...no sign of them, must've run off. Shit, alert the perimeter.*"

The Deputy spun around, heading back toward the art installation. "All units, be on the lookout for a suspect in a white hoodie. Height, sex, and race indeterminate."

Yeah, that'll fucking narrow it down, Cray thought. She'd have just ditched the hoodie in a trash can. Of course, that might leave DNA evidence on it.

The officers took off toward Jane Stanford Way. Cray followed along, trying to stay close enough to Reed and the lead Deputy to listen in.

"I want all units on the east side of campus to keep their eye out for any suspicious behavior. Suspect is on foot and may have ditched their hoodie, but I have report that they are wearing dark blue jeans."

Because no one wears denim in California. Cray rolled her eyes. Still, she supposed the Deputies were doing their best with what they had.

She glanced behind them. A student had come out of the library, but they wore a red hoodie, so Cray looked forward again. The group reached Jane Stanford Way, Hoover Tower to their left beyond some trees and the front campus buildings stretching off to the right.

The cops charged off toward the fountain to the left, Kaplan reluctantly in tow. Cray found herself left behind with Fraser, who looked deep in thought.

"It just doesn't make any sense," he said.

"Do you think it could be a diversion?"

"I have no clue what it could be." He looked at her. There was that softness in his eyes again. "And I hate having no clues."

"Can we pull fingerprints from the keyboard they were using?"

He shook his head. "Might've worn gloves. And there'd be hundreds of other prints on there."

"Security cameras?"

"Probably were careful to note them and hide their face. Especially if they had the hood up. Might've even had the escape route planned and just waited for signs that the guards were onto them to make a break for it. I bet there's not much time before they get off campus."

Cray scoffed. "I wouldn't even leave the building. Just throw open a window and hide, make 'em think you left, then ditch the hoodie and calmly walk out a couple minutes later."

Fraser stopped in his tracks, considering it. He glanced back along Jane Stanford Way and she did too.

A student in a bright blue hoodie came off the path to the library and continued across the road, heading south toward Lasuen Mall.

Cray paused, staring at the figure. There had only been one person behind them before, but they'd been wearing red.

Fraser followed her gaze, looking back and forth between her and the distant person.

"That's funny," she said. "I could've sworn they had a…"

It happened very quickly.

If she hadn't been scrutinizing the figure, she probably wouldn't have noticed it at all.

Several tiny blocks of white, then purple color flickered on the hoodie's left arm. Nobody else seemed to have seen it and the figure continued on as if all was normal.

Cray turned to Fraser and their eyes met. He'd seen it too.

Then they turned back toward the figure and headed after them, walking with a calm but steady pace.

12:05 PM

LEDs on fiber optic fabric.

That's gotta be it, Fraser thought, turning onto Lasuen Mall and following the figure south. Clothing like that had been popular at Burning Man for years, but it kept getting more and more advanced. You could have it blare graphic designs, display different patterns.

Or, evidently, you could set it to one entire color at a time and use it to evade police detection. And maybe that would've worked if not for the wind and rain. He bet that's what caused the glitch. It probably wasn't entirely waterproof.

Cray was right by his side, her gaze locked on the target, her face devoid of any emotion. Her demeanor reminded him of an animal on the hunt, closing in on its prey. It was a bit chilling, really, but he had bigger things to focus on.

"Will, where the hell are you?" It was Reed's voice in his earpiece.

"Cray and I found them. We're tailing right now."

"You're—Shit, where?"

"Heading into Lasuen Mall. Their hoodie changes color. I think it's some kind of LED setup. But the suspect looks about five-six, baggy blue jeans. Fairly slim."

"Alright. Stay on 'em."

The hacker continued past the entrance to a sandstone

building on the right, heading into a park. There were bike racks and trees everywhere. Pathways led off toward different parts of Stanford campus. The hooded figure kept glancing around, left and right, over their shoulder, somehow making it seem natural, casual.

Fraser did his best to look relaxed, sauntering and looking up at the foliage shielding them from the rain. Cray glanced at her phone as she walked, pretending to check messages. She looked less intense than she had a few moments ago, which relieved him. He still knew little about her, or why Reed had taken such a dislike to her.

The hacker froze.

Up ahead beyond them, some Stanford Sheriffs appeared out of a side path and entered Lasuen Mall.

The hacker turned around and started making their way back toward the pair of them. Then they stopped again. They were about a hundred feet ahead and between the gray day, the distance, and the hood, Fraser couldn't really make out their face. They looked white, though.

He and Cray continued walking casually, but he could tell the hacker was reading them, him in particular. He was the only suited figure in the whole park. They must be staring at his peroxide blond hair, he figured, wondering if any agent would actually show up to work like that.

Suddenly, the hacker turned on their heel and began sprinting south.

It was like an instinct.

The next thing he knew he was flying forward, legs pumping, arms swinging. Wind rushed by his ears. Stinging rain bombarded his face. It was refreshing—cooling, almost. Beats per minute ticked faster and faster, his entire body shifting to a higher gear as he sped after the suspect.

They had kicked it up a notch too. The Deputy Sheriffs saw them sprinting and increased their speed, but it was no use.

The hacker sailed by, barely missing an officer's out-stretched hand, dashing along another path toward a large fountain.

The cops gave pursuit.

Fraser watched them as he continued running, maintaining his velocity. He'd always been a good sprinter. Endurance wasn't his strength, but he tried not to think about that. Just had to keep going as long as he could. It was going to have to be enough.

The hacker screeched to a halt in front of the Cecil H. Green Library, swinging right back toward the fountain.

Fraser adjusted his course, realizing he had no clue where Cray was.

One of the cops cut across the lawn and leaped over a sand-stone bench ringing the fountain. He managed to grab the hacker's shoulder, but they spun around as they ran, shaking him off. The officer's inertia carried him forward and he toppled into the fountain with a splash. The other cop had fallen far behind, looking out of breath.

The hacker continued out from the fountain, dashing west as Fraser slid onto the path behind them. His lungs burned and his muscles ached, but adrenaline kept him going.

He was less than twelve feet behind the suspect now.

They dodged a cyclist coming out of a gate up ahead and Fraser veered right to avoid getting hit. The hacker poured it on, putting distance between themselves and the FBI agent as they dashed toward the archway to the Main Quad, tall palm trees soaring high above.

Rain mixed with perspiration on Fraser's forehead, his heart thumping from the exertion. Still, he didn't slow. Every ounce of his concentration was focused on the fleeing figure, LED glitches splashing strange color combinations across their back.

He followed them under the arch and the Main Quad opened up before him, an enormous courtyard with eight planting circles from which a variety of trees sprouted upward.

A tour group stood straight ahead, huddling in ponchos and umbrellas. The hacker managed to slide past them on the left before a family shifted, the entire space between two planting islands now occupied. Fraser swung to the right, jumping onto one of the islands and grabbing a lamppost to swing himself west again.

He ran, shoes tramping across muddy soil. When he leaped off the island and hit the ground, Memorial Church was finally visible up on the left. Its famous mosaic of Christ and his followers was displayed above stained-glass windows, rivulets streaking down the surface in the rain.

Dead center in the Quad stood an old, blue Volkswagen Touareg covered in corporate logos, an array of cameras mounted on top. The back of his mind recognized it as Stanley, the Stanford-designed autonomous vehicle that won the 2005 DARPA Grand Challenge.

He almost laughed. *These fucking things are everywhere.*

The hacker hadn't slowed speed, but was starting to stumble, the gracefulness of their motions disintegrating. They were heading straight toward Stanley, various bystanders in the Quad standing still and watching the chase with confusion.

Fraser's entire body burned, the rain unable to keep him cool. Wind swept down into the Quad, battering his face.

The gap started to widen. They were getting away, using whatever adrenaline they had left.

Goddamn it. He tried to push forward, his lungs screaming. The breaths were barely enough to satiate them, but determination propelled him. The hacker pulled ahead—

As one of the bystanders lunged for them.

Cray.

She caught the suspect by the wrist and the figure's whole body jerked back. They nearly got free, but she held firm, torquing the hacker's arm with a savage twist.

The hooded head tilted up and a cry escaped their unseen mouth. Sounded female.

Fraser had broken into a stumble, stretching his hand out toward Cray. But she'd already seized their other arm from behind, driving the suspect toward Stanley, past the information plaque, slamming them face-first onto the car.

He gasped for air, searching for the breath to tell Cray to be careful. But then she tore the hacker's hood back and he stopped in shock, blinking to make sure he wasn't seeing things.

The suspect glanced toward him, recognition flashing past the fear in her eyes.

It was Kayla Spencer.

12:11 PM

"You don't understand," she sputtered as a Sheriff came around with the handcuffs. "I was just trying to help."

"Funny way of showing it," Fraser said. He was still red in the face and breathing heavier than normal.

Cray stared intently at the murder victim's daughter. Between inhalations, Fraser had managed to tell her who she was.

"Why were you accessing his account from a Stanford terminal?" Cray raised an eyebrow. "How did you even get campus credentials? You're in high school, right?"

Kayla looked as exhausted as the FBI agent. She nodded. "They gave me leave because Dad died. I have a friend who goes here, and I asked if I could log in on her account to check something at the library. My stepmom came up to Palo Alto for the day and dropped me off here for a few hours."

"To do what?" Fraser asked, wiping sweat and rain off his brow.

"Walk around. Hang out in the bookstore. Keep myself busy." She scoffed. "Anything to get me out of her hair."

Fraser nodded, lost in thought. Cray wondered how the interview had gone with Tatum Spencer yesterday, if he and Quinn had gleaned anything useful.

"So why did you hack into his account?" Cray narrowed her eyes.

"I didn't. I knew his password. He kept them written on a sheet of paper in his desk. I know Asimov execs can access their accounts remotely. My dad did it all the time, said they implemented that after the pandemic."

"Alright, so why not access it from your house?" Cray asked. She wasn't quite buying this.

"I...I...wasn't sure if it would be traced. I wanted to see what he was working on." She grew angry. "He never told me. Kept calling it Catalyst. Now he's dead and I think it's why he got killed."

Fraser took a deep breath, standing up straighter. "Why?"

"Because he was anxious, paranoid that somebody was going to fuck—sorry, mess it up before the big reveal."

"But why did he think that?" Cray asked.

"I don't know." Kayla's frustration looked genuine. "That's what I was trying to figure out. I thought if I used a Stanford terminal, it couldn't be traced to me and I could maybe stay in the system long enough to figure out what Catalyst is. I can't wait until Friday. I *have* to know now."

Fraser gave a bitter laugh. "You and me both."

Whirring noises came from their left and they looked to see two golf carts speeding across the Quad, slaloming past the planting circles. Reed and Quinn rode in separate carts with the Deputies from earlier. When they came to a halt by Stanley, Reed got out and marched toward them.

"What the hell is going on?"

Fraser filled him in as Quinn sauntered over. "Hello, Kayla. Long time no see. I'm sure your stepmother's gonna be real happy about this." He took out his phone and started dialing a number.

She glowered at the detective.

Cray looked past her at the information plaque. Stanley had mostly resided at the Smithsonian museums in Washington, D.C. after its historic win, the first self-driving car to complete a race. Now it was on loan back to Stanford for the Fall Quarter, a reminder of one of the school's many achievements.

She glanced up at the mosaic on Memorial Church, men, women, and children gathering nearer to hear the word of Christ. It reminded her of her mother, who tearfully thrust a Bible into her hands when she was in college.

"I don't even care at this point if you believe, Izzy. But read it. There's a way people are supposed to act, values they're supposed to uphold. Without that, we're all just animals."

"We *are* all just animals," Cray had said, taking the book anyway. "Nothing you ever do will change that."

She glanced back at Kayla. She wondered what her stepmother would say to her after this, what beratement awaited her.

<···>

Tatum Leigh Spencer arrived about twenty minutes later, pulling up to the front loop in her Asimov F-Series. They were waiting beneath umbrellas beside Reed's SUV and Quinn's sedan.

She wore a dark Armani suit with her hair in a tight bun. The first thing out of her mouth was, "What the hell is wrong with you people?"

She went up to where Kayla stood beside a Deputy, handcuffs removed, and kissed her on the forehead.

"Did they hurt you?"

Kayla rolled up the hoodie, which glitched more frequently now, and displayed her right wrist. Cray's face remained impassive, but she wondered if she'd been a little aggressive.

"They grabbed me," Kayla said, her voice soft. She acted differently now that Tatum was here, almost childlike.

"Who?" Tatum stepped back, looking among the cops and the FBI agents. "Which one of you fascists did this to her?"

"Wasn't one of us, ma'am," said the lead Deputy. "It was her, and she's with Asimov." He gestured to Cray. "But your daughter was resisting arrest and nearly injured one of our own, knocked him into a fountain."

Tatum didn't care. She stormed right over to Cray and glared up at her, only realizing just how tall the younger woman was once she stood directly in front of her.

Cray dropped her mask, staring down at the actress with a blank expression. It seemed to chill Tatum and she backed off. Then she spun on Kaplan, who looked shaken by the whole ordeal.

"Maybe you should be a little more careful before you sic the dogs on somebody. I mean, what was she even doing for fuck's sake? She accessed her own father's account."

"She illegally used Stanford property," one of the Deputies began.

"This is a murder investigation, Mrs. Spencer," Quinn said. "We had reason to believe that whoever was accessing his account might have information on the case. Kayla fled the scene and resisted attempts to detain her for questioning, so we gave pursuit. Now, I'm sorry Ms. Cray over here got a little rough, but don't worry, she'll be reprimanded."

Cray narrowed her eyes at him. Reprimanded for what? Without her, the spoiled little bitch might've gotten away.

Tatum spun back toward her, but Kaplan walked up and put a hand on her shoulder. "I am so, so sorry, Mrs. Spencer. This whole thing got out of hand. We won't be pressing any charges."

She looked over to the lead Deputy. He opened his mouth to say something, then decided against it and sighed. "We won't be either. But if you're not committing a crime or you had a good reason to be accessing his account through one of our computers, please don't spark a campus-wide manhunt. We'd really appreciate it."

Kayla nodded softly, walking over to her stepmother and leaning on her shoulder.

That's it? Cray thought. *No bringing her in for questioning? Nothing more than a talking-to because Step-Mommy showed up?*

Then she wondered if Niall Spencer had been a donor to Stanford, presumably in the hopes of helping his daughter get in. She wouldn't have put it past him. And Kaplan didn't want to pressure the wife of the man whom she may or may not have slept with, who might now own a significant stake in her company.

"Sorry again, Mrs. Spencer," Kaplan was saying, even though it wasn't really necessary at this point. She looked like she was going to burst into tears. "I can't imagine the awful week you two must be having."

Tatum gave a thin smile. "It hasn't been a great one. See you Friday." And she led Kayla off toward her car.

Quinn lit a cigarette and took a drag, turning back toward campus. Reed and Fraser moved to discuss something with the lead Deputy. But Cray kept observing Kaplan, who was watching Tatum and Kayla go.

The redhead was gripped by an emotion Cray couldn't quite place, even though it was written all across her, clear as day. Then Cray realized it was because she had never felt it before.

Guilt.

6:47 PM

The breakroom was quiet save for the rain still drumming against the glass. Sitting alone, Cray found that she liked the noise. It was soothing to ears that rarely heard it, living down in L.A.

Night had fallen almost two hours ago and by now the HQ was mostly empty.

Not much progress had been made since they got back from Stanford. Fraser and Reed were aggravated by the wild goose chase, Quinn seemingly amused. The senior FBI agent had gone straight back to Graham's office to pester him for Catalyst access, which Graham had again flatly denied. After that, Reed made some phone calls to begin the process of obtaining a subpoena or a warrant.

Cray had been relegated back to babysitting the forensics technicians, who were doing fine on their own, even though there was still no trace of the virus code itself. They spent all afternoon digging into Telemetry, knowing part of it had to be there to delete any updates sent to hacked cars. Yet there were no more breadcrumbs extending back before the summer.

Kaplan had brought them some lunch, and afterward spoke with Cray privately outside the NOC. "I know you didn't mean to hurt Kayla, but you really have to be careful."

Kaplan's face was very close to hers, and Cray's heart beat as fast as it had back on campus.

"My bad," she said, managing a little laugh. "I don't know what came over me."

Kaplan lay a hand on her arm. "It's okay. The whole thing was crazy." And she gave her a warm smile before walking off.

Sitting there bored for most of the afternoon, hunger slowly sinking its fangs back into her stomach, Cray kept returning to that moment.

What did putting a hand on her arm mean? That was usually more intimate than a hand on the shoulder.

Or was it?

Cray hated trying to read signs from people she liked. One could run circles in their mind overanalyzing something, but she found that got boring real fast. She was always direct with people *she* liked. The sooner they got past the NT bullshit small talk, the better.

She was incredibly, *achingly* bored by dinnertime, when the forensics techs headed out and Kaplan ordered UberEats from a deli, which rolled up in an autonomous car. Cray now sat finishing her sub and wishing she'd ordered more than just a soda and chips with it. Though she'd probably get to raid the pantry at the loft tonight in San Jose.

Fraser walked in with half a sandwich still wrapped, reading something on his phone. He looked up, saw her, and said, "Hey. Find anything else interesting in the servers?" He walked up to the water cooler and tapped the touchscreen to fill a cup.

"Wouldn't Bailey or Levine have told you?" she said.

"They would've. But I'd rather ask you." He brought the cup and his belongings over to her table. "Mind if I have a seat?"

She smiled. "Only if you ask nicely."

"Well, in that case, I'll stand." He put the sandwich on the table and leaned back against the closest counter, sipping his water.

She shook her head. "How the hell did you become an FBI agent?"

"Well, there's this little thing called the Academy. I applied, got in, and then graduated and got assigned to the San—"

"No, I mean how did you *end up* as an FBI agent? What did you do before?"

He paused. "I went to MIT, comp sci and econ double major."

"So you hate sleep."

"Used to. Now I love it, whenever I actually get the chance." He grinned. "Funny how scarcity increases demand."

"Only funny if you didn't fall asleep in econ."

"Did you?"

She laughed. "I made it through the intro course, but I switched majors after that."

"Where'd you get your degree from?"

"Miami."

"Ah. So what brought you to the Valley?"

"I live in SoCal these days." She paused. "So that's the only reason why you're out here? You got assigned to the Bay Area?"

He shrugged. "That's how it works. Though I found it fitting they put me here. I've always hated the Valley."

"Why?"

Fraser drained the rest of his water. "This place did despicable things to our generation. I've experienced a number of them personally." He moved to the cooler to refill it. "I actually used to want to work here when I was growing up. Saw California as that shining spot on the Mainland. My father was from the West Coast, but up in Canada. I always thought Silicon Valley would be the place for me. Loved computers."

He returned to the counter with a full cup, leaned against it. "Let's just say by the end of high school, the rose-tinted glasses were off. Going to college, even out east, showed me where the groupthink starts. Smart people who think they know how to bring the world together, only to push it farther apart. Maybe if certain things hadn't happened in high school, I would've become just like them." He laughed. "Now I work cleaning up their messes."

Cray furrowed her brow. "Doesn't that get tiring?"

"Oh, it's exhausting."

"Then why do you do it? They've got enough rope. Let them hang themselves."

"Yeah, but they'll end up hanging the rest of us with them. Look at Asimov. Nearly a third of a million vehicles worldwide that some killer can now access. The cars can't be permanently shut off. We have no way of stopping this person until we find the virus. All because some fuckwits were too preoccupied with how visionary their ship was, they didn't notice the gaping holes in its hull."

Cray sipped her soda. "You said Mainland. Are you...?"

"From Honolulu. Canadian father, Japanese mother. I'm first-gen American. Had to give up the other citizenships to join the FBI."

"Ouch." She laughed. "I'm a dual. Scottish. My mother's parents are from Cuba, but they fled Castro in the 60s. My mom didn't get Cuban citizenship, but she wears American flags in public almost every day, so I don't think she's really minded."

His interest piqued. "So you're from Florida, then?"

"Born and raised."

"I've actually never been. What's it like?"

She thought for a moment, shrugged. "Humid."

"Miss it that much, huh?"

"I do miss it, actually. But I haven't been back in three years."

"Not even for Thanksgiving or Christmas?"

She shook her head, feeling a twinge of the only thing she could call sadness.

He frowned. "Who do you spend holidays with?"

"Friends," she said, just a little too quickly. Shit, it was harder to lie around Fraser. She wondered if other people felt the same about him. If so, that had to come in handy in his line of work. Or maybe she just kept getting distracted by his amber eyes. "Last year it was with my girlfriend."

"Ah." She saw something click in his gaze, realized it might be the wrong thing.

"The year before that it was with my boyfriend, though."

Fraser hesitated, nodded. "Right."

"I don't see either of them anymore. Or anyone, these days." She gave him a wry smile. "Graham's got me a nice place to stay tonight. Might be nicer with some company."

He opened his mouth, hesitated. Looked torn, uncomfortable.

Immediately, Cray backtracked. She was about to say something, but he moved off from the counter.

"It's getting late and I really should be going. I've got a fair bit of paperwork to do. Have a good night, Ms. Cray."

Fraser walked out of the breakroom at a brisk pace, looking flustered.

She sighed, disappointed more with him than with herself. The uptight types were usually the first to divert from professionalism. It would've made tomorrow so much more awkward and fun, especially with the digital forensics leads drying up.

Still, it had been impulsive to suggest that to an active-duty federal agent. If she kept a point system for High Functioning, she probably would've taken off several for that move. But if it became a true game, she might eventually get bored of it. It was better to keep it malleable, vague, a reminder rather than a checklist.

Cray sighed. Then she noticed Fraser had left half his sandwich behind. It was pristine, still wrapped. In his unease he must've forgotten about it. Or was just too embarrassed to come back.

Oh well, she thought, pulling it across the table. *More for me.*

10:14 PM

There would be no mistakes this time.

Sova gripped the steering wheel tightly, guiding his sedan from the Highway 87 off-ramp onto Santa Clara St. It amused him that people thought of San Francisco as the biggest city in the Bay Area, when San Jose was larger by both land and population. It was also less expensive, and in the wake of the pandemic many tech workers had migrated to the bright lights at the heart of the Valley, leaving the coast behind.

The sedan cruised past the AC Hotel on the right, continuing toward more high-rises. Tall palms lined the streets, but so did leafless trees. It was a strange mix down here, beneath the cloudy night sky. Proximity to the mountains provided rain shadow, and precipitation in the city was but a faint drizzle.

Sova glanced beside him at his passenger.

Quinn looked jumpy, anxious. He kept flexing his black gloves, as if they made him uncomfortable. A silenced pistol lay across his lap, pointed toward the door. Sova had his own beside him.

Another couple blocks and he turned onto Notre Dame, heading north. Once Racer had told him about the target's change in location, he headed straight out here and cased the place. Drove both this route and the getaway, mapped it all out. Then he'd headed back to the motel and run through the op in his head countless times. Figured out how to explain it to Quinn, to keep it real simple so even a novice like him could understand.

The detective had been put up in a Palo Alto hotel, so he left his car there and walked to the darkened Caltrain parking lot on Alma. Sova had been waiting with the engine off, the car completely dark. No passerby would've thought anyone was in there until he started the engine. But of course, there had been no one around when they pulled out. Palo Alto wasn't a place for night owls.

It was coming up on the right.

This area was quiet. The region had more corporate headquarters than clubs and bars anyway, and down this stretch there were several residential towers.

Sova turned down an alley behind the condo building. It was only five stories tall and so was the structure on the other side. The lane was deserted save for some dumpsters. Steam rose from vents on the ground. Ahead, the alley narrowed. Beyond it was a vast open parking lot across the street. An enormous digital billboard displayed an ad for Asimov Automotive, a car pulling up and the words *Driving your future* materializing above it.

Well, would you look at that? Sova almost smiled to himself, but he was too tense, too focused. He was in mission mode now. After an entire twenty-four hours of anticipation, the moment was finally here. He'd gone over the plan so many damn times, accounting for every contingency he could think of.

Sova turned to Quinn, who looked like he was psyching himself up.

"You ready?"

"Yeah, yeah." He nodded. "So Racer's unlocked everything for us?"

"Assured me they'd be in the building's systems by now. Cameras running on loop, back entrance unlocked. The suites have RFID locks, all connected to the master system in case of emergencies. If Plan A doesn't work, Racer will show us right in."

Quinn laughed. "God, I love technology." He moved for the door. "Alright, let's do this."

"Wait."

Quinn looked back at him.

Sova held the detective with a firm gaze. "You follow *my* lead. You're really just here to help me carry her down to the alleyway. There will be no fucking around, no unnecessary pain. We're just here to do a job. And we're gonna get it done smooth and fast. Got it?"

But Quinn only gave him a thin smile. "Of course. You're the professional. Lead the way."

They opened their doors and stepped out into the night.

"**S**hit."

Cray lifted the razor away, inspecting the wound. Blood trickled down her leg toward the drain and she sighed, reaching for a Kleenex, keeping her foot up on the edge of the tub.

On the TV in the bedroom loft, some talking head continued, "...raises the question of safety not only in Asimov vehicles, but in driverless cars by any manufacturer. Is that a legitimate concern?"

"I think it has to be," another said. "If it can happen to the CEO of a company, then I mean, how can they expect us to believe that any of these things are safe? I think that's what people are wondering right now."

Cray had turned her head when Spencer's name came up. Now she tuned the voices out as she dabbed the cut with a tissue and continued shaving.

When she finished and applied a Band-Aid, she strolled out of the bathroom and turned off the TV. They were going in circles on the news in absence of any progress on the case. Then again, they pretty much always went in circles. Fucking channels ran twenty-four hours a day and still all you got were talking points and cherry-picked data.

Yawning, Cray put on a comfy pair of black pajama shorts

and a gray tank top and headed back downstairs from the loft to the main floor. She'd spent much of the evening lazing around the various sofas. And the bed, which was incredibly soft. She'd nearly fallen asleep on it earlier, but knew she had to get more work done on the L.A. insurance company job.

She'd finally managed to breach the billing division and seize the credit cards, and now would have to write up a report with recommendations on how the company should improve its pitiful security.

But instead of thinking about that, her mind was repeatedly drawn back to the Spencer case. They hadn't found any evidence of a breach before the summer. The technicians hadn't been able to detect more irregularities anywhere else in the Ops department. It was as if the virus had suddenly appeared in mid-July.

Which, of course, made sense. It was unlikely whoever was behind this had been planning it for over a year. And that meant they hadn't breached the Catalyst servers after all. At least, not through the Telemetry data.

But if the virus only appeared in the summer and wasn't some long-buried Trojan, then how had it gotten there?

Cray flopped on the sectional sofa before the windows, offering her a view of the skyline. She put her feet up on the glass coffee table and leaned back, sprawling out. The pillows were soft and inviting, especially after her lack of sleep the night before. The past two days had been draining. She realized she hadn't had this much face-to-face interaction in a while.

Maybe it was better that she was spending the night alone. Cray needed a recharge after yesterday's run in with the Palo Alto prowler, and this expensively furnished penthouse was more than able to provide. It had a very modern feel to it, every appliance made from gleaming stainless steel, every counter or surface a smooth cut of stained concrete. Cray had eaten a sizeable snack from the pantry earlier and downed a glass of sauvignon blanc, the bottle still open on the kitchen island. She thought about getting up and having some more wine, or playing the PS6 upstairs, but for right now she was content to stare off at the rain.

It wouldn't be bad if she had some company, though. It just had to be the right person. There had been so few of them over the years.

The first one she really connected with was Tom, back in college.

Whenever they talked — whether in groups or otherwise — she'd felt a click, a chemistry. They discussed everything from movies to politics to philosophy, not always agreeing, but becoming engrossed in each other's words, in each other's company.

The only problem was that he was her boyfriend's best friend.

Looking back, she could see how much of an obvious mistake it was, how impulsive she had been to sleep with him. The harm it would do hadn't even registered. She hadn't meant to hurt anyone, even though her boyfriend, Michael, had been kind of a douche. It was like a line of code her computer couldn't process.

Tom had been racked with guilt afterward, insisting they come clean to Michael. She pointed out that telling the truth would only hurt him. They enjoyed being together. Why couldn't they continue in secret? All three of them would be happy.

But in the end, Tom had been weak. He broke down and confessed to Michael, who texted Cray to visit him at the frat house. He was already drunk when she got there. He screamed, swore, and hurled an empty beer bottle at her.

Along with Michael and Tom had gone their friend group, including the girls. One of them saw Cray at another frat party and spilled beer all over her while she was talking to some guy. "*Whoops,*" she'd said, flashing an evil smile and walking off.

Shoved out of her friend circle, Cray found herself isolated for a time again, like she had been in high school. Although this time she wasn't just a loner. She was a cheater, a skank.

And there was one thing she couldn't overlook.

She didn't *have* to sleep with Tom. The whole situation had been avoidable.

More than that, she learned not rely on other people. They inevitably fucked things up. Like Tom, giving in to the guilt.

But even after all that it didn't click, though the pieces were there. What actually pushed her over the edge, what finally made her seek a psychiatrist, was the death of her dog at the end of junior year.

Elsie had been a Border Collie, whip smart and sweet as they came. Her companionship was never unwelcome. She was one of the few things that instinctively drew affection out of Cray. Her family had her for nearly ten years, but she'd developed mast cell cancer so suddenly they hadn't even noticed anything was wrong until three weeks before she died.

Her mother had called her and asked her to come back home one Saturday, to join them at the vet. Elsie wasn't eating and was racked with pain. She couldn't even get up off the floor. They had no choice but to put her down.

When the vets finished and left the Crays to have a moment with her on the floor, Izzy realized she was the only one not crying. The others were on the ground with tears pouring from their eyes, but she only knelt there, petting the dead dog's head and feeling just a twinge of sadness. She knew she should feel something greater in that moment. *Wanted* to feel it more than anything else.

She looked at Elsie's open eyes, staring off into oblivion. The dog had been one of the few creatures on Earth she actually cared about, one of the few things that sparked joy. A thought struck her at that moment, colliding with profound force, piercing her to the core.

There is something very wrong with me.

A bell chimed and Cray opened her eyes, realizing she had dozed off on the sofa. Shit, maybe she was more exhausted than she realized.

Rubbing her eyes, she glanced toward the door. Who the fuck was coming over at this hour? Had Graham's friend forgotten to tell the neighbors he was out of town?

Slowly, she got to her feet.

Cray approached the door as quietly as she could, tiptoeing across the floor. When she got to the spyhole, she saw a tall man with a buzz cut standing on the other side. He had an Eastern European look about him and wore a gray trench-coat, black clothing underneath.

She looked around behind her. The only light in the kitchen was a lamp above the stove, reflecting off the stainless-steel appliances.

No, this man shouldn't be able to see any light coming under the door. He'd think no one was home and leave in a moment or two. Cray turned around, began heading back to the sofa.

The bell rang again.

She stopped and looked back at the door. Voices came from the hallway. It sounded like the man was conversing with someone else.

Tiptoeing again, she crept back over and peered through the looking glass.

The man spoke quietly. She had to keep her ear near the door to make out what he was saying. He had turned toward an unseen figure. "...cameras saw her enter earlier this evening, according to Racer. She hasn't left since, and there's a light on in the window."

Cray spun around. There was a lamp by the window, but the main light would probably be upstairs, from the loft. *Shit.* What the hell was going on?

She turned back to the spyhole. The man had taken out his phone and was typing something. He didn't wear gloves.

"She's probably taking a leak. We can surprise her coming out of the bathroom. Make this whole thing a lot easier." He lowered the phone, then looked down at it again a moment later. "Racer's working on it."

Suddenly, there was a *beep* and the door unlocked.

Cray's heartrate shot through the roof. She turned, striding as quickly across the floor as she could without being loud. The door swung open behind her, washing the room with light.

"Ah, there she is." Cray froze. She knew that voice. "Not very polite to leave guests waiting at the door."

She turned around. Two men stood silhouetted in the frame, but she could make out their faces. Both sported trench coats, but the second man wore beige. It was Quinn, a fedora on his head, closing the door softly behind him. And locking it.

Her mind raced to fit the pieces together. She turned to the first man, the one with the buzz cut, narrowing her eyes. She flashed back to yesterday evening, the figure racing after her. She hadn't caught much of a glimpse, but now, seeing him shadowed here, she wondered.

"You tried to kill me last night," she said matter-of-factly. Her mask had fallen and she wondered if playing scared would help her. The anxiety was back full force, tension racking her body, but she wanted to kill these men more than anything. Especially Quinn, who had evidently moved up from lechery to attempted homicide.

"No," said the first man. "We're not here to kill you, Isabella." His eyes looked sad, like he didn't want to be doing this.

"Yeah," Quinn chuckled, coming closer. "We're just gonna take you for a little drive, that's all."

Bullshit. They wouldn't have let her see their faces if they planned on letting her live.

Cray thought of exit strategies. She'd seen a fire escape stairwell, but it was in the hallway. The only way out of this penthouse was through that door, past both of the men.

The first drew a pistol with an oblong silencer out of his coat, bringing it up toward her. She prepared to dive for cover behind the island, but he held up a hand.

"Just do as we say, Isabella. And you won't get hurt. I'm not here to cause pain."

By the look on his face, Quinn didn't seem to share the sentiment. Maybe she could provoke him, get him to screw things up for his partner, who seemed more levelheaded.

"You never knew Spencer. And you're clearly not smart enough to code the virus. So who are you working for, Quinn?"

He laughed. "I don't even know their name, but they pay better than the Sheriff's Department, that's for sure."

"So much for serving and protecting."

Quinn shrugged. "Eh, been there, done that."

"Come on, get moving," the other man said to him, gesturing with the pistol.

"Right, right." Quinn drew out a rag and a bottle—chloroform, she guessed—and applied it heavily to the cloth.

She started to back up, but the hitman noticed. *"You* stay put."

Cray turned back to Quinn, who was now advancing toward her. "That's all this is for? Money?"

He stopped, snarled. "I had to find some way to pay for the booze, so I turned to poker. Now I gotta find some way to pay for the poker." His voice grew increasingly bitter. "Not my fault the bitch wife took everything in the divorce."

"Really?" She mocked sympathy. "I can't imagine why anyone would leave you."

He scoffed. "Yeah, right. But I realized something else too. I mean, what's this Racer person really done wrong? It's not like we got a shortage of asshole Valley billionaires. So what if they iced one? And who's the only other person Racer wants dead so far?" He glared. "Just a stuck-up slut with small tits."

"Ooh. Going right for the jugular, are we?"

"Quinn, *move*," the hitman snapped. He looked anxious. She had to be careful that he didn't just shoot her.

They were going to kill Cray, but they clearly didn't want to do it here. Too much mess, maybe? More likely, they just wanted her to vanish. Distract the investigation, have Fraser and Reed run around trying to find what happened to her instead of focusing on the case. Maybe they'd even try to pin this on her somehow, make it look like she fled.

Quinn was just a few feet away. She started moving back again, slowly.

"I said stay put," the hitman barked.

Cray didn't bother to look at him. He couldn't shoot her. Even a non-lethal wound would leave blood, and that would be a complication, something to clean up. They wanted to grab her and get her out as fast as possible. The hacker—*Racer?*—was already in the building systems. If they could access the locks, they could probably access the security cameras. These guys must have a car waiting, probably down in the alley.

"Come on, princess," Quinn was saying, staring at her with that same leer he'd given her before all this. "Time for a little nap."

He kept advancing. She kept moving back.

"Touch me and I'll scream."

The hitman shook his head. "It'd be no use. There are only two penthouses, and the other is unoccupied."

In that moment, Quinn lunged for her.

She turned, running back toward the sectional. The detective thundered after her.

Cray aimed for the stairs, ready to burst into a sprint—

As Quinn's hand grabbed her by the forearm, pulling her back toward him, jerking her shoulder. She struggled to break free. Even though she was a little taller, he was much stronger. He yanked her close and got her in a headlock.

Cray wriggled as much as she could, fighting from her core. Quinn seemed to have trouble holding her.

But the chloroform cloth was in his left hand. It came down toward her face.

If she inhaled that, it was game over.

Summoning all her strength, she jerked to the left just as the cloth nearly smothered her. Cray's mouth opened wide, chomping down on Quinn's exposed wrist. He yelled, the cloth falling from his fingers.

Cray slammed back against him and drove her bare heel onto the toe of his boot. Quinn cried in pain again, but held onto her, the two of them tussling against the back of the sectional.

The hitman held his gun toward them, hesitating. Then he slid it inside his jacket and rushed forward.

Tightening her abs, Cray lashed out with a kick just as Quinn spun her around.

The maneuver inadvertently strengthened the blow, delivering a roundhouse to the hitman's face. He toppled over the sofa, cracking his head against the glass table on his way to the floor.

Quinn got his chokehold tighter around her throat, the two of them stumbling back toward the stairs.

"I've got you. You're mine. Mine, you fucking bitch," he hissed.

She reached up behind her, dragging her nails down across his face, tearing the skin.

He pulled his head back, lost his balance. Then they were careening back, back toward the nearest wall. Tumbling in what felt like slow motion.

Then came the impact.

Quinn groaned and loosened his grip just enough for her to get her elbow free. She brought it back hard into his solar plexus, knocking the breath out of him.

Then she brought it back again, crouching as she did so, slamming her elbow into his crotch.

The detective howled and finally let her go. She burst forward, heading back around the corner to the kitchen, dashing across the floor. Blood pounded through her veins, her heart running like crazy. She'd never felt this alive.

Behind her came loud grunts and heavy footfalls. Quinn, still not giving up. And infinitely more pissed.

The door was right there. She slammed into it, yanked on the handle.

Locked.

Footsteps right behind her, a roar rising in Quinn's throat.

She turned the lock, heard the *click*. Tried the handle again—

As a meaty hand closed on her shoulder, tearing her away from the exit. Quinn dragged her to the kitchen island and threw her onto the surface. Her hip smashed the sharp concrete edge as she tumbled across, knocking the wine bottle over the other side. She went with it.

The bottle hit first, shattering, splashing sauvignon blanc across the tile.

Cray's right shoulder hit next, pain searing through her. She cried out, lying on the floor, white wine seeping into her hair.

Get up. He's going to kill you if you don't get up.

A figure stepped around the counter, his face shadowed by the stove light. Quinn wiped his sleeve across the darkened side of his face, coming away with blood. His fedora was gone. Must've fallen off earlier.

"You see, my buddy over there, he likes things done...the *clean* way. And I get it, I really do."

Get up.

But everything hurt.

Get. Up.

Quinn drew closer, got down on his knees. "And he thinks the only way to kill someone cleanly is with a bullet. But that would leave blood." He held up his gloved hands. "Strangling is personal, and he seems a little too...reluctant for that. But me? Oh, I'm real personal."

Then those hands were around her throat, and he was over her, still kneeling. "It's not that hard. All you gotta do is *squeeze*."

And he did. Hard.

She gasped for air, couldn't draw it into her lungs. Pain racked her body.

He was silhouetted by the light, but she could make out

his snarling smile. Cray reached back behind her, grasping. Quinn's shadow obscured what her hand was reaching for. Or maybe he was just so immersed in the kill that he didn't notice.

Her fingers gripped something, even as her strength weakened, blackness fading in at the edges of her vision. It was the top of the bottle. She lifted it slightly, got a feel for the weight.

And then, just as his eyes flicked up, just as he realized what she was doing, Cray swung it upward, driving the jagged edge into his neck.

Quinn immediately let go, his fingers clutching for the glass. Chokes and gurgles spewed from his mouth. Blood poured down his trench coat.

Cray gasped, heaving. Then she lurched up and slammed the bottle neck with her palm, ramming the shard in deeper.

He toppled over, falling back. Blood was everywhere. Down his neck, drenching his clothes, spewing out the bottle opening.

Rage and adrenaline lifted Cray to her feet. She towered over the wounded man, inhaling and exhaling, a leer coming to her lips. Quinn managed to get to his knees, desperately trying to remove the glass as he choked, expelling red liquid from his mouth.

The anxiety had dissipated, the danger vanished.

He was hers now.

She was still catching her breath as she came around behind Quinn, grabbing him by his hair, yanking his head back.

He looked up at her and she saw pure, delicious fear in his eyes. Her smile broke into a wide grin. No, he wasn't like her, she realized. Not at all.

That was going to make this all the more enjoyable.

She tilted her head, watching him choke, watching him silently beg for mercy.

Then, with sudden ferocity, Cray smashed his skull against the concrete corner.

〈••〉

Sova's head pounded as he pulled himself up, digging his fingers into the sofa for purchase. He was pretty sure he had a concussion, but he'd had them before and survived. The main thing now was to assess the status of the mission, to see if it could be salvaged. He didn't know how long he'd been out.

A noise came from somewhere, sounding like a cross between a *wham* and a *crack*.

Jesus, what the hell was going on? Where was Quinn? Had he gotten the target? Even if there was a mess, that was okay. Things had gone sideways before, and he'd still been able to clean them up. Operations rarely went smoothly. Tahoe yesterday had been an exception, not the norm.

There. Another *wham-crack*.

Slowly, Sova got up. He felt light and woozy, blood rushing to his head. He steadied himself against the sectional, looking toward the source of the sound.

As he watched, Isabella Cray slammed Quinn's head against a corner of the island. *Wham-crack.* A spray of blood shot in all directions, splattering her face, tank top, and arms. She released the body and it fell over to the side.

Sova felt himself drifting forward, walking to see around the counter, his other hand subconsciously reaching inside his jacket for the gun.

Quinn lay on the floor. Blood gushed from a gaping dark hole where his forehead had cracked open. Cray stood over him, smiling, as if proud of herself.

Then she finally looked up and noticed Sova.

It was as if she'd flipped a switch. Instantly, the gloating sadist was gone. In her place was a shy woman, retreating into herself and offering a weak smile. She even tried to laugh, to break the tension, but it died in her throat.

He knew it wasn't from embarrassment. People like her couldn't feel embarrassment. This was a cover, a ruse. He had seen a part of her others were not meant to witness.

In that moment, Sova knew he had been right about the eyes. He had been right all along.

This was not just a mission, a paycheck. It was a favor, a good deed he would perform for the world.

Before falling, he'd stashed his gun in an interior jacket pocket, a temporary holster. But when his fingers reached it, there was nothing there. It had fallen out over by the sofa.

He dove toward it, tumbling over the back of the sectional. This time, it was a controlled fall. Sova hit the pillows and reached down, grasping along the floor. Found the weapon. Shot back up, aiming toward the door—

Which swung shut. She was already gone.

Ignoring the pain in his head, Sova hurtled over the sofa and ran for the door. Reached the handle, turned it, aimed out into the hallway.

There, to the left. The stairwell door closing.

He checked the other way, just to be thorough. No one stood by the elevators. Too risky to wait for one for an escape. Too bad, too. Racer had control of them.

Sova sprinted down the corridor. Turned. Smashed through the door into the stairwell. He could hear her footsteps, bare soles slapping on the concrete.

He plunged down, taking them two at a time, his grip tight on the pistol.

He knew what he had to do. She needed to die. There was no question of it. He was doing the right thing. He wasn't a bad person anymore.

Maybe he never had been.

Cray turned down the next flight of stairs, her pulse racing.

There were only five flights and she'd just passed the third floor.

Keep going, keep going.

The walls were lit with vertical green LED strips. It was a new building, and the steps were clean gray, not grody. Dashing along the next landing, she shielded her eyes from the lime glow, continued down to Floor 2.

Come on, come on. Almost there.

She didn't use the railing. There was no time for safety. And Cray enjoyed the risk.

She didn't enjoy running for her life, but she would tell herself she did when she was bored again.

Assuming she lived to be bored again.

Another landing, another bar of bright emerald, then down.

One at a time, but rapidly, hoping there was nothing sharp to cut her feet. Trying not to lose her balance. If she fell, it would be over.

He would get her. He would kill her.

Finally, she reached the ground floor.

But this was a fire escape route. There was no door to the lobby. Instead, she found herself pushing off a wall, turning around. There was an exit beside the staircase.

She bolted through it, out into the alleyway.

A sedan waited in the dark, its lights out.

No point trying to steal their getaway car. Didn't have the keys.

She turned and ran to the right, where the lane narrowed. He probably couldn't get the car through, if he went straight for the vehicle.

But he could follow her on foot. No doubt about that.

She pushed herself harder, faster. Her muscles burned. Her right shoulder and hip were still aching from earlier. She'd never been more grateful for her pain tolerance.

Behind her, the door crashed open.

On impulse, Cray looked back. The hitman glanced left and right down the alley, pistol in hand, silhouetted by the glow from inside.

Just then, her leg struck something.

She went down, tumbling to the wet pavement. Her right knee scraped along the concrete, grazing off skin.

Cray clenched her teeth. She'd tripped on an overturned trash can. There were several garbage bags lying to her left.

Up. Now.

She didn't dare look back. Cray grabbed the nearest bag and launched herself forward, still gritting through the pain.

She hit the wall and pulled herself along the red bricks, into the darkness. Up ahead there was light from a parking lot, an Asimov ad blaring on a building at the back. The light might make her an easier target.

Would he use the gun?

Out of your control. Focus.

She pushed forward, gaining speed again. Her bare feet splashed through a puddle, light rain spattering her skin from above.

Almost to the sidewalk.

Blood rushed to her face, the anxiety cresting inside her. It was strange to be a bundle of nerves without feeling afraid. To know that death was imminent, yet to be somewhat clear-headed. Her heart pumped so quickly it was painful.

Then the alley gave way to the sidewalk and her momentum carried her forward, out into the street—

As a pair of headlights streaked toward her from the left. Cray turned, but she was caught in the glare.

Her hands raised, she braced for impact—

The vehicle suddenly came to a halt just a few feet away, its whir dying down.

Cray lowered her hands.

It was a Tesla Cybertruck.

Turning her head to the left, she saw headlights flash on back down the alley. The hitman's sedan tore into reverse, speeding back out onto the other road, turning around, and racing out of sight.

She was still staring after it as the Cybertruck's door opened. A man in a business suit got out, looking shaken. Cray bet the auto-braking had been what saved her.

"Excuse me, miss, are you alright?"

Cray didn't say anything, still processing everything that had just happened. She wondered what the man was thinking, given that she was covered in blood and standing out here in bedclothes.

Across the parking lot, an Asimov F-Series sedan swerved on the billboard screen. *Driving your future.* She stared off at the phrase, lost in a trance.

"Excuse me. Miss?"

Cray turned to him. She was starting to feel better already, now that danger wasn't imminent, but a neurotypical would still be extremely shaken.

Alright, Izzy. Let's play High Functioning.

The man was shorter than Cray was. She took him by the hand and lowered herself, staring into his eyes with an imploring look.

"Please help me."

11:51 PM

Fraser stepped over the blood on the floor and headed out into the living room. Evidence A-frame tents had been placed around the sofa, coffee table, and back by the kitchen island. The San Jose police were milling about, making sure everything was carefully documented. Reed stood in the kitchen, talking to one of the crime scene forensics staff.

They had just taken Quinn's body out. The image would stay seared into his mind, probably as long as he lived. But he had bigger concerns now.

He looked to the right. Cray was sitting on the stairs, wrapped in a towel but still not wearing any shoes. A large bandage pad was placed over her right knee, and she'd wiped most of Quinn's blood off. She stared out the window, a blank expression on her face. He wondered if she was still in shock.

Fraser made his way closer and she seemed to snap out of it. "Hey," she said softly, turning toward him. There were bruises on her neck and he'd glimpsed some on the rear of her leg earlier. Ones from the attack probably wouldn't have shown up this quickly, but he didn't ask her where she'd gotten them. Some of the ones on her neck looked like hickeys.

"Are you *sure* you're feeling fine? You've been through a lot."

Cray laughed. "I..." She searched for words. "I guess I lost control. I didn't mean to kill Quinn. He was still alive even with the shard and I...I just lost it."

Fraser shook his head. "No one blames you, Ms. Cray. It was either you or him." He glanced back toward the sectional. The glass table had cracked where the hitman's head struck it. "And you've already given a description of the other man to the sketch artist, right?"

She nodded.

"Good. Then hopefully we can find a match on the composite by tomorrow morning."

Fraser had gotten the call just over an hour ago. He was so harried getting ready, he nearly took the keys for his DeLorean instead of the Bureau's Crown Vic. By the time he got to San Jose, the police had already questioned Cray and she'd walked them through the crime scene, explaining what happened and where.

Reed had apologized for not believing her about the stalker last night.

Cray sighed. "It was just...a lot happening," she said, her eyes staring off. "I felt so anxious, I..." She laughed. "I thought I was braver."

"You are brave. Few civilians I know could've survived two hitmen coming after them. And you did it without a weapon." He smiled. "See, you didn't need me here tonight."

She smiled too, a genuine one. "You missed out." Then she looked down, sadness washing over her. "When I was nine, someone broke into our house in Miami. I don't remember much, but a man tried to come into the bedroom I shared with my sister. She was terrified. I kept hugging her, telling her to stay quiet. My mother killed the robber with a knife. I remember coming closer to stare at his body. It didn't seem real. And my mother pulled me away and held me, kept saying, 'Thank God you're safe.' Later, she thanked me for protecting Benita. My brother was still a toddler and he slept through the whole thing." She laughed, but anxiously. "I always thought I was brave after that. That things like this wouldn't get to me as much. That they shouldn't be able to."

Cray turned to Fraser, appraising him. "I've told very few people that. I don't know why I just told you."

"I'm glad you did," he said quietly. "It's only human to be shaken by this stuff. Trust me, I do it for a living." Fraser paused. "I'll be honest…I've never had to kill someone before. I'm afraid the day will come when I have to, in self-defense. If someone presents me with no other option. But I hate thinking about it—especially what it must be like after."

Cray looked down again. "It's strange. Maybe it just hasn't hit me yet, but right now I feel nothing at all."

Once she had left with a police escort, Fraser went to see Reed. He stood in the bedroom loft now, leaning on the railing and looking down at the living room and the city view.

"Some week this is turning out to be…" He sighed, shaking his head.

Fraser cracked a smile. "Would you rather be chasing another group of Russian hackers instead?"

Reed turned away from the railing, rolling his eyes.

The Bureau didn't usually send agents to Field Offices near where they had lived. When Reed applied to the Academy after his Valley days, he'd spent years on the East Coast, mainly in Boston and Washington, D.C. Then they decided it wouldn't be bad to have someone who knew the Valley working cybercrime there, and four years ago he ended up at the San Francisco Field Office. This wasn't the first case they'd worked together. They had discussed their backgrounds before over drinks.

Fraser hoped they'd do that again soon. The way this case was going, he'd need more than a few.

Reed rubbed his chin. "So Spencer's killer—'Racer,' Cray said—hires a hitman through the darknet. Probably pays him in crypto. Somehow finds out Quinn has gambling debts and uses that as leverage to get him on their payroll, keeping an eye on the investigation. But Racer really wants Cray gone, even though she knows just as much as the rest of us. There's only one explanation that makes sense of that."

Fraser nodded. "It fits with Cray's theory that the unsub wanted us running around trying to find her. Distracted by a missing person, maybe wondering if she had something to do with it."

"Yes, but distracted from *what*?"

"You already know the answer. It's obvious." Fraser leaned against the railing, looking out the window. He could see the blue and red lights of cop cars flashing up from the alley below. "Friday."

"But *what* on Friday? What is so important about this fucking product launch, or whatever it is?"

"Clearly someone knows," Fraser said. "And given the lengths they've gone to already, I think they're just getting started."

THURSDAY

8:12 AM

It was still raining when he got up. Sova closed the curtains back over and headed to the bathroom to splash some water on his face.

He couldn't get last night out of his head. Didn't know what was more horrifying: the way that monster had killed Quinn, or the fact that he had failed to put her down.

Again.

Two nights in a row he had missed his target.

Sova stood over the sink, shirtless, staring into the porcelain bowl and taking a deep breath. His pupils still weren't dilating properly, and his head hurt like hell. He examined the bullet wounds and scars on his torso. Whenever he bedded women, he found the old adage about chicks digging scars to be true. It helped that he stayed fit.

He'd ditched the Toyota last night in a lonely San Jose parking lot. Walked for an hour, keeping to side streets, before hailing a Waymo and riding it back to Palo Alto. Then he walked through the rain for another forty-five minutes to get back here, to the El Camino Motel.

Racer had asked for an update while he was in the auto-taxi. He was grateful the car wasn't an Asimov, lest Racer take control and drive him off the road right there. He spent most of the ride composing a message that clearly stated what went down.

Quinn broke protocol and fucked up. Sova did his best to salvage things, but Cray had reached another witness before he could neutralize her. Too much collateral, so he backed off.

How many people were around? Just her and the witness? Racer had asked.

Sova paused. Yes.

Then why not eliminate them both? Our purpose was to draw police attention. A double homicide, combined with the dead body of a cop, would have more than kept them busy. Not as perfect as the original plan, but Quinn was always expendable. You knew that.

Sova put a hand to his head. He hadn't expected this level of coldness from his client. Maybe he should've. There's no going back now. What should I do?

Racer hadn't responded until he was walking to the motel. He debated quickly packing his things and fleeing to the safe-house in Central Cali, lest his employer want him dead. But the hacker's next message changed things.

I still have use for you. I will contact you in the morning. Lay low.

With everything that had gone wrong that night, Sova was relieved. He had one last chance to redeem himself.

Out in the main room, his phone began to buzz on the nightstand.

He dried his face with a towel, hurrying toward it. He snatched the phone up, answered it, and brought it to his ear.

The voice was electronically distorted. "I'm beginning to lose faith in you."

"It won't happen again," he said, moving back to the window. He tore aside the curtains, looking out at the oppressive sky.

"You're right. It won't." A pause. "She saw your face."

A chill shot down Sova's spine. "Do they have a match?"

"They got your name by comparing a sketch to their database. You're a suspect in at least four different killings, Markus."

He was sweating now. "I operate underground. They've known my name for years. So what if I popped up in San Jose? I've popped up all over the country. But I disappear each time."

"This was supposed to be a simple job. How hard is it to kill one girl?"

He managed a laugh. "She's six feet tall and athletic, if you haven't noticed."

"And?"

"*And?* And she's a fucking *psychopath*. You never told me that part."

A pause. "How can you be sure?"

"The way she killed Quinn. She was standing over him with a smile on her face. He had to be dead after the first time she slammed him into the corner, but she kept going at it until his goddamn skull split open. And you know *why*? Because she was having *fun*. Any normal person would've run the fuck out of there. But she didn't worry about the danger. She doesn't get scared. Anxious, defensive, sure—but not scared. She's a fucking demon. All people like her are."

Racer was silent. Then, "It's not nice to make generalizations, Markus."

It suddenly hit him. "Of course. I didn't mean to offend—"

"I didn't realize Cray was a psychopath. I should've seen it in her eyes." A distorted laugh. "I meet so few others, it's almost a shame she's going to die."

Sova felt incredibly uncomfortable, but at that last bit his purpose returned. "I'll do it. I'll finish it."

"No. You will proceed with our initial plan. Evidently, I have to take care of certain matters myself." Racer sighed. "But don't you worry, Markus." He pictured them smiling. "I have something planned for her."

11:35 AM

The lobby doors opened and Cray stormed in, hair damp from the rain. She didn't even glance at the receptionist. She headed down the corridor to the left, badged in, reached the staircase, and took it up to the next floor.

She'd slept in late at a San Jose hotel with police protection, but a thought occurred to her this morning that she couldn't shake. Putting on her most charming mask, she convinced one of the cops to drive her to Asimov HQ. She needed to speak with Fraser.

Cray marched down the northern wing, past the break-room. Then stopped and walked back, hearing familiar voices.

Graham was in the midst of a heated discussion with the FBI agents. "...no goddamn point in it. No warrant, no Catalyst. That's final. It's irrelevant to the digital forensic investigation."

"But maybe not the investigation as a whole," Reed said. "You look pretty suspicious in this yourself, Mr. Graham. You've been making it exceptionally difficult for us to try to save lives. Your consultant was nearly murdered last night by a hitman and a corrupt police officer on the payroll of whoever killed Niall Spencer. Strange that they knew where she was staying."

"We've already been over this. It was a *friend's* penthouse. And why would I bring Izzy to the Valley just to turn around and have someone try to kill her? How would that serve me?"

"I think she'd like to know," Fraser said, nodding toward Cray.

Graham spun around. He went pale when he saw her. "Izzy, thank God you're alright." He briskly walked across the room and gave her a hug. She returned it. "I couldn't believe it when they told me. And Quinn. It wasn't your fault. I know you didn't mean to kill him."

Eh, she thought. *Kinda did. Not that I'm shedding any tears.*

Cray did her best to look distraught. She had to thread this needle carefully. No one could know how riveting it had been. For that moment, at least. Everything else about last night had driven her anxiety to levels she didn't know were possible, but now that it was over, she felt calm. And more determined than ever to meet this Racer prick face-to-face. The things she wanted to do to them would make Quinn's end seem tame.

"Thanks, Ted." Cray buried her face in his shoulder.

"You shouldn't even be here. It would be safer if you went home."

She pulled back. "I'm seeing this through. Someone's tried to kill me twice now. I won't sleep properly until we catch them."

"Alright." He embraced her again. "But I don't want to lose another friend this week."

"Mr. Graham?"

They turned around. Cheryl Acheson, the CEO's assistant, was standing in the door. "I've gotta leave now for my doctor's appointment."

"Yes, of course, Cheryl," Graham said. "Take care." He and Cray turned back to the FBI agents. "Catalyst is tied to the success of this company. If someone killed Niall because they wanted to sabotage Catalyst, then they are trying to destroy Asimov Automotive. I'm sure that's the only connection to Catalyst, if there even is a connection at all. I don't know if the killer is a disgruntled employee within the company or someone who left, but maybe you should focus on that."

"We have," Reed said. "I've gone through most of the exit interviews for Asimov for the past two years. Almost all of them called this a toxic environment where anyone who questions the direction of the company or its dominant beliefs is ridiculed and excluded from discussion. Many felt uncomfortable to speak up at all."

"Oh please," Graham said. "Niall and I had many thorough talks about what direction to take Asimov. And though he didn't always agree with me, he heard me out and considered what I had to say."

"Yeah," Fraser scoffed. "Because you were the second largest shareholder. He needed to keep you on his side."

"Look. This company isn't perfect. Nothing is. But we are creating something *important* here. If whoever killed Niall can't appreciate that and wants to ruin us, then do your job and arrest them. And let me do *my* job and make sure our roads become safer."

He stormed out of the room.

Reed and Fraser walked over to her, the senior agent giving a long sigh. "Well, this day's been a shitshow so far."

She raised an eyebrow. "Made any progress?"

"Actually, we have," Fraser said.

Right then, Cray's stomach growled so loudly the feds heard it, their eyes flicking to her abdomen.

She feigned embarrassment and laughed. "I haven't eaten anything all day. Can you fill me in over breakfast?"

Fraser glanced at his watch. "Sure." He laughed. "But it's basically lunch now."

"Let's all get something," Reed said. "I could eat."

As they continued down the hallway back toward the stairs, Fraser said, "We know how the condo building was breached last night. But Bailey made a discovery this morning. First real breakthrough we've had."

"What is it?" Cray asked, throwing him a glance.

Fraser looked grave. "He found the virus."

11:49 AM

The five of them pulled up chairs around a table in one of the first-floor breakrooms, just down the hall from the NOC. Software engineers milled about, grabbing slices of pizza that had been ordered or reheating food in the microwaves.

Cray had grabbed two bowls of ramen, three slices of pizza, and a soda, which she cracked open as she sat down. Fraser, Reed, Bailey, and Levine all stared at her.

"What?"

Fraser gestured to Levine. "You wanna start?"

The forensic technician nodded and turned toward Cray, who began eating. "I spent part of the morning in San Jose, going through the security systems of the condo building. This was clearly a quick and dirty job. The hacker must not have had time to cover their tracks. Several logs for door unlocks and camera resets were left in the servers. I could trace them all to a single user on the WiFi network, so they must've been sitting near the building, probably that big parking lot right near it, using a large antenna to hop on the network. The hacker must've figured out what type of router it was and found a zero-day exploit for it on the darknet. Which probably wouldn't have been cheap.

"But here's the real kicker, how we know they were in a rush: This is a previously unknown zero-day for this type of router. Because the hacker didn't cover their tracks, we now know this is out there. We'll notify the manufacturer, and they'll probably have a patch out in a few weeks. The hacker basically ruined this zero-day for anyone else who bought it, just so they—"

"Could try to kill me," Cray said, putting her pizza down. She did her best to look disturbed. And it did spike her anxiety, but it also amused her. It was kind of nice to be wanted so badly.

"Yes." Levine looked down. "They probably watched you escaping on the security cameras. And then if they were in the parking lot, they would've seen you get help when that truck pulled up. Do you remember a vehicle pulling out of there while you and that guy were waiting for the cops?"

Cray thought. "I don't think so. But they might've bailed as soon as they saw me run out into the alley."

"I imagine they didn't wait around for the cops to show up. That would've given them time to clear the logs," Levine said.

"Or they didn't care. Since they must've been in the actual vicinity, instead of accessing the security system remotely and leaving a traceable IP address, Racer would've known you couldn't track them as long as they got away. Maybe it was a calling card, a fuck you to us," Cray said.

Fraser nodded, considering. Bailey looked confused. "Racer?"

Reed sighed. "That's how Quinn and the hitman referred to their employer. We believe it's the hacker's handle. Speaking of which, we ran the sketch the police made of your description through our database." He pulled out his phone, tapped something, and slid it across the table to Cray.

"Say hello to Markus Sova, killer for hire." She saw the man from the night before, sporting longer hair on a captured security camera image. Reed swiped and another photo came up, Sova in a U.S. military uniform when he was younger. "Dishonorably discharged sixteen years ago. After that, he went off the grid for a while, but we've suspected him of various murders. He's turned up several times around unsolved killings, despite having no connection to the deceased. Too many times to be coincidence. But we've never caught him. He's a slippery fucker."

She didn't know what to say, but the table had fallen silent. They would expect some kind of reaction from her. Well, Reed wouldn't.

"That's him," was all she said, quietly.

Reed took the phone back.

"What about Quinn? He said something about gambling debts last night," Cray said.

Fraser nodded. "I spoke with the Monterey County Sheriff. Quinn had been a bit of a problem for several years. His drinking and gambling issues were well-known, but he had a high clearance rate, so they put up with him. And the union would've made it too hard to get rid of him anyway."

"How did Racer find out about that?"

"They must've breached the Sheriff's Department servers somehow. The lead homicide detective was out this week, sick. I wouldn't be surprised if Racer had something to do with that too. The SVRCFL is sending out a technician to Monterey to see if they can identify the breach."

She nodded, resumed eating. "You said you located the virus?"

"Yeah," Bailey spoke up, ecstatic. His eyes never maintained contact with hers, darting around, his cheeks growing red. "So...I ran the Telemetry data in a sandbox back at the RCFL and used an emulation technique to try to get the code to demangle itself."

Cray nodded along. Emulation techniques were considered one of the best ways to draw out polymorphic code. Run it in a virtual environment, hope the payload isn't designed to change with the algorithm. If it is, you're fucked. If not, it should reveal identifiable code blocks.

"And I finally managed to find the virus. I took the code blocks and ran them through the FBI database to see if they matched any previously used pieces of crimeware. And guess what?" Bailey shook his head. "Not even a partial match, so it looks like this was coded from scratch."

Reed sighed. "Which means if the same person who killed Spencer coded the virus—which seems the most likely explanation at this point—then we are dealing with a highly tech-savvy perpetrator."

"Well," Cray said, taking a sip of soda, "in Silicon Valley that really narrows it down."

Fraser winced. "We can probably rule out the MBA types. And the lawyers."

"This place is chock-full of software engineers." Reed gestured around, keeping his voice low. "Even most high-level Asimov execs have computer science backgrounds. We still have a large suspect pool within the company. And it must've been someone within the company in order to get the virus into the Software Update subnet in the first place."

Cray finished a slice of pizza, putting up a finger. "Not necessarily. Actually, that's what I wanted to talk to you about."

Every eye at the table was on her.

She took a deep breath. "So far, Racer has been willing to hire at least two people to carry out in-person tasks for them. Whoever they are, they seem more comfortable staying on the computer side of cybercrime. Don't wanna get their hands dirty. So...what if to get the virus into the building, they'd already hired a third?"

Fraser betrayed no emotion. "Go on."

"We haven't been able to find any traces of the virus before the summer. We also know that the last time Telemetry data was copied to the Catalyst servers to help build some kind of testing simulation was last December. So it seems that Catalyst hasn't been breached. But what if that's just what Racer *wants* us to think? What if they paid a software engineer who worked on Catalyst to upload a virus to the servers in person, then had him killed and staged his death as a suicide?

"Graham told me one of the Catalyst engineers died a couple months ago from carbon monoxide poisoning. Everyone assumed the stress had just gotten to him. Then Spencer got killed and I nearly did too. That's three people tied to

Asimov who have had brushes with death in the past several months. I don't think the engineer's death was a coincidence. It happened right between the summer hacks and Spencer's murder. I kept thinking this morning about how Racer got to Quinn, then wondered if they could've gotten to someone at Asimov the same way. Maybe the guy had gambling debts too, or something else they could've used as leverage on him. And then once he was done, they paid a hitman to take him out, staged it as a suicide."

Reed glared. "Graham mentioned a previous death, but he never said the engineer worked on Catalyst."

"But then how did the engineer breach the Update subnet?" Bailey asked. "It's one thing to plug a flashdrive with viral payload into your own workstation but getting access to the NOC would be another."

"He worked here," Cray said. "He could've connived some way to get it in there, or to swap out a flashdrive of a colleague who worked in Update. He'd have had to socially engineer it, but there are ways." She took a deep breath. "But I kept thinking about why Racer would try so hard to kill me. And the only thing I could come up with is that they want to distract the investigation."

Fraser nodded. "Reed and I agree with that. Digital forensics usually takes a long time, but we're working under a crunch here. We know hundreds of thousands of vehicles are at risk. And there's a big event on Friday that we think Racer is trying to sabotage. The hacker knows we're going to be pulling out all the stops. Sooner or later, we'd try to get access to Catalyst. But Racer clearly figured out that Asimov wouldn't let us get inside without a warrant."

"And we've been denied one," Reed said. "Judge told me yesterday there's no reason for either a subpoena or a warrant if Graham's gonna give everything to us this weekend. And there's no evidence that it's tied to the hack that killed Spencer, or that it would help identify the source of the breach, so there's no need to have it before the keynote tomorrow."

"And that's exactly how Racer wants it," Cray said. "By having two separate breaches, they can keep us running around trying to figure out how far back the Update infection went and how long ago Telemetry was compromised. But without any clue Catalyst has been infected, our attention would be focused *outside* the air gap. And if I disappeared without a trace—and I think that's how Racer wanted Sova and Quinn to do it—then your efforts would be even further split. Quinn would stall the investigation into my vanishing and the digital forensics part probably wouldn't advance much further before Friday either."

"But here's the thing that bugs me," Reed said. "If sabotaging the keynote has been Racer's plan all along, why kill Spencer so early in the week? Hell, why not wait until after the event?"

"I thought about that too," Cray said. "But if they killed Spencer too close to Friday, or even the day of, Asimov might've cancelled or postponed it. And if they waited until after they'd sabotaged the unveiling, then Asimov might have already implemented a crackdown in cybersecurity. Might've made it harder to kill him."

"I think it's more theatrical than that," Fraser said. "I think Racer is staging the whole thing exactly the way they want it. Whether they currently work here or not, they're tied to the company. They know Asimov. They know that if Spencer dies on a Monday, the new project unveiling will still happen come hell or high water on Friday. They know Graham won't let us into the Catalyst servers because that's how Spencer would've wanted it. The company is in denial of the danger, and Racer is giving Asimov enough rope to hang itself. Proceeding with a new unveiling after one of the most dangerous corporate data breaches in history, with hundreds of thousands of vehicles able to be compromised? The sheer *hubris* is staggering! And so on the big night, Racer can come in and deliver the fatal blow."

"And what is that?" Levine said, raising an eyebrow.

"Something we need to figure out, and *fast*." He stood up.

"We've gotta talk to Graham about the dead engineer, see if we can get anything more. You're right, Ms. Cray. That's our best lead."

"Sure," Cray said, covering her mouth. She swallowed, gave a weak smile. "But...can I finish eating first?"

Fraser waited for an Asimov employee to grab a cup at the water cooler, then began filling one of his own. He turned around, ready to head back to the table, but found Reed standing behind him.

"Will, there's something I need to talk to you about." He glanced back. Cray was chatting with Bailey and Levine between bites of ramen.

"Alright." Fraser wasn't sure what this was about.

"It'll just be a minute or two. But I think it's time I told you something."

12:02 PM

It was just the two of them in the war room. Reed closed the door, flicked on a light.

"What do you know about Picturesque?" He took a seat at the head of the conference table.

Fraser remained standing. "Used to be a social media company. Really soared after the TikTok spyware scandal. Rejected a $15 billion buyout from Facebook. Only thing that really gave Instagram a run for its money. Well, until they got exposed."

"Main selling feature?"

He sighed. "Ability to add people as friends by taking pictures of them. The app scanned their faces, matched them with user profiles in the company database. It allowed you to scan anyone and see if they were a user. The app rewarded people for scanning as many faces as possible, gave you points whenever someone you had previously taken a photo of joined the app." He winced. "Naturally, my generation ate it the fuck up. Rushed out to get all their friends to download it so they'd rise in the global rankings."

"And then?"

He laughed, remembering. "They had a big fucking breach. All their emails got leaked, along with their data and software. Turned out they were conducting massive facial recognition surveillance and getting high schoolers and college kids to do the leg work for them. They used location data, who was spotted where, amount of time active, number of friends, to create profiles estimating their social intelligence. Profiles that they then sold to other Valley companies." Fraser paused. "And, if I recall, the U.S. government."

"I was the lead agent on the case," Reed said, looking grave. "The whole thing skeeved me out. These people were spying on *teenagers*. My fucking kids used the app. But there was tension in D.C. Picturesque had a lot of lobbying power, contributed to a lot of campaigns. They wanted the flies swatted. I had no choice but to find whoever did it, but I secretly admired them. PATRIOT Act lets us search IP addresses even in other countries. We followed the VPN trail around the world, but one of the hackers got sloppy. Downloaded a Trojan we sent. We tracked them to Miami.

"So I flew there with my partner. We started surveillance on this guy, wiretaps, tailing, everything. The bigwigs at Picturesque wanted these people to burn. They'd been big virtue signaling types, always bragging how much they donated to social causes. But now that the curtain was pulled back, they were public enemy number one. The stock tanked. They were crucified by the press. These people wanted *blood*."

He shook his head. "They put a lot of pressure on D.C., who put a lot of pressure on the Bureau, who put a lot of pressure on *me*. So we watched this guy—early twenties, University of Florida dropout—found that he regularly met with this group of friends. We started spying on them, too. Got warrants, of course, and everything. We knew they'd done it. But we couldn't get proof of it for all of them. There was this one girl who seemed to be the ringleader, Simone Tessier. Her second-in-command was also her girlfriend." Reed looked up. "Isabella Cray."

Fraser stayed silent for a moment, thinking. The only sound was rain against the high windows. Then he grinned and said, "What, are you trying to make me like her *more*?"

But the serious look remained on Reed's face. "PATRIOT Act allowed us to access *everything* on these people. We went way back, got medical records and all. Psychiatric records too." He was quiet again for a moment. "We brought them in for questioning. I read the file right before the interview, and then I couldn't unsee it. She was so charming, so polite, so helpful. But her eyes were empty, cold, watching me like she was calculating a way out."

He looked back at Fraser. "She was diagnosed with anti-social personality disorder. Scored thirty out of forty on the Hare Checklist. She's a bona fide psychopath, Will. After that, I knew I had to lock her up. Sure, Picturesque needed to go down. I couldn't tell my bosses that, but fuck I was glad the truth came out. The company folded and those pricks became persona non grata in the Valley. But the whole thing didn't seem to be Cray's idea. She was following her girl-friend. It was Tessier's idea—or at least, I think it was. We could never prove it. We could never prove any of it. They all got away. The guy we had evidence on fled the country when we tried to get him to snitch on his friends. Still haven't found him. I got a stern reprimanding from my bosses, but as Picturesque tumbled, it lost influence in D.C. The pressure eased up. But I was on thin ice for a while. It was my biggest fuck-up, not because I let the corrupt people get what they deserved, but because I let something dangerous loose into the wild."

Fraser pulled up a chair, sat down. He was still processing everything, viewing his interactions with Cray in a new light. "I'd heard people at the office mention you were on the Pictur-esque case, but you never talked about it, so I never asked." He paused. "I'm assuming that's why you didn't bring it up until now?"

Reed put a hand to his head. "Shit, Will. It wasn't my finest moment. But then I found her here, working as a consultant for these Asimov fucks." He looked up, narrowed his eyes. "I thought she maybe had something to do with it, until last night. Any way I try to fit it, I can't see the evidence at the scene contradicting her story. But you saw what she did to Quinn. It wasn't an accident—not the last part, at least. I'm sure the glass to the neck was self-defense, but there was no need to do...*that* to his face."

Fraser nodded slowly. "He was a sick man, though. Depraved, even. The world is better without him."

"Of course, of course. But I think that she enjoyed killing him, that she's got this monster hiding behind her smiles."

"Well, in that case, maybe it's good she's on our side."

The senior agent leaned back in his chair, thinking.

"We're up against a dangerous criminal here, Reed. We need her help. I'm genuinely worried about tomorrow. If we don't get to the bottom of this, many more people could die."

"Then why haven't they already? If Racer has access to 300,000 cars worldwide and we can't shut them off, why haven't they created some car swarm or some other massive terror attack?"

"Because that would show a flaw in Asimov's *current* systems. They already demonstrated that by killing Spencer. Whatever they've got planned next has to revolve around Catalyst."

"But *why?* I get that there could be a motive for killing Spencer, but why all this?"

Fraser shrugged. "When Waymo started testing its driverless minivans in Arizona, back in 2017, the cars got attacked all the time. People would slash the tires when they stopped at intersections, hurled rocks at them as they drove down the street. As cargo fleets started getting automated earlier this decade, there were former truckers who protested and attacked the vehicles at charging stops, coming at them with metal pipes and even guns." He held up his hands. "Now, I'll be the first to question anything Silicon Valley claims is the future, but I'm not a Luddite. Some people, though, see any and all change as a threat to their existence. And what do people do when they feel their existence is threatened?"

Reed nodded slowly. "The same thing any animal does. They try to eliminate the threat. But that still doesn't explain why someone within the company would do all this."

"Maybe it's misdirection. A personal motive disguised as a political one."

"Either way, it had to be someone who knew Spencer." Reed nodded again.

"Cray's idea that the dead software engineer could be one of Racer's victims is interesting, though. We really need to dig deeper on that."

"Assuming Graham will tell us anything."

Fraser raised an eyebrow. "Do you think he could be Racer?"

Reed scoffed. "If he is, he's sure great at deflecting suspicion."

Fraser stood up. "Whether he is or isn't, I need to talk to him."

Reed got up too. "Alright, Will. But be careful around Cray. I think she's on our side this time, and I'd certainly rather she fight with us than against us, but still... Be careful."

‹••›

When they got back to the breakroom, Reed headed off to chat with Bailey and Levine by the water cooler. Fraser went back to the table but found Cray's seat empty. In front of it were two empty ramen bowls and a paper plate with pizza crumbs.

He turned around, looking for her—

As a figure suddenly walked up behind him. Fraser spun around, startled. "Oh, there you are."

"Did you guys talk to Graham already?"

"No, I was just on my way now."

"I might be able to help. He and I go back a few years. I'll try to convince him." She offered a charming smile, but to Fraser it seemed off this time. Now that he thought about it, her smiles had mostly felt like this before. There was always something about them he couldn't quite place, no matter how friendly she seemed.

They didn't reach her eyes, which stared at him coldly.

"Sure," Fraser said, trying to hide how unnerved he was. He couldn't unsee it. "Let's go have a little chat with him."

12:17 PM

Acheson was still out at her doctor's appointment, so the only voice in the CEO Suite reception was Graham's, audible through the polished wood door. Cray couldn't quite make out his words, but it sounded like he was having an argument. She exchanged a glance with Fraser.

Then they stepped closer.

"…still be in attendance. He's the mayor, Casey. He needs this for his re-election campaign. Toronto loves to think of itself as Silicon Valley North. They're not gonna fuck us on this."

"I'm just worried it'll be seen as too risky." Kaplan's voice now.

"Lots of Valley companies go to Toronto. Uber tested *its* autonomous cars there. The city will eat this up, I'm telling you."

"Are you worried about possible criticisms?"

A pause. Then Graham said, "I imagine some people will be skeptical. But there are always those who resist the future. It doesn't really matter though, does it? Because it comes for us all in the end, whether we accept it or not." Another silence. "Casey, you're not having last minute doubts about Auto—?"

"No, of course not," she snapped back. "But I'm worried someone's found out about this and is trying to sabotage everything we've worked for. I… Sorry, I've just been very tired lately."

"Of course." Graham's voice sounded understanding. "We all are, Casey. But we've increased security for tomorrow night. Every time we've scanned the air gapped servers, they've been fine. The breach didn't get to them. Everything will go smoothly at the event. I'm sure of it."

Cray heard footsteps, someone pacing the room. Kaplan, she guessed, given how her voice traveled. "I hope you're right."

"You're my favorite to replace Niall, by the way."

Silence.

"Figured you might want to hear some good news."

Kaplan gave a saddened laugh. "I can't even think about that right now."

"It has to be you, Casey. You're the only one who shares Niall's vision. You've managed the operations of this company for the past four years. You know it inside and out. You're more than qualified to carry Asimov forward. Next week, once all this is over, I'm going to name you as my official recommendation to the board."

"Thank you, Ted. I really appreciate that." There was a pause again. "I need to get back to work. We'll talk more later."

"Take care, Casey."

The door opened and Kaplan froze when she spotted them. Then she flashed a thin smile at Fraser, a warmer one at Cray, and continued on past them.

They headed inside, Cray briefly watching her go as she closed the door.

"Can I help you?" Graham said. "I'm a little busy at the moment."

"You told us one of the Catalyst engineers committed suicide a couple months ago, correct?" Fraser said.

Graham looked confused. "Yes, Greg Furman. Took his own life in September."

"What if he didn't?" The FBI agent pulled up a chair in front of the desk and sat down.

Graham shook his head. "What are you saying?"

"Ms. Cray has an interesting theory. You might want to hear it."

She sighed and took a seat, then explained to Graham her thoughts about Racer having Furman murdered.

Graham sat there in disbelief, but then it started to sink in. Cray watched his reaction, saw him tense, his eyes dart away. He was considering it.

Then he sat up straighter and adjusted his chair. "I'm sorry, Izzy. But the police found no sign of foul play. Furman had struggled with debt problems, overdue bills, that sort of thing. He and his wife were preparing for a divorce. It's quite believable that he killed himself."

Cray shook her head. "Come on, Ted. It's too many coincidences. Racer could've hired this Sova guy or someone else to come in and make it *look* like it was suicide. But if Furman had money problems, he might've been desperate enough to take a shady payment. He *worked* on Catalyst. It would've been easy to sneak a virus in on a flashdrive. And Racer probably told him it was something harmless. I bet he had no idea what he was doing. And then Racer had him killed before he could figure it out."

Graham put a hand to his head, closing his eyes. He stayed like that for nearly a minute. Then he said, "And you think he could've gotten a virus into the Update subnet? Sometime in the summer?"

Cray shrugged. "It would've been easier for someone inside the company than out."

"So if this is true, it means the hacker is someone outside of Asimov?"

"Potentially," Fraser cautioned. "Could be someone here who just wanted to be thorough in covering their tracks."

"Racer got to a Monterey County detective. They could certainly get to a corporate employee," Cray said.

"It's just…" Graham put a hand to his head again. "There's no evidence."

"I bet there is," Fraser said. "Go back inside the Catalyst servers and review Furman's logs for the last months of his life. Trace any suspicious activity on the air gapped network from his account outward. It'd be a lot easier if you let us use PrivateEye."

Graham stared at him blankly. "You don't know what we're building, do you?"

"No." Fraser gave a thin smile. "That's kind of what we're trying to figure out."

"No, I mean you *really* don't grasp how significant this is. We are on the verge of a revolution in transportation, in mobility. Niall always warned that others would try to stop us, that others would fear the disruption Catalyst is going to create. But he was extremely, crystal fucking clear that nothing was to touch those servers until tomorrow. You have no evidence that there's an infection. I will have my people purchase a commercial version of PrivateEye and we'll run it ourselves, doing exactly what you said. But no one outside the project team or the C-Suite is going near Catalyst."

Fraser restrained his anger. "If that's the best compromise we're going to get, then fine, I'll take it. But the standard version of PrivateEye isn't as good as what we've got. We can process large volumes of data faster. We can bring data back to the RCFL to demangle polymorphic code in a sandbox—"

"*Absolutely not*," Graham hissed. "Nothing is getting taken out of here. And no one is touching those servers but *us*. I'll get Ritter and Johnson to go through Furman's logs with the software, just as you specified. You can even give us a checklist. But you are not going anywhere near the servers."

"Where are they?" Cray asked, curious.

Graham paused. "They're in a separate area of the basement from the main servers. The Catalyst project is run out of offices down there. It occupies most of this wing on that level."

Fraser was still glaring at him. "You would risk *lives* just because you're paranoid about outsiders touching your belongings? Is that it? Your company has already endangered more than 300,000 people globally."

"No one is at risk for tomorrow, Agent Fraser. Not at the Catalyst unveiling."

"Why, because you're just demonstrating a simulation?"

Graham shook his head. "There is a...physical aspect to the keynote, but it's mostly a multimedia presentation. Unless this hacker has figured out how to kill people with a fucking PowerPoint, I think we'll be just fine."

"Then what's the physical aspect?"

"There will be..." He sighed. "Vehicles, but they won't have been compromised. And if they are, we'll find it by tomorrow. But I'm skeptical Greg Furman had anything to do with the intrusion in the Update Department, at the very least. We don't let unauthorized personnel walk around where they aren't supposed to."

Cray frowned. "I've been in and out of there since Tuesday and no one's questioned me being there once. All the badges look the same from a distance. He could've followed someone else in."

"Yes, but you walked in with *Kaplan* the first time. The NOC engineers were informed that investigators would be in and out. And, objectively, people are going to notice you, Izzy." He gave a brief smile, then turned to Fraser. "They'll also notice a federal agent with bleached hair. And two technicians wheeling a Snowball computer with *RCFL* stamped on the side of it. The Software Update NOC is adjacent to the main one. There are usually only about six people in there at a time. They would've noticed Furman coming in. Not to mention how he would've gotten past two levels of RFID locks from the main NOC to the antechamber.

"Maybe there's *some* way Furman could've done it, but it would've taken a fair amount of social engineering skills. And from what I heard, he was a fairly quiet, somewhat awkward guy. He was a good software engineer, otherwise Niall and Ritter never would've kept him on Catalyst. But it's very different for him to upload something on his own computer than to break into the Update NOC like some kind of spy. So until you can prove to me that Furman infected Update, I'm not buying that he was ever hired by Racer at all. And why would they wait *two months* after the intrusion to kill him?"

Fraser thought for a moment. "If we *could* get you proof, would you let the RCFL team run forensics on the Catalyst servers?"

Graham stared at him silently.

Cray shifted in her chair. She was starting to feel anxious again.

"Yes." He didn't look pleased. "Furman worked for a completely different department. The only reason he ever would've been in the Software Update NOC was if he'd been compromised. So if you can prove he was there, I'll believe you. There are cameras in the NOC. We keep security footage for six months. That'd probably be a good place to start." He turned to Cray. "This was your theory, Izzy. Why don't you sift through the footage?"

A pang of anger hit Cray. "I will," she said, standing up. Fuck, that was going to be tedious.

Fraser got to his feet. "Are you really willing to risk everything to keep a project secret for one more day?"

Graham scoffed. "I'm trying *not* to risk anything at all. I have to protect Catalyst. You'll understand why tomorrow."

They headed for the door, when suddenly it flung open. Adrian Johnson, the CSO, stormed in. Cray realized she was going to have to talk to him anyway, about seeing the camera footage, but he didn't appear to even register her and Fraser's presence.

"Ted, we've got a situation."

Graham sighed, aggravated. "Why are you always the bearer of bad news, Adrian? Who's trying to access our accounts now? The IRS?"

"No." He shook his head, looking tense. "There's been another incident with one of our cars. It's Cheryl Acheson's."

12:39 PM

Fraser stepped out of the Suburban's passenger door and came around the back of the vehicle, looking across the street. On the other side of the two-lane road were a couple cop cars and an ambulance, blocking the view of the crashed sedan on the median.

The SVRCFL van, long and white, pulled up behind the Suburban. Bailey and Levine climbed out and joined him waiting to cross. Cray and Reed stood at his other side. When the coast was clear, they briskly walked across the road to the other cars. Minus Cray, they all flashed their badges and the Mountain View police nodded as they drew nearer.

Reed and the others began speaking with the officers, but Fraser walked in between the cruisers and stared at the wreck.

No, wreck was far too strong of a word. Acheson's car had jumped the curb and collided with a large tree trunk. But given the minimal crumpling, it looked more like a bad fender bender than anything else. The passenger door was open, red light pulsing from within.

Fraser walked around the back of the ambulance, where Acheson was being attended to by an EMT. She displayed no apparent injuries but looked shaken up. Fraser showed the medics his badge and turned to Acheson, right as Cray came around the corner.

"Are you alright?"

She nodded quickly.

He lowered himself to her eye level. "How did it happen?" he asked softly.

Acheson glanced between him and Cray, who looked concerned. He wondered if that was just an act.

"I was coming back from a doctor's appointment—just a quick check-up. But I'd had it scheduled this week for a while, couldn't get it moved after Niall..." She shivered. Rain drizzled all around, but they were sheltered by the ambulance and the tree canopy branching overhead. "I was heading to HQ. And then suddenly the car just started swaying in the lane. And I knew something was wrong because Asimov cars never do that, unless they're trying to avoid something. So I started worrying. I figured I could maybe put it in manual mode, but before I could unbuckle my seatbelt—I was sitting in the rear—the car just veered to the left, went off the road, and hit the tree."

Fraser turned around, looked back down the road. The asphalt went along a bridge over a small creek. An overcrossing walkway traversed both sides of Central Expressway, the adjacent Caltrain tracks, and the street on the other side. Beyond that was an overpass for State Route 85.

"Where did it start swerving?"

"Back there," she pointed. "Just as I came out from the overpass."

"So it swerved through the off-ramp intersection right there?"

She nodded. "It must've been a green light. The car never slowed."

"Were there many cars in front of you?"

Acheson shook her head. "No, it was pretty light traffic."

Fraser stared back down the road. Electric cars could accelerate much faster than their gas-powered equivalents. If Racer began fucking with Acheson's vehicle before the intersection, they could have easily hit the same tree with enough velocity to kill her. Or at the very least cause serious injuries.

"Ms. Acheson, you should consider yourself extremely lucky."

She glowered. *"Lucky?* How the hell am I *lucky?* Someone just tried to *kill* me."

He shook his head. "If they wanted to kill you, you'd be dead."

Acheson went pale, staring off at the road. Cray tilted her head, watching her like a scientist might observe a specimen.

Fraser headed off to examine the car.

"I just don't get it."

Reed came around the tree, crouching to examine the damage to the sedan. Vehicles sped by on the eastbound lanes behind him.

"Why," he continued, "would they hack the car but not kill her?"

"It's not like it was hard for them. They already have access to any Asimov vehicle they want," Fraser said. "They select one, activate the Trojan, and once they're done, they log off and the virus automatically sends out an update wiping it from the car. Then another part of the virus in the Telemetry system deletes the update confirmation log. That all would've happened by now. I doubt there's any trace of the virus still in this vehicle."

"I want Bailey and Levine to run forensics on it anyway. We didn't get to examine the cars that crashed in the summer, and we didn't get to examine Spencer's either—for obvious reasons. Maybe there's something here still."

Fraser stared at the hood. "Definitely worth looking into."

"But you still haven't answered my question. What does this serve?"

He paused. "It's a reminder from Racer. They still have control of any Asimov car they want and there's nothing we can do about it. The patch Asimov sent out on Tuesday clearly didn't work. The virus in Update must've placed a Trojan in it too."

"So that's it?" Reed stared at the car in disbelief. "The killer's just fucking with us at this point?"

"Maybe they're a psychopath."

Both Fraser and Reed's heads whipped around. Cray stood beside them, running a hand along the side of the car.

She looked up. "The more I think about it, the more that makes sense. If their plan is to kill Spencer and then sabotage the Catalyst event, there a lot more straightforward ways they could've gone about it. They could've just tried to kill Spencer *at* the Catalyst unveiling. That would've been much easier."

He half expected her to say, *That's how I would've done it.*

"But they didn't," Cray continued. "They made it more complicated, killing him early in the week and toying with the company, trying to make a hired consultant disappear. Having us run around trying to find the source of the Update subnet breach, when Catalyst may have been separately compromised this whole time. And now, driving Acheson's car off the road while barely damaging it just to screw with us even more."

"Could it be a distraction?" Fraser said, trying not to show how chilled he was. "Luring us and the RCFL techs out here?"

"Possibly." Cray glanced at a passing car. "But killing Acheson would've been way more effective for that. A more serious crime scene to sort through. Would've created a bigger panic, too. So why do it this way? Why make everything so complicated? The more you toy with us, the more likely it is something could go wrong. Why risk it?" She looked between them. "Unless, of course, you're bored."

"What? Someone is doing *all* of this just because they're *bored*?" Reed looked incredulous.

Cray shook her head. "No, I wouldn't imagine *all* of it. I'm sure Racer has what they feel is a good—or even *necessary*—reason for killing Spencer and ruining the company. But they're enjoying this. They *want* to drag it out. There must be a lot of thrill in it for them, and they're trying to savor this as much as they can while it all lasts."

Fraser stared at her. Cray looked worried, but he could see no sign of fakery in her expression.

"It's something to consider," Reed said. He regarded her with a cold gaze. Fraser wondered if he was unnerved too.

Then all three of them headed back around the tree. Bailey and Levine were speaking with the police officers. They joined the conversation—something about getting a police tow-truck to bring the car back to the RCFL—but Fraser kept staring through the open passenger door. The dashboard light pulsed red every few seconds, then dissipated again.

Pulse, fade. Pulse, fade.

He couldn't help but think it looked sinister.

2:41 PM

The truck turned onto Deer Creek and Sova adjusted his baseball cap, glancing in the mirror.

The contact lenses had changed his eye color from brown to a muted green and his face was covered in a thick, reddish beard. The whole disguise looked fantastic, but he was worried.

Worried he would run into *her*.

It was painful Racer insisted on doing this their way. He'd much rather have snuck into Asimov to finish Cray, but he was needed elsewhere, and soon. He understood why Racer wanted to do it like this. It just disappointed him that he wouldn't get to neutralize the animal himself.

He'd been careful not to get blood on the trucker's jacket. The man it had belonged to lay dead in his garage, stashed behind a dumpster. He would be found soon enough, but that didn't matter. It would be too late to stop what was about to happen.

Sova grinned to himself as he pulled into the Asimov parking lot. The monster didn't know what was coming.

Buckle up, Isabella. You're going for a ride.

2:46 PM

There was a *whoosh* as the lobby doors retracted, then she and Graham were outside into the rain. The tow truck had arrived, the driver currently unloading Acheson's sedan.

At first, Bailey and Levine intended to bring the car back to the RCFL, but Graham insisted that it be driven to Asimov HQ so the company could run its own tests on it. Fraser and Reed had protested, but Bailey said it was alright. The RCFL's van was a mobile forensics lab anyway. They could get what they needed from the car right in the parking lot. After that, Asimov could do whatever they wanted with it.

Reed and Fraser were talking to the driver. Several other company employees were standing around watching. Ritter and Pawar, the legal counsel, were having some conversation. Kaplan stood by, her arms crossed, looking worried. Johnson was standing beside her, staring blankly as the scene unfolded. After the medics had ensured that she had no major injuries, Acheson had gone home.

With all the bureaucracy and working things out with the Mountain View Police Department, it had taken over two hours to finally get the sedan here. In the interim, Cray had begun looking into the NOC's security footage, searching for any trace of Greg Furman. Graham texted her a picture of what he looked like. Johnson had sat her down at a terminal in his department and showed her the basics of how to work the system, as if she couldn't figure it out, but assured her the whole thing was a waste of time.

"With our facial recognition software, you should be able to detect if he was ever in there pretty easily, though it's gonna take a while to go through six months of footage. But there's no way this guy made it within ten feet of the Software Update NOC, I'm telling you. He just wouldn't have gotten in without turning heads."

"If this is a dead end, there are other ways he could've gotten a virus into Update. He could've swapped somebody's flashdrive. They also have to patch those computers manually, since they're protected from the corporate network writ large. He could've sabotaged the hard disks used to deliver system updates to those computers," Cray said.

Johnson put up his hands. "Hey, it's your time to waste, not mine."

She glared at him. It was becoming harder to keep the mask fitted the longer this week wore on. "We have proof that the Update subnet was breached. Somehow, *somebody* got a polymorphic virus into there. If you've got any theories, I'm all ears."

He shrugged. "I have no clue. It just doesn't make sense. It shouldn't have happened in the first place."

"Well, it did. And there has to be an explanation."

Johnson didn't have any, so he left her alone. The system had scanned about a third of the footage and found no trace of Furman's profile, and Cray had mainly sat there watching the progress bar tick across.

Fuck, computer investigations were boring. It baffled her that Bailey and Levine did this shit as full-time jobs, sitting in front of screens all day, monitoring programs. Her respect for them swelled. Bailey hadn't been kidding when he said digital forensics wasn't sexy. Reed and Fraser had it easy, having underlings to do the grunt work and report back to them.

Cray tilted her head, wondering what it would be like to be an FBI agent. She looked good in a suit, she knew that much at least. But it wasn't as fun as it looked on TV. There was a lot more nitty-gritty to investigations that she didn't think she had the patience for.

Still, Racer had made it personal by trying to kill her twice. She just wished she could help the case in a more active way—not by spending hours staring at footage of the NOC, watching software engineers give themselves eye strain.

When Graham had come to tell her the car arrived, she practically leaped out of her seat.

The tow truck unloaded Acheson's sedan just to the left of the drop-off curve. Parked behind it was the RCFL van. Bailey and Levine wore ponchos, making sure the Snowball was shielded on the bottom of a carrel. The rain had picked up again. Cray had never seen it this bad here, but knew it was seasonal. The rest of the year there was rarely a cloud in the sky. Graham brought an umbrella, but she didn't bother to stand beneath it.

Cray walked onto the road, heading for the FBI agents and the truck driver. The man wore a baseball cap and baggy jeans, his face turned away from her. He nodded to Fraser, then went around toward the back of the truck as she approached.

"I'm not sure we'll find anything," Fraser told her. "But you never know."

She nodded, looking at the car. The truck driver was bent down, detaching it from the towing vehicle. Aside from the smashed up left side of the grille, it looked roadworthy.

"How do we make sure Racer doesn't take control of it again? Graham said the cars are never truly off without a dead battery."

"There's a wheel clamp on the front right. Car's not going anywhere, hacked or not," Reed said. "If your theory is right and Racer's toying with us, maybe they left a little gift to find. Maybe they secretly want to get caught."

I doubt it, she thought. Most psychopaths—if Racer truly was one—didn't care for notoriety. That was reserved for what Dr. Perkins called *malignant narcissists*, those who were comorbid with both ASPD and NPD. All the cold unfeelingness of the former, all the need for attention and grandiosity of the latter. Though Cray couldn't feel scared, the thought of such an adversary trying to kill her did no favors for her anxiousness.

If there was something in that car, she wanted to find it and find it *now*. All this standing around was really getting to her, cold rain drumming her skin. The truck driver moved around to the passenger side of the car, then looked back at her.

Cray examined the tall man. He had a red beard and green eyes and wore a jacket from the towing company the police had contracted with. For a moment, she thought there was something vaguely familiar about him.

He smiled, revealing a gold tooth, and tipped his hat toward her. "Hi there," he said with a Southern drawl.

Cray gave a thin smile in return, then looked back at Fraser, adjusting her turtleneck. "What are we waiting for?"

Bailey and Levine reached the car and were now opening the saloon-style doors on the driver's side.

"You alright?" Fraser asked, concerned.

Maybe he thought she was still shaken about last night. Maybe it had gotten to her more than she realized. But the longer they didn't know who Racer was, the worse she felt. Her stomach was tying itself in knots, her shoulders and neck so tense they gave her a headache.

Cray ignored him and walked forward, coming around the open doors and climbing into the car.

The four seats sat facing each other. The red lights from earlier were off, as the car had been powered down for transportation. Bailey was fitting an adapter onto the Snowball's connector cable, which he then plugged into the ethernet port under the touchscreen panel. He sat in the rear-facing passenger seat, Levine in the one across from him.

Cray settled down beside her. The leather helped her relax a little bit.

"Alright, let's see what we've got." Bailey turned the Snowball toward him, punching something in on the screen. Levine took out the laptop and handed it to him with another connector cord. "Since the cars are never completely off, we don't need to turn it back on to begin harvesting data," he explained.

"You're gonna need to activate Developer Mode for that."

Two people were approaching the open doors. Johnson climbed in and sat in the rear-facing driver's seat, looking over at Bailey's laptop.

Ritter was left out in the rain. She'd taken off her AR glasses. "Is there enough space for me in there?"

Johnson gestured to the seats. "Use your eyes, Mallory. Unless you wanna sit cross-legged on the floor."

She sighed, looking tired. "You know what, maybe I will."

The CTO climbed past Cray and sat in the center of the spacious cabin.

"Jesus, the doors are gonna get wrecked." Johnson reached out into the downpour, grabbed the handle, and pulled the door next to him shut. Cray thought for a moment, then did the same with the one beside her.

"The car's a write-off already," Ritter said, glaring up at him.

"It's got a fender. Once we get rid of this virus, we can get it patched up for Cheryl good as new." He was staring at the laptop, not even glancing at her. "Here, let me get you Developer Mode. That way you should have basically root access to the car." Before Bailey could respond, Johnson turned the laptop toward himself and entered the password.

"How many modes are there?" Cray asked, watching his fingers type, noting the keys. It appeared to be: *Tesl@suX.*

Seriously? Her face betrayed no emotion, filing the info away.

"Two," Johnson said, still looking at the screen. "User is just the standard operating mode, then Developer lets us go into the systems with a more hands-on approach. It lets us reconfigure everything from here." He gestured to the laptop.

Cray nodded. "So Racer's virus would've given them Developer access?"

Ritter turned and stared at her. "Racer?"

"That's what the hacker calls themselves," Cray said.

Johnson scoffed. "Fuckin' stupid name if you ask me. All these hackers think they're such edgelords."

Ritter laughed. "Well, one of them screwed your system pretty hard, so I wouldn't write them off just yet."

"Yeah, well I hope they brought cyber-lube, because they're about to get screwed back." He finished typing, then hit a key and returned the laptop to Bailey. "There you go pal, root access. Have fun. Let me know what you find." The CSO opened the door and climbed out, shutting it behind him.

Ritter groaned and climbed into his seat. "He's going to get fired when this is all over, and he knows it. He was friends with Spencer, but I bet whoever the next CEO is won't be so kind. Especially if it's Kaplan."

"Why?" Cray asked.

The CTO laughed again. "Don't let her soft demeanor fool you. When it comes to keeping projects on task, she cracks a whip."

Cray did her best not to smile, letting her mind drift off into fantasy. The tow truck was driving off. Out the window, Reed and Fraser were talking under an umbrella while Graham, Pawar, and Kaplan seemed to have headed back inside. Cray barely paid attention, thinking of one of the upsides to an autonomous car. She pictured one speeding along the highway, the two of them on a chair reclining back. Kaplan, pulling Cray on top of her with a leash, hooked to a black collar around her neck.

How nice it was, she thought, not having to take the wheel —

Levine clambered past her, climbing out the door.

Cray snapped out of her reverie. "Where's she going?"

"Just taking a water break," Bailey said, not looking up from the laptop. Suddenly, he stopped clicking and typing. "Alright, it's extracting logs from the car. Shouldn't be too long. There's not nearly as much data here as there was in the subnets." He gave an awkward laugh.

Ritter was staring at something on her phone. "Are you making backup copies of the Snowball data so that Asimov can review it?" she asked.

Bailey paused. "No, but we can transfer it afterward from the Snowball."

"Johnson's harping on my ass to get a physical disk copy from you guys as soon as possible."

Bailey hesitated. "I guess it would speed things up if we just duplicated it to a second disk from here. I'll go grab one from the van, be back in a sec."

He left the car and closed the door behind him. Now it was just Cray and Ritter.

The CTO sighed, leaning back in her seat. She stared at her phone, shaking her head.

Cray offered a smile. "Rough week?"

Ritter put a hand to her head. "There's not enough caffeine in the world to get me through it." She reached for the door handle. "Can you make sure they get us a copy?"

Cray nodded. "Of course." She glanced behind her. Bailey was almost to the RCFL van. When she turned around, Ritter was tugging on the handle.

"Hey, did you lock this?" she said.

Cray frowned. "I haven't touched anything."

She sighed, pressing the Unlock button on the door, trying the handle again. Still wouldn't budge. "What the hell?"

Cray suddenly became aware of a whirring noise and turned toward the center touchscreen panel. The Asimov logo appeared, then faded as the infotainment system loaded.

She blinked, her mind still processing it.

Someone turned the car on.

Tension gripped muscles across her body. Cray's heart pounded faster, fight-or-flight instinct rearing its head.

Get out of here. Now.

Ritter was frantically tugging on the door, her phone still in her other hand. But before Cray could move, before she could even say another word, the sedan lurched backward.

Cray spun around, gripping the headrest behind her. They were swiftly closing the forty-foot gap between the rear of the car and the front of the van. Bailey crossed the vehicle's hood, heading to the passenger side.

He turned at the last second, putting his hands out, his mouth going wide—

Cray braced for impact, ducking her head as the sedan rammed the technician against the van's grille. His pelvis was crushed between the vehicles, his head snapping back, then forward as he fell across the trunk. Blood spurted from Bailey's mouth, splattering the rear window. A hideous moan escaped his lips, his eyes pleading through the pain.

Ritter had been thrown to the floor by the impact. She scrambled up into the seat beside Cray, her hair a mess, her breaths coming quickly. Cray stared at the dying man, who was feebly trying to move. His mouth opened and closed, but nothing emerged save for red fluid. Rain was already washing blood off the glass.

"Oh my God, oh my God, oh my God..." Ritter covered her mouth.

Cray watched Bailey die with curiosity, her anxiety of the predicament failing to distract her from his final moments. He'd been nothing but kind to her, even seemed to have a crush on her, and yet she felt barely anything but shock watching him suffer. She probed deeper, trying to find something, anything, resembling empathy. There was only the logic in her mind, telling her that this *was* awful, that he didn't deserve this. That she should feel sad, or at the very least horrified. Maybe if she'd gotten to know him longer, this would've had more of an effect.

Slowly, she craned her neck around toward the touchscreen. The Asimov logo faded in again, then vanished. The infotainment system reappeared. The F-Series was rebooting.

Out the front window, Reed and Fraser were sprinting toward the car, almost reaching them. The bright yellow wheel clamp lay on the asphalt behind them.

Suddenly, the vehicle flew forward. Cray and Ritter were thrown back into their seats, Bailey's body sliding off the back.

The sedan veered left, avoiding the agents, and whipped around the drop-off curve. Ritter was thrown against the right door like a ragdoll. Cray lunged for the nearest roof handle and seized it, the sharpness of the turn nearly tearing her shoulder out of its socket.

Then the vehicle accelerated again, heading toward the northeastern corner of the parking lot and an even sharper turn up ahead.

Ritter was scrambling to get back into the other rear seat. Cray grabbed her, hauling her up. "Seatbelt, *fast*," she spat, trying to do her own.

She tugged it so quickly the strap halted. She tried again but was still too quick.

Goddamnit.

Cray pulled a third time, gentler now. It gave. Hurriedly, she jammed the buckle in. Heard the click just as the car braked, drifting around the corner.

Both she and Ritter were thrown to the side again, but the belts held them upright.

The sedan sped along the northern row, toward the western corner and the exit. Another turn was coming up.

"*Shit, shit, shit—*"

"Hold on!" Cray shouted.

She tensed just before the vehicle swerved again, throwing her to the left, the strap cutting into her shoulder.

Then the sedan shot forward, out onto the road.

2:53 PM

Fraser dashed for the nearest row of the parking lot. Reached his Crown Vic, tore open the door.

He was just turning the ignition when Reed opened the passenger door. "No, my car is—"

"Too big."

Reed glared. "This thing is a goddamn rust bucket."

"Can't hack it."

The senior agent gave an exasperated sigh, climbing in. He shut the door as Fraser threw the car into reverse. Slammed the accelerator. The sedan flew back. He braked, screeching the tires as the car aimed west.

Fraser hit the clutch, shifted into first gear and they raced forward. They were in fourth by the time he swerved out onto Deer Creek, and he put it straight to fifth as they began accelerating again. Though the car was unmarked, he activated the police lights in the grille and the windshield, the siren blaring into the rain.

Up ahead, the hacked sedan was already careening through the intersection onto Page Mill.

Fraser sped toward the T-junction, the light going yellow.

"Will…"

The light went red. Cars going each way began entering the intersection.

Fraser didn't slow down.

"*Will...*" Reed was clutching a roof handle.

The car whipped into the junction, Fraser hitting the brake and downshifting. Tires screamed as they drifted through the intersection, narrowly dodging vehicles on the left and right.

Fraser slammed the clutch, shifted back up, and accelerated, the car wobbling side to side as he regained control.

They raced up the hill. The fleeing sedan was already out of sight.

Fraser swore under his breath as they crested the rise, the engine roaring, rain slashing across his windshield. He activated the wipers at full blast.

The road curved back down toward the freeway, a guardrail looming to the right. Fraser kept his eyes fixed on it, looking for any breaks.

But as they rounded the curve, he saw Racer hadn't sent the car off the road.

There it was, slaloming past vehicles on its way toward the next bend. Its crumpled trunk was smeared with Bailey's blood.

"Fuck, are they headed for the...?" Reed let his voice trail off. Neither of them wanted to say it out loud.

Fraser floored the gas. He whipped by a bright green *Your Speed* indicator and it flashed *82*.

Avoiding an SUV, he came around the next bend, an overpass looming in the distance.

The Asimov F-Series was in the left lane. As the I-280 entrance ramp neared, it appeared to maintain its course.

Then, at the last second, it cut in front of the BMW i3 in the turn lane and accelerated onto the curve.

To her own surprise, Cray had remained paralyzed, gripped with anxiety through every sharp turn. She braced for oblivion, her entire body hot-wired, her hairs standing on end. Ritter was catatonic beside her, clutching her own roof handle and repeating, "*Oh God, we're gonna die, we're gonna die...*"

Yet after several missed opportunities to kill them and a sudden bank onto the highway, Cray snapped out of it.

They're toying with you before they kill you. They're having fun with this.

As the entrance ramp cut through dense trees and emerged onto the freeway, she unbuckled her seatbelt and leaped to the Snowball and laptop on the floor.

The cable had been unplugged by chaotic motion, but Cray further detached the laptop from the Snowball and fed the laptop cable into the ethernet adapter.

"We're fucking dead, we're fucking dead...," Ritter kept saying behind her.

The CTO was really getting on her nerves, but Cray tried to ignore her, buckling herself into the passenger seat and bringing the computer onto her lap.

There was light traffic at this hour. The sedan shot out into the four-lane freeway, gracefully swerving past and around other cars.

Oh, Racer was loving this, she could tell. Sitting somewhere at a computer—probably with an attached joystick, that's what she would've used—playing with the car like it was a video game. Keeping the driving smooth for now, but knowing they could cause chaos at any second they liked.

Where the hell were they going for the big finish?

Let's not find out.

Johnson said Developer Mode would grant her root access. She just had to activate the AutoDrive system and get it to override whatever control Racer had.

"We're gonna die, oh God please don't let me die..."

Cray clenched her teeth, trying to tune her out. Fucking NTs and their inability to remain calm.

Panic was pointless. You either dodged the bullet, or you didn't.

On the laptop she had access to the standard infotainment system. She needed something more powerful, pulled up the command prompt.

Guessing the OS was a modified Linux, she input `pwd` and hit Enter.

It listed her directory: `home/Dev`

The sedan cut off a speeding Cybertruck, earning a honk.

"Fuck, fuck, fuck…" Ritter was staring out the window, still clenching the handle. They were passing through open green space in the Valley, mountains off in the distance. Even in the rain, I-280's views were majestic. But they were getting farther and farther from Palo Alto, and closer to whatever Racer had planned for them.

She wasn't quite sure how the directory was organized, so she fired a shot in the dark: `cd AutoDrive`.

An error message flashed: `Problem opening the directory /home/Dev/Operations/AutoDrive (13: Permission denied by Administrator)`.

Her eyes widened, her anger soaring.

Administrator? Who the fuck is Administrator?

Racer's virus had somehow created a higher-level user than Developer. The only way to fix this would be to perform a privilege escalation attack on an OS she'd never hacked before.

While trapped in a compromised vehicle going a hundred miles per hour.

Wind and rain buffeted the car, the sedan continuing to dart in and out of traffic, gently accelerating and decelerating at just the right times with fishlike agility.

There were now tears sprouting from Ritter's eyes. *"Oh no, no, no, no, no…"*

Cray bent over, trying to focus on the screen. Ritter continued moaning. The exterior noise seemed deafening. She stared at the blinking cursor in the command prompt, trying to think of her next move.

"No, no, no, no, no —"

She couldn't take it anymore.

Her head snapped toward the other woman, obliterating the mask. *"SHUT THE FUCK UP!"*

Ritter froze, her lip quivering. She looked like she'd been smacked.

"You will stay quiet unless I ask you a question, or, so help me God, I will come over there and break your neck myself." Her face had flushed red with crimson, but her gaze never wavered, staring into the CTO's eyes. *"Do I make myself clear?"*

Ritter nodded quickly, trying to pull herself together. She was scared shitless.

Cray felt herself regaining control, but she was still incredibly tense, that sick unease gripping her. *If this is anxiety, I'd hate to find out what fear is like.*

Time to focus.

She returned her attention to the screen.

<··>

A Prius cut into his lane and Fraser took a hard right, veering off the road—

Right for a large interstate sign. San Francisco, thirty-six miles away.

He jerked left at the last second, narrowly missing the Prius's rear bumper.

"Jesus," Reed said, hunkering down in his seat, his phone pressed to his ear.

Fraser went into the next lane and accelerated again, overtaking the Toyota.

"No, it's a silver Asimov F-Series, speeding north on 280. Approaching Alpine Road. I didn't get the license plate. The occupants are not, repeat *not* in control of the vehicle. Alert all units that..."

Fraser stayed focused on the highway. They had to keep a visual. He had no clue if Racer's virus could wipe the car's tracking data out of Telemetry. It hadn't with Spencer's, but they couldn't risk that chance.

Racer could've easily killed Cray and Ritter by now, but hadn't. *Kidnapping, maybe?*

He couldn't rule anything out. Maybe the fucker just enjoyed having him and Reed play chase.

They want to drag it out, Cray had said. *There must be a lot of thrill in it for them, and they're trying to savor this as much as they can while it all lasts.*

The hell they will, he decided, ramming the pedal.

The engine snarled, the Crown Vic speeding forward into the downpour. Even in the gloom, he could make out the distant mountain range. Without suburban sprawl or urban rises, 280 was just his car, the one getting away, and moving obstacles in-between. His mind disregarded everything else.

He could see it up ahead, speeding like a bullet yet smoothly avoiding all collisions.

Fraser gripped the steering wheel, controlled his breathing, and overtook another SUV.

"This is an out-of-date browser," Cray said, wiping a bead of sweat from her forehead. Her heart was in her throat.

Ritter glared. "I've been telling Johnson to fucking fix that for a year."

No one noticed, Cray figured, *because who the fuck uses their car to browse the Internet?*

But that was good.

This had last been updated in 2026 and might have WebKit vulnerabilities. If she could download an exploit from a couple years ago, she might be able to get her own Trojan virus into the system, giving her a back door.

Yet as she tried to enter a search, the browser loaded a blank page:

No Internet Connection.

Fuck. Racer had full control. They were blocking any attempts to access the 5G network.

Unless...

"If it's Linux, you guys would've given the Developer account SUDO rights, correct?" she snapped at Ritter.

The CTO nodded nervously, stuttering, "It...it...should. I don't know, I'm focused on R&D—"

Cray held up a silencing hand.

Why didn't I think of it first? Fuck this anxiety, clouding her focus.

SUDO generally stood for "superuser do," granting permission to any account with such rights to act as a superuser—whether that account was the highest-level administrator or not. With any luck, Racer might've neglected to block these for lower-level users. It's not like they figured anyone would be trying to hack the car *back*. Though the blocking of outbound Internet was concerning.

The car swerved to the left and a truck horn blared, but Cray managed to keep the computer in her lap. She should be able to execute commands with superuser-level security, especially since Developer normally *was* the superuser.

She entered: sudo ps -aux.

Immediately, a line of text appeared reading: [sudo] password for Dev:

Cray input the phrase she'd seen Johnson type and the system accepted it. Then she entered sudo ps -aux again.

Now a list of every process running—and how many resources it was using—materialized.

"Oh fuck, fuck, where are we going?" Ritter moaned, staring ahead through the windshield. It made Cray glad she was facing the rear.

"Shut up," she said calmly.

The processes were sorted from highest to lowest memory usage. AutoDrive1, AutoDrive2, and AutoDrive3 were at the top, though the first two used far more memory than the third.

She entered sudo /proc/AutoDrive1/maps and a breakdown of the first process's memory appeared. It showed her everything from virtual memory addresses to permissions to the directory path where the process was located.

As the car swerved, braked, and accelerated, she did the same for AutoDrive2 and AutoDrive3.

And then it hit her.

Reactivating the AutoDrive systems wouldn't override whatever control Racer had.

Because Racer had seized control *through* the AutoDrive systems, making the car think it was being self-driven when it was actually being controlled by someone else.

Asimov vehicles employed three AutoDrive systems at the same time in case one malfunctioned. As long as at least two of the systems were working in harmony, the car would follow those systems.

But two of them had open socket connections to the same external IP address. They must be overriding the third, uncompromised AutoDrive system.

She just had to deactivate the first two processes.

For a brief second, she felt something approaching relief. She'd found a way to beat them.

Then the car took a sharp turn.

"Jesus Christ," Reed said, watching in disbelief.

Fraser stared in horror as the Asimov sedan cut hard to the left, drifting across the asphalt, then straightening again as it shot through a gap in the dividing guardrail.

Out into oncoming traffic.

A cacophony of horns blared as the vehicle straightened its course, speeding north on the southbound lanes. It dodged a compact car, then a station wagon, and faked left before jerking right to avoid a Hummer EV.

A shape grew in Fraser's peripheral and his eyes darted forward. The rear end of a truck was looming closer, his car about to plow into its rear.

Fraser spun the wheel, sliding the Crown Vic right at the last second, regaining control in the new lane.

"Shit," Reed said, pulling himself back upright. "*I* look, *you* drive."

"Got it," Fraser nodded, accelerating again.

They overtook the truck and the sedan came into view once more, barreling along into the face of death.

<···>

Don't think about it. Just don't think about it.

Cray gripped the laptop for dear life, hugging it close with one arm and typing with her free hand. She nearly lost hold of it several times with the car's increasingly erratic maneuvers, but maintained her grasp.

The Snowball kept sliding around on the floor. It collided with her shin one time, but she gritted her teeth through the pain.

As the car lurched right again, the machine crashed back against Ritter's foot. The CTO screamed.

Cray tried to ignore her, hitting the Enter key for her command `kill -9 2052`.

Immediately, `AutoDrive1`—process ID 2052—ceased to function.

The car began jerking left, right. Speeding up, slowing down. They swayed in one lane, an SUV racing toward them. It swung out of the way at the last second, but the sedan didn't respond at all, now zigzagging randomly.

Ritter turned to her, her skin white as a ghost. "What did you do?"

Sweat broke out across Cray's forehead. She felt like she might be sick. Heat flushed to her face and her entire body was so tense it hurt, a headache detonating in her skull.

She'd stopped one of the compromised AutoDrive systems. Now there were only two left, the one controlled by Racer and the one that had been previously overridden. They were grappling for control of the car, man against machine, as the vehicle headed toward oncoming traffic at ninety miles per hour.

Cray had hoped disabling one would be enough. Forsaking her firm hold on the device, she began typing on the keyboard with both hands.

```
sudo ps -aux
```

The list of processes appeared again. `AutoDrive2` was at the top this time, its ID reading 3478. She didn't need to delve further into it to know that it was still connected to that external IP address.

She began typing again. `kill  -9` for the kill signal, and lastly, the ID number—

There came a *screech* and a rending of metal.

A van raked along the passenger side of the car, tearing the mirror clean off.

The sedan jerked hard to the left, but it was already too late.

The laptop flew out of her hand, clattering to the floor.

Mercifully, the connector cable was long enough to keep it tethered. But as the car lurched to the right again, the device slid across the floor, the heavy Snowball skating after it—

Cray ejected her seatbelt, diving in front of the computer, her back taking the impact as she shielded the laptop. The car was still jerking left and right. An enormous horn blared somewhere ahead.

"Jesus, there's a t-truck!" Ritter managed to get out.

The command was still up on the screen, the cursor blinking next to it.

`kill -9 3478`

With her index finger, Cray stabbed the Enter key.

For a moment, nothing seemed to have happened.

Then the car swerved to the left as a cargo truck shot by, Cray glimpsing the Amazon logo along its side as it went. The word *Error* flashed on the touchscreen.

The car curved out to the right, then doubled back left, swinging in a big loop.

The Snowball slid along the floor, the edge scraping down her back. Cray gasped in pain, clutching the laptop as she slid into the base of the front seats.

Ritter was thrown against the door, restrained by her seat belt, closing her eyes in terror.

The tires squealed, the car still turning. It seemed like it would never end—

Then, suddenly, it slid to a halt.

Cray stayed there for a moment, breathing on the floor, waiting for a collision. Cars raced by on the freeway, some close enough to rattle the vehicle. Police sirens approached from somewhere in the distance.

Slowly, Cray turned around, glancing up at the touch-screen. It displayed the message *System Error—Please seek assistance.*

She stared at it blankly for some time. Then there came a gagging noise, followed by the sound of someone throwing up. Cray turned around and scrambled back up into the passenger seat, disregarding her pain.

Ritter had retched all over the floor, some of it getting on the overturned Snowball. A bunch was all over her hand, which she was still staring at. Evidently, she had tried to cover her mouth and failed.

"I'm sorry," she mumbled, watching fluid drip from her fingers. "I just…"

Cray felt sick too. The car's sudden movements while her eyes had been focused on the screen made her queasy. Now, with the smell of bile in the air, she couldn't take it.

She threw open the door beside her. The vehicle had come to a stop on the shoulder lane. There was a ditch beside the road, a cattle fence and farmland beyond. Rolling hills and trees stretched off toward the mountains.

Rain began to drench her. The sirens drew closer.

Tension dissipated as Cray kneeled on the pavement, a wave of relaxation washing over her.

Then her churning stomach became too much to ignore, and she bent forward to vomit into the ditch

4:02 PM

The Asimov HQ parking lot had been turned into a crime scene by the time they got back. Cray leaned her head against the glass as Fraser's Crown Victoria rolled up to the police cars. She was exhausted and wrought with unease. Though she felt less tense than she had been in Acheson's sedan, anxiety still wound its way through her body.

Still, she seemed to be faring better than Ritter, who was pale and quiet in the backseat, staring off into space.

Fraser and Reed had been right behind them on the highway the whole time, but got off at the next exit once they saw the sedan had stopped. Highway Patrol officers arrived first, but Reed had called ahead to explain the situation. When he pulled up in the Crown Victoria, Fraser had come straight over to Cray to ask if she was alright. He looked very worried, but once everything seemed to be in order and no major injuries were reported, his frosty FBI demeanor returned.

Cray would've been livid at the whole situation if she wasn't still recuperating. This fucker had tried to kill her on three separate occasions now.

But you failed, asshole. Each time, you've only succeeded in pissing me off more.

They passed the crime scene tape and pulled up to the drop-off curve. Reed had stayed behind to oversee the transportation of the sedan to the RCFL. Since Cray had forcibly disconnected Racer from the vehicle, the virus may not have wiped itself from the car's systems. And if that IP address she saw could be recovered, they'd have a trail to follow to the culprit.

Both FBI agents seemed incredibly tense. Though they were relieved that Cray and Ritter were unharmed, Bailey's murder had them fired up, out for blood. Once the hacked sedan had driven off, Reed dashed over to check on the technician. Levine had come running out of the van, telling him to help Fraser stop the car. Said she'd take care of Bailey, though he'd been practically sandwiched in two. Not much anyone could do about that.

Cray wished she felt sadder about him. He'd been nice.

And there was another matter. Once she emptied her guts, Cray had sat on the pavement waiting for the cops to arrive, realizing that as soon as the truck driver flirted with her, she'd turned away. But he'd been standing by the front right wheel, where the clamp had been located. He must've unattached it while they were busy looking elsewhere. Maybe even loosened it before he got to Asimov. She realized why he looked familiar now, angry for not recognizing it before.

The cops put out an APB on the truck, but Sova would've ditched it as soon as he could've. He was long gone by now. At least, until Racer needed his services again.

Fraser stopped the car and she turned to him. "Thanks."

"You did all the heavy-lifting, Ms. Cray. You deserve credit for ejecting a hacker from a moving vehicle." He managed a smile. "Every Bureau cybercrime agent's gonna hear that story."

About time something positive went on my file. She didn't know what else to say to Fraser, so she just smiled, nodded appreciatively, and climbed out of the car.

Neither she nor Ritter looked over at the crime scene around the RCFL van, instead heading straight inside. They walked past the receptionist and headed toward the staircase after badging in, making their way to the second floor.

Ritter continued on to her office, but Cray made a right

at the executive breakroom and went to one of the refrigerators. She took out a ginger ale, cracked it open, and started drinking.

"I've got something stronger than that, if you need it."

She turned. Graham stood there, leaning against the doorway. He looked as tired as she felt.

Cray laughed, put a hand to her gut. "I just need something to settle my stomach."

Graham nodded. He stepped closer. "Well, once you've done that, there's a bottle of scotch in Niall's office. Behind the painting next to the window. Code is 051212. Just leave everything the way you found it. I need to speak to your FBI friends." He headed for the door, then stopped and turned around. "I'm so sorry all this has happened, Izzy. I never should've brought you here."

She shrugged, gave a weak smile. "I'm in this till the end now, Ted. Whoever this person is, they've hurt all of us."

"We have to make sure tomorrow goes as planned. Catalyst is going to change the world and if this person sows distrust in our technology, society will never recover."

She was going to say that sounded a bit much, but it wasn't what Graham needed to hear right now. "Don't worry, Ted. I'm not gonna let that happen."

He nodded again, as if to himself. "Tomorrow's event will be fun. It's casual attire. Niall hated formality. He wanted to ban suits at the event. Wanted people to wear clothes expressing their uniqueness."

Cray couldn't imagine Fraser and Reed in anything other than suits, but she nodded again. "Looking forward to it."

Graham left, clearly lost in thought.

She stood there for a few minutes, gradually finishing the ginger ale. When she was done, she felt a bit better and tossed the can in the trash. Then paused.

High Functioning, Izzy.

Sighing, she fished it out and dropped it in a recycling bin.

Cray headed back into the hall and nearly collided with Ritter. "Whoops, sorry," Cray said, giving an awkward laugh.

The CTO had her purse over one shoulder and her phone in the other hand. She looked dazed. "I just wanted to thank you," she said. "I was so out of it earlier, I didn't get the chance. But thank you for saving us."

Cray smiled, shrugged. "It was nothing."

"No, seriously. And I'm sorry I threw up everywhere. And that I wouldn't shut up."

"I shouldn't have snapped at you," Cray said. She laughed. "I really blew a fuse there."

"I don't care," she said, looking like she wanted to collapse. A tired smile appeared on her face. "I'm just happy to be alive. Stay safe."

"You too." Cray continued past her, heading for the CEO Suite. She walked through the open frame to Acheson's desk, then looked back, making sure Ritter was out of sight, before heading into the office.

It was growing dark outside. With all the clouds there was no sunset, just a dreary day giving way to the gloom. Cray headed to the desk and tapped the power button on the lamp, casting a warm glow about the office. Then she made her way to the painting on the wall to the left of the west-facing window. It was modernist, depicting a blue square against a white background. She wondered how much Spencer paid for it.

She felt around the bottom of the frame and found that it opened like a door, revealing a safe behind it, just as Graham promised. It was a good place to hide one, she decided. She wondered if the FBI Evidence Response Team had bothered to look behind here. It wasn't a suspect's den, so they hadn't torn it apart. And they'd been focused on getting computer or physical files.

She wondered if Graham had told them about the safe.

He didn't seem to mind her having the code, so there must not be anything important in here.

She punched in the digits—051212—then stopped.

If she had to guess, it was a date. Probably May 12, 2012. Spencer's daughter was in high school, so Cray guessed it was her birthday.

Huh, she thought. For a man who'd positioned himself as the harbinger of the future, it was an oddly sentimental gesture. And a private one at that. Then again, she supposed NTs were supposed to feel sentimental about their children. Cray's parents certainly had toward her, when she wasn't making life difficult for them.

I should find it touching, she thought, staring at the code on the safe's display. She'd imagined having her own kids one day.

What had Niall Spencer thought, deciding the code for his safe? Clearly his daughter meant a lot to him. But Cray realized she didn't know that much about the man beyond how people here talked about him. And what people said didn't always reflect the truth.

Clearly, he had done something to piss Racer off. Even if the hacker was a psychopath, there still had to be a compelling reason why they would've gone to all this length. Maybe low-functioning psychopaths would snap and kill people over petty things, but whoever was behind this didn't strike Cray as low functioning.

It was either something Spencer *had* done or was *about* to do. Was this a plan to destroy Catalyst to sink Asimov and Spencer's legacy, or was Catalyst itself the endgame? She wished Graham had come clean earlier and explained what it was.

Even Kayla thought it was the key to his death. But she'd had no clue why. That's why she tried to gain access to his corporate account.

Find out what Catalyst is, understand the motive.

It seemed so simple, yet nobody was telling them anything.

The display had timed out, so Cray re-entered the code on the touchscreen and tapped *Unlock.* The safe opened with a hiss and inside she found a bottle of Macallan waiting.

Thank you, Ted.

She took the bottle and uncorked it. There were two glasses back there, but she didn't bother, bringing it straight to her lips and taking several long pulls. A pleasant sting seared down to her belly, and she lowered the bottle. Calmness flowed through her, easing her nerves. She let her shoulders relax.

Cray stared at the bottle, debating taking another drink. The full effect wouldn't hit her for a few minutes still. She didn't want to get drunk.

Fuck it.

She took a final large gulp and set the bottle back in the safe. This one went down rougher, searing her esophagus. Grimacing, she fit the cork back on top of the bottle. She grabbed the safe door, preparing to close it over, then stopped.

There was something at the back of the safe, shadowed in the dark.

Cray reached forward and grabbed it, drawing out a Moleskine notebook. She flipped through the journal.

Much of it was illegible handwriting. Spencer had made notes in scrawls and scribbles, and the only thing she could comprehend from the early pages were dates. One from February 2023 here, progressing on through 2024. By the end of the notebook, Spencer had gotten to 2025.

Why had he felt compelled to keep this in his safe?

She saw a drawing of a car from the top-down. It had wavebands emitting on all sides, probably for LiDAR. But what interested her most were the scribbles surrounding it. Spencer's handwriting was so terrible that one note looked like a check mark next to the number 2 and a slash beside it. Another looked like it read "U20."

Was this Catalyst, or at least part of it?

Footsteps thudded down the hallway, growing louder.

Shit. She closed the Moleskine and placed it back the way she found it, then shut the safe.

She was just closing the painting back over when Graham burst into the room.

He looked antsy. "Hi, Izzy. Find everything okay?"

"Yup," she said, deliberately acting a little tipsy. She came closer and tried to subtly exhale toward him as she spoke, hoping he'd smell the liquor on her breath. "Took more than a little. Hope Niall doesn't mind." She grinned.

"Did you see anything else in there?"

She turned around, back to the painting. "Uh…no." She looked back at him, raising an eyebrow. "Was there something there?"

Graham froze. Then he laughed and said, "No, no, that was just his little celebratory stash. He and Casey had it open when…" His voice trailed off. "Never mind. I'm glad you found it okay. Feeling better?"

She put a hand to her head. "I should really get back to scanning the NOC footage for signs of Furman. I bet the facial recognition software will have found something by now."

"Are you sure you don't want to go to a hotel? With police protection? This person seems to really want you dead."

She smiled. "I think they're pissed they had to up their game. And it's still not working."

He sighed. "Alright. I just want you to know that you don't have to stay here. You've done more than enough."

"Thanks, Ted. But I'm not leaving until this is finished."

Graham nodded slowly. "I really appreciate it, Izzy."

She made her way past him and back down the hall. She kept turning that vehicle diagram over in her head. There had been something off about it, and not just the serial killer-like handwriting. It didn't look like a regular car or truck.

Cray kept thinking about it on her way down the stairs and nearly bumped into Fraser.

He looked up at her. "Ah, just the person I wanted to see."

She smiled. "You flatter me."

"You looked lost in thought."

"Just trying to fit everything together."

"Well, so am I. How about we get out of here and chat about it somewhere else?" He looked around. "This place is getting to me."

She relaxed even further, and it wasn't just from the alcohol. "Sure, let's."

As they headed for the lobby, he turned to her and said, "Do you like milkshakes?"

Back in the CEO Suite, Graham punched in the code and opened the safe. The glasses were untouched, so Cray must've drunk straight from the bottle. Classy. Maybe she didn't let the bottle touch her lips. Either way, she'd just been through hell, so it was excusable.

What really concerned him lay at the back. There it was, lying just as it had been the last time he saw it. Graham had never actually flipped through it, but he remembered one time when Spencer mentioned the notebook to him.

It's a bit sentimental, I know, but I like to keep it there. It's important to remember how things began, to memorialize the inception of the future, Niall had said.

Graham forgot all about it until he was downstairs, speaking with Special Agent Fraser. He realized Cray might accidentally stumble upon it and had raced back up. Giving her access to the safe had been a cavalier move, but he trusted her. And it wasn't like Niall needed the Macallan anymore. Still, he didn't want Catalyst getting out before tomorrow.

Everything had to go perfectly.

He took out the notebook and flipped through it, just out of curiosity. Christ, Niall's handwriting was bad. He only grasped the notes because he knew what they meant, could approximate the shorthand. Or at least what he thought was the shorthand.

Graham exhaled. Even if Cray had looked at this, she'd have no clue what the hell she was staring at.

He put the notebook back in the safe and closed the door, sealing it inside.

4:38 PM

They were lucky enough to get a parking spot down-town, less than a block from the restaurant. Fraser held the umbrella over them as they strolled along the sidewalk. Pedestrians passed in ponchos and rainwear.

At the intersection of Hamilton and Emerson, they stopped. The Palo Alto Creamery stood across the street, its sign glow-ing yellow in the early evening semidarkness. The pair made their way to the entrance.

Cray told him about the notebook in Spencer's safe and the diagram she'd seen. It sounded to Fraser like Level 5 auton-omy, but he couldn't be sure. And he had no clue what the shorthand meant.

They'd chatted amicably on the ride here. Cray wasn't a natural conversationalist, but she always found something light to keep the flow going. How did he like working for the FBI? What was it like living in the Bay Area? He normally hated small talk, but with Cray the talk never felt small.

She must make a terrifying manipulator, he thought. Charm was an underrated weapon.

This had been Reed's idea, relayed over the phone.

"Take her somewhere, get a drink, get food, whatever. If she's hiding something, coax it out of her. If she's not, she's still our best bet for catching this fucker. One psychopath helping us get another. Hell, I'll forgive her for Picturesque if she helps us bag Racer."

The Palo Alto Creamery was one of Fraser's favorite spots in town. As they headed inside, Cray took it all in while he folded the umbrella.

"Oh, I like this," she said.

A 1950s-style soda bar with a wraparound counter and red stools sat ahead. A clock positioned at the vertex read *EAT-ANDGETOUT* in place of numbers. There were plush leather booths to the left and tables with green leather seats to the right. It was warm and cozy in here, away from the rain.

The hostess came up to them, smiling. "For two?"

Fraser eyed the back right corner. "Can we sit over there?"

She turned around. "Sure. Right this way."

A moment later they were settled by the jukebox, which serenaded the room to the tune of "Only You" by The Platters. The song echoed softly around the space, the rhythm almost omnipresent.

Fraser sat with his back to the wall, Cray across from him. The hostess gave them some menus and left them to decide.

"I'm actually pretty hungry," she said, looking hers over. "I've been running on empty thanks to earlier."

He smiled. "I'm just getting a milkshake, but I highly recommend one. They mix them in metal cans, like back in the fifties. It's actually written into the lease contract. There are two Creameries in Palo Alto. The original one was the Peninsula, which had a second location here for decades. They still own the land and require this place to keep the fifties soda fountain—and to make milkshakes the old-fashioned way." He glanced around. "No matter how much Silicon Valley disrupts the world, it's nice that some things never change."

Cray was still staring at the menu. "It's a comforting thought."

Fraser couldn't tell if she actually agreed with him, or if she was just trying to keep his opinion of her favorable.

Fatigue pressed down on him. He was nervous about the case, about tomorrow. If Cray was right about that software

engineer Furman, at least four people were dead in this business so far. Maybe five depending on what happened to the
tow truck driver. It needed to end before there were more.

"Why do you think Racer is a psychopath?" he said, cutting to the chase.

She glanced up. "It was completely unnecessary to kill
Bailey if they were trying to murder me. They also could've
crashed the car at any time they liked. We were going over
a hundred miles per hour. But Racer had something else
planned. They wanted to savor killing me, after I'd escaped
their clutches twice before."

He raised an eyebrow. "So all psychopaths are sadists?"

Cray paused. "I'd imagine not, but I'm sure a lot of them are."

"You seem to know a lot about psychopathy."

She shrugged, smiled. "Not really. Just used to read a lot of
pop-psychology articles."

"I thought those were all pieces like 'Does your ex have a
personality disorder?' That type of thing."

"Well, a lot of people hate dating psychopaths." She went
back to looking at the menu. "I'm sure they love misdiagnos-
ing their asshole, neurotypical partners, stigmatizing people
who actually suffer from mental illness." There was just the
faintest trace of bitterness in her voice.

Fraser hesitated, decided on a tack. "I can't imagine a psychopath making a good dating partner. I mean, how could
you love someone who thinks only of themselves?"

Cray paused. "Most people only think of themselves.
That's not exclusive to the empathy challenged."

"Most people don't date others just to get something from
them."

She laughed. "Are you kidding me? People *only* date others
to get something from them, whether they realize it or not.
We don't date to make our *partners* happy, we do it because
it makes *us* happy. That's why people leave when they no
longer feel a spark."

"You've never gotten joy out of seeing someone you love
happy?"

"Of course I have. I like seeing them happy because it makes me happy. But eventually they bore me, and so I leave. It's not their fault. We just part ways. Everyone's like that. Once interest wanes, you don't stay for the other person. You leave them because they have no more use to you."

"That's a pretty cold view of dating, wouldn't you say?"

She shrugged. "I think it's realistic."

A waiter arrived. "What can I get started for you?"

Cray gave him a charming smile. "Hey. Umm, I was thinking I'd get a vanilla milkshake, a California Burger with sweet potato fries, and the Roast Turkey Dinner."

"Those are separate entrees." The waiter gave an awkward laugh.

She stared at him, still smiling. "I know."

There was a pause. Then the waiter laughed again and said, "Coming right up." He turned to Fraser. "And for yourself, sir?"

He shrugged. "Just a strawberry milkshake."

"Excellent choice." The waiter nodded and walked off.

Fraser raised an eyebrow. "You didn't strike me as the vanilla type."

"Don't worry. Ice cream's the only vanilla I like." She winked.

He laughed and shook his head. "So that's what you're waiting for? Someone who won't *bore* you?"

"No, I've met a couple. Got close to one... What I really want is someone who I can be honest with."

"Oh, really? And how honest are you with others? Usually?"

She grinned. "About as honest as we're being with each other."

Silence fell across the table.

"Look at us," Cray said, giving a cold smile. She stared into his eyes, not blinking. Her pupils dilated within their blue and amber irises. "Both pretending Reed hasn't talked to you yet about the Picturesque case. About my file."

Fraser found the will to break eye contact with her. He stared off at the neon sign above the entrance, reading *Fountain*

– *Lunch.* Hard to think having a soda fountain was a selling feature back in the day. He wondered what people would take for granted seventy years from now.

I don't know what you're talking about, he almost said. But what was the point in that?

"Maybe he did. But maybe I never liked Picturesque and I'm not too sad no one got caught for hacking them."

"That's not the only thing Reed told you, was it?"

"No," he said slowly. He looked back at her. She hadn't broken her stare. God, it was magnetic. He couldn't look away, not this time.

"You already know what I am, so there's no point trying to hide it." Cray looked almost sad.

"No, but *you're* hiding it. I know enough about psychopaths. You're displaying too much affect. This isn't the real you."

She smirked. "You don't want to see the real me. I've been told it's too unnerving."

"By whom?"

"My ex-girlfriend. Reed met her."

"Simone Tessier?"

Cray winced at the name. "Yeah, that's her."

"You tested the real you out on her, and she didn't like it, huh?"

"No." Cray grew angry. "She opened up to me about some things she had kept hidden from everyone else and encouraged me to do the same. I tried to warn her. I even gave her all that self-pitying B.S. of"—she mocked a melodramatic voice—"'*You won't like me if you know who I really am.*' But Simone *insisted.* And so I started dropping the affect. I was still attentive, I was still committed. But she said I was too cold, too robotic. The iciest person she'd ever met in Florida."

"And so that's why you split?"

"No, that's not why." She took a deep breath, looked down. "We split because she asked me if I loved her."

Fraser hesitated. "And what did you say?"

"I told her the truth. That people like me can't feel love, not like everyone else can. I told her that I cared about her, that I really enjoyed being with her. That I would be sad if anything bad happened to her. That life was easier—hell, more fun with her around. But I didn't feel an intense attachment for her. I can't feel anything like that, even if I try. And I have. I want to, because it sounds beautiful the way people talk about it. I told Simone that I loved her in my own way." Cray looked back up at him. "And for her, that wasn't good enough."

The waiter arrived with a tray, setting down two metal cans full of milkshakes and two sundae glasses. "Enjoy," he said.

"Thanks," Cray said, suddenly jovial. As soon as he walked away, her cold expression returned.

"I'm sorry."

"Don't be. Psychopaths don't have feelings, remember?" She gave a thin smile. "Don't worry, I probably deserve the perpetual ennui, given the things I've done over the years."

"I know you have feelings. They're just toned down, but you're not a robot. You're not like the things the Valley wants to replace us with. You're still human."

Cray scoffed. "You think tech's gonna take over the world, right? That we're trading our autonomy for automation? Well, the truth is most people never really *wanted* autonomy in the first place. They're always happy to sell their own agency if they think it'll make life easier."

"That's an over-simplification," he said. "The companies here have coaxed that autonomy out of the rest of us, convincing us we need their latest toys, peer pressuring everyone into joining their social networks. They're playing society for suckers and winning."

"Maybe that's just because society *is* a bunch of suckers. Nobody held them at gunpoint and told them to get on Instagram."

"No, but there have been anti-competitive practices, groupthink, a constant push forward with no regard to where we're *actually* going to end up. They think if they just snap their fingers, the world will let them build the technocracy of their dreams."

"Yeah, but the thing is…even if we stopped buying their products, it wouldn't change who people are. Social media didn't *make* you waste hours scrolling through photos of friends pretending to be happy. Dating apps didn't *make* you ghost your matches or cancel dates at the last minute. Tech didn't *make* you harass people for offensive posts, just so you could convince yourself you're a good person. *You* did all of that. Silicon Valley gave you the gasoline and the lighter, but you set it all ablaze. You and everyone else."

"But these companies *knew* what they were doing and they fanned the flames anyway."

"Stop giving the Valley so much credit. You've seen the hubris at Asimov. These people aren't evil, they're just moronically arrogant. They think the petrol is sunshine fuel and the lighter sparks rainbows. To an outsider, what they are is obvious, but Silicon Valley is convinced it knows the truth."

"So why don't they take responsibility? Why aren't they held accountable?"

"They should be," Cray said. "Along with everyone else. But that won't happen because of human nature. It's not just psychopaths. I've seen it everywhere, with almost everyone. People *hate* taking responsibility. I know *I* do. It's painful to admit you're wrong. It took a lot of therapy for me to realize just how much harm I'd done to others. I still don't feel guilt for it, because I can't, but I *know* what I did was terrible. I cheated on partners, I manipulated people for fun, I hacked into my teacher's computer and leaked his porn stash to the district website…"

Fraser raised his eyebrows.

Cray poured her milkshake into the sundae glass. "He was an asshole. I kept asking too many questions, so he hated me. Specifically graded me harsher than the others. So I made sure to get back at him." She sipped her drink. "Holy shit, this is amazing."

"It is." He nodded, taking a sip straight from the metal can. The rim was ice cold.

"People blamed me for everything, even though I have an excuse. I have a mental condition. It didn't affect my academics, but it sure fucked up my emotions." She took another sip, a bigger one. "And yet that doesn't give *me* a free pass. If people find out what I am, I'm a monster to them. Everything I do is suspect. Everything I do is evil. So I have to lie to everyone and pretend to be someone I'm not just so they feel comfortable.

"But *them*? What do they have to blame when they treat other people like shit? They always find something, no matter how far they have to dig. Believe me, I'd *love* to make excuses. It's so much easier." She tilted her head down, but kept her eyes locked on him. "But, as my psychiatrist pointed out, that wouldn't be very high functioning of me."

Fraser sat there for a moment, sipping his milkshake and pondering. "I'm not saying people should make excuses for you, Ms. Cray—"

"Izzy," she said, staring directly at him. "My friends call me Izzy."

Sadness fell across his face. "I'm sorry few have given you the sympathy you deserve."

Cray looked stunned. She didn't say anything for a moment, lost in thought. Then she burst out laughing.

"Sympathy? What the hell have I done to deserve sympathy?"

It was getting increasingly dark outside. The waiter came with two plates, one with a Thanksgiving-style meal and the other with a burger and French fries. Fraser couldn't imagine eating that much in one go, not even when he'd been in high school. But she dug right in, keeping her eyes narrowed on him, waiting for his reply.

"Well, you *do* have an actual condition that affects your emotions. No one should expect you to be perfectly empathetic all the time. Calling you cold is pointless, and inaccurate. You're not a reptile. You still have feelings, they're just subdued. But if you actually try to be better, if you actually hold yourself accountable, they shouldn't hold it against you."

"Even if I'm better now, I've been a total asshole in the past. To friends, partners..." She winced. "Haven't been too good to my parents and siblings, either."

"Is it too late to fix that?"

She thought for a moment. "I haven't seen my family for three years, since moving out to California."

"Have you spoken to them since?"

"Occasionally. My mom asks me to call her once in a while, just so she knows I'm still alive."

He looked down, stirring his milkshake with the straw. "Well, that's something."

Cray studied him for a moment. "You're not on good terms with yours, are you?"

Fraser shrugged, looking up at her. "I was a caboose baby, the distant third child. Kinda felt like they didn't really want me sometimes."

"What do your siblings do?"

"Brother's in Hawaii, works in the family business. Sister's a Hollywood producer. Does pretty well at it, actually. You've probably seen her name in credits and not even realized it."

"Do you get along with them?"

He brightened. "Oh yeah, both of them are great. It's just the age difference was a bit jarring growing up. But they were always kind to me. Sometimes I feel my sister raised me more than my mother did."

Cray gave a weak smile. "I'm the oldest in my family. But I bullied them a little bit." She paused. "Okay, maybe more than a little bit."

"Like what?"

"Stole their Halloween candy, slammed the door in their face, that kind of thing."

"That doesn't sound…too egregious."

She looked down at her food. "One time when I was in high school, my brother Iain—he's the youngest, must've been like seven at the time—stole my phone. I grabbed his goldfish out of its tank. Dangled it above my mouth and threatened to eat it if he didn't give me the phone back. Iain loved that little thing, handed it over right away."

"And what did you do with the fish?"

She gave an embarrassed smile. "I didn't feel it swimming around, but I got a bit of an upset stomach."

He shook his head. "Who hurt you?"

Cray laughed. "No one. That's the worst part. Nothing to blame but genetic mutation. And, of course," she sighed, "myself."

"And do you?" He looked at her. "Honestly."

She paused, stared down again. "I don't think I am who I was back then. I used to be needlessly cruel—careless, really. I didn't mind hurting other people. It never bothered me. But I didn't know why I was like that. Ever since I got diagnosed, I've been better about controlling my actions. But it's not just about wearing masks. Every day I get up and have to simulate empathy. It comes so naturally to most people, but it's exhausting for me. For every little interaction I have to manually logic through both my behavior and the other person's. It's gotten easier over time, but it's still a deliberate process."

Fraser looked off at the soda bar counter, watching the cooks prepare meals through the ordering window. "I thought psychopaths hate revealing their true feelings. Why are you telling all this to a federal agent?" He laughed, turning back to her.

Cray stared at him with an emotionless expression, unblinking. Her voice suddenly lacked its friendly charm. It sounded monotonous. "When you spend most of your life telling lies, truth seems forbidden. I've come to appreciate it. And you already know what I am. There's no point hiding it. It gives me more of a rush, this way. I really shouldn't be telling you this. But I am. Getting myself into trouble is the only thing that makes me feel alive, though I hate it as soon as I'm in too deep."

Simone had been right. It *was* unsettling. And yet Fraser was somehow glad she'd showed this side of herself, a part of who she really was.

"I'd say we're all in pretty deep at this point. Wouldn't you?"

"Yes," she said, keeping her mask down. She looked tired but her eyes didn't plead. They were as cold and calculating as ever. "I want to kill this fucker like I've never wanted anything before. I don't want them to win. I don't want anyone else to get hurt. I want to do something good and enjoy it."

"I just watched a man get crushed in half today." Fraser swallowed, his mouth suddenly dry, trying to push the image out of his mind. He felt drained, like he wanted to lie down and sleep. "I saw Spencer's daughter devastated by his loss. I saw NOC screens with 300,000 cars ripe for hacking. It's not a want at this point. I *need* to stop Racer. If you really think they're a psychopath, then I can't solve this without you. You're my secret weapon, Izzy. You can put yourself into the killer's mind better than anyone else on the task force. I need you to help Reed and I figure out who's behind this. And fast."

She looked right into his eyes again, her own devoid of emotion. "It's Catalyst, that's the key. We figure out what it is before the keynote, we understand why someone's doing all this."

Fraser's phone buzzed in his pocket. "I intend to. Just one sec." He drew out the device. There was a new message from Reed:

Call me ASAP.

Fraser did so, bringing the device to his ear.

Reed answered quickly. "How soon can you be in South San Jose?"

He looked for the waiter. Saw him, started flagging him down. "We're at the Creamery on Emerson. Leaving now. What's going on?"

Cray started eating faster as the waiter came over.

"It's Racer," Reed said on the line. "We found him."

5:41 PM

It was a quiet night on the cul-de-sac. There had been no rain today, which he found baffling. He'd lived here for years now, yet still found it crazy when parts of the Bay got drenched while others stayed dry, just because of the rain shadow.

Up ahead, houses waited with lights on in their windows. Clouds drifted above, but they were scattered. Reed caught his first sight of sky all week. He could even make out a few stars.

They were in a middle-class neighborhood just west of Almaden Lake. From the map, Reed knew this cul-de-sac backed onto a fence, and beyond it, the road. Cop cars with lights off waited on the other side, in case the suspect made a break for it.

In the end, arrogance had been Racer's downfall. The sick fuck had been so preoccupied playing real life *Grand Theft Auto*, he'd never considered Cray might regain control and obtain his IP address. Hadn't even bothered to hide it behind a chain of VPNs. He probably thought his perfect little virus would take care of things once the car crashed, sending an update that wiped the infected software—assuming there would've been anything salvageable from the wreck.

The IP address led them to this house in South San Jose.

It belonged to one Kevin Reynolds. Age thirty-five, recently divorced, and owed taxes to the IRS. A few months before he and his wife separated, he'd been put on a 5150 during a domestic disturbance. He was involuntarily detained for seventy-two hours and stripped of gun rights for five years.

Evidently, he'd found other ways of killing people.

With Bailey's death and the highly public incident on 280, the San Francisco Field Office had thrown its full weight behind the case, which had remained in the headlines throughout the week. There were competing op-eds about autonomous vehicles and their vulnerability, scores of Reddit discussions debating how this would affect driverless acceptance. Reed's superiors wanted this wrapped up, stat. And they were prepared to give him whatever he needed to make that happen.

It had taken only a few minutes to dredge up what they knew about the suspect, once they traced the IP address to his house. Reed had the judge on his phone in a flash, obtaining an arrest warrant.

Then he'd hauled ass from Palo Alto with a SWAT team from the Field Office's Critical Incident Response Group. They'd called ahead to San Jose PD and requested urgent cooperation.

Normally, Reed would've liked more planning, more time to prepare. But he didn't want this piece of shit to slip away. He was worried Reynolds had already packed his bags by now, but there were still lights on in the house and a luxury sedan parked in the driveway, a Lucid Air. Given this man was divorced and supposedly lived alone, that was most likely his only car.

Maybe he could've fled on foot, but they'd find out soon enough. At that point, they'd tear the house apart looking for usable evidence.

Reed stared down the cul-de-sac from the end of the street. Then he turned and headed to the right, where a van waited around the corner. In the back, he found FBI Special Agent Ellis talking with the SWAT team commander, Bryant. Ellis was a stout white man with a moustache, Bryant a tall black woman with piercing eyes. They turned to him as he entered.

"How dangerous do we think this guy is?" Ellis said. "I mean, honestly. Just because he's good behind a keyboard doesn't mean he's gonna have a nuclear arsenal in there."

"I just want this to go as smoothly as possible," Reed said. "I'm not underestimating this guy, but I also want things done by the book. If he doesn't answer the door, we go in, we take him alive."

"Unless he shoots first," Bryant said.

"Right. Let's hope it doesn't come to that." Though secretly, after what happened to Bailey, he did.

There was a knock on the van door. Reed turned around and opened it. Fraser stood there, and he'd brought Cray with him.

Reed exhaled. He'd have preferred that she wasn't here, but after all she'd been through this week, he supposed she'd earned it. They all wanted this to be over.

"Glad you made it, Will." He gave a nod of recognition to Cray, but said nothing to her, turning back to the monitors instead. The SWAT team's feeds were transmitted here from their bodycams. They were currently seated in the back of the SWAT truck, parked across from them on the other corner of the cul-de-sac. Both the truck and van had police cars parked behind them for back-up. The authorities were taking no chances.

"We're really sure this is the guy?" Cray said.

Reed spun around, giving her a disapproving look. He'd told Fraser everything he knew over the phone, just before he left the Palo Alto Residence Agency. Fraser must've told Cray on the way here.

"We're not *sure*. He's just the prime suspect. But once we get in there, we'll find out." He returned his attention to the monitors.

But Cray pressed on. "It just...seems a little convenient, don't you think? This person is clearly a skilled hacker. We have evidence of that. Yet he didn't bother to hide his IP address behind even one VPN?"

Fraser didn't say anything, but he nodded in silent agreement.

"He didn't think he was gonna get caught," Reed growled, annoyed with both of them. "Like you said, the computer systems at Asimov always send a fresh update to wipe the virus off the cars—if there's anything left of them once Racer's finished. Then it deletes the log of the update in Telemetry. This guy thought he was safe. He didn't count on you overcoming his breach while kidnapping you. We couldn't have done this without you, Ms. Cray. You should be proud of yourself."

He looked back at the screens again, but deep down he knew she had a point. *I just want this to be over*, he thought, pushing the image of Bailey's death out of his head. *Just let this be the guy. Let's end it now.*

"Special Agent Ellis, hand me that Kevlar vest. And Commander Bryant, get your team ready. We're going in."

They made their way down the street in diamond formation, a fall breeze sifting through the air. When they reached the house at the very end of the cul-de-sac, they branched out. Bryant directed two to scope out the windows on each side while she, Reed, Fraser, and three others made their way up the driveway.

Fraser was tense, his entire body on edge. He tightly gripped his Sig Sauer P226, one of the Bureau's standard-issue handguns. This was only his second real raid. Back in the Academy, he'd scored highly in training exercises and on marksmanship, but these types of situations got him anxious. He was still recuperating from the 280 pursuit earlier, even if this beat doing paperwork.

The SWAT officers reached the front door. Fraser crouched off to the left, by the Lucid parked in the driveway. Bryant nodded to Reed and he made his way up to the entrance, drawing both his badge and the warrant that had been faxed to him.

Fraser took a deep breath, glancing at the SWAT officers. They wore full-body charcoal camo with the letters FBI stenciled on their armored vests. Their helmets featured sleek tactical visors with augmented reality heads-up displays. Fraser and Reed didn't have bodycams on, but the others were transmitting their feeds back to the van where Cray and Agent Ellis were watching.

Fraser couldn't get their conversation at the Creamery out of his head. He still didn't know what to make of Cray. She was deeply unsettling, and yet part of him found her oddly bewitching. He pushed those thoughts out of his mind, returning to the raid.

Reed rang the doorbell, then waited.

He let roughly fifteen seconds pass without an answer, then rang again, this time twice.

There were lights on in the windows, but the blinds were closed. It was a one-story house with an attached two-car garage and solar panels on the roof.

Bryant's voice came over the comm in his ear. "Garcia, anything on the north side?"

"Lights on in the windows, but no visual. Blinds are closed. Moving around to the rear."

"Taylor, south side report?"

"Nothing here either."

Bryant nodded to Reed, who stepped back. She got down on her knee and drew out a cable from a device on her wrist, a small camera attached at the end. She slid it under the door and stared at something on her visor, no doubt watching the feed.

"It's pretty dark in there. Switching to night vision." She pressed something on the side of her helmet. "Looks clear. Let's breach."

She pulled the cable back under the door, returning the camera to its wrist slot. The other SWAT officers drew nearer.

Fraser moved around behind Reed, keeping his Sig Sauer at the ready. Reed did the same.

Bryant kicked in the door shouting, *"FBI!"*

Four SWAT officers entered the foyer at once, crouching and aiming in different directions, making the sure the entire area was clear.

"Move," Bryant said, and they continued into the house. Reed and Fraser followed up the rear.

Inside, there were barely any lights on. An open space stretched across the length of the house, with a lamp on at the back. The kitchen took up the back corner and a sitting room with sofas and a TV were set up to the right. To the left was a billiard table and some bookshelves—and a corridor leading to the bedrooms, bright illumination spilling out across the tile floor. Bryant took point, leading the three other SWAT officers toward the source. The others were still outside, maintaining a perimeter.

Fraser and Reed followed them as the corridor hung a right. There were several bedrooms and bathrooms with doors open and lights off. The team systematically checked them one by one, aiming with flashlights attached to their machine guns. Fraser glimpsed an office with an array of curved monitors, though the screens were dark, a desktop PC powered down beneath the desk. Back in the hall, LEDs shone down from the ceiling, bathing everything in white light.

Soon the master bedroom was the only place left unchecked.

The door sat ajar at the end of the hall. Bryant and one of the other officers took cover on either side, nodded to each other.

Then they barged in, shining their flashlights around the room while the other two officers covered them from behind.

"Clear," Bryant said.

At the far end of the darkened bedroom was a closed door, light shining from the top and bottom.

"FBI! Come out with your hands up!"

There was no response.

Fraser and Reed entered the room. One officer checked the closet, another under the bed. Bryant and the fourth officer closed in on the bathroom door.

"Last chance to come out!"

Silence.

Fraser's heart accelerated as Bryant and the officer flanked the door. Here it was, the moment of truth. He looked to Reed.

He appeared equally tense.

Fraser thought of the FBI van at the end of the cul-de-sac, where Cray and Agent Ellis were no doubt staring at screens with the same anticipation. He could picture Cray leaning forward, watching with those cold, calculating eyes.

Bryant smashed the door open.

Immediately, bright light flooded the room and Fraser squinted, trying to get a better look inside. He saw the sink and the mirror, but no one was visible from this angle. Bryant and the other officer disappeared inside. Evidently the master bathroom was quite large.

There were no gunshots. No sound of a struggle.

Bryant's voice crackled on the line. "Oh, *hell*. Reed, you better come see this."

He glanced at Fraser, nodded. Then he entered the bathroom. "Well, would you look at that...," he said over the comm.

Fraser headed inside next, still holding his pistol at the ready. It was pointless though. As he stepped through the doorway, he knew he wouldn't need it.

His eyes adjusted as he took in the scene.

To the left by the shower, a man in his mid-thirties sat slumped on a toilet. His arms dangled limp at his sides, a pistol lying on the tile floor. A bullet had gone through the bottom of his jaw and out the top of his head, blowing blood and cranial matter all over the wall.

At the edge of the sink counter closest to him was an open three-ring binder with a thick sheaf of paper resting inside it. Fraser stepped closer so he could better read the title on the cover page.

Anti-Automata: A Manifesto.

"I'm sorry, miss. Nobody's allowed back here."

Cray stood with straight posture, trying to look as official as possible in her charcoal turtleneck and jeans. "I have special dispensation from Special Agent Fraser. He's standing right over there."

The cop turned around. Fraser was talking to Reed on the front lawn as the Evidence Response Team carried boxes out the front door. The entire lot had been fenced off with crime scene tape. The cop cars behind the back fence had pulled onto the cul-de-sac along with the ERT van. Residents up and down the street stood on their front lawns or stared out windows, trying to see what was going on.

It was a circus. Cray figured they didn't have long before local news showed up.

Fraser turned and spotted her. She gave a friendly smile and a wave. He nodded to the cop, who sighed and turned around, lifting the tape for her. "Alright, come on through."

"Thanks." She ducked under and continued along, making a beeline for the FBI agents.

Once the SWAT team had secured the house, Special Agent Ellis had left her alone in the back of the van making small talk to a technician. She'd watched the whole raid unfold without a comm to listen to, only hearing Special Agent Ellis make the occasional comment after they found the body. The driver's license in his wallet, sitting on a dresser in the master bedroom, confirmed the dead man was Kevin Reynolds.

Cray had heard Ellis say something about a "manifesto," which she presumed was the document she'd seen Fraser and Reed flipping through via Bryant's feed. She desperately wanted to know what it said—and what the hell was going on.

None of this made any sense. How was Racer just some random guy in San Jose? Had he ever even *met* Spencer?

Fraser turned as she approached. "Well, it seems to be over."

"What was in the manifesto?"

Reed sighed. Both he and Fraser looked exhausted. "It was a big tirade on how automation is ruining society. First it came for the truckers, now it's coming for the cab drivers and valets. Next, we'll all be slaves to Skynet. That kind of thing."

"Maniacs are prone to logical leaps. But why did he care? Did *he* lose his job to a self-driving car?"

"Unclear. Reynolds was a coder who lost money in a failed startup. His assets were whittling away, but he spent a lot of time blogging about how autonomous cars would destroy civilization."

Cray scoffed. "Why is it every time there's a new technology, people think it's the end of the world? The original car wiped out horse-drawn carriages, but it created an entire new industry that more than offset the losses. Autonomous cars will do the same."

Fraser shrugged. "Ignorance, but they do have a point. If automation happens too quickly, the economy won't be able to adapt to it. This Reynolds guy seemed to think Niall Spencer was taking us too far, too fast. Wanted to kill him before his big product launch so people would turn away from driverless cars."

"But then why hire Quinn and Sova? Why try to kill me if he wasn't distracting us from something else, something planned for tomorrow? What about the dead software engineer, Furman—?"

"Who we don't know for sure was murdered. That could be completely unrelated," Reed said.

Cray grew exasperated. "Yeah, but *still*. Doesn't this seem too easy, like it's what Racer *wants* us to think?"

"Racer is dead." Reed gave her a hard stare. "He was a nutjob. Probably did a little hacking here and there over the years, then turned to it full time once he didn't have a job or a wife. Lots of time to code a polymorphic virus. Lots of ways to scheme a path into Asimov's network—"

"We still don't know how the Update subnet was breached—"

"No," he said. "But we'll find out. The exciting part of the job is over. Now we'll have to pick through all the evidence, go through his computer, piece it all together. It'll take a while, but eventually we'll know—or, at the very least, have most of it figured out. But it doesn't really matter anymore, because it's over. He's dead. The danger is gone." He took out his phone. "Graham can rest easy tonight. He doesn't have to worry about cyberterrorism spoiling his little keynote."

Reed walked off, bringing the device to his ear. The conversation was finished.

She turned to Fraser, looking for support. "Come on, you can't actually believe it's over. Reynolds is a fucking patsy, and you know it."

His tired eyes met hers. "I don't know what to say. The evidence—"

"Is a forgery. Racer wants us to lower our guard for tomorrow. We can't stop the investigation now. They're still out there. This is just another distraction."

He looked off toward Reed, who was talking on the phone. After a few moments, he said, "Sorry, Izzy. I'm still processing everything. I don't know what's going to happen. I'll get an officer to escort you back to your hotel. We can swing by my car to get your leftovers from the Creamery."

She stood there, stunned. Her stomach tightened and her heart pounded faster, heat rushing to her face.

Something was very wrong here. It just didn't compute.

Fraser led her toward the officer who had let her under the crime scene tape. As they approached, she was struck by a terrible thought.

I never really escaped the killer today, hacking that car. It was all an illusion. Me, Fraser, Reed, Asimov—Racer's got us exactly where they want us.

11:08 PM

S ova watched the tip of the e-cig glow as he inhaled, sweet nicotine vapor filling his lungs.

A streetlamp spilled in through the gap in the curtains, light bisecting both the bed and his abdomen. He held his cigarette to the light and glanced over it absentmindedly.

Today had been a good day, and he felt relaxed. Racer would be pleased with him this time, though they hadn't contacted him yet. But that was okay. Right now, he had enough gratification from the TV screen across the darkened room, the only light inside.

"...other news, the FBI and San Jose police conducted a raid on the residence of Kevin Reynolds near Almaden Lake earlier this evening, where they discovered he had taken his own life before they arrived. The authorities were seeking to bring Mr. Reynolds into custody as a suspect in the murder of Niall Spencer and a related breach of Asimov Automotive corporate computers. The company is set to unveil a new project tomorrow evening at the San Francisco Auto Show, and has pressed on with the event despite Spencer's death and the possibility that other Asimov vehicles may be at risk.

"Answering the intense scrutiny her company has come under for this move, COO Casey Kaplan released a statement earlier today arguing that cancelling the keynote would only further the murderer's goals. Well, tonight, she appears to be vindicated. While the FBI and San Jose police are not sharing any details about Mr. Reynolds, KPTV has discovered that he maintained a blog for the last several years decrying the rise of automation in America—specifically the rise of driverless vehicles on our roads. It is unknown at this time if the authorities are investigating Spencer's murder as an act of politically-motivated cyberterrorism…"

His phone buzzed. Sova grabbed it off the nightstand, smiled as he read the messages.

Hook, line, and sinker. Tomorrow the real fun begins.

It's showtime.

FRIDAY

9:26 AM

Cray woke up to the sound of knocking on her door.

She groaned, burying her face in the pillow. She'd gone to bed early but took forever to doze off, waking up several times through the night. Her eyelids were heavy, and she just wanted to snooze. The bed was soft and comfy, inviting her back to sleep. She closed her eyes and breathed out, feeling tension flow from her shoulders, her mind floating away—

More knocking. "Izzy, it's me." Fraser's voice.

She opened her eyes again.

"I have food."

Damn you.

She kicked off the covers and climbed out of bed. "Just a second." She dashed over to her suitcase and fumbled through it, throwing on a T-shirt and jeans.

Cray's hair was still a mess when she answered the door, rubbing her eyes. He stood there in the hallway, already looking wide awake in his suit. The police officer guarding her room stood off to the side.

"Hey, good morning," she said, giving a tired grin. Her eyes darted to what was in his hand—a bag of Chick-fil-A—and widened. "You are officially my favorite person."

"I try." He held out the bag. "May I come in?"

"Absolutely." Cray took it and turned around, leading him

inside. She sat on the bed and tore the bag open. He'd gotten two chicken biscuit sandwiches with hash browns and an orange juice for her. She took out the bottle and twisted off the cap.

"Thought it would remind you of Florida," he said, leaning against the dresser beneath the TV.

Cray smiled at him, took a glug, and set it down. Then she unwrapped one of the biscuits and began devouring it.

"You might want to save the second one for the car. We've got a long drive."

She covered her mouth. "To where?"

"Reed is filing paperwork today, but he's allowing me to pursue one final lead, just for my own peace of mind."

She swallowed. "So you think I'm right? Racer set Reynolds up?"

"Yes," he said. "But everyone else wants this to be over. Levine is on leave after Bailey's death. It's officially the Monterey Sheriff's investigation, but they've said case closed after last night. Asimov is barreling on with the event this evening. Reed and I will be at the Auto Show, but in an unofficial capacity. You're the only other person who wants to keep investigating, Izzy. So, if we're gonna solve this thing, I need you to be my partner."

Cray ate the last bite of her biscuit, wiping crumbs from her mouth as she stood up. She stared right at him as a grin broke across her face, not needing a mirror to know that it reached her eyes.

"Well in that case, we better get going."

11:14 AM

The sky was overcast, but there was no rain as the sedan cruised south along CA-1, approaching the Monterey Peninsula.

"Do you have anything else besides eighties music?"

Fraser looked like he'd been slapped. "What more do you need?"

They'd been playing music from his collection the whole ride down. Depeche Mode's "Never Let Me Down Again" blared from the car stereo, which he'd modified to install a CD player.

She sat up straighter in the passenger seat and shot him a look. "I don't know, but maybe *something* from the past four decades?"

"Alright," he said, watching the road as he grinned. "What do psychopaths listen to, anyway?"

Cray paused, thinking. "EDM, mostly. But I also like trance-pop, stuff like Tame Impala."

"Is that an animal?"

She shook her head, laughing. "In my goth phase, I listened to a lot of industrial music. Cliché, I know. 'Every Day Is Halloween' was my go-to track for a while."

"That's an eighties song."

She brushed hair out of her face and smirked. "Okay, you got me. I like eighties music."

"There," he teased. "Now we can be friends."

Cray rolled her eyes.

The road took them inland and curved south toward Carmel-by-the-Sea. Continuing past it, they eventually reached Ribera Rd and Fraser hung a right. The street of multimillion-dollar homes took them west, then looped around and doubled back along a line of coastal estates.

At the gate to the residence, Fraser rolled down his window and pressed the intercom.

"Come on in." Cray recognized the voice of Tatum Leigh Spencer.

The gate opened and they drove down and around a bend, coming into an open area with a mansion by the shore.

On the way here from San Jose, Fraser had filled her in on everything he knew, including details from the first time he came here and his chat with Lucas Declan. In turn, she'd told him things various parties had said throughout the week along with observations she'd made. Once they felt they were both up to the same speed on the investigation, he finally explained why they were heading to Carmel.

Fraser parked the Crown Victoria and they climbed out. A breeze blew by, carrying a salt spray from the sea. The air was brisk out here and Cray rubbed her arms for warmth. She'd thought about grabbing a jacket before they left, but decided against it.

"You cold?" Fraser asked, concerned.

"I'll be fine." She'd only be out here a moment anyway.

They strode across the gravel drive to the front door. Before they even reached it, the entrance swung inward. Tatum stood there in casual attire.

"Thank you for having us, Mrs. Spencer," Fraser said. "I'm sorry to trouble you again."

She shook her head, smiled weakly. "Anything to help. It's so bizarre, hearing that a complete stranger took the life of someone you love. I guess it's an answer, but I still have so many questions."

He looked to Cray, then back at Tatum. "So do we, Mrs. Spencer. And we aim to answer some of them for you."

She led them inside and then up the stairs to the second floor. When they got to the office at the end of the hall, they found Kayla waiting inside, looking over her father's desk. She glanced up as they came in.

"Is that the one over there?" Fraser asked, pointing to a poster to the left of the ocean view window.

Kayla nodded. "That's it."

He walked across the room to the artwork, stopping to examine it. Cray walked around behind him to do the same.

It depicted a futuristic metropolis. Sleek skyscrapers stood tall across the landscape, lush greenery trailing down their sides and along streets. Solar panels were everywhere. Windmills loomed on distant mountainsides. Ground vehicles looked like two-seater pods, maneuvering alongside light-rail transit. It was an impressively detailed work. Maybe Spencer kept it here as his inspiration, the thing he got up every morning and told himself he was working toward.

At first glance, it seemed to be nothing more than paper stuck to the wall, like the kind of posters Cray had had in her college dorm room.

Then Fraser put his palm in the center and pushed.

There was a *click*. He stepped back as a door—concealed just behind the poster's edges—swung outward, revealing a safe behind.

<••>

"She was staring at something last time," Fraser had explained in the car. "Looking past me and Quinn at something on the back wall. She looked confused for a moment, hesitant, like maybe she wanted to tell us something. But she wasn't sure, so she kept her mouth shut.

"But then yesterday, you told me about Spencer's secret office safe at Asimov. And I wondered if he had something similar back home. Maybe Kayla had seen him opening it one time, or maybe closing it. Maybe she just suspected something was there. And given the stunt she pulled at Stanford, it seems like she really wants to find out who killed her father. So maybe, she might want to tell us after all now, if there really was something there."

He'd paused for a moment, changing lanes. "I called her stepmother this morning. Can't rule her out yet, but she'll want to be seen as cooperative whether she's behind this or not. I asked her if she knew of any hidden safes in Spencer's office. She said no. I asked if Kayla might know anything. She seemed incredulous but put Kayla on anyway." He glanced at Cray. "And guess what Kayla said?"

It looked identical to the one in the CEO Suite, Cray noted. And she bet it had the same code too. Most people didn't diversify their passwords very much.

"I have no clue how to open it, though," Kayla said, folding her arms across her chest. She seemed anxious.

Cray turned around. "Six digits. It's your birthday."

"My...? How do you...?" At that moment, Kayla broke, tears sprouting from her eyes. She caught herself, wiping her cheeks and stifling a sob. "I'm sorry," she said, embarrassed.

"Don't be," Cray said softly.

Tatum looked tense back by the door. She came over to her stepdaughter and began rubbing her shoulder. Kayla hid a scowl from her.

It must be awful, Cray thought, *losing a loved one. Especially if you actually loved them.* That was the price of empathy, she supposed. High risk, high reward. She didn't wish for a cure to her condition, given how much it had shaped who she was, but Cray never shied away from large risks. What must it be like to feel something that intense—happy or sad?

"May 12, 2012," Kayla said, looking at the floor.

Fraser punched it in. The door opened with a hiss.

Cray stepped closer, narrowing her eyes. Inside was a small, slim laptop. Fraser took it out and laid it on the desk. All four of them gathered around.

They each looked exhausted. Fraser's relaxed attitude from the trip down here had evaporated. Seeing the victim's family sobered whatever humor he had.

Reading the others, Cray determined that the mood in the room was of fatigue and anxiousness—which was exactly how she felt, too. A faint sense of kinship stirred within her, a rare feeling.

"Now how are we gonna access it?" she said.

Fraser looked at Cray and sighed. He gave her a sad smile. "That's where you come in."

11:36 AM

Reed stared out his office window at the rain.

He hated November. The Bay Area was beautiful in spring and summer, but the rainy season could be downright depressing. Still, it rarely—if ever—snowed here, and after several years in the Northeast he'd gladly take wet sidewalks over icy ones.

Sighing, he turned back to his computer and the report on his screen. He still hadn't even gotten one page done this morning. Reed massaged his temples, breathed in and out.

Though he'd only been put on the case Tuesday morning and Reynolds's body was discovered Thursday night, those three days had felt like three weeks. At this point, he was just thankful it was over.

Now came the boring part.

SVRCFL technicians were analyzing Reynolds's computer and the data they'd taken from Asimov's servers. He was sure they'd find similar polymorphic code on the perp's computer and that would be that. Case closed.

Though they still didn't know *how* he'd gotten into the Update servers in the first place. He kept thinking about Cray's theory. Maybe Reynolds had hired that Furman engineer after all, got him to sneak into Update and infect the computers using a flashdrive or something. He'd contacted

Asimov this morning about the work Cray did yesterday, going through the NOC security footage. She'd gotten stuck in Acheson's car before she could see the results, but when Reed called—just to be thorough—they'd put CSO Johnson on the line. He had reassured Reed that Furman's face never appeared once in the NOC in the last six months.

But maybe the engineer hid his face from the cameras, figured out their location and managed to get across the NOC without triggering the facial recognition software. It would take forever to manually go through those hours and hours of footage, but there might be proof buried somewhere in there. Might be.

But if that was true, why not hire someone who actually worked Update in the first place? If Racer had hired a Catalyst engineer to infect Update, surely they would've infected Catalyst too at that point, right?

If Furman had been killed to cover up his involvement, then a Catalyst breach was most likely the role he'd played. But there was no proof he'd been involved with Racer. None at all. It was all just Cray's conjecture.

There had to be another way Reynolds got into the Update Department. Even if he'd hired Furman, it *was* highly improbable that Furman had been the one to get the virus in there.

Okay smart guy, then how did he do it?

Reed sat there, lost in thought. Then he shook his head and took a sip of water. Surely, there would be some explanation in the dead man's computer. A phishing email sent to someone else in the company, who sent some internal memo to someone else, who inadvertently transported a flashdrive or external hard disk into the Update NOC with the virus on it. Something like that.

Still, he didn't like it. Something felt wrong.

Reed hated grueling cases, but he hated getting played even more.

Doesn't this seem too easy, like it's what Racer wants us to think? Cray had said last night.

It did, but he didn't want to believe her. There was no evidence. It was paranoia.

Reed leaned back in his chair, thinking. He went back through everything he'd learned this week about Niall Spencer, about Asimov Automotive. He thought of an angle, a reason.

After a while, his mind zeroed in on something Declan had said to Fraser. His junior partner had shown Reed his notes and given a full run down of their meeting, just as he had when he and Quinn interviewed Spencer's wife.

Something about the stocks, the Asimov stocks rebounding after the CEO's death. All because of Friday. Fraser had written a direct quote from Declan in his notes:

Not even his own death could derail the hype train.

The stocks were up, but if tonight went south, they would certainly crash again.

Reed leaned forward, pulling up a browser on his laptop. It was time to look into the short selling market for Asimov Automotive.

11:37 AM

Cray examined the laptop. It was a thirteen-inch Ultra-book, several years old. A sticker with the Linux penguin mascot Tux was slapped on the bottom right corner, below the numeric keypad. These machines usually came with Windows, but evidently Spencer had configured his to run one of the Linux operating systems. Or maybe it was a dual boot.

She thought for a moment, drumming her fingers on the desk.

"Are you gonna try and crack his password?" Kayla said. A look of expectation rested on her face.

Cray shook her head. "Don't need to. Hacking is a lot harder over the Internet. Once you have physical access to a device, it's pretty much yours for the taking."

She hit the power button on the side. Some form of Linux began booting up—looking like a Red Hat derivative—with no option to select a Windows operating system. Not that that would've made much difference. She'd hacked just about every OS at one time or another, some of them just to train herself.

A black-and-white grub screen loaded, and she tapped the E key on Advanced options, then went to edit the kernel. She added a "1" to the end of each line of code, which would force the computer to boot in single-user mode. When she was finished, she exited out of the kernel editor and tapped the B key to boot.

New lines of text appeared. To the right of [root@local-host/]# she typed passwd and hit Enter.

The computer displayed a prompt reading: Enter new UNIX password.

Cray now could create her own root password for the system, which would give her access to everything on the computer. She chose something simple, since this wasn't hers.

Catalyst

She retyped it to confirm, then hit Enter.

passwd: All authentication tokens updated successfully

Now Cray rebooted the system and logged in normally this time, using *Catalyst* as the password. The Desktop appeared with an array of files and programs.

Kayla looked over her shoulder. "You're in already?"

Cray nodded. "Don't ever leave your laptop lying around. Even Windows and Mac can be hacked."

"My computer's OS is cloud-based."

Cray shrugged. "If someone gets physical access to your device, and the hard drive isn't encrypted, it's hackable. End of story."

Fraser leaned closer as she began clicking through various folders on the desktop. If Spencer's notebook was where he first jotted down his ideas, this computer seemed to be where he fleshed them out. Cray saw diagrams for various computer networks and concepts of next-gen Asimov vehicles, including an even sleeker and more futuristic-looking F-Series. It looked less like a car than a spaceship with wheels.

But all the fuss, all the secrecy couldn't be over just an updated car. It had to be something entirely new. Fraser said Declan believed it would be a Level 5 autonomous vehicle, something designed from the ground up. A new concept car.

She went back to the Desktop, combing through the files. Unfortunately, the word *Catalyst* didn't pop out from anywhere.

Maybe it was staring her in the face, and she just didn't recognize it. Catalyst was the codename, not what the project was actually called. Its real name could be anything.

She clicked through more files, saw more diagrams. An F-Series police interceptor. A sleek fire truck with LiDAR emitters. A convoy of cars in traffic, all operating as one unit. Broadband towers casting down to city streets. An urban waterfront with a needle-like tower set farther back from the harbor.

"That looks like Toronto," Fraser said. "I have cousins there." He thought for a moment, turned to her. "Weren't Graham and Kaplan talking about testing something there?"

"They were," Cray said, growing increasingly anxious.

She continued clicking through folders, opening and minimizing diagrams. At one of them, she stopped cold.

It was a T-Series SUV beside a K-Series hatchback. Wavebands were transmitted between the two of them with the label *V2V* at the bottom.

It hit Cray all at once. A cold sweat broke across her body as she continued clicking through more images in the same folder.

She hadn't seen "U20" in Spencer's notebook. It was *V2D*, muddled by his shitty handwriting. The other scribbles had been V2I, V2N, V2P.

Vehicle-to-Vehicle. Vehicle-to-Device. Vehicle-to-Infrastructure. Vehicle-to-Network. Vehicle-to-Person.

She'd been staring at the same image for a while. Fraser leaned closer, scrutinizing it. "Is this Catalyst?"

"No. Not one of them is Catalyst."

She closed out of the image, then the window so that only the Desktop and its myriad files were visible onscreen.

"They *all* are."

11:56 AM

The Crown Vic swerved back onto CA-1 and Fraser gunned the engine, shifting straight to third.

The speedometer climbed rapidly. The engine protested.

He slammed the clutch, put it to fourth. The sedan raced north along the cypress- and oak-lined road.

"Declan figured they would unveil Level 5 autonomy, but not even he realized how far Spencer was going to go." He shook his head.

"It's V2X, right?" Cray said. "Vehicle-to-everything? I've heard that term before."

"Yeah, but that was supposed to be a gradual thing, developed over time and across systems, different computers and vehicles communicating with each other even from different manufacturers. This goes way beyond that."

"It seems to be a unified system, like an Internet of Things for cities," she said, looking at the device in her lap. Tatum had let them take it as evidence. "With AI keeping everything flowing: the traffic, the infrastructure, the—" She stopped. "Jesus, even the *police cars and fire trucks*. How the hell are they gonna automate that?"

"Don't let the name fool you. Asimov Automotive was never really a car company to Spencer. It was just a means to an end. You saw his office. Not one of those posters depicted automobiles as anything but parts of a cityscape. He wasn't a car guy. He was a *technocrat*. Vehicles were the key to his grand dream of disruption. But this was always the endgame: He wanted to create the cities of the future and monopolize them under his company—not just the roads, but the very essence of urban mobility itself."

Cray raised an eyebrow. "You make him sound like a megalomaniac."

"In a way, I think he was. Not like a Bond villain, but he clearly believed he knew how to fix the world's problems better than anyone else. This thing, Catalyst—or whatever they end up calling it—will centralize city infrastructure under automation sold and controlled by his company."

"But there will be push-back when they announce this tonight," Cray said. "It's classic Valley bullshit. They think everyone will accept this, so they'll unveil it at a big splashy event. Then the next day everyone on social media will freak out and they'll have to walk it back. Or the test run in Toronto will draw skepticism. Just because Spencer wanted the world to work his way, doesn't mean that it actually will."

"Valley companies do this all the time. They reveal something. People cry out, say it's too far, too fast. So the tech bigwigs dial it back, start releasing it in smaller increments so that it sneaks up on society."

"But then eventually people catch wind of it. Others will raise awareness. And then the public can decide whether they want to sell their souls to the Valley or not. They might think a system like this is safer and more convenient. Or they might think it'll be too vulnerable to hackers or give rise to AI overlords. But one way or another, it will be *their* decision to make."

Fraser shook his head. "It doesn't matter what you, or I, or even the public believes. The only thing that matters is what *Racer* thinks. And clearly, they decided it wasn't enough just to kill Spencer himself. They had to destroy both the man and the *idea* of the man. Catalyst is the thing that will make or break his legacy. Racer won't stop until they've buried it, and Asimov Automotive along with it."

Cray nodded. "And that means everyone at the event tonight is in danger."

The road widened into four lanes and Fraser shifted to fifth gear, speeding on beneath the dismal sky.

1:38 PM

On the way back, Fraser had Cray call Reed using his phone. But when she put it on speaker, Reed said he was in a meeting and that he'd call back later.

They arrived at Cray's hotel in downtown San Jose before he phoned. When Fraser pulled up to the porte-cochere, she climbed out, shut the door, and then tapped on the window. He rolled it down.

"Are you sure I can't help with anything?"

He shook his head sadly. "I've gotta head back to the Palo Alto Residence Agency, talk to Reed. I'll probably be making phone calls all afternoon. But I'll see you at the keynote tonight."

She nodded, expressionless. "Pick me up at seven."

"Um, alright—"

Cray turned and strode toward the entrance, throwing a smirk back over her shoulder.

Fraser shook his head, grinning, then put the Crown Vic in first and drove off.

Cray walked out to the porte-cochere, drawing a deep breath. The only other people out here beside the bellhop were a couple. The man was in his early thirties, dressed in an expensive blazer with a graphic tee and jeans. The woman on his arm was younger than Cray and looked way out of his league.

Cray sighed, glancing to the road and cars going by. She saw many people on their phones, letting autonomous mode take the wheel. A number sat in Asimov vehicles.

She was anxious again, jittery. She hadn't heard from Fraser since he dropped her off, though Graham had texted her to ask how she was doing and to see if he needed to arrange transport for her this evening. Cray told him she had a ride, but didn't mention anything about Catalyst. She'd left the laptop with Fraser but couldn't stop thinking about the diagrams and notes she'd seen.

The afternoon had been terrible.

She spent most of it pacing her room, bored and unbearably tense. All she wanted was for evening to arrive. She tried to get more sleep, but couldn't relax, so she resorted to other means of passing time. After a while, she wondered if the policeman on guard was pressing his ear to the door. When she went downstairs to pick up Uber Eats for dinner, the cop smiled at her but looked uncomfortable.

Cray pulled out the flask she'd brought in her suitcase, unscrewed it, and took a long pull. When she lowered it and exhaled again, she noticed the couple glancing at her. She must look out of place in Silicon Valley with this outfit, but Graham did say attire was meant to express one's *uniqueness*. She was dressed in all black, with a leather jacket, a T-shirt depicting bloody vampire fangs, tights, a leather skirt, and high-top sneakers—in case she needed to run. She wore red lipstick and heavy eyeshadow, mainly to distract from the bags, along with a black choker. She nodded to the couple, taking another swig and smirking.

A car pulled into the porte-cochere and Cray turned, recognizing Fraser's Crown Victoria. The windows were tinted and she peered closer, trying to see him. The car came to a stop and the driver's door opened, the FBI agent stepping out.

Cray nearly blinked in shock.

Fraser wore a white suit that looked tailored to fit his tall, slim frame. His shirt was sky blue, unbuttoned at the collar, and his espadrille shoes matched his suit. His bleach-blond hair looked less neatly combed, more casual, like he was going out for a night on the town—but a night decades ago, in a different town.

Her heart beat faster and she didn't bother to hide her smile, looking him up and down as he came around the car. "I'm *from* Miami and yet you look straight out of an eighties postcard."

Fraser laughed, opening the passenger door for her. "Well, a little more leather and you'd *really* be ready for San Francisco."

"Why do you think I usually go there?" She climbed into the car.

Fraser closed the door and came back around to the driver's side. When he climbed in and shut his door, Cray noticed the couple and bellhop were staring at their vehicle, baffled.

"Graham said it was a casual event, no suits. But I think he'll make an exception for this."

"And Reed is letting you wear that?" she asked.

"I'm officially off-duty."

"Don't undercover agents try to, you know, *blend in?*"

He gestured to himself. "Do I *look* like an FBI agent right now?"

She shrugged, took another swig of her flask. "Good point." She placed it back in her jacket pocket and put on her seatbelt.

"I thought ancaps and libertarians hate seatbelts," he said, doing his own.

"No, just seatbelt laws. Anyone who's too stupid to wear one deserves to die."

He turned to Cray, scrutinizing her. "Were you one of those people who refused to wear masks during the pandemic?"

She laughed. "I wear masks every day of my fucking life."

"Fair enough."

They drove off, leaving the puzzled-looking couple and attendant behind.

"What happened this afternoon? Did Reed believe you?" she asked.

"He thinks something's suspicious, but no one else does. They all want this thing wrapped up. There will be heavy security at the event and Asimov apparently ran through their Catalyst presentation several times, but nothing happened."

"The virus could release its payload at a certain time."

"It could, but they haven't found any virus. So they don't think anything will happen."

"And what do you think?"

Fraser glanced at her. "You and I both know this is exactly what Racer wants. Everybody's lowered their guard, thinks Reynolds was the perp, case closed."

"Did he have any connection to Spencer or Asimov?"

"None that we've found, but they think he was just some wack job."

"And there's been no sign of Sova?" she asked.

"None. He's a hitman. They figure he's fled the area, laying low or maybe even preparing his next job for someone else."

Within a few minutes they were on Highway 87, heading north.

"I got a bulletproof vest in the backseat for you, if you

want it. I'm wearing mine. They make them pretty thin these days, but just as effective. We can pull over somewhere for you to—"

"Nah, I'll just change in the backseat." Cray unbuckled her seatbelt and began climbing over the center console.

"Don't worry, I won't look." He gave a lighthearted laugh.

Oh, really? She positioned herself in the center of the back row, remaining seated upright as she shrugged out of her jacket and pulled her shirt over her head. She glanced at the rear-view mirror. His eyes remained forward.

She put a hand on his seat to steady herself, staring, waiting. Fraser kept his gaze focused on the road ahead.

After a few moments, she smirked and said, "Aren't good drivers supposed to check the rear-view mirror every eight seconds?"

Fraser laughed. "You got me, Izzy. Don't tell my insurance."

His knuckles were snow-white on the wheel.

7:35 PM

Highway 101 snaked its way up the peninsula, bringing them alongside the darkened Bay. Rain had started almost as soon as they cleared San Jose, but grew more intense the closer they got to the coast.

Cray stared out the window as they reached the city limits, houses densely packed into the hillsides like upscale favelas. The skyline loomed as they merged onto I-80. The lights of skyscrapers glowed through the rain, the top of the Salesforce Tower shining an effervescent blue.

The freeway curved east and soon they took the exit for Fourth Street. When they came to a stop at the light, she glanced out the window and saw a dead homeless man lying beneath a lamppost. Even from here she could make out the needle sticking from his arm.

"Welcome to San Francisco," she muttered.

Fraser glanced past her and sighed.

The light turned green.

The sedan cruised through city streets, hanging a left at 3rd. At the Folsom intersection, the Moscone Center complex came into view, its name written in big letters on the side of the main building.

Cray's stomach tightened. She contemplated stealing one more swig of vodka before they arrived, but resisted the urge.

Fraser turned left again on Howard, which bisected the complex. Up ahead, a glass walkway connected Moscone North and South. Cray looked up as they drove along. The South building was three stories tall, glass panes stretching across the north side overhang. There was a long drop-off loop and cars were unloading eventgoers.

"Here we go." Fraser turned the wheel, swinging around into the loop. "Oh, would you look at that. They still have human valets."

"Almost old fashioned for the Bay Area."

"Wonder how much longer we'll still have those," he muttered.

Most of the cars pulling up drove themselves, but at the sight of a late-2000s Crown Vic, the two valets hurried over. They wore ponchos over suits and were by far the most formal people Cray saw around.

"Good evening, sir," one said, opening Fraser's door. "Welcome to the Moscone Center."

"Thank you," Fraser said, climbing out.

Cray was about to open her door, when the other valet got it for her first. "Thanks," she said, stepping from the car. The two of them hurried to get under the overhang, away from the rain, following the other attendees.

Cray and Fraser reached the entrance doors, strode inside as they opened automatically.

It was bright in here, both from the ceiling and the glowing screens along the walls. Most of them displayed an image of an Asimov F-Series speeding through a light tunnel next to the auto show logo. Others teased upcoming conventions and events into the new year.

They walked to the left, toward the escalators. One set had been blocked off, railroading all attendees through a security checkpoint on the right. Once they got their names checked on the guest registry and moved to the metal detector, Cray emptied her pockets and put everything—including the flask—into a bowl.

"Can't bring that in here," one of the guards said, holding his hand up.

Fraser leaned over, flashing his FBI badge. "She's with me."

The guard looked surprised. "Um, alright."

Once they were through and riding down the escalator, Cray turned to him and smiled. "I owe you one."

He shrugged. "I think we're both gonna need that flask tonight."

At the bottom, they got off and walked toward the giant opening of the massive exhibition hall. When they reached the threshold, Cray stopped and took it all in.

The lighting was darker in here, magenta beams shining down on the walkways while car exhibits remained in shadow. The area to her left was entirely dark. To the right, all the way at the end of the hall, was a stage with a massive screen displaying the Asimov emblem. The lights were brighter over there, people milling about a reception. Enormous support arches all around fortified the ceiling in case of earthquakes.

"I went to the auto show in Honolulu every year as a kid," Fraser said. They started walking forward. The light path led to the center of the hall, then turned right. "Loved it. Used to wanna work in the car industry."

She looked at him. "Why didn't you? Why does someone like you join the FBI?" She laughed. "You don't give me fed vibes the same way Reed does."

He hesitated, looking uncomfortable. The nearest people were about twenty feet ahead or behind them on the path. "I got cyberbullied for years. Badly. Let's just…leave it at that."

They reached the center of the hall, turning and continuing toward the reception and the stage.

"And you blame the Valley for what your classmates did to you?"

Fraser sighed and said, "No. I know tech companies didn't aim to create platforms for abuse. But they didn't realize how easily things would spin out of hand, what they could be used *for*. They think they're making the world a better place. Instead, they just create an endless supply of messes. *That's* why I joined the FBI, to help clean them up. Because at the end of the day, for all the good it brings, tech makes it easier for bad people to do bad things."

They came out into an open area with hors d'oeuvres on tables. Rows of chairs sat before the stage. The lighting wasn't too dim. She could easily see everything and everyone through the magenta hue. Guests milled about, some with press badges, chatting with each other and eating appetizers. Attire ranged from casual to business casual.

Cray saw a number of familiar faces. Johnson was hitting on Cheryl Acheson by one of the hors d'oeuvres tables. Ritter and Pawar were chatting over by one of the rows of chairs. Tatum and Kayla had already taken their seats.

Graham was nowhere to be found, but as they continued forward, someone placed a hand on Cray's shoulder. She turned around.

"Hey!" Kaplan said. She looked a little drunk. "You made it!"

Heat flushed to Cray's face, and she laughed. "Yeah, been a long week."

"It's been a rollercoaster for me," she said. "I'm *so* glad they found that asshole dead yesterday. Niall can finally rest in peace." She looked like she was holding back tears.

Cray nodded, softening her expression. "Are you feeling okay?"

Kaplan looked around sadly, nodded. "I'm a bit better now. I'm very excited for Au—I mean, Catalyst. You're not gonna believe it."

"Have you seen Graham?"

"He's in the control booth. He's doing the keynote in place of Niall."

Cray took her hand and held it. Fraser had wandered over to a nearby table. "Stay safe. And I'll see you afterward, yeah?"

Kaplan nodded, smiling. She'd definitely had a few before coming here. Cray didn't blame her. She leaned closer to whisper something and Cray leaned in too, her heart accelerating.

There was the stench of alcohol on the COO's breath. "I just wanted to say…you look *super* hot in that outfit."

Cray threw her head back and laughed, some tension leaving her shoulders. *Oh, if only this was any other night…*

She leaned back in. "You don't look so bad yourself." She kissed Kaplan on the cheek, then headed over to where Fraser stood.

He looked up as she came closer. Cray detected a flash of jealousy on his face.

"Graham's at the control booth," she said, trying not to smile. "We won't find him here."

"Alright, we need to talk to Reed. He's over by the front row." Fraser moved off, but she stayed behind for a second, staring off at Kaplan, who was now chatting with Acheson. Fraser came back. "You can talk to your crush again later," he said. "We've got a crisis to avert, remember?"

She faced him and smirked. "Buzzkill."

He walked away again, and she nearly followed but stopped and grabbed some food off the table. To her dismay, as she bit in, she discovered it was some vegan oddity instead of a bacon-wrapped scallop. She ate it anyway and threw out the toothpick, heading after Fraser.

They walked down the center aisle between the chairs. It wasn't too large of an event. Didn't look like there were more than 200 people here, but she'd seen photos of Moscone Center conferences where this entire space was lined with thousands of seated attendees. Granted, the rest of the hall was occupied by cars from major manufacturers.

Reed spotted them and made his way closer at a brisk pace. It was the first time she'd seen him in business casual.

"Graham's at the control booth if you're looking for—," Fraser began.

"Forget Graham. Luther tracked down the owner of that shell company, Grand Prix Investments."

Cray looked between the two of them, confused.

"Someone recently bought a lot of short stocks against Asimov," Reed explained, lowering his voice. His eyes darted around, making sure no one else was listening. "They used a number of shell companies to obscure the purchaser, but we just tracked down who owns the holding company. And get this…"

He looked between the two of them. "It's Lucas Declan."

Fraser thought for a moment, nodding. "Well, I guess that makes sense. Graham always considered him his main suspect."

"Come on," Cray said. *"Grand Prix Investments?* If he's Racer, why would he call attention to himself so easily?"

"I don't know," Reed said. "Why don't we ask him? He's standing over there."

He pointed to where a fortysomething guy with a man-bun was chatting up a blonde reporter.

"Might as well," Fraser said, starting to walk back down the aisle.

Then, right at that moment, the entire hall went pitch black.

7:47 PM

Sova stepped out from the stairwell onto the parking garage's third floor. The Moscone Center had been almost entirely reconstructed and refurbished a decade ago, but this adjacent structure had seen better days. The floor was grody, the walls covered in grime. The stairwell smelled with the piss of homeless men and women.

But here the air was cleaner, tempered by zero emission electric cars and a wind blowing through with the rain. Sova walked to an unmarked white van by the railing and punched in the code Racer had given him on the keyless entry pad.

The door unlocked. He climbed in and turned around to see a duffel bag waiting on the floor behind the passenger seat. The rest of the van was full of moving boxes he assumed were empty, just for show.

Sova reached around and grabbed the bag, hauling it over the center console onto the passenger chair. He unzipped it, smiled.

A security guard outfit sat neatly folded. A metal syringe with clear liquid rested on top, a keycard beside it.

He already wore a moustache, a dirty blond toupee, and color-changing contacts. His silenced pistol was stashed in his jacket pocket. Sova climbed into the rear of the van and got changed. Then he stepped out and locked the van, heading back to the stairwell.

His watch told him it was 7:53. The power would be going out in there any minute now.

By the time he reached the ground floor and jaywalked across the rainy street, he figured it was dark down in the exhibition halls. The car show took up A, B, and C, used together in one big, long run.

An angry driver honked at him, but he held up his hand and dashed across, heading for the gap between the two buildings of the Moscone South complex. Beneath a short glass walkway, he turned left and swiped his keycard through a reader.

Nothing happened.

He sighed. The power must not be back on yet. A moment later, an orange light beside the reader came on and he swiped the card again.

This time, the maintenance door opened, and he made his way inside.

He moved quickly, reaching a staircase that took him below to a stark white corridor. Sova hurried along, making his way to the next door and a staircase that led down, down into the Earth.

7:56 PM

As soon as the lights came back, Cray gathered her bearings. She'd stumbled into the row of chairs to her left, nearly knocking one over. It felt like the lights were out for a long time, but it was probably only thirty seconds. She'd spent the time crouching, listening, waiting. No one had screamed, but there had been loud, concerned chatter.

Now everyone was looking around, startled.

Reed hurried back up the aisle while Fraser glanced around to find her. She rushed over to him, and they followed Reed toward Pawar and Ritter.

"Where's the control booth?" Fraser asked.

Both the CLO and CTO looked concerned.

"It's over there." Ritter pointed toward a large, raised stand behind her, to the left of the row of chairs. It was mostly hidden in the dark, but computer screens illuminated the faces of three people. Cray saw Graham bent over a technician's shoulder.

"Attention, everyone," a female voice said over the loudspeakers. "We had a momentary power outage, but everything is alright and on schedule. The keynote will begin shortly."

"We need to move," Fraser said.

Reed glanced around. "Shit, where the hell did Declan go?"

Cray scanned the crowd. She couldn't see him either. Even the reporter he'd been chatting with seemed to be searching for him.

"You find Graham, get him to shut this down," Reed told Fraser. "I'll find Declan." He moved on, walking at a brisk pace.

Cray and Fraser made their way down a row of chairs, then rushed past some hors d'oeuvres tables toward the raised booth. Away from the lights, darkness engulfed them but they kept on toward the computer glows, looming nearer.

Fraser led her around the back. There was a staircase up into the booth, lit below from some lamps. Gripping the railing, they hurried up two steps at a time.

Inside, they stopped and Cray looked around. Graham had already left. It was just the two technicians, one of whom came up to them, angry as hell.

"Excuse me, just who the hell are you?"

Fraser whipped out his badge. "FBI. You need to shut this presentation down."

The tech stared at him, then burst out laughing. "Are you kidding me, man?"

"Everyone here is in danger," Cray said, trying to hide her impatience. "A blackhat breached your systems and they'll—"

"This is bullshit. You can't just barge in here and tell us what to do. Don't you know what this *is?*" He gestured toward the stage.

Fraser stepped forward. "I'm one of the few people here who knows *exactly* what it is, and why someone's prepared to kill over it. Just delay the start of the presentation. Will there be cars onstage?"

"Yes, of course."

"Are their controls accessible here?"

"They're *only* accessible here. But they're just driving themselves up the back ramps. The main part of the show is the—"

"Doesn't matter. That wasn't a random blackout. The hacker is in the Moscone's systems somehow. They already breached the keynote files earlier. Something terrible is about to happen, and if you don't step aside and let us stop it, it'll be *your* fault."

The tech paled. The other one had turned around, staring between all three of them.

"I need to speak to my supervisor." He spun to his coworker and said, "Don't let them touch a thing until I get back."

The other tech nodded.

The guy brushed past Cray, heading down the stairs. Her fury was rising. She turned back around, but the lights were already beginning to dim.

"I'm sorry," the remaining tech said, working the light-board. "They'll fire me if I don't do this."

Spotlights faded in on the stage as Ted Graham walked out to the center, wearing a blue-gray collared shirt, chinos, and a transparent headset microphone.

"Good evening, everyone," he said amiably, facing the seated crowd. "Welcome to the San Francisco Auto Show. Thank you for coming." He smiled. "We have something very special to share with you tonight."

8:00 PM

"It's been a difficult week for us at Asimov Automotive. We lost our leader and dear friend, Niall, the architect of what you're about to see."

Graham didn't need to look behind him to know the screen displayed the deceased's picture, looking pensive. To the right would be his name, and below it the years of his birth and death.

"His vision led our company forward. Every day, he inspired those who worked with him to better not only themselves, but their world. He was a man of dedication, not only to his work, but to his family and his friends. He was a man of tolerance and inclusion, working ceaselessly to create a better future for us all. We choose to remember him for what he stood for and what he gave us." He lowered his gaze. "Thank you, Niall. Rest in peace."

Silence hung over the crowd. Graham let them feel it, then continued.

"But his death will not be in vain. He lives on in the reason we've all gathered here tonight." He looked up. "Niall strived to make the world a safer place, to use technology to cure society's ills. Every year, tens of thousands of people are killed in car crashes, while millions more are injured—and that's just in the United States alone. Around the world, our safety is threatened by one of the most dangerous forces on the planet: the human driver."

Graham started pacing. "Under Niall, Asimov Automotive was the first car company to bring Level 4 autonomy to the consumer market. Over-the-air updates meant that even older models received this benefit. Today, our entire global fleet runs the safest driving operating system in the world, AutOS. Our vehicles have *never* caused a single accident.

"Niall recognized that autonomous vehicles were the key to our future—a safer world with less gridlock, fewer vehicles, and reduced emissions. A world where no one owns a car, where vehicles do not sit idly parked for 95% of their lifespans. A world where only all-seeing, never-sleeping artificial intelligence transports us and our loved ones from A to B. For years we have pursued what was thought to be the ultimate goal: Level 5 autonomy, vehicles with no need of any steering wheel, capable of safely driving us rain or shine, day or night.

"But Niall realized this wasn't enough. One of the largest fears for these cars has been the so-called 'trolley problem.' It's a far-fetched argument that asks what would happen if an autonomous car had to choose between plowing into an obstacle and killing its occupant or swerving and hitting a bunch of schoolchildren and puppies on the sidewalk."

There were laughs from the crowd.

"This moronic fallacy was once the greatest barrier to the acceptance of self-driving vehicles, even though a car with LiDAR that sees more than 200 feet ahead at all times would easily brake long before it came to such a dilemma. Still, even as the concern over this has waned in recent years, it has been replaced by a new one: How can we be sure that cars will *always* be able to respond to threats? Even if their systems are infallible, they can't account for the unpredictability of human drivers they share the street with. And so Niall realized that in order to make roads safe once and for all, we need to abolish the concept of driving altogether."

He paused. For a moment there was silence, then the crowd broke into applause.

"Anyone can tear a system down. But to create something new is a Herculean task, one that we at Asimov Automotive—along with our AI partners at Wintermute Research and the urban planning firm at PBP Group—have worked tirelessly toward for the past three years. And next summer, the Harbourfront district of Toronto will be the first to bask in a safer future."

❬••❭

Out there, the screen changed to show a high-definition simulation of the Canadian city, glass condominium skyscrapers towering along the lakeshore, the CN Tower set farther back.

The technician was still working the controls.

Cray was tense, her pulse throbbing. She felt like she might break into a cold sweat at any second, her eyes darting back between Graham's presentation and the technician. The other man hadn't returned. Even if he did, she was sure the answer would be no. Fraser looked on edge beside her.

Fuck this.

She strode forward and crouched beside the tech, putting on her friendliest face and brightest voice. "Hey, when do the cars come onstage?"

"In just a second," he said.

"Where are the controls?"

"On the laptop, but—"

"I need to see them," she pleaded. "It's really important."

"We've run the presentation several times. Everything's on a closed system. Nothing is going to happen."

She contemplated smashing his face against the desk, knocking him out, but that might get both her and Fraser in trouble.

On the stage, Graham continued, "Using real world data collected by our vehicles, we've created a breathtakingly realistic simulation to test our new project. Imagine a world where every vehicle communicates not only with cars of all brands, but with pedestrians via their phones and wearable tech, with the roads, bridges, and traffic lights, with buses, trains, and light-rail transit, with cell phone towers, with satellites…The possibilities are *endless*."

"Just let me look at the cars' running processes for peace of mind," Cray told him, still watching Graham.

"I…" The tech looked conflicted.

Graham said, "But what would a world with universal Level 5 autonomy look like? It's easy to picture driverless buses and vans, but what about police cars, fire trucks, and ambulances? What will happen to them? Level 5 will bring about a world without speeding tickets, but aren't there situations that require high velocity? Niall saw through it all. Imagine a future where cars automatically pull over, not at the sound of a siren, but by a digital proximity alert distributed through a shared network. Where fire trucks douse flames of their own accord, allowing fighters to focus efforts on civilian rescue."

On the screen, a futuristic-looking truck pulled up to a burning building, water cannons folding up out of the roof and blasting liquid at smoky windows. All other cars in the area were alerted by the Catalyst system, which automatically directed them on detour routes to save time.

"There will always be criminals who try to subvert the system, who possess dangerous old-fashioned cars and attempt to use them in getaways. But we've thought of that too."

The screen displayed footage from a simulated car chase along an expressway downtown, an F-Series police interceptor bearing down on a sedan. It smoothly weaved in and out of traffic, pursuing its target as other cars automatically drifted to safer lanes, avoiding the chase altogether. The getaway car's position was tracked by the interceptor and alerted over the network to all automated police units.

Cray reached around to the laptop and pulled up the remote Developer Access application, monitoring the three vehicles backstage.

"Hey, you can't—"

"Stop me," she said.

He didn't.

"Using machine learning in every vehicle to adapt to any and all threats, and a distributed intelligence AI network to keep everything flowing smoothly, efficiently, and safely, we have successfully simulated the future. Now, we're ready to bring it into the real world."

Cray glanced up as three sets of headlights flared on in unison. The vehicles crawled forward, driving up ramps from the darkened area behind the stage. Even she paused.

In the center, directly behind Graham, was a life-size recreation of the fire truck from the simulation. It was smaller and stouter than most American trucks. The cockpit looked like an extended glass pod. The interior lights were on, revealing eight seats and no steering wheel. The ladder sat folded on the back next to two water cannons, which looked almost like weaponry from a science fiction movie.

On the left was a boxy vehicle with sliding doors and no windows, stark white save for the hospital red cross glowing on each side. Like the Cruise taxi she'd ridden in the other day, it didn't appear to have a front or back either, taillights on both ends.

To the right was the most normal-looking vehicle, an F-Series souped up as a black-and-white police car with red and blue lights flashing on the top.

Cray looked down at the screen and saw she had entered the interceptor's Linux system. She used Johnson's bullshit *Tesl@suX* password to authenticate the SUDO rights, then typed in sudo ps -aux and hit Enter. The list of processes appeared.

Just like last time, the top three were AutoDrive systems.

And just like last time, two were using far more memory than the other.

Graham let the applause die down before speaking again, watching the camera flashes fade in intensity. There was excited chatter among the audience. He couldn't wait to see what the response would be online tomorrow.

"We begin testing these vehicles in Toronto next summer, along with standard Asimov vehicles equipped with our V2X technology. But that is only the dawn of this new future."

He'd seen the presentation so many times, he knew exactly what was happening behind him. The view of Toronto was gradually dwindling as the virtual camera retreated into the sky. He'd seen Niall practice it so often that he was merely repeating his rhythm, his cadence. In a way, it was still him delivering the unveiling. Graham was just a stand-in.

The view pulled back to the globe at night, arcing lines jumping from Toronto to other cities. "We will move forward, and quickly—to San Francisco, to Los Angeles, to New York. To Austin, Atlanta, Miami. To London, Paris, Rome. To Africa, Asia, Oceania…"

The world was glowing, covered in connections. "It's not just around the corner anymore. It's here. It's now. And it will be better and safer than even Niall could've dreamed. Ladies and gentlemen, welcome to the future."

He spread his hands. "Welcome…to the AutoNet."

The Earth turned gray inside a large O on the screen, the other silver capital letters fading in around it.

The crowd stood up, thunderously clapping in applause.

Graham exhaled, tension streaming out of him like a river. They'd done it. Despite everything, they had actually pulled it off. Pictures were snapped, people were talking, and hands continued to clap. It had gone perfectly. Not even that bastard Reynolds had been able to stop this. If anything, he'd probably increased interest in the event.

Still, it wasn't the same without Niall to see the fruits of his own labor. Graham thought about one of the last things he'd said to him, back on Monday night.

Just remember that no matter how advanced a world we create, at the end of the day, we're all still human.

He hoped people wouldn't read AutoNet as misanthropic. This was to save lives, not reduce their worth. AI was simply more trustworthy. Bugs could be corrected, but people always made mistakes. This was for a better tomorrow.

They'll see that, he told himself. *Maybe not at first, but they'll realize. They'll come around eventually.*

He was so lost in thought that he didn't notice the whirring behind him, not that it would've been easy to hear over the crowd anyway. It wasn't until Graham sensed something big moving that he spun around —

As the fire truck shot forward, straight for him.

He never even got the chance to scream.

8:07 PM

Cray had never watched a friend die before.

She had killed the AutoDrive processes for the police car, and one of two for the fire truck. Still, it was no use. Just as she typed the command, the technician beside her had said, *"Holy shit."*

Her head snapped up just in time to watch the impact. Thanks to its electric motor, the fire truck had accelerated with frightening speed. It continued off the edge of the stage and slammed down, its bumper getting caught on the ground as Graham's body went flying like a ragdoll. People screamed and started running while the ambulance sped down the right stage ramp and swerved back toward the chairs.

She was more startled than anything else. Maybe an NT would've told themselves it was the shock, that it would come crashing back later, but Cray knew it never would.

Instead, anger seared through her. She liked Graham. Yes, he drank the Valley Kool Aid, but he did it in the memory of his wife, not out of arrogance. Racer had swatted him like a fly, and for what? Her list of grievances against the hacker only grew.

"Izzy," Fraser said, anxious.

She snapped out of her daze. The fire truck was spinning its wheels, trying to free itself.

Cray rapidly typed in kill -9 and the process number, shutting down the last corrupted AutoDrive. Abruptly, the vehicle's wheels ceased spinning.

The ambulance crashed through several rows of empty chairs, sending them flying through the magenta hue.

She clicked into its remote-controlled OS, both Fraser and the tech leaning over her shoulders.

Like clockwork, Izzy. Just do it again.

The tension all over her body was unbearable. Her throat and stomach clenched, sweat seeping from her pores, her legs shifting in her seat.

Her eyes remained glued to the screen as she typed sudo ps -aux, pulling up the processes. *There, get the number IDs.* She stared at the two top AutoDrive systems, trying to burn their four-digit codes into her memory.

Then she typed in kill -9 and the first ID, hit Enter.

"Shit, it's coming for us now!"

Cray didn't dare look, but she heard it barreling through chairs, crushing some and knocking past others. She heard people screaming, running, tripping over each other as they scrambled for the exit.

She input kill -9 again, followed by four digits as she remembered them for AutoDrive2.

Error: Process ID 2346 does not exist

Cray blinked. Shit, had she gotten the numbers mixed up? Maybe the ID was actually 2364. She'd have to go back and check.

"*Izzy...*" Both Fraser and the tech were looking out from the booth. She heard the ambulance plowing through the hors d'oeuvres tables. There were only seconds before it struck the control booth.

No time.

She typed in kill -9 2364.

Then hit Enter.

Immediately, she shot to her feet, looking down from the platform.

At the last split second, the ambulance swerved right. It

gradually decreased its speed, rolling to a halt twenty feet away.

Cray collapsed back into the seat, catching her breath.

"Holy shit, holy shit, holy shit," the tech said, stumbling back against some equipment.

Fraser put a hand to his head, walking off.

Staring off at the magenta lights, she drew her flask out of her pocket, unscrewed the cap, and took a massive gulp. Some of it went down the wrong pipe and she doubled over coughing.

"You okay?" Fraser asked.

"Yeah," she said, hacking some more. "I'm fine." She glanced over at him, realized he wasn't looking at her.

He was staring off to the left, toward the southern wall of the exhibition.

"Izzy, you need to see this."

Coughing once more, she stood up and came over.

A shadowy figure ran for a maintenance door. Pushing it open, they ducked left and disappeared down a corridor.

"How the hell was that unlocked?" she said.

"Maybe it was left that way earlier. Or when the power went out, Racer unlocked it through the system. We need to get the building shut down. No one in or out."

They both looked toward the hall entrance, where people were escaping, still in full charge. Police officers and security guards were ushering them through, silhouetted by the brighter lighting at the base of the escalators.

"We don't have time. We need to follow that person *now*, or they might get away."

Fraser hesitated.

"Do you have a gun?"

He nodded, sliding up the side of his suit jacket to reveal his holstered Sig Sauer.

"Then let's catch this son of a bitch," she said.

Fraser took a deep breath, like he was psyching himself up. "You're right. Let's finish this."

8:09 PM

Everything was falling apart. Everything.

Lucas Declan hurried down the back hallway, sweating all over. His heart was palpitating, and he felt delirious.

It's okay, he tried to tell himself. *You'll pull out of this. Somehow, it'll all be fine.*

But first, get a fucking lawyer.

Today could not have gone worse, there was no denying that. But it wasn't over yet. He could still survive.

Suddenly, he heard voices up ahead and ducked to the side, hiding behind an equipment locker. *Please don't be cops, please don't be cops...*

The talking grew louder.

He heard a woman's voice. "...the hell did you run this way, Adrian? Everyone else was going to the lobby."

Now a male voice. "I saw some guy running for one of the other doors and it opened. It's safer here than with the crowd. They're all gonna get mowed down by that fucking fire truck. If this was such a bad idea, why the hell did you follow me, Mallory?"

"Because I was panicking and clearly not thinking straight."

"You know, I think you like me."

"Shut the fuck up."

They came around the corner of the locker. The woman noticed him and stumbled back, startled. *"Shit."*

Declan held up his hands. "Hey, it's just me, sorry." He'd met them both at events before. Mallory Ritter and Adrian Johnson, the current CTO and CSO of his old company.

"Jesus, what the hell are you doing back here?" Johnson said. He looked shaken, accusatory.

"Same reason you are." He swallowed. "Figured it would be safer back here from the cars."

He needed to ditch them and get out of here. *Fast.*

"Yeah, well great minds think alike, huh?" Johnson said.

"Or fools seldom differ." Ritter folded her arms.

"I wouldn't stand too close to him if I were you," came a voice.

All three turned to see two figures approaching them down the hall. It was that weird FBI agent who interviewed him, wearing a white suit beside a tall goth-looking chick with blonde hair. This day really couldn't get any stranger.

"What's going on?" Ritter said, confused.

"I think it would be best if Mr. Declan explains that himself." The FBI agent gestured toward him, moving his jacket up to reveal a sidearm as he did so.

Declan burst out laughing. "Okay, okay. You want me to explain the short stocks? Because that makes me look pretty guilty, right?" He laughed again. "Well, here's a hot take for you..."

He looked between all four of them and, registering the mania in his own voice, said, *"Someone is setting me up."*

Cray figured as much, but she looked closely at him anyway, searching for signs of duplicity. None were evident.

Her mind was still processing the events in the exhibition hall. There was something that bugged her about the AutoDrive systems, something staring her in the face. But her mind was still too harried to connect the dots, her nerves too frazzled.

"Then just come in for questioning, and we'll sort this all out, Mr. Declan." Fraser kept his face a cool, calm mask. She noticed his left hand had tightened its hold on the gun.

"One of my financial advisors told me today that Asimov short stocks were going up despite the normal stock rising too. I asked them to track down who, and they said it was me. *Me.* That someone was using my fucking name to buy them. It's not hard to guess why. Everyone knows I hated Niall. Everyone knows how much Asimov Auto meant to me. It'd be easy to frame me for murdering Niall. I've been anxious people might think that all week. But when I found out about the shorts, I just about lost it. This must've all been part of their big plan, sabotaging the event. And they want *me* to go down for it."

"We stopped the vehicles," Cray said. "All three have been disabled. Graham might've been the only person killed, but—"

Declan burst out laughing again. "It doesn't matter how many people they killed tonight. The murderer won. The company is finished. Between Niall's car getting hacked and *this* fucking nightmare, it's dead. It's through, man." He turned to Ritter and Johnson, who both looked pale. "I hope you've got your fucking resumes ready, because you all are going to be seeking new employment come Monday."

He returned his gaze to Cray and Fraser. "Who the hell would ever set foot in an Asimov car again? Fuck, who would ever want to set foot in *any* autonomous car again? Do you realize what's just happened? That keynote was being livestreamed. The whole world saw Ted Graham die on fucking YouTube. This will set the acceptance of driverless vehicles back by *years*."

"But it...it wasn't the cars that failed," Ritter said, disbelieving. "It was someone. A *person* did this."

"So what?" Declan said, glancing at her. "You think the public cares? The media headlines will read 'AUTONOMOUS CARS BAD' and everyone will run for their Model Ts."

Fraser gave him a sympathetic look. "I know this is distressing, Mr. Declan. But if you want to help us catch whoever did this, then please just come in for questioning so we can sort it all out."

Declan paused, looking back down the hallway past him. "I hated Niall, but I didn't hate the company. Self-driving cars were going to help the world. Why did they have to push that AutoNet bullshit? Why did they have to take it too far? Maybe we'll never have true Level 5 autonomy if there are still human-driven cars on the road, but that's not so bad. Even if most cars drive themselves, it'll be much, much safer. That's attainable. Why didn't they just...?"

He seemed to be talking to himself at this point, like the others weren't there.

Cray stepped closer, softening her expression. "Please, Mr. Declan, just come with us."

He turned to Ritter and Johnson, who nodded gently. They both looked uncomfortable.

Declan turned back to her and Fraser. "Alright," he said. "If it helps get everything cleared up, I'll do it."

He walked over, starting to lead the way back to the door he'd come through—

And abruptly turned, punching Fraser across the jaw.

He fell back as Declan escaped in the other direction, smashing past the Asimov execs.

Declan raced down the corridor, ignoring the yells behind him. It was a long stretch of dimly lit concrete hallway that ran the entire length of Halls A, B, and C—the whole auto show exhibition.

He tried not to think about what he'd just done. He had to keep running now.

Running was all that mattered.

Soon he noticed the footfalls behind him. He laughed as he ran, hoping this was somehow all a crazy dream. One with mysterious goth girls and FBI agents in white suits. He was gonna wake up any second now.

Any fucking second.

But he was still running, still being chased. His lungs burned and his legs were giving out. There was no point in stopping, though. Stopping meant death. Whoever set him up would have enough faked evidence to put him away. He had to go on the run, sort this out from a non-extradition country. Then he could return.

Finally, he reached the end of the corridor, turning a sharp left and crashing through a door. Now he stumbled along a new hallway heading north—

And faltered into a stumble, panting. Up ahead was a security guard.

Think fast.

Declan raised his hand toward the man, who was getting closer. "Oh, thank God you're here," he said, smiling. "I got lost after all the chaos started and—"

"You're not supposed to be back here, sir. Don't worry, follow me." The guard was still coming toward him.

The footfalls grew louder from the other corridor.

"Sir?" the guard said, coming beside him and putting an arm around his shoulder. "Just follow me." He guided Declan forward.

"But I..."

"Don't worry," the guard said.

And then his other arm moved and suddenly there was pain in Declan's neck, something sharp plunging through skin and vein.

When they turned the corner and pushed through the door, all three of them froze.

"What the hell happened?" Johnson said, peering. "Is he dead?"

Declan's body lay on the floor by the end of some equipment lockers, across from a large heating pipe.

Ritter walked closer, leaning down.

"Be careful," Cray said, looking farther down the corridor. Fraser was still behind them in the other hallway, catching up. He'd fallen against the wall and hit his head, but he'd told them to get after Declan while he gathered his bearings.

Ritter glanced behind her. "I'm just checking his pul—"

A security guard leaped out and pulled her into a headlock, forcing a silenced pistol to her skull.

"Don't fucking move or she dies," he hissed.

The CTO swallowed, squeezing her eyes shut.

Cray stared closely at the man. He had a moustache and different colored hair now, but she recognized him. "You're Markus Sova."

"Shut up," he said, backing away—and taking Ritter with him. There was a door not too far behind him on his right, leading back into the exhibition hall.

"Just let her go," Johnson said, holding up a hand. His voice seemed almost preternaturally calm.

The hitman was still backing up, pushing the weapon tighter against Ritter's head. She looked petrified, clutching the arm across her throat. Sova gave Cray a hard stare.

Then there was movement behind her.

Fraser smashed through the door, aiming his Sig Sauer. *"Drop the weapon!"*

Sova aimed toward him and fired, the suppressor muffling the gunshot.

Cray dove for the ground, scraping her wrists as she landed. There was the sound of a door opening and she glanced down the hall.

Ritter had been thrown to the ground and the door to the exhibition hall was closing behind her. Fraser leaped over Johnson, who had also ducked to the floor, and charged after the hitman.

He disappeared through the door, leaving the three of them alone in the hallway with Declan's body.

Cray got to her feet and walked over to Ritter, helping her up. "You okay?"

She didn't look it but rubbed her throat and nodded anyway. Cray immediately moved past her to Declan and knelt down, feeling for a pulse on his neck.

There was one.

"He's still alive. Come on, we've gotta get him out of here."

"What the fuck is going on? What was that guy doing?" Ritter asked, incredulous.

"Let's find out later," Johnson said, coming up behind them.

They started to pick up Declan, holding him under his shoulders, but he was a deadweight.

"Come on, put your backs into it," Johnson said.

"Trying, asshole," Ritter grunted. They managed to get him off the ground, Johnson holding his legs. "There's gotta be a way out that direction." She nodded straight down the corridor.

That should bring us north out of the exhibition halls, Cray thought. "Then let's hurry."

She didn't want anyone else showing up. As they made their way down the corridor, Cray glanced behind them. So far, there hadn't been any other audible footsteps.

But that didn't mean they were alone down here.

8:17 PM

The showroom floor was dark save for reddish-purple lights, but it was bright enough to see. At the far end, Hall C and the Asimov stage had been blocked off by a sliding partition wall, no doubt the police cordoning off the crime scene. Halls A and B were devoid of life, a sea of cars and information booths shadowed in the magenta glow.

And so was the hitman, fleeing toward a sportscar exhibit. Fraser altered his course, sprinting after him.

Sova glanced back, spotted the FBI agent, then slid for cover behind the nearest vehicle.

Fraser kept his gun close, slowing his approach. The sportscar Sova had ducked behind was obscured by another car on a raised circular platform.

He breathed in and out, coming closer, lowering his center of gravity, his footsteps dampened by the carpet. He reached the raised platform and kept close to it. Fraser took a deep breath, then leaned out.

No sign of him.

He came around the sportscar, aimed again.

Still nothing.

His pulse soared. Sova could be anywhere.

Fraser's eyes swept his surroundings, scanning the darkness for any signs of movement. The hitman was nowhere to be seen.

Keeping low, he ran for a nearby exhibit of Mercedes-Benz sedans. Violet light reflected off their exteriors, increasing visibility.

Fraser looked back—

And saw Sova, silhouetted, aiming something toward him—

He turned on his heel as a bullet whizzed by, dashing for the nearest car. He tried not to think about Sova lining up the next shot, his finger tightening around the trigger—

Fraser dove the last several feet, crashing down on the carpeted floor beside the sedan.

The rear window shattered from Sova's bullets. The car alarm went off, echoing around the hall.

Fraser stared at the carpet, taking deep breaths. *Stay focused.* He lowered his head to look under the vehicle.

Out there, boots advanced toward him at a cautious pace. Sova knew he was alive. It wouldn't be easy to get a drop on the hitman.

Fraser glanced behind him, saw a rack of Mercedes information flyers. He figured they were out of his enemy's line of sight.

Scurrying across the carpet, he snatched a hefty booklet and retreated to his cover. Then, slowly, his heart pounding, he raised it up beyond the trunk.

A bullet tore through it almost immediately.

Fraser screamed, trying to make it sound like he'd been hurt.

Sova's footsteps came faster now. He must think he had the upper hand. Now it would be just a matter of finishing the job.

Fraser gripped his gun with both hands, took a deep breath—

And then swung out of cover, aiming over the trunk.

The hitman darted for the other side of the car as Fraser squeezed the trigger. The Sig Sauer roared, the bullet drawing blood from Sova's left arm as he dove for the ground.

Fraser pulled himself up, moving around the car, aiming the gun—

The fucker was gone.

His eyes darted up, saw a shadow hurrying away toward the next exhibit, toward the center of the hall. Fraser followed, keeping his gun at the ready.

Suddenly, more lights came on overhead. Fraser shielded his eyes as they adjusted. Halls A and B seemed completely empty of people, save for himself and Sova. Even the cops had disappeared, probably waiting for a SWAT team. Reed must be with them.

But backup wasn't here yet.

Drops of blood made a trail toward the next display, BMW. He crept closer, keeping the Sig Sauer aimed ahead.

The trail went around behind an iX SUV with a rack on the top. He tried to look beneath the carriage as he drew nearer, spotting nothing. The hitman might be behind one of the wheels.

Fraser was wound tight as a wire, blood thumping in his ears. This was nothing like back at Quantico. This wasn't even like the staged scene at Reynolds's house. This time, it really was life and death.

Remember what they taught you at the Academy. Ready, aim, fire.

Movement flickered out the corner of his eye.

He brought the gun around just as Sova lunged for him from behind a 7 Series to his right—

But the hitman caught his weapon and pushed it up, the gun discharging into the air. At the same time, he brought his own pistol up and fired it point-blank into Fraser's chest.

"We must've taken a wrong turn."

They'd come out into a loading bay. Pipes and ductwork ran across the ceiling. Harsh white lamps shone along the walls, but the light only pierced so far. More illumination came from around a corner, leading deeper into the underground level—and, eventually, to the street ramps. A truck sat parked to one side, next to some shipping crates.

Cray turned to Johnson, who seemed aggravated. "No," she said. "I looked at maps of this place earlier. That door over there should lead back out by the escalators. Or we could drag him a block and up an incline to 4th Street, if you'd prefer."

He scoffed. "Fuck that." The CSO nodded toward the set of double doors to their left on a raised platform, up a ramp. The auto show cars must've been loaded in through there. "Let's get the hell out of here. This place creeps me out."

"Can't we put him down for a sec?" Ritter nodded toward Declan. "My arms are gonna give out."

"Oh, fine," he grunted, dropping the unconscious man's legs.

Ritter and Cray gently set his upper body down, then breathed sighs of relief. Cray looked around. They should be safe here, but her anxiousness hadn't waned. She wondered where Fraser was, if he'd caught Sova. She'd be disappointed if the FBI agent died. Hopefully, he was okay.

Johnson took out his phone. "Shit, there's no reception down here. I can't call 9-1-1."

Cray's arms were tired, and her heartrate was just beginning to slow. She took a couple deep breaths, trying to calm her nerves.

Let's just get out of here.

She turned to the others, but they were staring at something ahead now. She looked too.

A set of headlights grew larger on the far wall. Then a black Asimov F-Series sedan rounded the corner. Its beams were glaring and Cray couldn't make out who sat inside.

The vehicle slowly cruised toward them. All three exchanged glances but remained still. The car blocked their exit through the rest of the loading level, and it could easily swerve and kill them if they made for the ramp.

Cray turned for the steel double doors that had closed behind them, tugging on the handle.

They were locked.

She spun around, the anxiety crashing back. She shook her head to Ritter and Johnson, who turned back to the advancing car. It had slowed its speed but continued crawling forward.

Racer wanted it this way, Cray realized. *Declan couldn't be killed because he had to disappear, to turn up dead later. Sova was supposed to bring him here, to let this car take Declan away to complete the set-up.*

But on the orders of *who*?

Cray closed her eyes, thinking. She had all the pieces, she could feel it. What was so strange about the AutoDrive systems back there? There was something, something—

Her eyes flashed open. The car was still advancing. She stared at the vehicle, working through it.

I'm a psychopathic hacker. I placed a virus in the Update subnet—but I didn't hire Greg Furman to do it for me. It would've been too difficult for him to get access, so I only used him to infect the AutoNet demo.

But that didn't matter. I already had access to Update myself. I placed a virus there years ago, just for fun. What is hacking if not the joy of doing things just to see if you can? But I didn't have a purpose for the virus, not then. Until I found one, earlier this year.

It was just sitting there, beaconing, undiscovered, like Fraser theorized. I had left myself a backdoor into the Update Department. I had a means of getting access to every Asimov car worldwide. So I did.

The sedan was pulling up alongside them, coming to a stop about fifteen feet away.

I had access to everything all along. I knew Catalyst was AutoNet and what Spencer was all about, what kind of world he was leading us toward.

The saloon-style doors opened outward slowly. The cabin lit up, illumination spilling out into the gloom.

I convinced myself it was up to me to stop him. Only I had the means. Only I had the motive. Only I could get away with it. So I killed him and the others because it was the only way to save society from technocracy. Or at least, that's what I told myself. Deep down, I might not even realize why I actually did it.

The doors came to a rest, revealing the interior cabin and all four seats facing each other.

I did it because I was bored.

The vehicle was empty. All was quiet in the loading bay.

After a moment, the others looked back at her, confusion written across their faces.

"But...I don't get it," Ritter said. "Who the hell summoned this car?"

"Haven't you figured it out yet, Mallory?" Cray shot her a wicked grin. "It was you."

For a moment, the CTO just stared at her. Then, slowly, the mask dissolved. Pretend shock faded, a conceited smile forming on Ritter's lips. Come to think of it, her eyes had always been slightly cold behind those AR glasses, but now they were downright chilling.

"I'm impressed, Izzy." Her voice was flat, monotonous. One corner of her mouth curled even higher. "Can I call you that? You seem to be on a first name basis with me."

Cray returned to her natural, flat affect. "I'd say so. We're a rare breed. It's fitting we should be cordial."

"Okay, what the fuck is going on?" Johnson backed away, glancing between the two of them.

"You know, you should thank him, really," Cray said. "He made your job so much easier, playing the part of the high-strung female executive."

"Oh, it's easy to be overlooked in Silicon Valley if you're a woman," Ritter scoffed, not even glancing at him. "I just finally found a good use for it."

Johnson looked antsy, like he was about to make a break for it.

Without even glancing at him, Ritter drew out a gun she'd hidden on her back, under her sweater. "I wouldn't do that if I were you," she said, aiming it at him.

"Jesus Christ, Mallory, what are you—*Why*?" He was shaking, on the verge of a panic attack. His eyes turned to Cray for support, but her expression must've been just as disturbing as Ritter's.

"I'm sorry, Adrian. I don't have time to monologue." She raised the gun.

"But you'd like to," Cray said, before she could fire. "You want to gloat. We're the perfect audience. You tried to kill me, yet I'm the only one who understands you. He's been a prick to you, but you want to show him just how well you played him, how you dangled it over his head the whole time."

Ritter looked back at her, cracking a smile. The gun was still pointed at Johnson. "Why don't you explain it, Izzy? If you really do understand me."

"Oh, it was very clever." *Appeal to her ego. But not too forcefully.* "My favorite was putting yourself in Acheson's car with me. If I hadn't deactivated the second infected AutoDrive in time, we would've been hit by that truck."

"A little danger is what makes life worth living. But you know that. And it was worth it, watching you let your mask down. I was ecstatic when you lost your cool. Sova told me you were a psychopath, but I had to see you stripped down, under pressure, just to be sure. And it was beautiful. I know we suffer more anxiety than our male counterparts, but you seem to have it especially bad, Izzy. If I could feel sorry for you, I would. You're kind of adorable. Wish I had been there to see you kill Quinn."

"Oh, but let's talk about your feats, not mine." She added some charm to her smile. "You're the mastermind, I'm just a pawn. You took the AutoNet's police interceptor protocols and modified them into an escape mode, didn't you? That's why you could sit there with me, throwing any suspicion off your trail, pretending to be scared. You weren't trying to cover your mouth when you threw up. Your hand got puke all over it because you'd just stuck fingers down your throat."

"Very good, keep going."

"The car evaded everything so smoothly on 280, but I didn't put it together at the time. I was too shaken. Only autonomous vehicles drive that perfectly, especially when they're going down the wrong side of the highway. The simulation footage of the police chase in Toronto reminded me of how Acheson's car drove. But that wasn't the only thing tonight that tipped me off. The hacked AutoDrive systems were operating just like the ones yesterday. Though here's the thing: *the AutoNet demo wasn't connected to the Internet.* Graham kept stressing how everything was air-gapped to maintain security. So how was someone able to remotely control the cars?

"The answer: they weren't. They were preprogrammed, just like the car we were stuck in yesterday. You set a route, probably would've had the car just stop eventually if I hadn't been in it, made it seem like Racer lost their connection. Or you would've done what I did myself. It doesn't matter. The whole point was that they'd find Kevin Reynolds's IP address, and that you would be cleared of suspicion. Funny how the car didn't start moving until we were the only ones left in it. Funnier how it didn't start moving until you'd taken out your phone."

Ritter looked like she was about to say something, but Cray continued, talking faster.

"After Sova took the wheel clamp off the car, he must've gone straight to San Jose to kill Reynolds and stage the scene. You needed a scapegoat so there wouldn't be too much security tonight. You needed everyone to think the crisis was over. So you found the perfect patsy, some idiot who ran an anti-autonomous car blog. You wrote a fake manifesto to make him seem like the killer, but you'd need another fall guy after tonight. So you went to the most obvious suspect, the person who openly hated Niall the most: Declan. You had Sova come here to kidnap him and place him in this car right here, though now you're gonna do it yourself."

Johnson was completely startled. Ritter's smile had only grown. "Alright Izzy, you've mostly got it. Not bad for an amateur detective. But how did you figure out we're alike?"

Cray smiled. "You were having fun with this, Mallory. You couldn't resist. You had to draw it out over the week and savor it, the most thrilling thing you'd ever done. But what really convinced me Racer was someone like me was when you killed Bailey. That wasn't programmed into the route. There was no way you could've known he'd end up standing right there. You manually locked the car from your phone and drove it backward into him, then activated the virus and let it go to work. That's why the car rebooted after ramming the RCFL van. It was loading your program. But there was no reason to murder Bailey. I knew Racer would've only done that for kicks. A true sadist."

"Playing psychiatrist now, aren't you? Alright, what's my motivation? I did this all for my own amusement?"

"Of course not. You were the only executive who openly disagreed with Spencer, but it wasn't just about commercial viability, was it? I think it was deeper than that. You argued with him about where he was taking society. You oversaw AutoNet as CTO. You knew the implications better than anyone else. You realized Niall wouldn't stop, that this was just the beginning. You were Greg Furman's direct superior—you would've known who on the AutoNet team could be compromised. You were bored with life, tired of your job.

Everything had become tedious. But if you killed both Niall and his legacy, you'd be saving the world. That must've sounded fun, Mallory." She paused, softened her voice. "I know it would've to me."

"Come on, Izzy." Ritter grew angrier, but remained calm, barely blinking. "You and I might have issues, but we're still *human*. People like Niall don't care about our species. Only *they* can save us. Only *they* know what the future looks like, and goddamnit it's going to look exactly like they say it is—or else. They want to automate everything—cars, planes, trains, retail, farming, manufacturing—hell, they want AI to write books and movies. What's next—music, painting? If there's something humans can do, Silicon Valley will find a way to replace us with computers. They're not gonna stop, Izzy. *Someone* had to send them a message. *Someone* had to have the *guts* in that little cult of personality Niall called a car company to tell him his ideas were shit, that he was sending us down a slope we couldn't climb back up. And of course he didn't believe me, so I knew he had to die. The logic of it just hit me one day, after a meeting earlier in the spring. He said AutoNet was only the beginning, that one day we'd have the whole world moderated by AI."

Cray shook her head. "He was delusional. Society won't automate *everything*. People will just pay a premium for human service. And those displaced will find jobs in new fields that haven't even been invented yet. Society always adapts to innovation. There might be growing pains, but in the long run it will be worth it."

"We won't get the chance, Izzy. People like Niall genuinely want our world to be run by AI. They say they're not religious, but they throw themselves on the altar of the singularity. I'm sure *you* feel the same way about life that I do: It's not worth living unless you can enjoy it, and it'll be pretty fucking miserable answering to Siri and the Terminator."

She said everything calmly, barely raising her voice. Johnson was staring at her in shock, his mouth slightly agape.

"Just because Silicon Valley pushes something, doesn't mean the world will take it," Cray said. "Let them try. If their ideas are too radical, people will turn to saner competing companies instead. We just have to keep the public informed—"

"Oh please, people are fucking idiots."

"And so they need *you* to save them? I don't like neurotypicals either, but I don't hate them. I just want to be left alone, so I treat them the same way. Let them live their lives."

"It doesn't work, Izzy. Society flocks to flashy products and people who make big promises. That's how it's always been. At least I'm actually *doing* something to help them. I'm taking action."

"And you're getting off on it. All of it."

"So? Why not? Why can't I fix the world and have a little fun?" Ritter smirked. "Niall figured out it was me in those final moments on Monday, when I *disrupted* his ride home. I shot him a look when I was leaving that afternoon and said 'Goodbye' with a little more finality than usual. He seemed confused, but I'm sure he thought nothing of it until that evening, when I disguised my voice on the speakers. It was so fun sending his SUV off the cliff. Once I lost the feed, I had this incredible rush come over me. Killing him was...*exciting*. Niall always thought he was so *inevitable*, that he was destined to bring about the future."

"And you thought it was your right to decide whether he did or not."

Ritter sighed. "You're starting to bore me, Izzy. I've got more interesting things to do."

She turned the gun on Cray.

Outwardly, she showed no change in emotion, though her stomach clenched so hard it hurt. "That's it?" she said. "You finally meet another female psychopath and you're just going to shoot her?"

Ritter laughed. "When I realized you were like me, I knew even if I couldn't get you during all this, I would still track you down later. I would find you and we'd have a little chat before I killed you." She swallowed. "That would've been fun. The next step. I'd gotten away with remote-controlled murder, but doing it with my bare hands? To someone like *you*?" She grinned. "That would've really been something. Face-to-face always beats virtual. But I'm glad we've had this chat, Izzy."

She started backing up the ramp, drawing out her phone while aiming the gun between both of them. Ritter pressed something on the phone and the sedan's doors began to close. The car began backing up, turning so that the front was angled toward them.

It suddenly hit Cray. The 280 route might've been pre-programmed, but the vehicle behavior during the keynote seemed too erratic, too unpredictable.

"You modified the pursuit mode again," she said flatly. "Not to evade pedestrians, but to kill them."

"Very good, Izzy. Oh, I am going to miss you. At least it'll be fun watching you scream."

And the sedan accelerated toward them.

8:21 PM

It was as if a massive fist had slammed into his chest, but the Kevlar held firm.

Grunting through the pain, Fraser seized Sova's gun-wielding arm with his other hand and pulled the man closer, slamming his foot down on the hitman's toes.

Sova gnashed his teeth and snarled. For a moment they grappled, their weapons aiming in different directions.

Then Fraser kneed him in the crotch. He reeled back against the nearby 7 Series, both weapons falling in the separation.

Fraser doubled over, reaching for his Sig Sauer. Fuck, his chest hurt. The bullets had driven the breath out of him, and it hurt to breathe. His head still pounded from earlier.

Just as his fingers brushed the grip, something swung in on his right. His face just barely dodged Sova's knee as he fell over backward, scrambling away. Fraser turned over, trying to get back to his feet.

Hands grabbed his shoulders, hauling him back up. He barely tensed his abs in time before Sova socked him in the gut.

The bulletproof vest helped, but pain exploded in his core, winding him. Sova hit Fraser again, this time even harder. Between that and the ache in his ribs, he wanted to collapse.

The hitman dragged him forward, picking up speed, then

threw him against the hood of the iX SUV. Muscling past the pain, Fraser pulled himself back up.

Sova was glaring at him, drawing something out of his jacket, fitting it over the fingers of his right hand. For a second, Fraser thought they were brass knuckles, but then he recognized the dull metallic sheen and swore under his breath.

Titanium. Illegal in several states, but the darknet always found a way.

The Kevlar would mostly shield his chest, but one blow to the skull from those and he was good as dead.

Sova threw a punch and Fraser ducked, the death knuckles missing his face by inches. But the hitman's left hook caught him across the cheekbone.

The hit knocked him against the SUV's mirror. He edged around it, trying to ignore the pain all over as his opponent swung again. And again. Fraser dodged both times, but barely.

Just keep him going. Sova was starting to look tired. That was good. Now he had Fraser against the iX's back left door, maintaining a defensive stance.

Anger seared in the hitman's eyes. What must he be thinking right now? This week had been one fuck up after another. Now he was taking it out on Fraser. *He's lost his touch. He's losing it. You can beat him.*

Sova screamed and swung the titanium knuckles.

Fraser waited until the last split second to move, the side of his assailant's fist grazing his left cheek. Then it smashed through the window behind him, the car alarm blaring, deafening in his ears.

Fraser channeled the pain into his right hook, grunting as he clobbered Sova across the face. The fake moustache dangled above his lip, more than half of it unstuck. Fraser immediately followed with an uppercut. The hitman stumbled in reverse and Fraser finished with a right cross, knocking the man flat on his back, his toupee falling off.

He stood over him. Sova merely lolled his head from side to side, losing consciousness. The moustache was gone too.

Turning and clutching his torso, Fraser limped as fast as he could back to where the pistols had fallen. He snatched his up, kicked Sova's away under the 7 Series. Then he hurried back to the iX—

The hitman was gone.

Slippery fucker, Reed had said.

Fraser sighed in exasperation. His opponent was unarmed this time. At least that was something.

He went around the iX, searching for a blood trail. There was none. He continued through the BMW exhibit, looking left and right. All around him were idle vehicles, displayed in the dim light.

Fraser thought back to shows like this in his childhood, how he'd loved climbing around the cars and dreaming of having his own someday. Now he'd never look at an auto show the same way again.

He came back out onto one of the walkways between the exhibits, over by the enormous column of a support arch. There was a crashing noise off to his left and he turned just in time.

An electric sportscar raced toward him, Sova snarling behind the wheel. It knocked past an information stand and glided forward at a startling pace.

He hadn't even heard it until it was this close. Now the whir was unmistakable, the last sound he would hear before the breaking of his own bones.

Unless—

Ready.

Instinct took over and suddenly he was back at Quantico, lining up for a shot on the target, looking down the sights.

Aim.

Sheer determination etched itself across Sova's face, his hands gripping the wheel. The vehicle was less than thirty feet away now. It would strike him at any second—

Fire.

Something cracked through the windshield and pain seared in Sova's right shoulder. A hand came off the wheel, clutching the wound, the car swerving. Sova slammed both feet onto the brakes. He glimpsed a white-suited figure diving the other way—

As the sportscar plowed into a support column.

Every airbag in the car detonated, cushioning Sova's head as it whipped forward. The impact jarred his body to the bone, and he blacked out.

Sometime later—he didn't know how long—he regained consciousness, blinked blood out of his eyes.

He lifted himself up from the airbag, his neck aching. His head still hurt from the concussion two days ago. The sportscar was totaled, the front mangled into a mass of unrecognizable steel.

That's a shame.

He felt down along the floor of the passenger seat. *Come on, come on.* But it was still there. He'd watched the FBI agent kick it under the 7 Series and doubled back for it as soon as the retro-looking fucker had come around the iX.

Sova kicked the door open. It hurt like a bitch all over, but he clenched his teeth and hauled himself out of the car, staggering to his feet.

The FBI bastard was waiting for him, pistol raised with both hands, which were trembling. A rookie, probably. He looked young for a fed. Sova had been surprised when Racer sent him photos of both him and Special Agent Reed.

"Drop the gun and put your hands up," Fraser said, an edge to his voice. His white suit was bedraggled, dirty, and spattered with bloodstains.

Sova's eyes flicked past him. Across the hall, a SWAT team was rushing toward them, armored in heavy gear and wielding submachine guns. The cavalry had arrived.

He laughed, shook his head. So it had come to this.

Sova stared off at the ceiling lights. "I didn't choose this life," he said, not sure if was to Fraser, himself, or no one.

The FBI agent shook his head, a sad look on his face. "We all have a choice."

Sova nodded slowly. The SWAT team was getting closer. He took a deep breath and turned back to Fraser.

"Then this is mine."

He raised the pistol toward him, aiming for the head.

A shot rang out through the hall.

Sova dropped his gun, smiling. Warmth bloomed inside his chest. He looked down, saw blood seeping through his security uniform. It spread quickly, darkening his shirt, gravity drawing it down.

Suddenly all the soreness and fatigue caught up with him. He collapsed to his knees, then onto his stomach. His head was turned toward the back wheel of the sportscar, light reflecting off the hubcap.

The footfalls of the SWAT team slowed as they approached, though he didn't see them.

Blackness closed in.

And as it did, he wondered if—just maybe—it was better this way.

<⋅⋅>

Fraser lowered his weapon, staring at the man he had just shot. It seemed unreal.

The SWAT team stood behind him. Someone lay a hand on his shoulder.

"You had no other choice, Will. He did that on purpose."

He nodded slowly, then all his other concerns and questions raced back. "Where are Cray and the others?"

Reed looked confused. "What are you talking about?"

"Shouldn't they have reached the lobby by now?"

"They weren't there a moment ago."

"Shit, we need to check the back tunnels. They were helping Declan. Sova attacked him."

"Was there anyone else back there?"

"Didn't seem to be."

"Alright, we'll go check it out right now," Reed said, wiping sweat from his brow. He looked utterly exhausted. "But don't worry, Will." He cracked a knowing smile. "I'm sure she's safe."

8:27 PM

Her body lowered into a defensive posture, but she didn't
move.

Johnson screamed and ran to the side, as she expected he
would. And, as she expected, the car swung toward the moving target, not wanting to let it get away.

Cray sprinted forward, past Ritter, past the rear of the
vehicle, dashing for the corner. She glimpsed Johnson hiding
behind some crates, but the vehicle rammed them back anyway, nearly crushing him.

She'd tried to help him earlier, but she figured he wouldn't
make it far at this point. Besides, Ritter would want to save
her for last. She was the real prize.

Cray was almost to the corner. Ritter wouldn't use the pistol on her. She had no silencer, and they weren't far from the
escalators. It was just in case of emergencies, probably plastic
so she could slip it through the metal detector. It was easy to
make guns and bullets on 3D printers these days.

Behind her, Johnson screamed and there was a hideous
crunch.

She looked back at the corner. The vehicle was already
speeding after her, blood smeared across the damaged
grille.

Cray turned forward as anxiety reared its ugly head. She

felt physically sick as she ran, with a splitting headache from neck tension and her heart thrashing inside her ribcage.

Yet her mind was strangely calm. *Just keep running. Turn left up ahead.*

Around the next corner was a long tunnel, running to the other end of Moscone South. There was another truck parked on the right up ahead and a forklift farther back. To the left were several smaller loading bays with more crates and forklifts.

Tires screeched behind her.

Don't look back.

Cray darted to the left, heading into the nearest loading bay. A maze of cargo crates, steel beams, and loading equipment awaited her.

She slalomed through the labyrinth, her lungs burning. She gasped for air, pushed off one crate, then another, then pulled herself along the side of a forklift for support.

Back there, the car was prowling, scanning for a way to get through.

Cray fell back against a packing crate. She took a moment to catch her breath, thinking.

The car's kill mode probably wasn't that advanced. It was just something basic Ritter programmed, modified from the original police pursuit code. Its purpose had been to create chaos at the event, not to hunt people down like predator drones.

Therefore, it probably wouldn't calculate the best way to create an opening for itself here. She was hidden too far back. So the car would just wait.

And that's what it seemed to be doing, its headlights shining through the gaps in the maze.

Ritter would probably have camera access on her phone. Once she hid Declan back there, she'd come over and finish Cray herself. This area was farther from the escalators. She wouldn't be afraid to use the pistol here. She'd want this to be over quickly so she could get Declan into the car and have it crash somewhere near here. With the blood all over it, it wouldn't get far without drawing police attention.

But that would be okay instead of a more elaborately

staged death. The authorities didn't need to know for sure if it was Declan. Ritter just needed to be cleared of suspicion.

Which meant unless Cray got out of here alive, she would be. She'd thrown them all off earlier. Maybe Fraser would put it together, but without hard evidence they wouldn't be able to arrest Ritter. She'd get away with it, find a job at some other company. Or just work as a blackhat. Now that she'd gotten a taste for this level of crime, Cray doubted she would stop. She was too into the thrill. Cray had had the good sense to quit after Picturesque, but maybe Ritter enjoyed close calls. Regardless, one thing was sure.

She had no intention of letting Cray get out of here alive.

"Izzy," her voice cooed down the tunnel. She would've taken care of the security cameras. She would've taken care of everything. "You're too old for hide and seek."

Cray looked around for anything she could use as a weapon. Everything seemed to be packed up.

On top of a small crate, a toolbox sat in the far corner.

She stumbled toward it, running on adrenaline. Part of her was enjoying this, she realized. At the same time, another part of her wanted to curl up and clutch a pillow. Suddenly, she missed Simone again. Not just the way she made Cray feel, but being in her company, hearing her laugh.

Cray reached the toolbox, unlatched it, threw it open.

On the upper level were several screwdrivers.

"Izzy…don't make me come in there. There's no way out."

She grabbed one, a slot. Looked it over—

As high beams enveloped her. She squinted, looking ahead.

The sedan was there, aiming its battered nose at her like a hunting dog, pointing through a gap in the crates. The vehicle whirred forward and backward, trying to calculate a way of reaching her.

"Oh, *there* you are!" She sounded amicable, excited even.

Footsteps clacked on the pavement.

Cray spun to her right. Ritter didn't sound far away.

She pressed her back against the nearest crate. Took a deep breath in and out. Then another.

Beside her, a gun appeared around the corner, followed by Ritter's outstretched arm. Then the woman herself appeared, staring ahead. Her gaze was intense, but devoid of expression.

Ritter spotted her, turning around—

As Cray screamed, slashing with the screwdriver. Ritter lurched back, firing the gun away from both of them. Cray leaped forward and slammed her back against the next crate.

Ritter snarled, trying to move her gun-wielding arm. She was shorter than Cray, but strong nonetheless.

The pistol went off again. Now that she was up close, Cray saw it was plastic but painted to look like a metal gun. There were lots of those she'd seen out there on the Internet and darknet.

Ritter kneed her in the gut. The vest beneath her shirt shielded some of the blow, but it still hurt. She grunted, forcing Ritter back against the wall, digging her fingers into the other woman's wrist.

Ritter clenched her teeth, held firm. She probably had a similar pain tolerance, Cray realized.

Suddenly, the gun dropped from her fingers. Cray lunged down for it, realizing the ploy too late. Ritter tackled her to the ground. The impact knocked the breath out of her.

But the screwdriver was still clenched in her grasp.

Ritter grabbed it with both hands, twisting it toward Cray, forcing the blade down toward her face. Her expression was blank again, save for the cold vehemence in her eyes behind the glasses. But, as the tip descended closer and closer to Cray's blue right eye, a contemptuous grin sliced across her lips.

Cray struggled, her arms shaking, the tip hovering larger and larger in her vision.

"I'm glad it ends this way, Izzy," Ritter breathed. "I'm glad it came down to you and me, alone."

The blade was less than an inch from her eye.

Cray swallowed, her teeth clenching, her muscles straining.

"You never...told me," she managed to get out, "why you call yourself...Racer."

Ritter smirked, letting up just enough. "It was—"

Cray brought the screwdriver to the right and down, the tip slamming against the concrete. She let go and smashed the bottom of her fist into Ritter's face. The woman reeled back, clutching her nose. Then she came down again, snarling—

As Cray rammed the screwdriver upward, into her stomach.

Ritter gasped, something between a grunt and a hiss escaping her mouth.

Cray jerked the handle up and down, feeling resistance from her innards. Blood gushed all over her right hand. Her other reached up into Ritter's jacket.

Her opponent fell over, clutching her abdomen. She turned and desperately crawled away in the other direction.

Cray got to her feet, standing over her with the bloody tool in one hand. Ritter was making her way toward the gun.

In a few quick strides, Cray reached it and kicked the weapon away.

But Ritter was still crawling, faster now, back toward the tunnel. Trailing crimson in her wake.

She clawed her way out of the loading bay, clenching her teeth and doing everything she could to ignore the pain.

The car awaited up ahead. High beams shone blinding light in her face. She'd programmed Kill Mode in this car to spare her. Hadn't done the same for the ones in the AutoNet demo, of course. Forensics would be run on them. They were air-gapped, no way for a new update to wipe the virus off their systems.

But that didn't matter anymore. Nothing mattered except escape.

Izzy was still behind her. Fucking bitch, watching her suffer. If she was going to kill her, just get it over with already. *You're just as much of a sadist as I am, you hypocrite. You're no better than me.*

Adrenaline powered her now. She was bleeding, but the damage to her organs might not be that bad. She would get patched up. She would survive. She had half the short stock funds she put in Declan's name. That had always been a contingency, in case things went south. Flee the country, start a new life with millions of dollars, change her hair color.

Ritter made it to the car.

Grunting, she reached up and grasped the handle and tore it open. Left a bloody smear, but she didn't care. Just had to get out of here.

She hauled her way into the nearest seat, her muscles straining. It felt like a gaping tear had been made in her stomach, but she tried not to think about it. The fact that she'd been able to make it this far was a testament to her pain tolerance and adrenaline. She smiled. No one else could do things like she did. Not even poor, fucked up Izzy.

"SALLY, close the doors," she yelled, her voice hoarse. "And get me to the nearest hospital."

"Confirm destination—"

"*Confirmed!*" she screamed. Fucking stupid car. At least there *was* ultrawideband reception down here for it to chart a course. Johnson hadn't been able to use his phone because of the signal jammer Ritter had in her pocket.

Everything all planned down to the letter, and yet it had gone to shit anyway. And all because of *her*.

The doors closed. Suddenly, the front seats began turning around, back to their forward-facing position.

What the hell was going on? She hadn't ordered it to—

Now the seat was sliding forward. Ritter tried to climb aside but was too weak. The next thing she knew, her body was pressed against the steering wheel until it hurt. She summoned her strength, trying to wriggle free.

It was no use.

She looked up and her blood boiled.

Cray stood in the headlights, giving her a hard, unblinking stare. Her lips formed an evil smile. With all the eye shadow, dark clothing, tangled hair, and her hand covered in blood, she looked like the goth girl from hell.

But then she held up her other hand and Ritter's entire body tensed.

It was a phone. *Her* phone.

Izzy's smile grew even wider. "I just wanted you to know, before I kill you, that this has been the most interesting week of my life. So I'd like to thank you, Mallory. You really did me a favor."

Ritter said nothing, glaring. She'd never hated anyone so much before.

"But that being said, you *did* try to kill me. A lot. And you killed a friend. And Bailey. And though he was probably a prick, Niall didn't deserve to die. But you do."

Ritter started to feel woozy. The blood loss was finally catching up with her.

"I'm sure the authorities will be here soon enough, so I can't make this as slow as I would've liked. But you were right about the thrill. When I killed Quinn, it was like an electric charge. I'll never tell anyone else it felt like that, not even lovers. But I'll tell you. You're the only one who understands."

Ritter started to laugh, but still gave Izzy her most wicked stare.

Cray looked down at the phone. "Nice little UI you made for yourself. Like a fucking universal remote. That's going to make this even more fun. Goodbye, Mallory. I enjoyed this time we spent together."

Then she stepped aside, holding the phone with both hands like a game controller.

The car moved forward. It turned to the right and began picking up speed with smooth electric acceleration.

Looking ahead, Ritter saw what Cray was up to.

She struggled in her seat, her laugh becoming more desperate. The tunnel whipped by on both sides, the forklift getting closer and closer.

At the last second, she let the laugh morph into a scream. It was cathartic, liberating—

Then the sedan impaled itself on the forks going seventy miles per hour.

⟨••⟩

Cray came up beside the wreck. Both vehicles had spun out into the center of the tunnel on impact.

The lift truck had extended forks, and one skewered Ritter through the driver's seat. Her limbs twitched, her eyes staring off blankly as blood poured from her mouth. The AR glasses were broken, dangling across her face, the lenses glitching.

Cray sighed, tension escaping her shoulders. There was only one thing that remained. She needed to exit out of controlling the car so that the virus would send an update, wiping all logs. The police wouldn't be happy if they knew she had Racer trapped and killed her anyway.

She tapped the icon at the top of the screen, her finger hovering over the Log Off icon.

Footsteps came behind her.

"Freeze and put your hands up!"

Shit. She turned, raising the device above her head. "I'm unarmed."

Several members of a SWAT team had come around the corner from the first loading bay, led by Reed and Fraser. His white suit looked worse for wear, and as he got closer, she saw he did too. She wondered what she looked like herself.

Fraser motioned for the SWAT officers to lower their weapons. "Jesus, Izzy, we've been looking everywhere for you."

"What the hell happened?" Reed said, looking past her at the car. "Holy shit, is that *Ritter*?"

"It's…a lot to explain." Cray lowered the phone, keeping her eyes on him. Without looking, she tapped something on the screen, hoping she'd remembered where the Log Off icon was.

She held the device out to the FBI agent. "But it's all on here."

And she gave everyone a weak smile.

SATURDAY

Kaplan looked up at her, across from the CEO Suite desk. "I guess that's it, then."

Cray sighed wistfully. "Yeah, I guess it is."

She nodded slowly, glancing back down, like there was something she wanted to say. "What took so long at the FBI Field Office? They had you there most of the day."

Cray shrugged. "There was a lot to sort out. But once they got a warrant for Ritter's place and searched her computers, everything backed up what I said."

"What, did they think it might be you?"

She rolled her eyes. "They just like to be thorough. I was the only one left alive at the crime scene. Except for Declan, but he was unconscious."

"I can't imagine what that was like... When she tried to kill you." Kaplan looked at Cray in disbelief. "I always liked Mallory. She seemed incredibly dedicated to the company. I know she and Niall had their disagreements, but I can't believe she...I can't believe she was responsible for all this."

Cray sighed. "How much can you really know anyone?"

"I knew Niall well," Kaplan said. "I think he would've wanted me to take his place. Ted thought I would become the new CEO anyway. I'm officially Interim for now, but the board will probably confirm it this week."

"You deserve it, Casey. Ted spoke really highly of you." She paused, smiled. "And it's been nice getting to know you this week."

Kaplan smiled too, standing up. "Yes, I'm glad we got to work together."

Cray got to her feet and together they headed to the door. Kaplan reached for the handle, then stopped. She turned away, hesitating. There was something she *really* wanted to say. Cray smiled and put a hand on her arm.

Kaplan turned to her, nervous. "Last night, what I said to you…"

"Yeah?" Cray was leaning closer, smelling her perfume.

Kaplan leaned in too, their faces close together. Cray nudged forward, going for a kiss—

As the other woman stepped back, giving an awkward laugh. "I…wanted to clarify some things."

Cray froze.

"When I complemented your outfit at the keynote, it was just because…I thought it looked cool. But the more I thought about it, the more I got worried that I was…giving you the wrong impression."

"About what?" Cray said, trying to maintain her smile.

"Well, you're very pretty, but I, um… I don't…go for girls." She laughed.

"Oh." Cray laughed too.

"I just thought you were being friendly all week. I didn't…I didn't realize you *liked* me. But then you kissed me on the cheek, and I got worried. That, maybe, you were reading things the wrong way."

"Whoops, my bad." She forced a laugh again. "I do that all the time. Sorry, it's…"

"No, no… I mean, you seem really great. And I hope we can work together again someday. But I just don't want you to get the wrong idea."

Cray raised a hand. "Totally my fault. Sorry if I made you feel uncomfortable."

"Oh no, you didn't. You were great. I just…"

"Take care," Cray said, opening the door and walking out. She gently closed it behind her, then sighed, clenching her fists.

After the long, agonizingly boring morning at the Field Office—sitting there hungry, getting asked more and more questions—she just couldn't take it. She strode over to Acheson's desk and kicked the trashcan, sending it flying against the wall. It fell on its side, spilling Post-It notes and pieces of paper.

Real mature, Izzy.

She turned and stormed out of the CEO reception, past the breakroom. At least she would never return here again. Kaplan wouldn't bring her back even if half the C-Suite hadn't died this week. It would've been too awkward. But now Cray's face would only remind her of everything that happened since Tuesday. Granted, the company was pretty fucked at this point.

At least her fee had been paid, direct deposit. As Graham had promised, it was triple her usual. So it had been a financially productive week. And Cray discovered things about herself she hadn't known before, things she was still thinking about.

Things she'd be thinking about for a while.

No doubt now would be a return to boredom. Back to inane whitehat work. To pointless hookups like Marcy.

Still, it could be worse. This week had also shown her that.

Her suitcase was waiting at the reception desk in the lobby. She'd spent the night in a hotel in downtown San Fran. The FBI had her luggage brought in from San Jose, and she'd now brought it with her here, dotting the I's and crossing the T's with Kaplan. Asimov was sending her back to L.A. via the corporate jet. *That* was something to look forward to.

As the receptionist retrieved her luggage, she heard a familiar voice off to her right.

"Oh, there you are."

She turned, and immediately her spirits lifted. It was Fraser. Today, his wardrobe was back in black.

"I could say the same for you." Cray smiled. "You disappeared around lunch time."

"Reed said I'd done enough, that I should take the rest of the day off."

"Then why are you here?"

"I came with the ERT. We were returning a few boxes of Spencer's stuff. Not relevant to the investigation now that we know who killed him."

"Then why are you here?"

He shrugged. "Thought I'd swing by this place one last time."

"You just wanted an excuse to see me, didn't you?" Cray smiled, tilting her head.

"I wondered if you'd be here."

"Uh-huh." Her grin widened.

Fraser laughed, shaking his head. "Anyone ever tell you that you've got an ego?"

"All the time."

The receptionist handed her the suitcase. "Here you go, miss."

Cray thanked her and took off her lanyard badge, leaving it on the desk. Then she and Fraser made their way to the doors. The rain had finally vanished by morning and it was a gorgeous day. Blue sky stretched as far as the eye could see, shadows growing longer in the late afternoon sun.

A cold breeze cut through the air and Cray huddled in her sweater for warmth, the last clean turtleneck she'd brought.

Fraser tensed, then seemed to relax into the chill. "So the RCFL team found the source of the Monterey Sheriff's breach."

"Oh really?"

"Yeah, a phishing email disguised as one from a local animal shelter, all the way back in June. After that, Ritter worked her way through the Department, collecting all the info she needed, including Quinn's file and the concerns about his gambling issues. That's also how she would've found out about the meds Richie Liu, the lead homicide detective, was taking. The Sheriffs found that he'd been sent a tampered supply of blood pressure medication."

"Ritter really went all in, huh?"

"No kidding. We also talked to the wife of Furman, the engineer who supposedly committed suicide. Turns out he paid off a number of bills in September, about a week before dying. He'd seemed on edge about something, like he was guilty. There were encrypted messages between him and Ritter on her phone. She pretended to be someone outside the company, implied she was Declan. Furman never knew what he was getting into. He thought it was for corporate espionage, not murder. Ritter instructed him to delete the messages on his phone once she wired him the payment. Then she contacted Sova. That was the first job he did for her."

"September... So the AutoNet demo was only infected two months ago?"

"Seems so. We just assumed it was around the same time as the Update breach because if Furman had done both, Ritter probably would've had him do them around the same time. But she was the CTO for the last five years. She put a Trojan in the Update Department back when security was laxer, teased Johnson about not focusing enough on safety measures the whole time—because she *knew* they had a breach."

"Have you found the virus yet?"

"Not in the Update system. We'll get the RCFL on that next week. Shouldn't be too hard now that we know what we're looking for. We'll also have to find the bug she placed in the CEO Suite for listening to conversations, but we have the recordings from that on her computer, along with all her other files. It's how she knew Graham was putting you up in that penthouse."

Cray nodded. They'd stopped at the edge of the drop-off loop. She looked around at the various Asimov cars in the parking lot. Now that it was the weekend, far fewer were here. "Did she sell backdoors to the cars anywhere?"

He shook his head. "Not that we've found. I think she thought herself above that. The way you described her, she sounded like a self-righteous megalomaniac who thought she was saving humanity."

"No, she was an extreme sadist who *convinced* herself she was a self-righteous megalomaniac saving humanity."

"Well, that makes sense, doesn't it?" Fraser said. "Self-righteousness always stems from a lack of empathy, a refusal to consider any other perspective than your own."

She sighed. "I guess you're right. But you don't have to be a psychopath to be self-righteous."

"Of course not."

"So, do you really think she won—like what Declan said last night? That nobody will want to sit in a driverless car again after this?"

Fraser thought for a moment. "I don't know. But probably not. People didn't stop sailing passenger liners after the *Titanic* sank. They just added more lifeboats. The Asimov cars themselves didn't fail, it was a malicious human element that killed Spencer, Bailey, and Graham. I think cybersecurity in this industry is going to become the main focus for a while, before anyone tries anything crazy like AutoNet again. And I don't know if we'd ever fully accept a society with no steering wheels. But maybe that's just me."

He looked past her to the building. "Asimov, though, is definitely finished. They fucked up big time. In the future, there will be many self-driving cars on the road. Just not theirs."

Both of them were quiet for a moment, the wind blowing past them. Cray was thinking of something else to say, when Fraser added, "Declan's getting charged for punching me, by the way. Battery of a federal officer."

"Serves him fucking right."

"Not sure how harsh the sentence will be. I'm sure he'll get a nice, expensive lawyer who will plead temporary insanity. And I'll have to spend a fun day in court."

"I just would've beaten the shit out of him and called it even."

He stopped and turned to her. "Maybe it's a good thing you don't have a badge."

She burst out laughing. "Yeah, you're probably right."

They continued into the parking lot, her suitcase rolling behind her. Cray guessed she was walking Fraser back to his car. Her eyes scanned the vehicles, but she didn't see the Crown Victoria anywhere.

"Izzy? Over here." He gestured to a vehicle hidden behind two SUVs.

She followed him around and stopped. "You have got to be fucking kidding me."

Before them stood a silver DeLorean, the sun glinting off its hood. The car looked in excellent condition.

"The Bureau let you take this here?"

"No. I'm officially off duty. I just swung by to see how the ERT was doing. And I needed an excuse to drive these roads." He looked off at the sky. "Most beautiful day we've had in a while."

"And, of course, you wanted to see me." She smirked.

"I plead the Fifth Amendment, Izzy," Fraser grinned, walking toward his car.

"You call me Izzy, but I don't know what to call you." She tilted her head. "Special Agent Fraser sounds a bit too formal."

He stopped and turned back to her. "My friends call me Will."

"Well then *Will*, what's your car run on? Nuclear paranoia?"

"Oh please, there's so much more to be afraid of now."

Cray hesitated. "What's it like having a life ruled by fear?" She meant it as an honest question.

Fraser paused. "I wouldn't say *ruled* by fear. But small doses of it are good. It reminds me that not everything is wonderful, that not everyone can be trusted. That we have to look before we leap."

"And where's the fun in that?"

He laughed, shaking his head. "Can I ask you a question?"

"Of course."

Fraser looked right at her, softening his gaze. "When was the last time you felt truly happy?"

The words hit her in an unexpected way, piercing a shell she hadn't paid attention to. Cray stood there for a while, staring off and thinking, combing back through her memories to find that last genuine spark.

Finally, she shook her head. "I...can't remember."

He looked sad. "When was the last time you talked to your family?"

"It's..." She lowered her head. "It's been a while."

"Why don't you call them up, see if there's one seat left at the Thanksgiving table. That *is* next week."

She hadn't thought about it. "I...I don't know. It'd be pretty awkward, me coming home out of the blue like that. I haven't seen them in so long."

"I thought psychopaths don't feel awkwardness."

"No, but I can sense it."

"Are you afraid? Anxious?"

"No, but..." Cray still didn't know why she liked telling him things. But she didn't want to stop, either. "It's an unknown, but not a fun unknown. It probably wouldn't be very enjoyable for any of us. And I bet it would be tedious for me. I'd just want to leave the whole time."

"You know, I read an article this morning about pro-social psychopaths."

She raised an eyebrow. "I definitely wouldn't call myself *pro*-social."

"It's a relative term. Introvert doesn't mean antisocial. Pro-social psychopaths are the highest functioning, the ones who are productive members of society. But in most cases, they were raised in good households. Their parents brought them up right, taught them to care, called them on their bull-shit. Basically prevented them from becoming—"

"Like Ritter?"

He nodded. "We pulled everything we could on her today from national databases. If she was ever diagnosed as a psy-chopath, it's not in our records."

"She probably figured out she was one and thought it wouldn't be good to have that written down anywhere."

"Right. Though we did find her foster care files. She was removed from the custody of her parents because they both abused her. She probably developed psychopathy as a coping mechanism, if she wasn't already a genetic case."

"That still doesn't excuse what she did. There are lots of people who had bad parents who didn't become psychopaths, and others like me who became fucked up anyway. Even with good families."

"My point is, you should really appreciate your parents and siblings more, Izzy. Three years is a long time to never see them once in person. At least give them a call. I mean, how many times did you nearly *die* this week?"

She paused. "I'll think about it. I have to be in a certain mood to talk to my mother." She looked back at him. "What are *you* doing for Thanksgiving?"

"My brother and I meet up at my sister's family's place in L.A. every year. But then for Christmas, she and I trek out to Hawaii to meet my brother and parents for the big family reunion."

She was lost in thought. "That must be nice."

"It is. Even though I wouldn't call us the most functional group of relatives."

"I'm assuming mai tais and beach sunsets go a long way for coping with that."

"You wouldn't be wrong." He turned to his car, opening up the gull wing door and climbing in. "But seriously, Izzy, give them a call."

She looked down at her feet.

"Oh, and one last thing."

Cray glanced up.

"I just wanted to say, we couldn't have solved this without you. Ritter might've gotten away with it. You were a really great help, and even Reed is impressed."

She gave a soft smile. "Thanks, Will."

"Who knows? Maybe we'll cross paths again someday."

The smile widened. "I'd like that."

"I would too. Take care, Izzy." He pulled down on a dangling handle, closing the door.

A moment later, the engine started to purr. Fraser pulled out of the spot and rolled down his windows. He waved goodbye, then drove off toward the exit. The car turned onto Deer Creek, speeding toward the intersection. Cray watched him hang a right on Page Mill and accelerate north.

The throaty roar of the engine dwindled the farther he got, driving off into the afternoon. She pictured him behind the wheel, shifting the gears, the wind blowing through his hair. He must feel genuinely happy, she thought, savoring every moment of the experience while it still lasted, before that day when the driver became the driven.

Cray sighed and made her way back toward the drop-off loop, enjoying the breeze. She'd have to go into the lobby and get the receptionist to hail her an autonomous chauffeur to the airport. The corporate jet should be ready by now.

But when she stepped over the curb, she stopped and turned around, staring off for a while.

Then, sighing, she drew her phone out of her pocket.

She pulled up the contact information and sighed, psyching herself up. This was going to take some effort. She tapped the call icon and brought the phone to her ear.

It rang and rang. Cray was suddenly tense again. Maybe she wouldn't pick up. That would be the easiest—

"Hello, Izzy?" Her mother's voice sounded surprised, concerned.

For a second, she didn't say anything. This had been so much easier in her head.

"Um…hi, Mom. I, uh…I'm sure this is kind of last minute, but…" She took a deep breath, forced a laugh. "Is it too late for me to come back for Thanksgiving this year?"

Her mother paused and for a moment Cray wondered if she was angry, calling her up out of nowhere like this. But then she broke into a fit of tearful laughs, which gradually slid into outright sobbing.

Cray laughed along with her, her eyes watering ever so slightly. It was such a good release, she realized, tension vanishing all over her body. She stared off past the parking lot, past the green hills, up at the endless blue sky.

Bravo, Izzy, she told herself. *Very High Functioning.*

ACKNOWLEDGEMENTS

Writing *Auto* has been a three-year long process and it wouldn't have been possible without the help of certain people along the way.

I'd like to thank Jeffrey Carr for discussing vehicular cyber-security with me as well as his advice for striking a balance between accuracy and entertainment.

The FBI Office of Public Affairs, for having a Special Agent walk me through the digital forensics process and discussing the anticipated cyber-threats of tomorrow.

My father, for letting me pester him with questions about IT, his experiences working in Silicon Valley, and for providing insight on earlier drafts.

To my beta readers: Chloe Bray, Everan Michalchyshyn, Claudia Pileggi, Julian Russell, Rory Tassonyi, Harry Twyford, as well as my mother and sister—thank you all for taking the time to give feedback on this novel's various iterations.

Any liberties or inaccuracies taken with regard to hacking, digital forensics, criminal procedure, or Moscone Center back corridors are my own.

VISIT

www.alexanderplansky.com

FOR UPDATES AND NEWSLETTERS